almost
PRETEND

MORE BOOKS BY NICOLE SNOW

Bossy Seattle Suits

One Bossy Proposal

One Bossy Dare

One Bossy Date

One Bossy Offer

One Bossy Disaster

Bad Chicago Bosses

Office Grump

Bossy Grump

Perfect Grump

Damaged Grump

Men of Redhaven

The Broken Protector

Knights of Dallas

The Romeo Arrangement

The Best Friend Zone

The Hero I Need

The Worst Best Friend

Heroes of Heart's Edge

No Perfect Hero

No Good Doctor

No Broken Beast

No Damaged Goods

No Fair Lady

No White Knight

No Gentle Giant

Enguard Protectors

Still Not Over You

Still Not Into You

Still Not Yours

Still Not Love

Marriage Mistake Stand-Alones

Accidental Hero

Accidental Protector

Accidental Romeo

Accidental Knight

Accidental Rebel

almost
PRETEND

NICOLE SNOW

Montlake

Published by Montlake, Seattle

www.apub.com

Amazon, the Amazon logo, and Montlake are trademarks of Amazon.com, Inc., or its affiliates.

ISBN-13: 9781662516405 (paperback)
ISBN-13: 9781662516399 (digital)

Cover design by Hang Le
Cover photography by Wander Aguiar
Cover image: © Nadia Yong, © LUMIKK555, © Art_girl / Shutterstock

Printed in the United States of America

almost
PRETEND

I

HELLO, MR. BRIGHT SIDE

(ELLE)

I'm going to be brutally honest.

I have a track record of making bad decisions.

Usually, I don't mind it. There's always something right side up in upside down.

One door opens, another closes.

You know how it goes.

Like when I was five, and I decided to make a net trap out of sticks, yarn, and cheese to catch the raccoon in our yard. Sure, I wound up with two spitting-mad raccoons, my mother shrieking, and my dad lecturing me for an hour about rabies while he freed the little beasts from a safe distance with a rake.

But I learned that I loved being a little spontaneous—pretty important for a lifelong love affair with the arts.

Or maybe when I was twelve and I asked a classmate, Kenny Purdue, to the Sadie Hawkins dance. He laughed, called me a *zombie vampire bitch*, and threw mud on my dress.

He also taught me how to tell which boys suck real fast.

Plus, the fact that splattered earth tones look pretty cool on fabric.

Oh, and my gothy phase in high school?

I'm a master at pairing contrasts. I had to do *something* with the anemia and pale skin. Fashion forward, always.

I think I'm still looking for the bright side in the fact that I chose to go to art school and graduated just in time to be replaced by an AI algorithm that can whip up a masterpiece in a fraction of the time it would take any human. Luckily, it hasn't totally stopped me from finding freelance work as a children's illustrator with my uniquely human imperfections—so it can't be all bad, right?

Right?

Like I said, I can find the good in any situation.

Even the tattooed stoner rock star wannabe I dated in college because I forgot how to tell which boys suck, a guy who cheated on me with *two* of my friends, taught me a valuable lesson. I don't need a boyfriend, or friends with grabby hands.

That was also the first time I tried painting angry.

It landed me an exhibit in a New York art gallery. The perfect dot on my résumé to keep the freelance work rolling in for the last few years.

So, sure.

I've made gallons of lemonade out of my weight in lemons.

Right now, though, I'm having a hard time finding the good in a cross-country flight when we're not even done boarding and my eyes are aching with the spangly white flashers again.

That's what I call them before the headache from hell hits.

This time, it started in the terminal at JFK before my red-eye flight.

So much noise and motion, all of it bouncing off high ceilings. Just a dull throbbing behind my eyes, but it's the only warning I get that I need to hydrate and lie down in a cool, dark place to head things off before the pain turns volcanic.

But I didn't have that option today.

Not when I had to slog through security, check in, and run to my gate just in time for the boarding call. By the time I got on the plane, my head was spinning.

Now, as I wedge through the aisle and try not to gag, and the sounds of someone's upset, teething baby pierce my skull like an ice pick, I wonder why I didn't just book a train.

A nice, leisurely Amtrak ride from NYC to Seattle. It would take almost a week. No sudden takeoff, no noisy crowds, no screaming anything.

But noooo. I had to be Efficiency Girl and book a flight, forgetting that in her off time the fantabulous Efficiency Girl moonlights as Mistress Migraine.

So I grit my teeth, squint, and force my eyes to focus so I can count down the steps to my seat without vomiting.

At least I booked a window seat.

Sometimes watching the clouds helps ease the earthquake in my head, and if that doesn't work, I'll still have a nice corner to hide in.

When I get to my row, though, the aisle seat is already occupied by my seatmate.

It takes me a second to process the big, stiff man perched in the seat when there are sparks popping across my vision like the Fourth of July.

But when I finally see him—

Holy hell.

Did I *say* there was no bright side to this flight?

I was very, very wrong.

For a split second, I forget I'm battling the mother of all migraines.

My seatmate looks to be around his late thirties.

He's *tall.* So tall that his knees press against the back of the seat in front of him, even with the extra legroom in business class.

He's got a face cut from granite, stern and so handsome and intimidating he could be peeled right off the pages of a fashion magazine—especially with his perfectly tailored clothing.

A dark three-piece suit with a gorgeous dark-blue silk tie brings out the cutting, icy tints of blue in eyes brighter than the summer ocean. The suit is all angles, but it fits him in a way that says he's nothing but solid muscle underneath.

3

Of course, he's got the devil's lips. Cruel, sensuous, and framed by a dark, close-cropped beard just beginning to pick up a few streaks of silver here and there.

His brows are decisive, dashed thick and dark under striking black hair swept neatly to one side, though one unruly lock arcs over his brow.

A flaw in his armor? Imperfectly perfect?

He's killing me already.

And he does it again with his posture.

There's something broody and furious about him.

The lines carved in his face tell me this is just his default look. It's not whatever he's glaring at on the laptop settled on the tray table in front of him that's putting it there.

The stranger just flipping *smolders*.

There's a visceral simmer radiating off him, taking up even more space than the man himself.

Hello, Mr. Bright Side.

Can you go from zero to daddy issues in thirty seconds flat?

Someone bumps into me from behind, and my headache drags me back to earth.

I wince—and not just because I've been gawking at a total stranger who isn't acknowledging my existence while I'm next to him, blocking the aisle.

Right.

I need to sit down, take a deep breath, and swallow a couple of the Imitrex I barely managed to get through security. Dry, if I can't flag down a flight attendant to ask for water in the middle of people getting seated.

Sighing, I adjust my carry-on and pin on a smile for Jet Daddy.

I always try to smile like I'm not in excruciating pain, but today I probably resemble a demented carnival doll with the way my left eye keeps twitching.

"Excuse me," I say softly.

He doesn't answer.

He doesn't even look up.

It's like I'm not even here.

Except the people behind me waiting to climb into their own seats make it crystal clear I didn't just turn invisible. While someone at my back coughs and curses for me to hurry it up, I clear my throat and try again.

Louder this time.

"Excuse me."

Nothing.

"Sir? *Excuse me.* I'm in the next seat. Can I squeeze in here?"

He doesn't even lift an eyebrow, let alone look up.

What the hell?

Is he deaf? Is he ignoring me intentionally?

No one can possibly be this oblivious. His screen looks like nothing but Excel charts and spreadsheets, so it can't be *that* fascinating.

"Sir?" I try again before I sigh and reach out to tap his shoulder. "Hi, sorry to bother you, but—*eep.*"

I never make contact with his shoulder.

His hand snaps up and locks around my wrist, stopping me in my tracks.

My first impression is that his hands are enormous.

More like paws with fingers, but his fingers are thin with large knuckles, giving them a sort of brutal elegance.

They wrap around my wrist so fully that his fingers overlap the heel of his palm. The pads of his fingers are callused, shredding the image of the pampered suit. The graze of his thumb against the pulse point under my wrist turns my breath into a stutter.

My second impression is that even though he cut me off before I could touch him, he's holding my wrist so gently I can barely feel it.

No matter how quick and sharp that slashing movement was, he doesn't want to hurt me.

Again, those glacial eyes slide toward me without his head ever lifting.

They watch me from under decisive brows with a cool, penetrating look that feels like being dunked in arctic waters.

I'm about as overstimulated as I can get between the noise and the headache and his touch and the way his indecipherable look cuts through me.

If I don't sit down in the next thirty seconds, we're going to have a much bigger problem than me blocking the aisle.

Thankfully, he seems to get the message.

He lets go of my wrist with a light push that sends me back a half step, clearing the aisle so he can lift the outer armrest and slide his legs out, making room for me to slip past. *Barely.*

Like I said, he's not a small man.

My knees still brush his outer thigh as I edge past him with a flustered "Thank you."

I try to tell myself my face only feels so hot because the migraine has all my wires crossed, especially when my blood pressure is likely plunging and I should feel cold.

But even with my distracting seatmate, it's a relief to throw myself down in my seat.

I can't be bothered to toss my bag in the overhead bin. Not when that would just piss off the horde behind me even more while I fumble to get my little carry-on packet of pills out.

Which I do now, hefting the bag into my lap and then digging inside.

Please. Please let me get this medicine down fast enough to stave off the worst of it.

I find the prescription bottle, fight with the childproof cap, then shake out a dose and gulp it down.

Closing my eyes, I go limp, hugging my bag close and idly listening to the caveman next to me moving back into position and the faint rainfall of his fingers on his keyboard.

The darkness behind my eyes is soothing.

The violent flashers slowly fade.

The worst is over.

I hope.

I can't do anything about the noisy people settling in, but I can at least choose which noise to focus on. Jet Daddy's typing is actually pretty soothing.

It's rhythmic and predictable. As long as I focus on that, I won't jolt every time a toddler shrieks like they're trying to turn my head into a broken Easter egg.

Once we're in the air, I'll be fine.

I will.

Cabin pressure will even out, and, assuming the migraine hasn't put me in a coma by then, I'll be able to ride it out like I always do until this flying metal tube drops me off at SeaTac.

I stay still until the telltale ping tells me the *Fasten seat belt* lights have come on, and I wince as the captain's voice rattles over a staticky loudspeaker.

Not helping, but at least some of the pounding has stopped. Enough that I feel more human and less like a reanimated corpse.

Opening my eyes, I fish my laptop out, then tuck the bag under the seat and the laptop against my hip while I fasten my seat belt.

Next to me, Jet Daddy has finally closed his laptop, put his tray table up, and tucked the laptop away in the seat pocket in front of him so he can fasten his own seat belt.

I could almost live with the migraine just to watch him move.

There's a flexing flow under his suit that's fascinating. He's thick enough in the waist—no, *thicc*, like muscle *thicc*—that he has to yank the seat belt tight just to fasten it comfortably.

I catch his head starting to turn slightly toward me when I realize I'm staring again.

Yikes.

I look away quickly, riveting my eyes on the window and holding my breath. It's at least a solid thirty seconds before I dare to glance back at him.

Now, he's not looking at me at all.

Welp.

So much for hoping I could distract myself with a little light flirting.

Still, I should try to be friendly.

Even though he's looking straight ahead, I offer my hand and try another smile.

"Hi. I'm Eleanor Lark, but you can call me Elle," I say. Then it hits me how weird it must be that I'm talking to him after I dove into the seat like I was falling and immediately went for my pills. I let out an embarrassed laugh. "Sorry if we got off on the wrong foot. I just really needed to sit. I know I was being, you know, kinda weird. I'm not a nervous flier or anything. I just get these nasty headaches and needed my meds."

Jet Daddy lets out an almost imperceptible sigh.

He turns his head, just enough to look down at my outstretched hand like a prince contemplating why any mere mortal would be so stupid as to try to touch him.

There isn't a flicker of a reaction.

No smile, no frown, no *Ew, cooties, get your dirty paw away from me.*

He just looks away again without making eye contact.

O-kay, this guy is weird.

Frowning, I pull my hand back, curling my fingers against my palm.

Hey, I tried. Hot pricks and me don't mix, I guess.

His attitude problem doesn't need to make my bad day worse, when I've got better things to focus on.

Like the fact that the engines are whirring and the airplane's jolting to life, this giant steel dragon with us in its belly.

Overdramatic?

Yes.

I get a little dramatic when I'm praying my skull won't implode at thirty-six thousand feet.

Ready or not, though, it's coming.

That powerful push forward, faster and faster, gravity pinning me to my seat.

Most people don't get that migraines aren't just in your head.

When they hit like this, they attack everywhere. It's like being crushed in a trash compactor until your entire body rings with pain, blindness, nausea, throbbing, dizziness.

I dig my fingers into the armrests as we take off. I close my eyes and try to time my breaths in deep, slow movements.

I try to find my happy place where there are no soul-shredding migraines or antisocial sexy freaks cramping my breathing space.

It's not much, but it helps with the pressure changes.

It still sucks.

So I just try to keep my internal organs in one place as the pressure builds, peaks, and—

Then it just bursts.

The worst migraine ever slugs me dead in the face before we hit cruising altitude.

I'm reeling, sick, trying not to cry.

I hate this.

I hate this so much.

All it takes is a change in the hydraulic pressure in my veins to turn my world into a special hell.

It's why I try so hard to just be happy when I can.

To counterbalance these moments of sheer torture and enjoy the good times while I have them.

That's definitely not now.

It feels like years pass before I can breathe again.

I can't stop the tears that leak out, trickling down my face. The pain is too deep, but it starts to ease up, so I no longer feel like I'm going to shatter by the time the *ding* sounds that tells us we can unbuckle our seat belts, use our devices, and enjoy a six-hour nonstop flight from coast to coast.

I'm suddenly glad I picked a night flight. Even without opening my eyes, I can tell the people around me are just settling in to sleep, and those who aren't sleeping will stay quiet for those who are.

By the time we land, I'll be stable again.

Until then, I can at least keep my overhead light off and try to settle in.

I hear a faint click over my head, followed by a second one to my side, grounding me where I am. I'm still clawing armrests.

I'm also holding my breath.

I exhale in a rush and slowly peel my fingers loose from their death grip one by one. Wary of the lights, I crack one eye open—but my overhead light is off, though I'm sure I didn't turn it off.

As I open my other eye, I realize the overhead light next to me is off too.

Oof.

Jet Daddy knows I exist.

He's watching me so intently my lungs stop working.

He still has that cold, reserved look of disinterest bordering on disdain. His winter-blue eyes could gut someone if he glanced at them too fast.

But he's holding something out to me.

Something that resembles the same dark-blue silk as his tie.

The pocket square from his suit?

Oh.

He noticed.

He noticed I was crying, and I don't know what to make of that. But if he's offering . . .

My movements are creaky as I reach for the silk gift with a trembling smile.

"Thank you," I whisper.

Amazing how a headache on steroids can screw up my entire body this badly. "Sorry, mister. Um, like I said, migraines. The medicine hasn't kicked in yet."

He doesn't say anything.

He just looks away from me and leans forward to retrieve his laptop and fold his tray table down.

Seriously, this guy is *weird*.

But his strangeness is a welcome distraction, if I'm being honest.

Though I have to look away from the brightness of his screen when his laptop wakes up. I close my eyes again, dabbing the wetness from my cheeks.

I feel self-conscious giving it back to him when it's wet with my tears, so I curl the silk against my fingers and bite my lip, opening my eyes again.

"I can have this cleaned and return it to you, Mr. . . . ?"

He'd started tapping on his laptop—is it me, or is he deliberately typing with a lighter touch?—but now he stops.

Still no eye contact.

His screen is way more interesting than me. I mean, I know I've already made too awful a first impression to hope for a little flirting, but *man*, this guy is hell on a girl's self-esteem.

"Keep it," he rumbles.

Whoa.

For a second, I wonder if audio therapy is a real thing.

Because his voice . . . it's like standing under a waterfall that's the same dark blue as the pocket square in my hand. Deep, soothing, heavy with this scorched sensuality that makes even those two mundane words feel like a caress.

It's an odd contradiction when his tone is just as cold as his eyes, but the timbre and resonance are all heat and whisper-sweet darkness.

It messes me up so much I forget my headache again in the sound of his voice before I really process what he's said.

Keep it?

He can't be serious.

I bite my lip, but I'm too tired and hurt to protest.

So I tuck the silk square into the pocket of my jeans and mutter another "Thanks."

I don't expect him to answer.

I'm absolutely right.

I don't exist in his bubble yet again, but for some reason, I'm still smiling.

I guess even weird stuffy Jet Daddies can be kind, now and then.

I'm pretty sure he turned the lights off for me too.

Someone else who's kind: the stewardess who passes by and leans past him to look at me with a worried smile. "Hon, are you all right? You look pale."

"Kind of my default," I say dryly. "I get bad migraines. Already took some pills, but if I could please ask you for a water, a pillow, and a blanket, I'd be so grateful."

"Of course!" She reaches over Jet Daddy and lightly pats my shoulder, then bustles off.

A minute later, I've got an ice-cold water bottle, a little airline pillow, and two blankets. I glug down the water and tuck myself into the corner, nesting with the pillow cushioning my skull.

It's not perfect, but a little rest in Satan's own jet is better than none at all.

Hopefully by the time I wake up, the meds will be doing their job.

And maybe Jet Daddy will remember how to grunt more than two words at me.

For now, I pull one of the blankets over my head, willing myself to sleep with the sweet distraction of his gentle typing in my ears.

◆ ◆ ◆

When I wake up, he's still on his laptop.

I'd almost think the whole flight hadn't passed and I'd only been out for a few minutes. But the sky is turning pink outside above the pillowy clouds.

We'll be landing soon, which means I'd better brace for round two of crushing pressure changes.

At least my own brain isn't trying to claw its way out of my head like a starving animal.

With a heavy yawn, I poke my head out of my blanket nest. My hair floofs into my face as I peer out from the hood the blanket's turned into. I'm sure I look deranged.

Good thing Jet Daddy doesn't give a damn if I'm cute or not.

I peek at him, rubbing one sandy eye, and consider trying to talk again. But I think I've learned my lesson.

So I watch him tapping away for a few seconds, check my watch, and wiggle my laptop out from under my hip and prop it open on my tray table.

As soon as the in-flight Wi-Fi connects, there's an email waiting from my grandmother.

Subject: Dinner tonight

From: Grandma Jackie

Elle Dear,

I hope you'll see this before your flight. I wanted to make your favorite for dinner tonight, but I do hope you still love five-cheese tortellini. Please let me know before your flight lands, my darling. If you have something different in mind, we can always stop by the grocery on the way home.

Yours always,
Your loving Gran

My smile feels too big for my face.

Jacqueline Lark always talks that way, like she's trying to remind me how much she loves me with every word. She's practically my mother at this point, although my real mom is happily retired with my father down in the Florida Keys.

I tap out a quick reply.

Subject: Re: Dinner tonight

To: Grandma Jackie

Gran,

You know I'd never turn down your tortellini, especially if you're making your special cream sauce. But I told you—**no coming to the airport**. You shouldn't be on your feet if you're still in your knee brace. I'll Uber, and we can order anything else. See you soon. Love you!

Elle

Knowing Gran, she's probably already at the airport, and I'm too late to stop her.

I'll just have to take the keys and drive so she's not hurting her bad knee. After her hiking accident last summer, her doctor hoped that she'd be able to walk unassisted with her new knee plate after recovery, but she refused the surgery in favor of other options.

Over six months of physical therapy and she's still struggling— which is partly why I'm here.

Sure, life wasn't working out that great in NYC.

But I could've roughed it out until things started looking up.

I just didn't want to, not when Gran needs me more.

I glance at the time again. I should have a few more minutes before I have to put everything away, so I kill time looking for local jobs.

Might as well get a jump start on settling in. As I sink back in my chair, I prop my elbow on the armrest between me and Jet Daddy.

He's so quiet I'd forget he's there, if not for the heat of his thigh stretched out next to me and my aching skull quieting enough to be very aware of just how close his mile-wide shoulders are to touching mine.

But I remember him well when my elbow bumps his and knocks it off the armrest.

"Oops," I say. "So—"

I never get the word out before he plants his elbow back down and sweeps mine off. He never stops typing—and he's still not looking at me.

I narrow my eyes.

Look, I'm grateful to him for turning off the lights and giving me his pocket square, but a single human sentence from him would be nice.

Annoyed, I nudge my elbow back on the armrest and send his dropping back down into his lap.

Then he does it right back without missing a beat.

Oh, now it's on.

Hiding my smile, I sweep his elbow back off again, this time more forcefully—and there he is again, his huge arm brushing mine as he pushes right back.

Again.

Again.

Again and again and again until I'm hard pressed not to grin. He never pushes hard enough to come close to hurting me. Mostly, this feels like some weird game.

Okay.

I may look like a corpse and my hair is probably sticking up everywhere, but maybe I *am* getting to flirt with Mr. Walking Daddy Issues a little bit.

Even if he's still no closer to showing the slightest hint of a smile, let alone breaking that no-nonsense expression. He still wears the same broody look of intense concentration as he scrolls through the data on his screen.

It looks like financial projections and profit reports that seem negative, I think.

But our weird little game ends as the *Fasten seat belt* light dings on, and my amusement turns into dread.

Here we go.

I just hope I don't cry this time when the shifting pressure crushes my head like a grape.

As the pilot announces our arrival, we put our laptops away.

Jet Daddy keeps very pointedly ignoring me, but as we both fasten our seat belts, it happens.

He leaves the armrest free.

I smile slightly and hold on tight, bracing for pain.

But the pressure change doesn't hit me as much like a plane crash to the face. I still end up clawing at the armrests until my fingers hurt, pinching my eyes shut.

The vise squeezing my skull only lets up once the wheels touch down on the runway and we start taxiing in.

My mouth feels sour, but I think I'll make it to the terminal without showering Jet Daddy in my last meal.

I do go fuzzy and dark for a second, though.

Maybe more than a second—or is it a few minutes?

When I pry my eyes open again, people are disembarking and Jet Daddy is gone like a ghost that never existed.

Did I imagine him the whole time?

I smirk a bit to myself.

Never had a guy so eager to get away from me before, but I guess if I were him, I'd want to lurch away from the sick girl too.

Steeling my dizzy vision, I get my bag and stumble through the aisle and off the plane.

Until now, I thought I was okay, holding it together long enough to make it out on my own.

I was wrong.

Because the second the noisy terminal hits me in the face, the migraine gnawing at the back of my brain charges to the front again.

I make it out of the gate, swaying violently, bumping into people who shout their irritation as I weave through the crowd.

Then that red flood over my eyes becomes a drowning roar.

I'm blind.

Blind, fighting for breath, and going down.

My mind feels like it's swirling down the drain as angry red fades to bitter black.

II

NO RAIN, NO FLOWERS

(AUGUST)

I have a big damn problem in my hands.

Literally.

Considering I made it exactly three steps toward Miss Lark just in time to catch her as she fainted, and now my arms are full of a soft young woman who isn't able to move.

When the slender blonde introduced herself on our flight, I never expected to wind up in this predicament—even with her silly-ass attempts to distract me from my work.

She's got my full attention now.

I don't have time for flirtatious women. It's nothing new to me, and all they do is break my focus.

Fate's decided I don't get a choice right now.

This girl—Elle Lark—is alarmingly light in my arms. Trim, pale, and tangled up in me like a tree branch.

Her wispy strawberry blonde hair floats over my arm, so light and fine it wants to defy gravity rather than falling down gracefully.

What the hell did she say her health issues were again?

Headaches?

She certainly feels fragile.

Blue veins glow against thin wrists. She's long legs and not much else, a girlish frame that would make my gaze linger if she wasn't out cold.

Before, I thought she was young—too young for my hungry eyes—but I realize now as I look at her face that it was simply her ivory color and smallness spinning that illusion.

For someone so pale, she's surprisingly warm against me, a living sunspot draped against my arms and chest.

"Sir?"

Blinking, I look up.

I forgot we're in the middle of a busy airline terminal, fainting girl or not.

People are staring at us like the slack-jawed paralyzed slugs they are.

Everyone except my driver and personal assistant, Merrick "Rick" Adams.

He looks at the girl. Looks at me. Looks back at the girl and steeples his fingers together.

Then he moves closer, wisely choosing not to comment, waiting for me to speak first.

"I've got her, Merrick."

He offers me his usual gracious smile.

He's a thin, lanky man who often reminds me of an overly friendly cat.

"So then," Merrick says, "your luggage already arrived a day ahead, as planned, and it's been transported to your residence. Will we be making any additional stops on the way to the office, considering the—the situation, sir?"

"Yes. Change of plans," I say dryly, shifting the negligible weight in my arms so I can balance Miss Lark and the laptop bag slung over my shoulder. I nod at her carry-on, which is currently resting on the floor with its strap crumpled on top of it. "Would you?"

"Of course."

He bends and scoops up the bag, then turns to lead me through the terminal, threading a path that avoids the thickest clusters of staring, muttering idiots.

Not an EMT in sight, of course.

Knowing how slow things move around here, it's one of many reasons I decide to deal with Elle Lark myself.

That doesn't stop people from looking, but I don't have any time or fucks to care about gawkers.

Since I'm not an authorized care provider or emergency contact, I'll have to deliver her into the hands of someone who knows her and her medical needs before being on my merry way.

Which is why I avoid the nosy TSA agents as well, brushing them off.

Her breathing is fine, at least.

She isn't bruised or suffering a concussion, and I know it's not diabetic shock, a heart attack, a stroke, a seizure, or anything requiring instant intervention.

For her, it's still a medical emergency.

For me, it's trouble.

More trouble finds me as Rick takes us to the cold parking lot and the dark-blue Genesis G80 waiting to ferry us from the airport.

It's not the way the girl shivers and curls up closer, tucking herself against me for warmth, that bothers me.

The real irritant is that I've got no clue where this girl lives.

That will be a problem.

While Rick deposits her bag on the pavement and holds the car door open, I settle her in the back seat, sitting upright. A quick, non-intrusive search inside her bag reveals nothing. The bulge of a wallet makes a faint outline against the back pocket of her close-fitting jeans.

Fuck.

She's going to make me touch her, isn't she?

Pinching the bridge of my nose, I draw a deep breath.

Annoying.

"Forgive the intrusion," I mutter, despite knowing she's unconscious.

Then I slip an arm around her delicate waist to lift her up, just enough to slide my fingers into her back pocket.

I try to make as little contact as possible, yet it's impossible to avoid the soft, warm flesh through denim, curving against my fingertips.

I damn sure don't linger.

Half a second of annoyingly enticing warmth dipping under my touch, and I snag the barest edge of the wallet and yank it out quickly before settling her back down in the seat.

When I flick the wallet open, her license tells me nothing except that I was correct about her age: twenty-three.

The address on the license is in New York City.

Not helpful.

With a disgusted sigh, I drop the wallet into her bag.

"Problem, sir?" Rick offers a sympathetic smile.

"I have an unconscious stranger in the back of my car and no idea where to drop her off, so yes, I have one," I retort.

Rick only smiles and shrugs.

I suppose he's used to my barbs by now.

"We could simply leave her with airport security," he points out.

We could.

Hell, maybe we *should*, especially since we have no idea if she's meeting someone here who might be looking for her and panicking by now when she isn't responding to texts.

I thin my lips.

Simply abandoning her to the whims of overworked TSA agents or an expensive ambulance ride she doesn't need ticks at my morals.

She shouldn't be my problem, but she is now—and I don't leave problems unsolved.

"Check with airport security," I say. "Her name is Eleanor Lark. Ask them to page anyone waiting for her. If there's no one here, then we'll get her wherever she belongs."

"Understood." His nod might as well be a crisp salute.

Rick turns and speed-walks back into the terminal. I sink down into a crouch outside the open car door, watching the unconscious girl with her head tilted against the back of the seat.

"You," I mutter, "have been a pain in my ass ever since you stepped on that plane. What am I going to do with you?"

She actually responds and startles me—though I don't think she's aware.

"Gran? Grandma?" she mumbles in her sleep. "No, no, I told you . . . stay. Stay home."

I arch a brow.

Her grandmother must be pretty formidable, if I somehow remind Miss Lark of her.

"I'm not your grandmother," I point out firmly. "If you could provide her address, that will help us resolve this dilemma faster. You don't need a doctor, right? The ER?"

"No. No hospital." She mouths the words more than she says them. "Home. Grandma."

Shit.

"Where is home, Miss Lark?" I try.

She doesn't answer.

She only lets out a soft, pained sigh past her pink lips.

I notice she has a small mouth, a little bud of a thing with a plump upper lip tapering sharply down to peaked corners.

I wait for those lips to move again.

They don't, not even as I hear the echo of her name over the PA system from inside the terminal.

"Problem," I mutter, shaking my head. "You are a *problem*."

"Bite me," she mumbles back, and I blink.

Is she actually awake now?

"Miss Lark." No response. I suppose this is revenge for ignoring her on the plane. *"Miss Lark."*

Nope.

She's truly out—either asleep or unconscious or in some haze of pain in between.

It makes me wonder what her life must be like if *that's* her reflexive response.

I feel a touch of déjà vu as I reach in to shake her shoulder lightly, though no hand rises to stop me. "Miss Lark, wake up. Just enough to tell me your destination so we can be free of each other. Take my hand."

I grab her fingers and fold them around mine. She grips them weakly.

"Nnh?"

I sigh.

She's like a helpless little bird.

This is so not my wheelhouse.

I have zero talent for managing small, fragile things. I'd prefer to put this delicate young woman in the hands of someone more gentle before I accidentally rupture something. Either in her fragile body, or in my exasperated brain.

"Home. Where? Talk to me." Maybe if I keep it simple, the question will penetrate her fog. I just need to leave her wherever she's meant to be.

With a strangled sound, she turns her head and falls to rest against my hand on her shoulder, using it as a pillow. Her skin is soft and feathery warm against the backs of my knuckles. Her slow breaths stir the hairs on the back of my palm.

". . . wanna go home."

"Then tell me where home *is*," I grit through my teeth.

"Huh?"

"*Where.*"

Her lashes flutter. They're several shades darker than her hair, with a deeper red tinge, almost russet, making the glinting hazel underneath look closer to the rusty golden orange of a wildcat's fur by contrast.

Then she mumbles an address—I think.

23

I recognize enough of the street name to know it's in the Queen Anne neighborhood.

I only hope I'm not about to deliver her to some psycho ex-boyfriend's house or the place she shared once with a roommate who's long gone.

While I wait for Rick to return, I ponder what the hell to do before I buckle Miss Lark into the passenger side, carefully shifting her into place.

I don't let my hands linger a second longer than they want to.

I've already been touchy, digging around in her pocket. By the time I slide her bag under her legs and around to the other side to deposit my own bag behind the driver's seat, Rick returns, sighing and running a hand through his short crop of greying hair.

"No one answered the page, Mr. Marshall," he says. "Seems like we're on our own."

"I have an address," I say. "One where we can hopefully leave her safely. It shouldn't be too much of a detour."

Rick's pleasant facade actually cracks—something I've rarely seen in the years he's worked for me. No matter where I travel on the job, Rick is on the ground a day or two ahead of me.

He handles my accommodations and transportation, discussing any local legal issues when I'm contracted out to corporations outside the United States.

When I come home to Seattle, he keeps my house in order, and any business matters that have followed me home from my contract assignations are well sorted and ready for me to handle on my own time.

The man is unflappable, and he typically handles anything without protest.

I'm not used to seeing dismay and concern cross his face.

Just a flicker, but it's there, glaring and unmistakable.

Still, he smiles again and says "Of course" before moving to open the driver's side back seat door for me. "Just let me know where, and we'll be on our way."

I give him the address and slide into the back seat, well aware that I'm typically alone in these instances. But considering Miss Lark is sleeping off her migraine attack, I can at least *pretend* to be alone until the time comes to deposit her in someone else's hands.

As Rick settles behind the wheel and drives us into the light traffic that comes with a cold Seattle dawn in February, I retrieve my laptop and settle in to review a few reports.

I've mostly closed out my last contract—a major semiconductor chip manufacturer in Taiwan that hired me to step in as temporary COO for a six-month stint to reverse a revenue decline caused by material shortages.

So I restructured their manufacturing processes to reuse waste and scrap materials in new manufacturing, launched multiple new products with tiered pricing models to capture new markets, and sourced previously unknown suppliers who were willing to sell off key materials to help fill the gaps.

Four months in, my client hit breakeven.

By the time I booked my flight back home, they were seeing a profit again.

I'd just like to keep an eye on their actual revenues versus projections over the next six months. Too many companies that bring me on to sort through their chaos like to fall apart again the second I'm out the door.

Technically, not my problem. I've done the job I was hired to do.

I have zero responsibility to stay and hold their hand, but there's nothing I hate more than good work going to waste.

As we take a corner, a soft weight flumps against me.

My laptop veers off to the side, bumping against the door.

That weight slides down my chest, settling in my lap.

I freeze, just staring.

Miss Lark has slid down the back of the long bank of seating in the car's rear passenger area, shifted by the momentum of the turn.

She's so slender there was too much slack in the seat belt, tumbling her down until she's now pillowed on my thigh, with her gold hair spilling over my dark slacks in sunrise tones.

Goddamn.

She still hasn't opened her eyes the entire time.

Even I can't work like this.

"Miss Lark," I say pointedly. Surely, she must be awake by now.

She only gives back a sleepy exhalation and curls up, snuggling into me with her cheek rubbing my thigh.

The sound of soft skin against fine wool is damnably distracting.

The sensation even more so.

I grind my teeth.

"Miss Lark, up. Wake *up*."

She doesn't.

If anything, my words only push her deeper into sleep. Her lips curve up as she lets out a drowsy mumble.

"Daddy."

"No." My eyes widen. "I am not your father, woman."

Just what the hell have I gotten myself into?

She still isn't moving. I can't prop the laptop on her head and press on with my work, can I?

Swallowing a growl, I close my computer, tuck it back in my bag, and then settle in to look out the window. Somehow, I must endure this until I can hand this impertinent brat with no boundaries off to someone who can help her annoy the rest of the world.

I catch Rick watching in the rearview mirror with clear amusement and bare my teeth.

"Not one word," I bite off. "Drive."

"Of course, sir."

He tries not to smile.

He fails miserably.

That was three words, when I said not *one*.

What the fuck ever.

Grumbling to myself, I glare out the window, trying like hell not to breathe in her sweetness. She's wearing some scent that's floral and sweet like apples.

I try my damnedest to ignore the soft bundle of woman in my lap while I watch morning struggling to break through a light rain in golden sheets over the hills of Seattle.

III

BE MY SUNSHINE

(ELLE)

I was having the nicest dream.

My parents were actually home for Christmas. Dad wasn't staying overseas at one of his company's corporate offices handling trade negotiations. Mom wasn't in her city of the month as a traveling nurse. We were at our old house in Laurelhurst, almost as cozy as my grandmother's cottage on Queen Anne Hill.

Gran was there, too, of course.

We were laughing and sharing hot apple cider. The whole house smelled like baking cookies and Mom's fancy perfume. We opened presents together at home, instead of my gifts coming by mail from two separate addresses with two separate apology notes.

It's the family life I never had but always wanted.

For a hot minute, the dream is so deep and rich and wonderful that I almost believe it was real.

Gran opens her mouth to say something. I expect to hear *Merry Christmas, my little Elle* in her happy, slightly warbling voice.

Instead, the sound of a blaring car horn comes shrieking out of her mouth, louder and louder, until it jolts me awake.

This is not helping my head—though at least it's a normal headache now and not the sledgehammer migraine I remember having before I fell asleep.

Wait.

. . . when *did* I fall asleep?

My last memory is getting off the plane at SeaTac, staggering through the terminal, and—

I think I passed out as the migraine got the better of me?

I don't know what happened after that.

But why do I hear traffic noise and feel motion like I'm in a car?

What's this dark, musky sandalwood smell?

Whose lap am I resting my head in? And whose very male bulge am I staring at?

"Sorry, sir. Seems to be a traffic issue up ahead. You know Seattle drivers and slick roads."

"Yeah," a chocolate-silk masculine grunt acknowledges.

I freeze.

Those slacks. That warmth. The raw power of a hard-muscled thigh under my head . . .

Jet Daddy?

Oh my God, say it isn't so.

Carefully, I peek up without turning my head.

Sure enough, I'm treated to a view of his sharp beard and strong throat from below.

He's leaning against the door in the back seat of whatever car we're in, his elbow against the bottom of the window and his strong, stark knuckles curled under his chin.

His blue eyes reflect back the icy drizzle misting the city streets.

He's taken off his suit coat, revealing a crisp white shirt and dark vest underneath, both fitted to his powerful body with trim precision.

His coat is draped over me as a blanket, I realize.

My heart thumps with confusion before it stalls like it's too baffled to really know what to do.

How did I end up in this situation?

Where is he taking me?

He answers that question for me a minute later.

I don't think I've given away the fact that I'm awake, but the man must have freakishly good senses—or a really prickly personal space bubble—because without even looking at me he rumbles, "If you're awake, Miss Lark, kindly get out of my lap."

"Um!"

My whole face burns.

I snap myself upright so crisply that I not only make myself dizzy, but I get myself tangled in both his suit coat and the seat belt strapped across me.

Holy hell, shoot me now.

I spend a few more seconds squirming like I've got ants in my pants, embarrassing myself even more, before I manage to fight upright.

Exhaling roughly, I blow my hair out of my face and look out the car window.

I recognize these streets.

We're about two blocks from Grandma's house.

"I'm sorry, I—"

"We're almost to the address you gave me," he interrupts. "I hope the address was correct, anyway."

"We're almost to my grandmother's, so yeah." Wide eyed, I stare out the window, then glance back at him. "I don't remember giving you her address. I don't remember anything."

"Yet you speak with remarkable lucidity in your sleep." His words are as frigid as ever, creating this confusing contrast with the sensual roar of his voice. His expression is pensive as he keeps his gaze trained out the window. It's almost like if he looks at me, something terrible will happen. Like a man avoiding his own power to curse. "You were quite serious about the severity of your migraines. I caught you when you fainted in the terminal. When we paged the airport PA system and there was no one there to fetch you, I asked for an address so I could drop you off. Along the way, you slept on me in traffic three times and decided to use my lap as a pillow." *Definite* touch of icy offense there. "Since you were so stubborn about waking up, I had no choice but to accept the situation."

Dude.

You could've just said I passed out, so you're taking me home.

I smile faintly. It's like talking to someone negotiating a legal contract, stating every word carefully to avoid misinterpretation and possible liability.

"Thank you," I murmur. "I'm sorry for inconveniencing you. That's twice you've saved me now."

"Bull. Offering you a handkerchief isn't an act of heroism. Had I left you with the TSA, you would have been fine, minus a far less comfortable nap."

My smile strengthens at the scowl on his face.

So, so *stuffy.*

"Well, thanks anyway. I appreciate everything. You're a really nice guy."

"I'm anything but," he retorts. "I'm simply doing what's practical."

"Okay. Whatever you say."

I want to ask more—I'm suddenly so curious it's practically eating me alive—but the car pulls up right outside Gran's sweet little blue cottage, with its arched wrought iron entryway and a fence covered in climbing jasmine vines that, even in a cold late February, are green and waiting to bloom once the season warms up.

Grandma Jackie is just coming out the door, leaning hard on the forearm crutch she now uses after refusing a walker. She's got her keys in her other hand, and she turns to lock the door while fumbling to keep her purse on her shoulder when it keeps sliding off the slickness of her bulky jacket.

All while she's also trying to hold an umbrella over her head without dropping her crutch.

Crap.

She probably intends to pick me up at the airport, even though I told her not to.

She looks shaky. She definitely shouldn't be standing, let alone driving.

My stomach sinks.

I don't have time to be curious about my bizarre benefactor, or even to carry on a longer conversation expressing my gratitude.

Definitely no time to get his number so I can pay him back somehow, take him out to lunch, buy him a new pocket square, get him some facial therapy so he can relearn how to smile, whatever.

The moment the car stops, his assistant barely gets out one syllable before I fling the door open, letting in a chill breeze.

"Sorry!" I throw back. "She's hurt and I have to help her, thank you guys again, I'll find my own way to—" I stop.

Repay you, I want to say.

But the moment I grab my bag and tumble out on the slick sidewalk in front of the house, the door to the car—a *nice* car; I'd barely noticed the luxurious interior, but I definitely notice the swanky exterior—shuts.

I stand there staring with my mouth slightly open, rain plonking down on my head in freezing droplets as the car pulls away.

Dang.

That was the nicest rude thing anyone's ever done for me.

Also, I have no idea what just happened.

I didn't even catch his name.

But I only give myself a few more seconds to wonder before I dash through the gate and pelt down the stone path bisecting Gran's beautifully cultivated garden lawn and dash up the short front steps to her porch.

Just in time to catch her as she starts to turn and her crutch slips on the edge of the top step.

"Oh!" she cries.

"Gotcha!" I catch her by the shoulder and steady her.

Gran blinks up at me through her round spectacles.

She's a small, slim bird of a woman with a thick tumble of wispy grey hair that refuses to stay in the bun she's twisted it into.

"Elle?" She reaches for me, but her hands are still a little too full. "I was just on my way to get you. I'm so sorry I'm running behind. I still move so slow, you know—"

"I told you, you didn't have to come at all," I chide gently, taking the keys from her to fit the house key in the lock and push the door open. "You shouldn't be driving. I got a ride, and it was fine. But it's cold out here. Let's head inside before we get too wet and catch a cold."

Gran looks past me at the bag I dumped on the walk in my sprint to catch her. "Of course, my love, but . . . is that all you brought with you?"

"Huh?" I glance over my shoulder and groan.

Right.

Of course, Jet Daddy wouldn't have gotten my luggage at the baggage claim.

"No, but I'll go back to the airport to get everything tomorrow. I just stole your keys, so I'll steal your car too." I smile brightly.

With a fondly exasperated look, she cackles and nudges me on, then lets me take her bag and umbrella inside. I duck back out to get my carry-on, then follow her into the cozy warmth of what was basically my childhood home.

The familiarity instantly feels like a hug from an old friend.

I'll worry about arguing with Delta over claiming my luggage tomorrow.

For now, my head still hurts, and I just want to lie down, relax, and enjoy being home.

◆ ◆ ◆

I've never been happier to put a whole twenty-four hellish hours behind me.

Yesterday, I spent the day catching up with Gran—helping her around the house, finding out where she needed me most, convincing her it's fine to take a load off her knee and let me do anything that requires more mobility.

Yes, I get it.

It hurts her that she can't prep her garden, but I'm working on finding a little comfortable chair she can sit in to prune her petunias. Preferably one made for rolling through the soft earth of the yard.

She's too stubborn to consider a wheelchair, but if I call it a *gardening chair*, I might make some headway.

By lunch, my migraine slithers back into the hole it crawled out of.

Gran knows better than anyone that a gently lit, low-stimulus environment helps keep them at bay—and she'd already stocked the fridge with the protein drinks that help keep my anemia from knocking me flat too.

When I was a kid, I used to feel like an old grandma myself, drinking protein formulas and popping iron and B12 pills every day just to keep myself baseline.

But now a lot of brands make light, refreshing fruit-flavored drinks. A few of them paired with cold chicken salad sandwiches have me feeling better in a heartbeat.

I even decide to make the trip to grab my luggage today.

I fuss Gran into staying home while I borrow her cute little light-green Audi to make the run back to SeaTac, where I navigate to the baggage claim with much less difficulty than yesterday. The lack of staff and airline delays work in my favor.

I'm able to grab the bags with an agent just before they fall deeper into the chasm of lost property claims.

Overall, it's a pleasant day.

It feels good to be with Gran again.

Later, I feel at home, making tortellini with her special vodka cream sauce before we curl up in front of the fireplace to eat dinner together and catch up with our lives.

I go to bed content with my belly full, my head clear, and the sound of late-winter rain pattering against the window of my childhood bedroom.

◆　◆　◆

I wake up to my phone shrieking and the doorbell ringing so many times it sounds like a whooping ambulance.

I fumble for my phone first because that's the first sound I can make *stop*.

My foggy brain thinks it's my alarm, but then I remember I fell asleep without setting one. I guess the bright side here is that whatever's making that racket has kept me from sleeping too late.

Groggily, I look at my screen as I punch the volume down.

What the hell?

I have over *seven thousand* Twitter notifications—and twice as many on TikTok?

But I have less than three hundred Twitter followers. Mostly all people I met through school or work, or a few art comments.

And I don't even post to my TikTok account; I just use it to follow creators I like.

What gives?

I don't have time to read the notifications and find out, though.

Not when I hear Gran's crutch thumping against the hardwood floors. I need to get down there ASAP and answer the door before she overexerts herself.

I fling myself out of bed, grab the robe I dug out of one of my suitcases last night, drag it around myself, and drop my still-buzzing phone into my pocket as I dash downstairs.

I slip past her on the landing with a quick smile.

"Don't worry, Gran, I've got it!"

"I've got a bad knee, girl, I'm not *dead*!" Her voice drifts after me with playful irritation.

But I'm already to the door, pulling it open.

Before I can blink, Lena Joly flings herself at me, pulling me into her arms with a gasp. "Oh my God! Oh my God, Elle, I was so worried, you weren't answering your texts. I thought something happened to you . . ."

Did I wake up in the twilight zone?

Numbly, I hug my childhood best friend—and try not to sneeze as the ends of her cute little dark-brown bob of hair tickle my nose. "Uh? What would have happened? I was just asleep."

"Asleep? Very funny—oh, you're serious? How can you sleep when you're—" She pulls back, and her eyes search mine frantically, her freckled nose wrinkled. "You don't know, do you?"

"Know what?" I throw my hands up. "Lena, I have a bajillion notifications. I haven't been able to look at them yet, and now you're here talking like the Mafia might have murdered me or something."

"Girl, I don't know. I thought the 'billionaire pick-me' fan club might have kidnapped you." Then, like she didn't just say the most outlandish thing in the world, Lena leans around me and smiles brightly, wiggling her fingers in a little wave. "Morning, Miss Jacqueline."

Gran's crutch thuds closer.

"Good morning, Lena," she says warmly, completely indifferent to Lena's ranting. "Have you had breakfast?"

"I have, ma'am, but I always have room for your lemon poppyseed muffins, if you're offering."

Grandma cackles. "You know my baking habits too well."

"I could smell them coming up the walk."

I just take in this exchange like I'm watching a Ping-Pong match before I clear my throat.

"Guys, are we talking about breakfast or talking about why apparently there's some kind of crisis? What billionaire? Am I getting dragged on social media? Did someone leak my nudes to Elon Musk?"

Lena pauses. ". . . you have nudes to leak?"

Grandma blinks. "You have nudes to leak, and they're accessible in the cloud?"

I bat my eyes right back at her. "You know about the cloud?"

"Young lady, how old do you think I am?" Grandma clucks her tongue and thumps her cane emphatically. "Please lock down your phone. At least have a little common sense if you're sharing a little spice."

"I don't have nudes!" I hiss. Groaning, I drag a hand over my face. "Could someone please just explain what's going on?"

"Perhaps," a silky-dark voice interrupts from behind Lena, "I could be of assistance."

Oh, crud.

That voice isn't so comforting this time.

That voice darts through me like I've just grabbed an electrified fence.

Lena and I both go stiff, while Gran only looks mildly amused.

I stare past Lena in absolute horror at the man standing on the last stone before the front steps.

He's just as impeccable as he was two days ago, even if he looks a bit more casual and relaxed.

His slacks today are still black, his shoes perfectly polished, his waistcoat a dark silvery slate grey, and he's not wearing a tie this time.

His starched white dress shirt has precisely one button unfastened at the neck, exposing his Adam's apple and the corded tendons in his throat.

Also, he's carrying something under his arm. What looks like several stacks of newspapers folded with splashy cover pages just barely visible.

There's also something in one of his angular, graceful hands.

A little grey velvet box.

I have no earthly idea what's going on. No clue how he's involved in this or what he's doing here.

Oh, and I *still don't know his freaking name.*

But I can't stop the small squeak that spills out, turning into a strangled mumble.

"Jet Daddy," I say instinctively.

"Jet *who?*" he snaps, his eyes widening, before he scowls. "Miss Lark, that's not my name."

Lena looks over her shoulder and echoes my squeak.

"Holy shit, it's you!" She stares at him, going so pale she could give me a run for my money.

This is just getting weirder and weirder.

"You know him?" I demand.

"I know *of* him," Lena strangles out. "You don't?"

Then Jet Daddy turns his hell-glare on Lena. She recoils, blushing, sudden color painting her face in vivid red as she makes a choking sound.

Gran lets out an aggrieved sigh. "You young people, always making such drama of everything." She turns away, thumping her crutch definitively toward the kitchen. "Come inside. Let's not have this conversation on the front stoop like heathens. I'll make tea. There's enough muffins for everyone."

Lena just looks at me incredulously.

"You always fall into the weirdest messes," she says before she brushes past me to the kitchen—though that doesn't stop her from catching my hand for a moment and giving it a warm, reassuring squeeze.

That just leaves me standing in the entryway more numb than I've ever been in my life.

Jet Daddy stays rooted to the front step, watching me with those penetrating blue eyes.

"Um," I say. "Is this like a vampire thing? You can't come in without being invited?"

"You," he mutters thinly, "have the oddest imagination, Miss Lark. My name is August Marshall."

I blink at him. "If that's supposed to mean something, it doesn't."

"Don't know if I find that a relief or—fuck, forget it." He pinches the bridge of his nose. "I don't have time for muffins. I have a full schedule today, and this is an unplanned detour. If we could stop wasting time, I'd like to ask you to marry me."

"What?" I yelp loudly.

"What?!" Lena echoes from the kitchen.

But August what's-his-face's stone-cold expression doesn't change.

I don't think he's joking.

I'm sure I make every last face under the sun for him while my stomach and heart do a twisty tango that leaves me feeling breathless and stunned and just a bit sick.

"You heard me," August Marshall says, opening the box in his hand to reveal a diamond-encrusted silver band.

The thing almost blinds me. I'm sure it could retail for seven solid figures.

We're beyond numb now.

I'm not sure how I still have a pulse.

Even in the dim grey Seattle morning, the ring—*the flipping ring!*—glitters impossibly.

"Are you crazy?" I force out slowly. "Like, are you having some kind of breakdown?"

"Crazy? No." He cocks his head like I'm the insane one. "This is a proposal, Miss Lark. I need you to say yes."

The words are already receding.

My head might pop off and spin away to the moon.

I am *so* confused.

"Excuse me," I whisper faintly, even as the world tilts sideways.

"Miss Lark? Are you—"

"I'm going to faint again," I whisper, barely catching my balance.

IV

CALM BEFORE THE STORM

(AUGUST)

This woman brings chaos wherever she goes, like a sweet but deadly perfume.

It's been a morning.

First, Merrick called me in a panic.

Let me be clear—I'm not a morning person.

There's a special place in hell for whoever invented them.

Mornings are a waste of time. Everything is still beginning, nothing solidified, and anything worth happening still can't be dealt with until it's had more time to develop.

What's the point in waking up before I can take immediate action on pressing issues?

Plus, Rick typically reviews our global business and financial headlines affecting whatever industry I'm contracted out to now. He has a list of relevant articles and publications compiled in my inbox before I even sit up and yawn.

However, today he was browsing the gossip rags. Social media. Some odd little thing called *Clubhouse*, and something else involving a tick-tock.

All because people are talking about me for no good reason, and on a clock app where ten-second dog videos rack up more views than State of the Union speeches, no less.

Dammit, not again.

Regrettably, this time they aren't *only* discussing me.

They've dragged Miss Elle Lark into my shit show, and that means I had to pry my eyes open before eleven. Not happily.

That also means I'm standing on her doorstep with the perfect solution to our crisis in hand, while she goes chalk white and sways like a sapling about to fall over.

Not a-fucking-gain.

This time, I'm glad I'm only one step away to catch her.

In one movement, I pocket the ring. In another, I step forward, sweeping an arm around her waist before she can do more than dip to the side.

She doesn't fall as far or as hard as I expect.

I pull her up more sharply than I intend, right as she reaches for the door to brace herself in the frame.

Instead, she falls into my chest.

She reels to a halt with her nose pressed to the top button of my waistcoat.

We're both frozen.

I'm struck once again by that damnable heat radiating off her, especially when people as frail and pale as she is typically have lower body temperatures.

"Um." She stares at the base of my throat, not at my face. Her own face is redder than a fire engine, bringing out the strawberry blonde undertones in her hair. "Mr. Marshall, I . . . I wasn't going to fall. I just . . . I get a little faint." She swallows hard. "You can let me go anytime."

"Right."

Why haven't I immediately?

Clearing my throat, I release her and retreat down one step, placing us a little closer to eye level. My skin remains oddly warm where her frame was just pressed.

"Sorry," I say gruffly. "I didn't mean to be overly familiar."

"What?" She stares at me. "You show up asking—no, *demanding*—to marry me, and you're worried about being overly familiar?"

Her eyes are saucers.

Their hazel is so close to orange it makes me think of a tiger. A tiger cub, maybe.

Only that cub has kitten claws, needle sharp but harmless. Her brows lower fiercely, unexpectedly.

She still has my hand. Her fingers are little slips of warmth gripping at mine with their softness while she pulls me forward with surprising strength.

"Muffins. Now," she bites off, dragging me into the house.

What the hell is happening?

I nearly trip on the steps.

For a moment, my sheer surprise lets her haul me several steps up into the little cottage and down a hall painted in a soothing deep rose. It's festooned in wall-mounted planters that drip flowering vines down the walls under the golden glow of tiny sun lamps.

I pull back, freeing my hand from hers and stopping firmly. "I told you I don't want muffins, Miss Lark. There's no time."

She whips back, glaring at me.

"Don't let Gran hear you! There's *always* time for muffins."

I clench my jaw.

She's an honest mess right now—her hair sleep mussed, falling out in tendrils around her face. An enormous fuzzy bathrobe in pale peach wraps around her, trailing to the floor over a thin white silk camisole and shorts set. Her feet are stuffed in floppy, oversize fuzzy peach slippers that match the robe.

No, she's not a tiger kitten after all.

She's a bunny sent to bring a whole lot of hell into my life.

A small, fuzzy, hell-raising bunny.

If I were still prone to enjoying such things, I might find her cute.

Especially when her pink-tipped nose twitches just like a bunny's as she plants her hands on her hips.

"Look, if you're gonna show up on my doorstep with a ring, you're gonna eat muffins while I try to decide whether or not I'm dreaming." She closes her eyes, huffing and rubbing her temples. "I have anemia. It's why I get the crappy migraines. But it also means that until I get proper nutrition, my blood runs thinner than chicken broth and my brain isn't getting the oxygen it needs. So if you want to explain why you decided to go completely insane in my corner of Seattle and expect me to actually understand, *we're making time for breakfast.* Got it?"

Damn, she's a forceful little thing.

She does, unfortunately, have a point.

Considering how early it is, I don't actually have any pressing scheduling conflicts. That was simply my excuse to get through this quickly, negotiate a deal, an understanding, then extricate myself from this fuckery ASAP.

Perhaps *ASAP* can involve a muffin.

One.

"Fine," I agree reluctantly.

Elle Lark immediately lights up with a brilliant, cheerful smile.

"Good." She turns and tromps away, following where the other girl and the old woman disappeared. "I'll introduce you to my grandmother and Lena. She's my best friend."

I can't do anything but blink.

Her moods change on a dime.

Another potential land mine.

I'm actually starting to wonder if I might be better off weathering the storm of the tabloid toss-up alone.

Still, I follow her deeper into the house.

The entire place is filled with flowers. Wicker furniture nestles everywhere among the greenery.

Soft golden light gives the illusion of sunlight pouring down through garden bowers, reflecting from polished oak floors.

The kitchen is half kitchen, half dining atrium, the circular space glassed in to look out over the views of the lush city below. Mount Rainier rises in the distance, surrounded by hints of hazy clouds and sunlight above the city skyline.

The other girl is helping the older woman set the table and puts out a large basket of muffins and an enormous skillet of scrambled eggs, along with teacups and a teapot with steam drifting out of its spout.

There are four places.

It's like they knew Miss Lark wouldn't take no for an answer.

Damn.

I'll treat this just like a business meeting.

In front of me, Miss Lark stops where the living room blends into the dining area. She makes an awkward sound.

"Um. Mr. Marshall, this is my grandmother, Jacqueline Lark. And my best friend, Lena Joly. Lena, Gran, this is August Marshall."

Miss Joly gives us both a strange look, lingering on me with her eyes still wide.

"I know who he is," she says, and she throws herself down into one of the seats. She's a coltish woman with what seems like a short fuse. "The question is, How do you guys know each *other*?"

"Pure happenstance," I clarify quickly.

"Hmm," Jacqueline Lark says, easing herself down into the chair next to Miss Joly, handling herself deftly with her cane. "Sometimes it's chance. Sometimes it's what needs to happen."

I wrinkle my brows. "I'm not certain what that means."

"It's nothing," Miss Lark says hastily, moving to take one of the two remaining chairs. I can't help but note that the other two have arranged it so we are sitting next to each other. Miss Lark smiles sheepishly. "Sorry. The pills didn't work as well as I'd hoped after the flight yesterday. I passed out in the middle of SeaTac. Mr. Marshall saved me from cracking my head open, then gave me a ride home. That's all."

Miss Joly snorts. "Well, that explains the cover story on the *Seattle Sauce* today."

Miss Lark blinks, then coughs into her hand. "There's a cover story? About him? About *me*? Is that why my notifications went berserk?"

I sigh, pulling out the tabloid sheafs tucked under my arm. "Let me shed some light on this situation so you can understand my proposal."

"Sit, sit," Jacqueline Lark urges. "Don't look so awkward, boy. Food first. Explaining later. Or are you telling me you don't like good home-cooked eggs?"

I find myself sitting without even thinking about it.

Perhaps because she reminds me a little too much of someone else so close to my heart.

Guess all it takes is a fussy older woman to render me into an obedient little boy again.

Still, I'd rather not get too familiar or dawdle too long.

One muffin. That's all I agreed to, and one damn muffin is all I will eat.

Leaning forward, I set the tabloids in the center of the little round table. My elbow brushes Miss Lark as I do. The table is small enough to bring her scent to me, more of that biting sweetness I can't quite identify. "If you'll—"

"Didn't I say explanations later?" Jacqueline says with mock sternness. With one hand, she plucks the papers from me and turns them face down before anyone can see more than a flash of the covers. With the other hand, she scoops up a huge serving of steaming, cheese-threaded, bacon-flecked scrambled eggs onto my plate. "Don't be rude, now. Eat."

Sighing, I glance skeptically at Miss Lark.

She flashes me the same sunny smile and plunks a muffin down on my plate. "Don't be such a grouch. If you really want me to marry you, she's going to be your grandmother-in-law."

"You're enjoying this, aren't you?" I scowl.

The giggle she can't suppress says everything.

I hate my life.

Across the table, Miss Joly had started to pick up her fork as Jacqueline Lark served her. Now it drops to the plate with a clatter. She stares at us with her jaw hanging open.

"Okay. No. Explanations *now*. Elle, you—I thought you didn't know each other! He proposed?" Her jaw hangs open.

"Guess so," Miss Lark answers with a shrug as she reaches for the pan of eggs to serve herself a heap. "No idea why, but he'll explain after we eat, won't he?"

Jacqueline chortles and scoops up a forkful of her own eggs right before she drops a second muffin on my plate and fills my cup with a rich, orange-brown tea with a citrus scent.

"Imagine that. My little Ellie, my first grandchild to get married. And to bring me such a handsome grandson-in-law too!"

Fuck.

My lips work incoherently, then slump.

I pinch the bridge of my nose so hard I'm shocked it doesn't bleed.

How did I lose all control of this situation so catastrophically and so fast?

They've cornered me.

I don't normally bother with breakfast, considering how late I sleep, but I'll indulge this once since it seems to be the only way I'm getting through this alive.

I pick up the little sugar shaker on the table and dash some into my tea, just the way I like it.

"Thanks for breakfast," I say grudgingly. If only because the woman Jacqueline Lark reminds me of would rap my knuckles red for forgetting my manners.

I settle in to eat, remembering my manners only because I won't embarrass myself by wolfing down the food in order to get this over with ASAP.

Miss Joly clearly has no reservations.

She stuffs enough muffin into her mouth to look like a chipmunk, still watching me and Miss Lark with wide, curious eyes.

It's a textbook case of awkward silence, broken only by clinking forks and teacups plinking on the dark cherrywood table.

The food is good.

The tea, a delicate Ceylon with hibiscus.

Once again, it reminds me of better times.

I wasn't always a C-level corporate consultant.

The Fixer, I'm called in some circles. Less kind four-letter names in others.

Regardless, I've staked my name on working corporate miracles.

Before that, there was a time when I was a boy sitting around a table in a homey kitchen just like this, watching the rain patter against a different set of windows while a gentle reminder told me to tuck my napkin in my lap, keep my elbows off the table, and always thank the chef for the food.

After a few bites of flavorful eggs, I look up. "Delicious, Mrs. Lark. Thanks for sharing your table with me. It makes this easier."

I'm not sure there's any way *this* could ever be easy, but it's a start.

I'm surprised to feel a wizened hand patting my knee. Jacqueline Lark smiles at me, her wrinkled face creasing up, and in that moment I can see the resemblance between her and Eleanor quite strongly.

"There now, isn't the morning nicer when you slow down?"

"I'm not a morning person," I say. "So I don't really have anything to compare it to."

"Oh, I love a good morning," Jacqueline says. "Right at dawn, before the morning glories get frightened and curl up. They're gorgeous with fresh dew gleaming on their petals. Perfect little magnifying glasses that highlight every delicate color."

To my other side, Miss Lark laughs softly. Somehow it evokes the image Jacqueline just described: morning glories in the palest blue violet, a few diamond dewdrops along the rim of their trumpets, enhancing every subtle detail until it shines.

I shake myself from my thoughts.

Where the fuck is my head?

I don't daydream. The creative, artsy gene in the family skipped my DNA, and so did any special appreciation for delicate, breakable things.

If anything, they've been my curse.

But when I glance at Miss Lark, she's smiling at her grandmother with an affection that makes her ivory face shine. "Don't mind my grandmother, Mr. Marshall. She loves her flowers more than she could ever love any human after Gramps. She used to be a botanical illustrator before she retired."

"Nonsense," Jacqueline chides with an amused cluck of her tongue, pointing her fork at Miss Lark. "I certainly love you as much as I love my begonias." She frowns, tapping her lower lip. "Almost. On a good day."

"Gran!" Miss Lark laughs brightly again.

Miss Joly chokes out a sound. "How do you—"

Then she simply *chokes*.

A few muffin chunks fall out of her mouth as she goes into a purple-faced coughing fit, her eyes bulging.

Again, I act without thinking, launching myself from my chair. I round the table to hoist her up out of her seat, pulling her back against my chest and embracing her with my hands clasped together for the Heimlich.

One, two, three quick thumps that make her gag—then she spits out the enormous bite of muffin she'd choked on, sending her fork spinning off her plate as it strikes like a meteor.

Miss Joly slumps against me, sagging down into her seat as I gently let her go.

Wiping at her mouth, she clears her throat a few times, coughing out a "Thank you."

Miss Lark and her grandmother were half out of their seats, expressions of frozen concern on their faces, but now they sink back down.

Miss Lark lets out a relieved sigh, brushing her mussed hair back, while Miss Jacqueline just looks at me with a penetrating gaze.

"My, you truly are quite the knight in shining armor, aren't you?" she muses.

I'm not sure what to make of that.

Miss Lark glares at her friend. "That's like the sixth time that's happened. You have got to stop eating like that."

"You've been telling me that since we were eight. Guess what? I still haven't." Miss Joly takes a sip of her tea. Afterward, her scratchy voice sounds much smoother, and she seems completely unbothered by the incident. "Maybe next time it'll be a hot guy coming to the rescue who *isn't* engaged to my best friend."

Next I think it's Miss Lark's turn to choke.

"We *aren't* engaged!" she throws back.

"Yet," I point out as I reclaim my seat. "Will you let me explain now, or do we have to clean our plates a second time? I'd prefer to avoid Miss Joly asphyxiating herself in her curiosity."

Miss Joly says nothing. Her blush betrays her.

Smirking, she flips her middle finger at me from across the table.

Miss Jacqueline swats her shoulder lightly. "Don't be so crude at the table, Lena," she fusses, then nods to me. "All right. Let's hear this, before I give consent to marry my granddaughter."

I start to protest that it's not a real marriage and I don't need consent, but fuck.

I have a feeling that if I let this conversation fly any further off the rails, there's no telling what these women will badger me into.

So I lean over my half-empty plate and turn the tabloid pages over, fanning them out so they're all visible.

The three women all gasp.

Who could blame them?

Every last cover page is splashed with an image of Eleanor Lark either already in my arms, or else falling into them.

I have no idea who took the photos. I wish I did.

They'd already be dead.

But in such a busy terminal, it could've been anyone.

I do have a mighty good idea who slipped them to the trashier arm of the press, but that's a worry for later.

The headlines are our problem now.

IS HE BACK ON THE MEAT MARKET? BILLIONAIRE AUGUST MARSHALL RETURNS TO SEATTLE WITH A DRUNKEN DAMSEL! WILL SHE BE HIS NEXT VICTIM?

VULNERABLE VIXEN IN VICIOUS VILLAIN'S GRASP!

MAY–DECEMBER MAYHEM! WHO IS AUGUST MARSHALL'S MAIDEN?

THE BLACK WIDOW BOSS STRIKES AGAIN!

That last one knifes me in the guts.

Fuck them entirely.

One dead wife does not a black widow make.

Also, FYI, it's the female black widow spider who's always deadlier.

Miss Lark presses her fingers to her mouth.

"I don't understand," she whispers slowly. "I wasn't drunk. You were just helping me. You aren't a villain. Why are they doing this?"

The hurt tone in her voice gives me pause. She may be twenty-three, but at the moment she sounds like a young girl meeting the ugliness of the real world for the first time.

Shame *I* have to be that ugliness.

"My reputation has caught up with you," I say. "An unearned reputation, I promise. I'm not in the habit of preying on random women at all. But a certain business rival has a vested interest in spreading this dreck, and you've been caught in the crossfire. You came to Seattle seeking employment, correct?"

"Well . . . yes," she says faintly. "I mean, I'm also here to help out Gran, but I was going to take a few days to settle in and then start looking for jobs."

She goes paler as the realization sinks in.

Somehow, her pallor only makes her look more unreal, bringing out shades of red in her eyelids, her cheeks, the tip of her nose, and her lips, as if colored with natural makeup.

She's pretty as hell, and I need a firm slap across the face to quit staring.

"Oh. Now I see. So I guess Twitter figured out who I am from the photos." She swallows visibly. "And that means if any employer googles me, that's what's going to come up. That I'm some drunken ho-bag sleeping with—whoever you are." She stares at me. "Who *are* you, August? Why are they saying all these crazy things about you?"

"Rumors. Just like I said. A little blackhearted business dispute. Again, I assure you there's no trail of victims littered in my path. Not even one." I sit back in the hard-backed chair, lacing my fingers together over my stomach.

That part is true.

Mostly.

Whatever guilt I carry doesn't necessarily reflect the honest facts of the situation.

"I do, however, need to recover my reputation in some way, Miss Lark. My family runs a children's publishing house, and it's currently on the ropes. I've been called in to reverse its fortunes, but I can hardly take over Little Key Publishing when the tabloids are telling every bored bystander in the world that I'm a predator who takes advantage of vulnerable young women." I incline my head. "Not exactly someone who should be selling books to kids."

"Hold up," Miss Joly cuts in. "How does getting married fix that? Like . . . did you snap under the stress? Is this you having a psychotic break?"

I eye her. "Your sense of humor is interesting." Then I turn my attention back to Miss Lark. "We don't need to actually get married. An engagement is enough—and a *temporary* engagement at that. If we're engaged, there's a plausible explanation for why I was carrying you in the airport. Far more plausible than me helping a total stranger in medical distress."

They all look at me like I've grown a second head. I'm not winning hearts and minds.

"Look, I have enough contacts in the mainstream press. If we do a joint press release, any searches for your name will return tons about the engagement. Far more than the tabloid mud trying to fabricate a scandal. In the meantime, I can announce my takeover of Little Key Publishing as a family man intending to make a fresh start with a lovely young woman at my side. After an appropriate period of time, we'll stage an amicable breakup. Our relationship couldn't survive the fact that I'm away for months, working on huge turnaround projects for global companies. You will be well compensated for your time, and in the end, I might have contacts who could assist with your career. Easy."

It's not, but I need to sell this.

I pause.

It hits me that I truly know absolutely nothing about Miss Lark or what she might want in life.

I wasn't nosy enough to see what sort of jobs she was looking at on the flight, and I glanced away after noticing the logo of the career site at the top of the page.

"What exactly do you do, Miss Lark?"

She's listened to my proposal in complete silence, just looking at me with the strangest expression on her face, but now she shakes herself, blinking through her daze.

"I'm an illustrator . . . ," she says slowly.

Fuck me, I almost smile.

"Interesting coincidence," I say. "Have you heard of illustrator and author Clara Marshall?"

"Oh no. Stop," Miss Joly interrupts, dragging a hand over her face. "Now you've done it."

Miss Lark brightens instantly. "Clara Marshall? The same one who did Inky the Penguin? Oh my God. I sent so many pen pal letters to Inky—I *loved* those books! They were the whole reason I wanted to be an illustrator in the first place. They made me so happy, and—*wait*." Her lashes tremble as her eyes widen. "Marshall. You mean you're—"

"She's my aunt," I answer. "Also, we're currently looking to revive the Inky brand."

"Oh my God. So cool!" Miss Lark curls her fingers against her chest. "So if I pretend to be your fiancée for a little while, I get to meet *Clara freaking Marshall?*"

I quirk a brow.

I'd almost be insulted that she cares more about my aunt, if this weren't convenient.

Most women would consider me one of Seattle's most eligible bachelors. More than one single woman—and a few not-so-single women—have made plays for me, and they were hardly happy about being rebuffed.

Miss Joly clearly recognizes me for my reputation.

And Miss Lark is more interested in my aunt.

It's simpler that way. There'll be no misunderstandings. I have no desire to get involved with a woman this young—or any women at all. I don't need distractions, complications, deceptions, lies.

I don't need entanglements.

But Jacqueline gives me another strange look.

"Hmm," she says.

"Hmm?" I repeat.

"Nothing, Mr. Marshall. Nothing at all." She smiles mysteriously.

I frown.

The Lark women are damnably cryptic.

Since Miss Lark does, however, seem to have warmed to my scheme after hearing about my aunt, I slip my hand into my pocket and retrieve the ring box. I set it on the table in front of her lightly.

"Do we have a deal?" I growl. "Give me a few months. That's all I ask. I'll pay all expenses, as well as a stipend of twenty thousand dollars per month so you can live the life appropriate to a woman engaged to someone with my particular means. This doesn't need to be difficult. We'll have a press meet; we'll make a few public appearances; we'll be seen together. You will reside partly here, partly at my home. And if you'd like, I could hire you as a temp to work with Aunt Clara. I imagine she'd enjoy having young blood around to revive her inspiration. After our time is up, you'll return home in better shape than you left. A month later, once I've done what I can at Little Key and departed for my next contract, we'll quietly leak news of our breakup while we go about our normal lives with our reputations and sanity intact."

Well, *sanity* may be doubtful when I'm inviting this chaotic woman into my life for a few months.

She gazes at the ring, then looks at me, her eyes shining as she lights up with the brightest smile I've seen yet.

"Okay. Deal!"

"Then get dressed, please." I push my chair back and stand, dusting off my clothes and straightening the creases in my slacks. "Unless you have appropriate wear for meeting the press, I'll need to take you shopping immediately."

"Oh my Gawd," Miss Joly mumbles, pressing her face into her hands. "You guys have both lost your ever-fucking minds."

"And isn't it delightful?" Jacqueline chuckles.

V

GIRLS JUST WANNA HAVE SUN

(ELLE)

See? I *told* you there was a bright side to everything.

Okay. Sure. Maybe Lena's right.

Maybe this is absolutely batshit insane.

But it's also crazy cool.

I get to have fun swanning around pretending to be Mr. Marshall's spoiled fiancée for a while.

I get to meet smart people in children's publishing, and if I'm lucky, I'll even get a shot at building a strong network of referrals.

I get nice new clothes. Nicer than my standard interview pantsuit and my small collection of eclectic business casual wear.

I might even get to find out what's under his grouchy exterior, assuming Mr. Marshall just has to defrost enough to talk to me like a normal human being. Pretty much required, if anyone's going to believe I know him well enough to call him *August*.

And best of all?

I get to work with the *Clara Marshall.*

I can't stop grinning as I watch Seattle slide by from the back seat of that slick car—which was waiting for us outside with the driver, Rick.

I'm still trying not to hyperventilate.

Inky the Penguin practically shaped my childhood.

The whole series of illustrated children's books follows an adorable emperor penguin like no other. Instead of being black with a white belly, Inky was born white with a special black belly that doubles as a magic inkwell for writing letters.

If it sounds weird, don't worry. Inky only uses his powers for good.

He travels all over the world, finding new places, new cultures, new friends, always carrying pen pal letters. His backpack bulges with envelopes overflowing with cheerful messages from folks who would've never met without his help.

I remember it like yesterday.

Even though we only lived a few houses apart, Lena and I would write letters and leave them in each other's mailboxes, pretending that Inky himself had delivered them. When we played together, we'd tromp through the woods, imagining we were Inky's little companions on his long hikes around the globe.

If we had to cross Puget Sound on the ferries with Gran or Lena's parents, then we were Inky on a great steamship crossing the oceans.

"Do you ever stop smiling, Miss Lark?" August mutters without looking at me.

"Do you ever start?" I throw back, tossing a grin over my shoulder. "And I mean a real smile. Not that creepy Mr. Burns thing you did when you found out I was a children's illustrator."

"Burns? As in Lincoln?" He's on his laptop. *Again.* I don't think the man knows how to take a break.

"No! Not the fashion CEO. *The Simpsons?*" When that gets me a blank look, I laugh. "Wow. We are *so* different. How are people ever supposed to believe we're engaged?"

"'Opposites attract' is still a thing, isn't it?" He frowns. "Of course, it's bound to end in divorce as soon as the novelty wears off, but since we're breaking up anyway, we don't have to worry about that."

How romantic.

"Ugh, you're such a pessimist." I shift in the back seat to face him, drawing one leg up and hugging it to my chest. "People should believe we're engaged because . . . because we met and something too powerful to ignore swept us up in this crazy attraction. You, this dashing, handsome man. Ice cold on the outside, but when you met me, you melted. And I saw a touch of heart in you that thrilled me and made me want to know more. While you . . ." I toss my hair playfully. "You were confused and annoyed because you found me irresistible. You couldn't stop thinking about me for a single second."

I hold up my hand with a sliver of space pinched between my fingers.

August is not amused.

His stern blue eyes drill through me with his dead stare.

"While you're clearly a very lovely young woman, Miss Lark, you're also cursed with an overactive imagination."

The gruffness in his voice makes me smile.

"Sad you think that, but okay. The more you ice me out, the cuter I think you are."

"Fuck that." Both of his starkly defined eyebrows rise sharply. "There's nothing *cute* about me."

"That's a lie! There's plenty." I wiggle more comfortably into the almost sinfully plush seats, settling to sit cross-legged as I face him. "Now why don't you close the laptop and tell me what's wrong at Little Key?"

"I have a meeting in—"

"Not for three hours," Rick calls from the front seat. "Listen to the lady, sir. She's right."

"This is a two-way conversation," August growls, shooting a glare at the driver's seat. "Traitor."

Rick just flashes me a smile in the rearview mirror and winks.

"Sorry." I lean over to thunk his laptop lid down firmly. "You're outnumbered two to one, and this is a democracy. So, what's up? Why is the company struggling?"

August sits stiffly for a moment, then sighs out half his soul.

"Because my aunt hasn't published a book in over a decade. You can only revive your backlist for so long before you're spending more on advertising than you're making, no matter how famous your books are. Originally, they planned to expand the Inky line from young readers into middle and young adult with illustrated short novels and new characters. That plan died when Clara lost her ability to work on new stories."

Clara Marshall has lost her mojo? The news almost rocks me back.

"Why did she stop?"

"It's complicated." He presses his lips together. For such a grumpy-looking man, he has a surprisingly full red mouth. The framing of his dark, trimmed beard makes it stand out even more. Pressing his lips together does little to thin them and just makes them look fuller. "The Inky concept had a rough start that led to some personal complications. Those complications spiraled, eventually leading to my aunt losing her inspiration until she no longer wished to work on new concepts at all—even if the loss clearly pains her. But I've said enough. The rest isn't my story to divulge."

Vague much?

Even so, a little pang plucks at my chest. I rub at the ache, biting my lip.

"Wow, that's heartbreaking. She made something that meant so much to so many children—and adults too. My walls used to be covered in my own drawings of Inky. Just scribbles, but Lord knows I tried. Oh, and I'd write letters to the address in the back of the book all the time. It always made me burst with joy when 'Inky' wrote back, and it was real, handwritten. Not just a form letter. Those stories, your aunt, they're the reason *why* I'm a children's illustrator. She inspired me. I want to make people feel happy the same way she did with me."

August just looks at me in grim silence—and is there something different in his eyes?

It's like spring coming to a frozen glacier, warming its frigid blue shadows into something softer.

But he looks away abruptly like he wants to hide that softness.

He gazes out the window. Seattle light at this time of day turns silver, tinted by rain, and it pours in pale edges over the sharp, decisive lines of a strong, masculine profile.

"You should tell her that, when you meet her." His fingers drum lightly against his closed laptop. "I think it would matter a great deal to her. She answered every last one of those letters herself, you know."

"Wait, what? You're kidding?" That ache in my chest flips, turning into a sweet flutter. "You mean the real Clara Marshall actually wrote back to me?"

Though he's hiding his face from me, I think I actually catch the corners of his mouth turning up.

"You know, it's charming that you're more starstruck by my aunt than by me."

"Bleh. If you find me charming, we're getting somewhere." I snicker. "But I mean, c'mon. I grew up with her books! I'd never even *heard* of you until this whole flap set the internet on fire." And I haven't had a chance to check my phone and see what all the fuss is about, considering how quickly he whisked me out of the house. Plus, I'm still scared to look at my notifications and sift through the endless DMs from trolls. "Why does everyone in Seattle but me know who you are?"

Wrong question.

Wrong question.

That glacier goes arctic again, and his strong shoulders stiffen.

"Shit happened. My personal life was tabloid fodder for a while," he says tightly. "If you don't know, you don't need to pry. Besides, I have an eleven-figure net worth, Miss Lark. I'm single, in moderately good shape for my age, and apparently I have a reputation as a bit of an asshole in my line of work. People talk. Bullshit travels at the speed of lies."

Oof.

I'm so, so curious about this personal stuff, but he's asked me pointedly not to look.

I'm not completely insensitive, even if I may be a little too tactlessly extroverted. This is also hardly the time or place.

I'd have to say that he's in more than *moderately* good shape, though.

Not to mention the flight, where I was thigh to thigh with him. His impeccable style may slim him down with the sleekness of perfectly cut suits, but underneath there's a solid stack of muscle. He's a powerhouse of steel with a delicious taper from his broad shoulders to the sleek, straight waist and narrow hips.

"How old are you, anyway?"

"Thirty-four, if you must know," he grinds out.

I burst out laughing.

"Oh my God." I press my fingers to my mouth, trying to stop my giggles. "You act like you're sixty with one foot in the grave. Thirty-four is still young. You're not an old man. Stop being so stuffy—even if *that's* pretty cute too."

"I am not fucking cute," he snarls.

Very cutely.

"Also," he continues, drawing himself up almost pompously, "Aunt Clara raised me to behave like a gentleman. It's served me well, and I dare not disappoint her."

"Um, okay. Either way, I bet she didn't raise you to keep a permanent stick up your butt, but hey, we just found out something we have in common, *fiancé*. My parents didn't really raise me either." I stick my tongue out at him playfully. "You'd probably like them. They were all over the world instead of at home with me. Total money-obsessed workaholics. Even if I still don't quite get what you *do*."

August's sigh is long, aggrieved, and pissed off.

Oh boy.

I'm having too much fun with him.

He gives me a weary look. "They call me the Fixer."

"That sounds like a nickname for a plumber. Or a hit man?" My smile wilts. "You don't actually kill people, do you?"

His stare turns flat.

"You're not as funny as you think, Miss Lark. As I said at your grandmother's, I do turnaround projects. Failing companies hire me to reverse their fortunes and set them on the right track to profitability and market dominance. Once I've finished, it's on to the next miracle."

"Commitment issues. Got it."

He narrows his eyes. "It's work. Work that has nothing to do with my personal life."

When I just grin at him, he scowls.

"Brat. You're trying to rile me up."

"Caught me." I wink.

"Why?"

"Because." I flop myself back against the seat, letting my feet fall to the floor again. "No one's going to believe we're in love if you don't stop trying to pretend you hate everything and you're too dignified to come down from your ivory tower. So if you won't come willingly, I'll just have to tear down those tower walls until you do."

"Must we be *that* convincing?"

"Yes, we must." I tilt my head against the seat back, eyeing him with amusement. "Again, you're not that old. You know people pick everything apart on social media. It's just going to make things worse if they can tell we're faking it. Then this whole thing will be for nothing."

"How is it that this was my idea, yet you're planning for more complications than I am?" Huffing, August mutters something under his breath and glares out the window again. ". . . parents."

"What was that?" I blink, leaning toward him.

"My parents died. I was so young I don't remember them," he growls. "There was an accident. So my aunt Clara raised me and my younger sister, Debra. Clara was more than an aunt to us. She was practically our mother."

It takes a minute to sink in.

It's not about his parents at all. He can't miss what he doesn't remember.

It's about what he cares about.

"Oh. So saving Little Key means a lot to you," I murmur. A softness wells up inside me, and I think I like it. "It's not just another fixer job. You actually want to save the company because it's your aunt Clara, not just for business."

He doesn't answer, just swallows roughly like a sulking boy who's been caught caring too much.

"You understand. I'm glad."

"Yeah, I do. It's sweet, August." I smile. "For the record, I'd do the same thing for Grandma Jackie. I moved back here to look after her."

"Is she ill?" August glances at me, and there's a flicker of what might be genuine interest in his eyes.

I shake my head.

"Nope. She just busted her knee hiking around Olympia. She never could sit still, and now it's driving her insane that she has no choice but to take a little downtime. So someone's got to stay with her to make sure she doesn't kill herself, since she's being stubborn about surgery, and since my parents are retired and soaking up the sun in the Keys, it has to be me."

"You uprooted your entire life for this? Where were you before?"

"New York. I lived there through college and a little after." I shrug. "There wasn't much to uproot, honestly. I was just doing the freelancer grind. And at least if I'm going to live somewhere with a stupidly high cost of living, it'll be at home, where I don't have to pay rent."

"Hm." He looks puzzled. "Why does your grandmother refuse surgery?"

"My grandfather died during a routine medical procedure." I smile sadly. "He ended up with an air embolism. Ever since, she's afraid of going under anesthesia because she might not wake up. She misses Gramps, but she always says she's not ready to join him yet. Her flowers might miss her too much."

"I see." There it is again—that barely there softening. I don't think he realizes it's happening, but I want to see more of it. "She reminds me of Aunt Clara. Strong willed and lovably eccentric."

I smile. "That's the best description of Gran I've ever heard."

It's sweet that underneath his gruffness he actually seems to like and respect my grandmother after such a short meeting.

But I shouldn't be thinking he's sweet at all, should I?

Although if we're going to fake it for a few months, we can at least *try* to like each other and get along.

Before we can say anything else, though, the car stops on the curb.

We're close enough to the Seattle–Bainbridge ferry that I can see the glinting water through the window, just past the cluster of high-end boutique shops surrounding us on all sides of the street.

Although I know the neighborhood, shopping here has never been in my budget, except for that one time Mom and Dad sent home a big cash envelope for my sixteenth birthday and told me to buy the nicest dress I wanted for homecoming.

I wound up going to homecoming alone. Lena did too.

We went to a bonfire with a bunch of our friends and got stupid drunk and cried over finals and bad breakups. We had the best night of our lives before waking up hungover the next day.

Bad decision?

Yes.

But I still remember that night with a fond smile.

Back then the shops here were swank. Now they're couture and European—very high fashion.

I already feel like I don't belong in my cute cuffed jeans and clumpy Doc Martens, my pretty lavender shirred sweater, and my mangled military-style grey canvas jacket with artsy patches all over it.

Then again, some trendy designer would probably take one look at what I'm wearing and call it boho, then sell it for ten times what I originally paid.

"So, what's our budget?" I stare up at the sign on the shop closest to the curb.

"Budget?" August asks dryly. "Miss Lark, I could buy the entire store. Don't bother looking at the prices; just focus on finding what makes you look—acceptable."

I notice that pause before the last word.

He stops and makes a low, almost embarrassed sound deep in his throat.

I glance at him with a smirk. "You were about to say something insulting, weren't you?"

"I was not," he insists so firmly that he most definitely was. "Your style suits you. It simply doesn't suit me for this arrangement."

"Oh, okay. And if I'm going to be your arm candy, I've got to match the rest of your accessories, right?" Laughing, I reach for the door handle. "C'mon. Let's go make me look like I could actually attract some rich pill like you, and then you can make your big meeting on time."

The door latch clicks, but before I can push it open, I feel it again—that long, warm hand wrapped around my wrist. The calluses on his fingertips brush my pulse like he's trying to fan sparks into flame, searing my blood.

I have to stop and remind myself this isn't real.

Sure, I've thought he was hot since the moment I saw him on the plane.

But this man is completely indifferent to me, and as far as he's concerned, I'm about as attractive as a ruffled legal document.

I'm surprised he hasn't made me sign anything in blood yet.

When I swallow dryly and look back, he lets me go quickly, like he hadn't even realized what he was doing.

"Miss Lark?" He brushes his hand lightly against his slacks.

I glare at him. I've had *enough* of this uptight *Miss Lark* thing.

"Elle," I correct.

"Miss Lark," he repeats.

"*Elle*," I hiss.

His brows set. I swear to God, he looks like a stubborn bison who's just stepped onto the highway and won't move.

My mouth opens again, but he speaks first.

"Eleanor," he concedes, almost under his breath.

"Nope. That's not good enough." I fold my arms over my chest and lift my chin. I'm not going into the store until he says it. "Elle. Say it, August."

"On one condition." Another of those long sighs that tells me I'm driving him insane rolls out, and it feels like victory.

"Conditions already? Such a businessman." Groaning, I flop back against the seat. He's probably going to tell me to always call him *sir* or something like that.

Which. Hey. If that's his kink, I could get into it, but I doubt that's the case.

"Lay it on me, boss man." I roll my eyes.

He pauses.

"The ring," he says softly. "We'll be seen together in public. You should be wearing it."

Oh.

Oh, crap.

I'd almost forgotten all about it in my pocket.

I haven't even tried it on.

For all the heavy meaning and expense, he might as well have gotten it for a quarter out of one of those toy machines with fake princess rings in plastic bubbles.

I slip the little velvet ring box out of my pocket. I never expected that putting it on would feel like signing away my soul.

I'm not sure how to feel about that, but I did agree to this insanity.

I just never thought the first time a guy put a ring on my finger, it'd be with such weird strings attached.

That makes it hurt more than it should.

Why?

I'm only twenty-three. It's not like I was looking to get hitched anytime soon, and I won't actually be off the market after we end this little charade.

It's just a few months.

It's just a little game of pretend with a man who doesn't love me.

Fun times ahead.

But maybe wearing it will just drive home the fact that there's no one who loves me right now.

"Miss Lark—Elle." The inside of the car is so quiet when he speaks. Rick is just a ghost in the front seat, so I feel like I'm alone in a small space with a voice that doesn't match the detached distance this man wears around him like a prison wall. "Is something wrong? If the ring isn't to your taste, we'll find you a better one."

"No, no . . . it's not that." I look up, smiling faintly. "It's just . . . you didn't even ask if I had a boyfriend before throwing this whole idea at me. So it makes me wonder if I'm just that unlovable—is it so easy to just assume I'm not seeing anyone else?"

August blinks like he's just been slapped.

"Elle Lark," he whispers almost gently. "You weren't subtle about flirting with me on that damned flight. You seem like a woman with integrity, even if you drive me up the wall. I assumed you wouldn't flirt with me if you were attached to someone else. You wouldn't—would you?"

"Yeah, no. No way. I get it now."

Why doesn't that answer totally satisfy me?

It's perfectly logical. It's correct.

I'm definitely not that kind of girl.

If I'd been seeing someone else, I'd have never looked at him twice besides distantly noticing he's easy on the eyes.

So what did I want him to say?

Sure, you're erratic and whimsical and annoying. Possibly completely fucking crazy.

But you're so intensely lovable that I don't know how I'll keep this pretend *for the next two months.*

You're irresistible, Elle Lark, no matter how many ex-boyfriends called you "weird" and "impulsive."

Nice fantasy.

Instead, I get, *Yes, I wasn't oblivious to your wiles. I just didn't care.*

"Elle." It's the third time he's said my name in just a few minutes, almost like he's practicing it. Each time gets more of his chocolate voice on it until my own name sounds dark and decadent. His hand covers mine on the ring box, and we lock eyes. "Stop doubting. Let me."

"Huh?"

I don't realize what he means until he takes my hand.

His grasp feels different from the other times. Before, when he caught my wrist, it was always to stop me from falling on my face—but now he does this to hold me, to keep me still, to spread my fingers with a gentle touch that makes my skin ripple and steals my breath.

Not real, not real.

But it feels like something tangible as he carefully pries the box open, revealing that weighty silver band. He plucks it out and slides it onto my ring finger with something like—

Reverence?

I don't know.

It would've made more sense for him to just jam the thing on my finger as quickly as possible, but he's slow and careful and ceremonial.

When he's done, he still doesn't let go.

He just looks down at the ring on my finger, glittering there in the low light. I can't tell what he's thinking, but these mixed signals are messing me up.

At least it fits.

Lucky guess.

"You'll have to excuse me for not getting down on one knee," he says. "I couldn't be sure if the paparazzi stalkers followed me to your house, and it would seem odd if they'd caught me kneeling on your front step. It might have blown our cover when we were already engaged."

That's when it hits me.

The fancy sleek sedan has tinted windows, but they're not totally opaque.

He's being like this just in case someone's snapping photos of us through the windows.

That knocks the butterflies right out of me.

I smile brightly and free my hand from his, curling it against my chest. The added weight of the ring and the sharp glint of the diamonds both feel strange. I'm sure I'll get used to it.

"I don't really do formal anyway," I say cheerfully, ignoring the strange scratchiness in my throat. "Okay, let's go dress me up like a proper lady."

"Wait here."

Puzzled, I watch as August opens the door and slips out, moving with a litheness that seems to belong to a much trimmer man than this hard-cut giant. But I get an answer to my unspoken question when he slips around to the curbside door and opens it for me, reaching inside for my hand.

Oh my God.

The gentleman doting on his fiancée, after all.

I do my duty and play along.

With another smile I slip my hand into his. The little flip in my stomach isn't fake when he lifts me out like I weigh less than a ladybug.

He's *strong*.

Strong enough that I can't help but call him *Jet Daddy* in my head, even if it would piss him right off if I said it to his face.

I guess my expression gives me away, though. Because even as he guides my hand to his arm and escorts me to the closest fashion shop, he eyes me suspiciously.

"That smile does not inspire trust, Elle Lark. What are you thinking?"

"Nothing good. But I'll behave myself for your sake." I giggle.

He rolls his eyes.

So dramatic.

We step into a brightly lit couture shop with scents of sandalwood and vanilla everywhere. The bell over the door jingles, announcing our arrival among artfully staged displays showing off unique pieces that don't have price tags on them because if you need to ask, you can't afford it.

Several shop attendants drift around, wearing clothes just as nice as what's on display. They move with this fairy-tale grace that makes me feel like I'm watching elves in *The Lord of the Rings*.

One of the slender, statuesque women glides closer, her perfect shell pink manicure gleaming. Her neck is so long she looks like a sculpture, and as her cool gaze flicks over August with interest and me with a touch of confusion—*What is this urchin doing in here?*—I have a terrible thought.

She'd look way better on August's arm than I ever will.

She flashes a smile. "Welcome to—"

"We're fine." August cuts her off. He's not even looking at her as his gaze drifts over the store, moving from one display to the next. "We'll let you know when she's ready to try something on."

The woman blinks rapidly. Her smile freezes, then relaxes with professional practice.

"Of course," she says smoothly, inclining her head in a way that might as well have said *Well, fuck you too.* "My name's Angelique. Call me if you need anything."

August doesn't acknowledge her.

He just turns and leads me deeper into the store.

I press in a bit closer to his side—not for appearances, but so I won't be heard in the echoing space over the distant tinkle of some astral-sounding soothing music.

"Did you have to be so rude?" I hiss. "She was only trying to help."

"She's trying to make her commission," August points out flatly. "I was saving her the effort and the breath. She'll earn without hovering over us. Can't stand being badgered while I'm making purchases."

"You can at least be polite about it."

"Why bother when you can just get to the point?"

I side-eye him hard. "Where are you in such a hurry to be that makes every second spared a second wasted?"

He pauses and gives me the oddest look.

Then he moves on without answering, leading me to a display where a dress of deep-scarlet chiffon courses over a headless mannequin's body. It's sleeveless with a plunging V in the front, loosely belted and backless.

Before August opens his mouth, I shake my head.

"Absolutely not."

"Why not?" he demands, scowling.

"For one, wearing red doesn't flatter my complexion. It makes it worse. Trust me. I look like a zombie-girl in red. Even worse, I look like a zombie-girl covered in *blood*." I tick off the points on my fingers. "Two, that's not a dress for introducing your fiancée to the press. That's a dress for taking your fiancée out to a fancy dinner and then bringing her home and ripping the dress off her to fuck her on the couch before you can even make it upstairs to the bed."

August had been opening his mouth—to argue back, I'm sure—but he chokes on his stalled words. His eyes widen as he shoots me an absolutely searing look that might be anger if it's not—

Hm.

Are Grumpy Boy's cheeks a little red under that beard?

He stares at me like he's waiting for me to apologize for being so crude.

I just smile, sweet as pie. "What's the matter, Auggy dearest?"

"*August*," he snaps, and I swallow my snicker. "And my house is single-story. There are no stairs to the bedroom."

. . . what?

70

A smirk flicks over his lips, then vanishes.

He lets my arm go, drifting away calmly toward another display while I stare after him with my mouth open and my face too warm.

God, he's confusing.

That just makes me want to mess with him more.

So I skip after him to the next display—and immediately grimace at the dress.

It's this flared skirt thing like a fifties housewife's, complete with a lace bib collar and the most awful shade of mustard yellow.

"Nope."

"What's wrong with *this*? It's more reserved, isn't it?"

"It's ugly," I say. "Dresses that length make me look stumpy. I know my own body, thank you very much. I know what looks bad on me. I just don't know what would look *good enough* on me."

Clenching his jaw, August darts me a look like he thinks I might just be doing this on purpose—I promise I'm not—and turns to another display. Before he even moves toward the weirdly duck-patterned mini-dress, I shake my head.

"Don't even think about it."

August turns back to me with a hiss, throwing his hands up. "Well then, what *will* you wear?"

"Don't know," I chirp back. All his hissing and scowling and grumping just doesn't work on me. "But I have an idea."

"Enlighten me," he retorts.

"Hmm . . ." Kicking my feet lightly, I lace my hands together and turn to slowly survey the shop. There are some pretty things in here, not just outfits that are weird for the sake of being weird because *fashion*. "Why don't you dress me in what you'd like me to wear? Not what you think I should. What you want to see."

I swear to God, August could singlehandedly cause a polar vortex with those man-freezes he does. I glance over my shoulder, and he's gone cold again. I can practically feel my skin icing over, prickling with shivery goose bumps.

"I have no opinion on your dress as long as it's press appropriate," he growls.

He says it without ever unclenching his teeth or changing his flat tone.

Wow, I must really annoy him.

With a small smile, I decide to dial it down a notch.

Poor August.

He just tried to help a sick girl out at the airport, and now he's stuck with a hyperactive artist who isn't intimidated by him.

"August," I murmur, stepping closer to him. "Just humor me, please?"

He purses his lips but relents, shaking his head. "I have a feeling I'll be doing a lot of that in the coming months."

I grin. "It just means your lovely fiancée has you wrapped around her little finger already."

And I can't help but run my thumb over the ring as I say it.

So weird.

Even if it's just an act, I'm *engaged*.

August flashes me another resigned look before he shakes his head and wanders away. I let him, just watching his tall, agile figure as he moves from display to display, studying each dress and coordinated outfit with a thoughtful gaze.

That's just how he is, I guess.

The man takes everything so seriously, even a silly request from a girl he feels obligated to just because we got our lives tangled up in the weirdest way.

Is it strange that I find that endearing?

He's fascinating to watch. Mr. Buttoned Down, but he still seems like he's going to realize how much he confines himself and come busting out of that tight-stitched shell with a primal roar any second.

It's that one lock of hair that always falls over his brow, I think.

He's so stern and buttoned up, but he just can't tame that one glossy arc of black. Almost like it's his own internal rebellion screaming to let loose and be the wild, sexy, dominant man he was always meant to be.

. . . have I mentioned I have a very active imagination?

August pauses on a pale flapper-style dress covered in tiny seed pearls, studying it intensely before moving on.

A high-waisted jacketed pantsuit with a silk neck scarf and legs so wide and flared each one could be a skirt.

A Lady Gaga–worthy *thing* that looks like a minidress made out of giant cotton balls—I bet that would itch like mad. I'm glad he moves past that one fast, and I watch curiously as he settles on a dress that makes me think of a moth under a tree, dappled in moonlight.

It's lilac, but just barely. If not for the fact that its soft-shimmer gauze is layered, the color would never show through. The dress is sleeveless, with a high, demure neckline and a gathered waist. The skirt trails down in layers with tattered, pointed ends and a faint shirring.

On the mannequin, it falls just below the knee. On me, it would fall to just above midcalf.

Subtle hints of color speckle the fabric, hints of pink and peach and gold that disappear if you stare at them too long.

Silent, motionless, August looks at the dress for so long without his expression changing before a sudden knit to his brows tells me he's made his decision.

He turns to look at me.

"This one," he rumbles, his silky voice resonating.

I step closer, moving to his side, and look up at the dress. When I touch the trailing ends of the skirt, they're so soft. It'll feel like wearing a breeze.

"This one it is," I agree.

It's honestly lovely, and it suits me.

I'm actually getting excited about wearing something he's picked out.

I just hope it looks as good on me as it does on the mannequin.

I look around for Angelique—but she seems to materialize from between two displays, moving as silently as an assassin.

I leap back with a squeak, letting go of the dress guiltily.

She smiles like nothing happened.

"You wanted to try this one on?" she asks. "Please, follow me to the fitting rooms. I'll have my assistant bring the dress." She flashes that *fuck you* pleasant smile to August again. I honestly think no matter how creepy and stuck up she seems, I might just like her. "If you'd like, you can wait outside the fitting rooms, sir. We keep refreshments for our shoppers' gentlemen partners."

I start to protest that he's not my partner, then shut my mouth so hard my teeth click.

For now, he absolutely is.

That shouldn't make me blush like an apple.

August trails Angelique and me like a silent hunter as she leads me on a weaving path to the back. The fitting area looks like a cozy, comfortable waiting room, with lush seating, an espresso machine, refrigerated drinks, snack trays, and even a chocolate fountain arranged against the back wall near the curtained-off changing rooms.

I nearly jump out of my skin again as another tall, statuesque elf-woman appears from behind one of the curtains with the dress draped over her arm.

Where did she come from? I look over my shoulder where the dress had been, then back at her, then—?

Elves.

She smiles knowingly and beckons.

"In here, sweetie." Her voice is warmer than Angelique's, though I can barely tell them apart except by their outfits. "Will you need help changing?"

"No, I'm okay," I say quickly. I cast August a nervous glance, but he's reading something on his phone.

Yep.

We look like a real couple, all right.

74

The married ones where the husband just wants to get out of here before his wife steps on his last nerve.

The second woman gives me a wry, knowing look as she passes the dress over, then pats my arm. "Don't worry, sweetie," she whispers. "Once you put that on, he won't be able to take his eyes off you."

Do I want that?

Or do I just want to fit the image August needs?

Stop overthinking it.

Once I duck inside, my inner frustration becomes a second presence in the decorated, highly scented fitting room. I keep asking myself why I'm being so weird over this, but it's pretty obvious.

Sure, I'm taking this all in stride.

Yeah, I'm calmer about it than August himself is.

But it's also a lot to take in.

August is a human tornado: dark and broody and destructive, touching down wherever he pleases and tearing up everything in his wake.

He's spun me completely for a loop, and even if I am keeping my equilibrium, I'm in shock and still trying to process all of this. It makes me wobble back and forth, getting the *now* all tangled up with those hopeful *what-ifs* when I first saw him on the plane and my crazy, romantic imagination thought, *Wow. I wouldn't mind starting something with him.*

Well, I've definitely started something.

A flipping mess.

It's only been a few hours since he showed up with the ring on my doorstep.

Once I have time to get used to this, I'll treat it like what it is—a job.

For now, as I look in the mirror with the dress draped over my arm, I linger on the ring, glimmering in the mirror like a dream.

If this were real, if it had been some other girl August loved and who loved him, she'd have broken down in tears and said, *Yes, yes, yes!*

I'm not her.

So I just smile at my reflection and get busy transforming into the girl August Marshall wants me to be.

I plaster the dress on like I'm handling a gossamer spiderweb. I don't know how much it costs, but I don't want to rip it if I'm not going to wear it.

Shoes go too. My clunky shoes couldn't possibly look good with this.

I'm barefoot as I slide into the delicate dress and gather my hair up off my neck, though I can't stop a few wavy tendrils from falling into my face and trailing down to my collarbones.

There's a long, nervous pause before I glance at the mirror again.

Holy crap.

I look pretty.

I look the way I wanted to look that night when I got smashed at homecoming because I spent my birthday money on an ugly dress I thought would make me look grown up.

I don't just look grown up now.

I look *beautiful.*

It makes me feel like I'm made of moonlight. The outfit flows around me like wings waiting to carry me to the stars.

As I twirl I even *feel* lighter, like it gives me a grace I've never had before.

I mean . . . I know how to make myself look cute. Hot, even, if it's a good day.

But this . . . this is that moment where you wish you had a man just so you could steal his breath away.

I guess I do have one, a man who can sign off on this part of our deal and then be on his merry way to his meeting.

My chest shouldn't be a bundle of nerves as I push the curtain open and step outside to see what August thinks.

He's settled on a long low leather bench, reading something on his phone with an impatient knit to his brows, sipping from a small espresso cup.

He doesn't notice me—but he looks up as I clear my throat.

"So." I smile, turning to let the skirt swirl around me. "How do I look, Mr. Marshall?"

VI

THE STORM APPROACHES

(AUGUST)

It's a minor miracle I don't face-plant on the floor.

Look, I've seen legions of beautiful women in dresses that cost more than the GDP of a small country. Women whose job is to be beautiful; who wear the very best like they were born to, their bodies and faces crafted to model perfection so elegant it's inhuman.

Yet none of them have ever made me do a double take the way this messy little firecracker does when she sails out of the dressing room wearing gossamer and a smile.

When she clears her throat, I glance up at first without registering anything besides how well the dress fits even before any alterations.

Only, my fucking eyes get stuck.

I can't look down again at the chart on my phone mapping years' worth of Little Key's quarterly reports and their ugly downward trend.

". . . how do I look?" she asks again, shy and beguiling.

That's when what I've seen really sinks in, and then I can't look away to save my life.

She's goddamned stunning.

Not messy.

Not infuriating.

Not dolled up like a scruffy art punk.

She's a wind-tossed force of nature, delicate and too bright.

The dress swirls around her like an angel's robes, this soft madness that makes me want to break down into writing sappy poetry if I don't just throw her against the nearest wall and rip it off her with my teeth.

It's all the light she exudes so naturally that sometimes just standing close to her burns.

Her arms are pale and slender, willowy things that flow with her movements and make her too graceful.

Her legs are slim and silky, demanding greedy caresses as they flirt in and out of the dress's layered hem.

The modest neckline flatters the fragile line of her collarbones, extending her slender neck until it holds her finely crafted face up on a pedestal to be worshipped.

Although the dress isn't made to be form hugging, her curves are as disobedient as the rest of her. They play fucking peekaboo every time she turns and the material hugs her chest, her hips, her sleek thighs.

She's innocent and sensual, surreal and earthy.

I don't understand why my eyes won't work.

Why I can't look away.

Why my heart beats so violently and my body tightens as I lose blood to a thrumming hard-on designed to torture me.

This is hell itself distilled into roughly five feet of sweetness too gorgeous for life.

Elle twirls one more time, just to finish me off.

Her strawberry blonde hair kisses her throat as she stops, a touch flushed and breathless, her hazel eyes glittering like stars.

"Well?" she asks—teasing as always. "I hope I don't look half-bad. It's a nice dress. And I think it makes me look pretty respectable. Hopefully?"

Right.

We're here to make her fit in my world. It's not about making her look beautiful, according to my tastes.

It's just about her fitting in.

Yet when she told me to choose what *I* wanted to see her in, I rebelled at the idea.

Normally, I don't care to see a woman in anything except stark professional attire when they're working in my offices or on site with my clients. I have no use for pretty things flitting around, glancing at me with beguiling eyes and ruby lips, their soft hands an invitation to heartbreak and betrayal.

I'm over and done with that shit.

Yet when I saw that dress draped against the mannequin, looking like someone had teased a sunset into silk and spun that thread into cloth, it made me think.

It made me imagine the sunset hues of her hair.

Hell yes, I thought. *This will suit her perfectly.*

The end result turned out infinitely better than expected.

And I'm still staring at her blankly when she falters, her smile wilting. "August? Oh God, does it look bad?" She catches the skirt of the dress and spreads it out, looking down at herself, her gaze searching. "I didn't get lipstick on it, did I?"

"No," I snap off, shaking my head. That's something my inside-out brain can still do.

Focus, man.

What the hell is wrong with me?

Clearing my throat, I stand, then tuck my phone into my pocket and set my empty cup on the nearby table. I take a longer look at her, trying to be objective before I look away.

"The dress works. Buy it and let's get out of here," I clip out tightly.

I choose my phrasing very deliberately.

I don't want her to know I'm battling a case of blue balls from polar hell—let alone flirting—or it will just encourage her impish fuckery. Not to mention the issues I've had in the past with women reading interest into my complete *lack* of any.

I need to keep my head out of strange places.

Looking down, I fiddle with the already perfect crease in my cuffed sleeve.

"If you're content with it and comfortable, then we've found what we're looking for. You'll need a jacket to go with that. The weather, I mean. It's still February. We'll likely be outdoors for a small part of this."

I want to punch myself in the face.

How am I tripping over my words like a boy with a prom date?

I stare at Elle, willing myself to look at her without falling to pieces. She's smiling again, looking quite pleased with herself.

"You're right," she says, twisting to look down at her feet.

She really does resemble a wild modern bohemian flower child. I could picture her barefoot in this thing, racing through the grass, laughing as she takes long, leaping strides like she's trying to fly.

Fuck me.

Maybe Aunt Clara isn't the only one in the family with a dangerous imagination.

"Hmm," Elle muses. "Maybe we'll add some low slingback heels in a nice color. Nude pantyhose. It's too cold to go bare." She looks up at Angelique. I hadn't even realized the woman was still hovering to assist, standing with her hands clasped together and looking far too pleased. "Do you sell that here?"

Angelique beams, sweeping a hand out. "If you'll get changed, I can have my assistant package the dress and help you find everything you need. We can also schedule an appointment for tailoring to alter the fit."

"Thanks." Elle flashes her a sweet smile, then turns it on me. "Just give me a few minutes, okay? I'm not a fussy shopper. If it matches and it fits, I'm good."

"Take your time," I say, still dazed.

She only smiles wider, her eyes creasing into warm pools before she flits away inside the fitting room again.

Both shop assistants look far too smug. The shorter one with the happy face leans into me with a mock whisper too loud to be secretive.

"It's wonderful, isn't it?" she says. "Seeing the woman you love treat herself? I've never seen a man look as smitten as you. Have you been together long?" She dimples at me.

I don't answer.

"Congratulations on your engagement!" she gushes.

Shit, here we go.

But at least if we're supposed to be believable, these people are eating it up.

I'm sure I do *not* look remotely smitten, though I keep that to myself and force a smile that feels like rusted gears grinding to a halt.

I also try not to be obvious about edging away, putting a few more precious inches of space between us.

"Thanks," I manage.

Right before I'm saved by Elle, who apparently changes with lightning speed. She's back in her eclectic outfit, punky and trendy and—if I'm being honest—it's just as suited to her as the gravity-defying dress. She hands the dress over to the shorter assistant before raising a hand to me and joining Angelique.

"I'll meet you at the register," she calls out.

Then she's gone.

The other assistant delicately folds the dress over her arm, beaming at me. "If you'll follow me, please."

I trail her to the register, trying to shake this unsettled feeling.

That feeling doesn't ease up when Elle returns with Angelique, a shoebox, and something else that none of the women will let me see.

In fact, it only intensifies.

Elle is smiling and pleasant to the women, and her helpers are politely efficient, but somehow I feel like everyone is staring at me buck naked, even though I'm fully clothed.

I suppose I wasn't prepared for the scrutiny involved in playing Mr. Right.

Once everything's been bagged up and we turn to leave, I'm definitely not ready for the small, warm hand that slips casually into mine, instinctively lacing our fingers together.

I stop in my tracks and look down at our twined hands.

Her fingers are so pale against mine, so small, engulfed by my palm.

I remember my wits and, instead of jerking away, I keep walking, trying like hell not to focus on the soft heat soaking my skin.

"Sorry," she murmurs from the corner of her mouth. "Just felt like the thing to do."

"You're doing fine, Elle."

Fuck, can I say the same about myself?

This is just business.

A Hail Mary to save my reputation.

We'll survive these two months.

We will.

◆ ◆ ◆

After we've left the store, Elle seems surprised when Rick drives us toward the business district rather than back to her grandmother's house.

She twists in the seat, peering back through the rear window.

"Where are we going? I thought you had a meeting?"

"I do," I say. "But I thought you should come to the office and meet my sister first. The staff should see my devoted fiancée at work. Aunt Clara won't be in today, but you'll meet her soon enough. Rick will drive you home once you've toured Little Key." I pause, frowning. "You didn't have other plans today, did you?"

"Not really. I was just going to sleep in, bum around, and do some unpacking. The rest of my stuff hasn't gotten here yet. I shipped it through Amtrak to save money on movers, but it takes a little longer."

My frown deepens. "Is money a concern for you? I can raise your compensation for the next two months."

"Huh?" She whips her head around and blinks at me. Her hair's still bound the way she tied it in the store, and it frames her face in an alarmingly attractive way, soft wisps bringing out delicate cheekbones. "Oh no. No, that's totally fine. You've already offered more than enough, August. Money isn't a huge problem any more than it is for, um . . ." She clears her throat. "Normal people, I mean. I just try to be thrifty." Then she giggles. "Though it's funny you can say that like it's nothing."

I grumble, looking away.

My upbringing was normal enough, despite growing up with a famous aunt for a stand-in mom who banked serious money early on.

Sometimes discussing my net worth embarrasses me. Though I suppose that's why I give it away so easily, especially if it helps someone close to me.

Money matters a hell of a lot less than other things in life. It's a means to an end, nothing more.

I feel Elle leaning closer now, her warmth and that damnably sweet floral apple scent washing over me.

"Sorry. Did I embarrass you?" she asks with a wink.

"No." A little. "I'm simply thinking of your grandmother and her care, if she ever decides to take the plunge with surgery. Surely, insurance won't cover the full costs?"

I feel her pulling back and glance at her. She's blinking at me like she's seeing me for the very first time.

"What?" I ask.

"Nothing." She shakes her head slightly. "I just didn't expect you to be—well, *nice*."

I glower at her. "I'm not. I told you, I don't have the time or patience to bother with any complications, including family ones."

That doesn't deter her.

If anything, her smile only warms.

"All right, all right. So you're not nice, but you're still a good man. Good enough to worry about me falling at the airport. Good enough to fret over what a scandal could do to my job prospects. Good enough to consider my finances and Gran's surgery. Sorry, Crankyface. You're not going to convince me otherwise."

Damn.

And I'm sure she'd finish driving me stark, raving crazy if I tried.

I huff, muttering under my breath, and fish my phone from my pocket.

"I need to make a phone call," I say.

Elle settles back in her seat and looks out the window with a secretive smile.

I try like hell to distract myself from her by calling one of our print production suppliers to ask why, exactly, we're being charged double for cream-colored page prints over flat white.

Thankfully, the call lasts the entire drive to the office.

Once Rick parks and lets us out, I take Elle's arm and escort her to the elevator.

It's starting to feel surprisingly easier and more natural touching her like this, though that brings its own problems and its own distractions.

Christ, what *is* that scent on her? And how is she always so warm?

There's still an awkward silence in the elevator, but it's a short trip up.

We're on the top floor of the high-rise neighboring other corporate titans like Winthrope International, the high-end hotel chain. It's all the space we need for a lean operation with global distribution. When we step off onto our floor, the receptionist in the small front waiting area looks up with a smile and a "Good morning, Mr.—"

She stops, just staring at us with her mouth open and her eyes bursting with questions.

I decide to ignore them all.

"Hi," Elle says shyly.

She lets me lead her through the double doors into the open-plan main floor. All the editorial, sales, marketing, design, and administrative staff are already here, hard at work.

As we head through the space, a thick silence trails after us. Then stares. Then whispers.

By the time we're almost to the executive wing, it's so fucking quiet I can hear Elle swallow.

"Breathe," I clip. "They're only staring because you're with *me*."

". . . but they're *staring*," she whispers, keeping a plastic smile in place.

Just then the door to one of the three private offices at the far end bangs open. My sister steps out, a blue-eyed whirlwind with her long tail of black hair lashing. She stalks toward us, her heels clacking irritably.

"Finally!" Debra snaps. "August, we've got a huge—" She stops in her tracks, staring at Elle. "Wait. That's the girl from the papers, isn't it? Why is she here?" She rounds on Elle. "Why are you here?"

"Um." Elle holds up her hand and waves weakly, letting the ring shine and offering a nervous smile. "Because we got engaged?"

Debra gawks at her, completely dead for the longest second.

Then she whirls on me.

"Office. *Now.*"

I incline my head to Elle and nod, urging her to follow my sister's cutting steps.

Elle looks poleaxed.

"Am I in trouble?" she whispers.

"No," I whisper back. "I probably am. Just stay out of the crossfire. We've been bickering since we were babies. Let me calm her down."

If I survive.

Inside Debra's office—open, airy, decorated in pale tones—she waits just long enough to slam the door behind us before she points at Elle like she's brandishing a dagger.

"You. Sit." She jabs her finger at the soft easy chair in one corner and turns that accusatory finger on me. "You. *Explain.*"

Apparently, whereas I don't intimidate Elle, my sister does, because she obediently drops into the chair. She gives me a look, wide eyed like a little girl trying to take up space in an adult's seat.

Sighing, I rake a hand through my hair.

It's all I can do to avoid cursing a blue streak.

"It's a ruse, Deb. Relax," I grind out. "Social media already unearthed Elle's identity. She's just returned home to Seattle and needs a job. We need a reputation fixer. Her, for the sake of her career, and me for the sake of Little Key and Aunt Clara. We'll be engaged for a few months, just enough to give things time to simmer down. Then we'll break it off and go our separate ways. Eleanor is a children's illustrator. She'll be working here during that time. She might even be able to help Aunt Clara."

Debra's eyes narrow. She gives me a foul look, but instead of arguing, she just throws her hands up—which tells me something else is wrong.

Fuck.

"Whatever," Deb says sharply. "Do what you want. I'm going to laugh when it blows up in your face. This is the dumbest thing ever, and frankly, I can't believe your stick-in-the-mud ass thought of it." She pivots back to Elle, flashing an almost patient smile. "Hi. I'm Debra, this idiot's younger sister and current head of Little Key. I'm sorry. Seriously sorry my rockhead brother dragged you into this. When it *does* blow up in his face, I'll take you out for drinks and let you vent the whole night, okay?" Her smile turns cutting. "And I'll hold him down so you can punch him to your heart's content."

"Uh . . . thanks?" Elle lets out a shaky laugh.

I drag a hand over my face.

"You done shitting on me yet? What's put you in such a mood?"

"Oh, now you ask?" Her smile looks ready to slit my throat. "Well, since you asked so nicely . . ." Deb stalks away, snatches up a manila envelope from her desk, then stomps back over and thrusts it at me so fast the papers inside rustle. "While you were out dicking around with your fake *fiancée*? We've officially been sued."

VII

HALF AS BRIGHT

(ELLE)

I haven't seen August for three days.

From the whirlwind way he swept me up shopping that first day, I thought the press conference was so urgent it would happen the day after at the latest.

But after his sister, Debra—a force of nature in her own right—slapped the lawsuit news on him, I didn't even get the grand office tour he promised.

Instead, I got to see August Marshall in all his workaholic glory.

I thought he was sharp before.

But he was like a living weapon then, launching himself into reading all the papers Debra threw at him. On the phone, stealing his sister's laptop to fire off emails like a human Gatling gun, barking sharp words with this fierceness that told me if his sister is a force of nature, this man is more.

August is an angry god.

It was all there. That intense energy I felt caged inside him, bursting to get out. Directed entirely at this new problem, this threat.

The tailored suits and creased slacks are a total front for a warrior general scowling with determination.

Somehow, the angrier and bossier he gets, the more raw emotion carves his face.

Handsome lines and power ripple like live currents in the tense lines of his body as he assesses, drives battle decisions in a split second, and gathers his assets to draw blood in the most lethal, efficient way possible.

A little awe inspiring, if I'm being honest.

It's also made me realize just how little I'll ever fit into his high-stakes world.

This sham engagement really is a side game to him, and I'm sure it'll be the biggest relief when it's over.

Heck, I don't think he even noticed when I left, after Debra remembered I was there and apologized, smiled, and called Rick to drive me home.

I'm not a part of August's real life.

I'm a freaking prop with some awesome benefits.

Even when I went off alone to get the dress adjusted, Angelique didn't bat an eye over the fact that he wasn't with me.

Typical rich guy's woman stuff in an atypical rich guy's world.

So, why the hell haven't I been able to stop thinking about him for even a second?

"You're moping, dear," Gran says from across the dining room table.

"I promise you I'm not, Gran," I lie firmly.

I look up from the puzzle piece I've been turning over in my hand, pondering it without really seeing it, then offer it to her.

She's putting together a thousand-piece puzzle of blooming hollyhocks. It's one of the many things that keep her busy so she doesn't go stir crazy from not being able to spend as much time outdoors with her plants.

"Eleanor Lark. Haven't I known you since the day they cut your umbilical cord?" She gives me a knowing look over the rims of her glasses, then plucks the puzzle piece from my fingers. "Stop moping and call that grumbly young man right this instant."

As if.

I refuse to look at her.

I only have August's number because Debra hastily tucked his business card in my pocket before I was ushered out the door that fateful day.

"Let's say I do. I pick up the phone, I call, I pester him, and what then?" I prop my chin in my hands, waiting for her wisdom. "Say, 'Hey, casual business partner paying me to be his fake fiancée, missed you really hard. You're kinda weird and grumpy, but I have a lot of fun poking you. Wanna talk for no reason at all?'"

She gives me the patient look only saintly grandmothers can, then inspects the bright-pink puzzle piece and sets it aside in a pile of other pink pieces.

"That's a sensible start. It's honest." She picks up a green-and-yellow piece, studying it a bit too deliberately. "He *is* a handsome young man, you know."

Holy hell, I can't.

I stick my tongue out.

I know what she's trying to suggest, but it's not going to work.

"Did you miss the part where he's not the least bit interested in me, Gran?"

"Ever the pessimist! What makes you so *sure* of that, Elle?" She smiles with mock innocence and works the piece in. She's making her way from the outside toward the center, the border already assembled in a rectangle.

My jaw drops.

I try to dredge up an answer, but the words won't come.

She's got me good.

"Some men don't always say what they mean, dear. Many boys can barely read their own feelings."

I snort. "Well, he's made his pretty clear. Honestly, I wonder if he likes women at all . . ."

Grandma was reaching for another piece—but now she freezes, blinking at me. "Oh. *Oh*, I see. So it's *that* kind of situation."

"No!" I hiss back immediately. "I'm not his companion beard."

That much, I'm sure of.

So maybe I'm exaggerating, and I know it.

He may not like me as a person, but I'm still a woman, and August Marshall isn't *dead*.

He's just the next best thing—entirely wedded to his work, far too busy with his demanding empires to cast a longing look at the army of supermodels fawning over Mr. Eligible. Let alone boring old me.

Chewing my inner cheek, I eye my amused grandmother sourly.

God, I'm so confused.

It's like being his fake fiancée has turned me into a mini version of August today. All grumps and glares and sad thoughts.

Gran's teasing isn't helping, either, but I guess I really am her grand-daughter, since I enjoy messing with him like this far too much.

"I think he was married once," I continue, reaching for one of her unsorted pieces. It's dark green with yellow speckles. Part of the background, I think, where the little yellow flowers create a backdrop for the hollyhocks. I sort it into the right pile for her and sigh deeply. "I think the headlines were calling him a 'black widow' or something. I don't know. I just don't think he has any use for a woman in his life right now, practical purposes aside. Especially not *me*."

"People aren't made to be used, dearest heart. Women, like men, are made to enjoy," Grandma says firmly. "Frankly, I can't imagine any man who wouldn't cherish your company."

"You haven't met this guy, Gran." I cough. "I mean, you have, but you haven't spent enough time around him." I shrug. "If he wanted to talk to me, he'd have called me."

"Does he have your number?" Grandma quirks a brow and fits in another puzzle piece.

I blink, sit up straighter, and replay the entire chaotic morning in my memory.

Showing up at my door, whisking me off for a shopping spree, talking in the back of the car.

Oh, plus the way he looked at me and made my stomach go weird with butterflies when I walked out in that dress, went into his office, and met his sister, and then *she* gave me *his* number, but I never gave either of them mine.

Ugh.

I smack my hand against my face—then yelp when my forehead stings. "Ow!"

"I take it that's a no," Grandma says wryly.

"It didn't come up, okay?" I rub my forehead. "I have his number but never got around to giving him mine."

"You should correct that, hm?"

"He still won't want to talk to me."

"Eleanor Jacqueline Lark." There it is. Not just my full name—which I share with her—but that *grandma look* over her glasses. Her mouth compresses. "Since when are you afraid to go after what you want? Regardless of the complexities or this man's history, you like him, don't you? You're attracted to him?"

Annoyingly attracted. Ready to keel right over on the spot.

"I . . ." It's mortifying to admit it out loud. But I can't lie to Gran, especially not when she looks at me that way. "Maybe. *Maybe*, Gran. As much as you can like a guy when you barely know him. I mean, I get on his nerves, but it just makes me want to do it more because the way he grumps is so *cute*."

With a satisfied smile, she nods. "Go on."

"Like that one morning I spent with him. It was more fun than I've had in forever. And even if he is kind of a surly a-hole, he's honestly a decent guy. He thinks about things other people don't, and he just—he helps people like it's the most natural thing ever, and then he calls it 'practical.' That tells me he's someone worth getting to know. Never mind the weird way we met."

"Hmm." Grandma's smile is pleased, almost secretive. "I do wonder if he's able to see himself the way you do."

I frown, tilting my head. "I don't know? I'm not sure what that means, honestly. Like, you think he doesn't realize he's actually a good guy behind all the roughness?"

She nods heavily. "The good ones rarely do, dear. Those are the men who do what's right because it's in their nature. Not because they want a reward or a nice pat on the head."

"Oh yeah. I get it." And I can't help how I smile, thinking of all the little things August did in just two days. "Yeah, I think that's him."

"Call him," Grandma insists.

I wrinkle my nose at her. "I'll text him."

She sighs deeply. "You kids these days with your texts and tweets and Tic Tacs and toots."

". . . I don't think Tic Tacs or toots are a thing, Gran."

Laughing, I shake my head and lift up in my chair to wriggle my phone out of my jeans. I have August's number saved in my phone under *J.*

Jet Daddy, of course.

I stall for a second, flipping through Facebook, Twitter, Instagram, and TikTok. I want to delete my notifications in one quick swipe.

The onslaught has slowed down a bit, but it's still more than any sane person can keep up with. I've given up on trying to read any of them. Half of them are pretty nasty anyway. I also haven't posted anything in ages and have no desire, when it'll just open me up to more criticisms from the worldwide peanut gallery.

Plus, some of the things they've hinted about August . . .

I know, I know.

I said I wouldn't pry—and I mean it.

But the curiosity eats me alive, and reading those cryptic messages implying something bad is going to happen to me because of him?

I might not be able to resist forever.

Right now, though, I can't stall any longer.

My notifications are cleared, no new emails, and just one text from Lena promising she'll stop by after work tonight with takeout so we can watch a movie over Thai kebabs. Just like when we were kids and we had to keep it down and not scream at the scary movies so we wouldn't wake up Gran.

Some things never change.

Weird how my life has come full circle while also turning into something insanely different.

I pull up his name and number, then tap a new text into that fresh, empty message window.

> Hey. It's Elle. It just hit me that I have your number, but you don't have mine.

I'm expecting to get ignored.

So I set my phone down and reach for the unsorted puzzle pieces again, but I've barely picked one up before my phone vibrates, and my heart jumps.

Oh God, oh God.

Why are my palms sweating? Why am I snatching my phone up so quickly? Why is Gran looking at me like—

Okay, I know why she's looking at me that way.

I scrunch my nose at her knowing little smile, then read the new text.

> Jet Daddy: Useful. Thanks.

I let out a deep, dramatic groan, rolling my eyes and throwing my head back before thrusting my phone at Grandma.

"See? *See?*"

"He's being polite and responding directly," she retorts blandly. "If you want to talk about something else, say something interesting, girl."

"You are the worst dating coach ever."

"Considering the two of you skipped past dating and went straight to marriage . . ."

"It's fake! And I shouldn't be trying to figure out how to get my fiancé to notice me!"

Grandma chuckles, still patiently setting out her puzzle pieces. "Be yourself. The rest will happen naturally."

"Thanks, Jack Handey," I mutter, staring down at my phone.

What am I supposed to say to a brick wall?

Hey, are we still supposed to do that press conference thing? It sounded pretty urgent but then you fell off the map, I send.

Jet Daddy: Distractions of the legal kind. The conference is scheduled for tomorrow, even if it is less of a conference and more of a meet.

Oof. His texts are just as formal and no nonsense as the way he talks.

I'm not smiling at it.

I'm *not*.

Elle: So when were you going to tell me so I could get ready?

Jet Daddy: I would have arrived early enough to pick you up so you'd have time to get dressed. Unless you need help with that too.

Dead.

His response hacks me down to a nub.

Somehow, my fingers keep typing.

Elle: Um. I still would've appreciated a note beforehand. A carrier pigeon. An Inkygram. Whatever.

Inkygram? Hmm.

That gives me an idea, something small teasing at the back of my mind, percolating and waiting for me to figure out what it is. But I'm too distracted by August's answer to think too deeply.

Jet Daddy: Obviously, I didn't have your number.

Elle: Ha ha ha.

Jet Daddy: Did I say something funny?

Of course he didn't.

"You're smiling," Gran points out. "Is he wagging his tail now like a good boy who's happy to see you?"

"Gran, he's not a dog." I laugh. "I don't know why I think it's so cute anyway."

So what's going on with the lawsuit? I text. Why the hell would anyone sue Little Key?

Jet Daddy: I'm heading to a meeting. I'll pick you up tomorrow at 7:30 sharp.

Nice nonanswer.

I wrinkle my face up, glaring at the phone.

"Well?" Grandma asks just a little too mildly.

"He's picking me up in the morning," I say with dread numbing me. "Then I guess the whole world gets to meet August Marshall's fiancée as she falls on her face."

◆ ◆ ◆

I'm so not ready for this.

God, what was I thinking? Why are all these people staring at me?

The cameras pop like fireworks every three seconds.

Just how rich is August to have this many people obsessing over his personal life?

I thought I could handle this.

I mean, I've made it through an art exhibition full of snooty rich people who'd only come to gawk at the ordinary girl's art and pretend they were getting culture by slumming it.

I didn't even have a nice dress then. Just a basic glittery black cocktail dress that was a little too slutty for the occasion but was perfect for what I normally used it for—the one date-night dress that worked reliably every time.

Back then I could feel them looking at me with thin-lipped suspicion that said I hadn't actually been chosen for that exhibit based on any kind of *talent*.

No, they just liked feeling good about themselves by plucking up some little street urchin and making her sparkle like she mattered for a few nights.

Still, I breezed through it.

I laughed.

I smiled.

I was awkward and silly and brazen and I let myself have fun. Because no matter their reasons, I still had a gallery exhibit, and the rich bitches weren't the only ones who showed up.

Plenty of other folks came because they wanted to appreciate the art. I couldn't be miserable about any extenuating circumstances when I got to hang back and watch people stop to study my paintings with that thoughtful look that said they honestly appreciated what they saw.

This time, at least I have a proper dress.

Somehow, I survived putting on that dress while Lena helped me with a more demure makeup style than my usual colorful eye shadow wings and bold pink lipstick.

Once Lena did my hair pretty in a delicate chignon with sideswept bangs, I felt like a real lady.

Once I put on the pale-lavender open-weave cardigan to go with the dress and added my pantyhose and the pretty off-white slingback heels Angelique helped me pick out, I felt like a goddess.

When August came to the door to escort me to the car and stared just a few seconds longer than he really needed to, and he handled me like he was grasping something delicate?

I was breathless.

Gratefully trapped in a thrill I can't describe.

Maybe this is my Cinderella moment. Maybe once he saw me as a princess, the prince would easily fall in love.

But no.

I'm not Cinderella, and this is no fairy tale.

I'm not even the ugly stepsisters, the stepmother, or the fairy godmother.

I'm the damned pumpkin, and there's no one here to make me shiny while I stand in front of this podium with August by my side and my face frozen in a smile that will turn into a grimace if it gets any wider.

It's the relentless flashing that kills me.

I didn't know cameras not attached to phones could still blind you.

We stand outside the office building where Little Key leases the top floor. There's an overhang fronted by polished sandstone columns. The paving underneath forms a small outdoor entryway leading up to multiple sets of double doors.

It's here that August chose to hold the press meet, keeping them from snooping and prying around the Little Key workings.

It also creates a dividing line that invisibly says *Do not cross.* Over three dozen reporters and cameramen are out on the smooth grey pavement in a plaza centered by a fountain.

It keeps them from crowding us, and the building itself blocks the biting late-winter wind to give us shelter. Not to mention an easy escape route so they can't follow us into the building. The plan is to take off in the getaway car waiting on the curb together after we've made our statements—and let people assume we've run off to our lovers' nest.

It also makes the flashes that much brighter, with the overhang casting its shadow over us.

August is saying—something?

I don't know what.

I caught my name; then the flashes from hell melted my eyeballs again, turning me into a frozen statue.

My head rings horribly.

My vision swims, exploding with spangles.

Someone's barking questions at me, but it's not August. I think he's answering for me, but I can't tell, when his voice is just this hollow cadence that doesn't form real words.

It hurts.

It also makes me think of this Reddit post I saw once about this guy who got off on his wife's migraine pain, so he'd wake her up in the middle of the night with a flashlight in her face, flicking it on and off quickly while turning the alarms as high as they would go so she'd burst into an explosive migraine and be helpless while he fucked her.

Honestly, I don't think a single court in the world would have convicted her for cutting his throat. But I feel like I'm being tried and sentenced right now.

Because I haven't said a single word through the chaos, and I'm failing spectacularly as August's imaginary fiancée.

I want to say something.

I want to help.

I want to be *myself*, extroverted and chirpy and happy to meet these pushy asshats.

I want to be able to walk away from this with August feeling triumphant that we pulled it off without a hitch.

I want to see him give me a real smile just once.

But all I can do is stand woodenly, fighting the urge to burst into tears from the invisible knife plowing through my eye.

Did I mention it hurts?

Everything is red-white, receding into this awful sea, like the whole world drowning in the light of a blood moon.

My knees go weak. I have to lock them to stay up.

Damn, say something.

Tell August what's happening and apologize for failing already, but every time I try to even form a sentence in my brain—I can't.

Another acid flash goes off.

Even closing my eyes and lifting my hand to shield them doesn't stop my brain from getting blown to bits.

". . . lle. Elle. *Elle!*"

My name?

I realize it's my name because it's the only sound that doesn't peel my face off.

That chocolate-silk voice pours over me, trying so hard to erase the pain.

Then there's a huge hand at the small of my back. Hot as sand- and sea-washed rocks left baking under the sun all day, easing that warmth back into me.

It's all comfort.

And suddenly, the flashers stop assaulting me.

Because there's a tall body moving between me and the source like a wall.

I don't think anything could ever get through August Marshall.

My senses are a stained glass window after a shattering gunshot, but I know the scent of sandalwood and the crispness of his suit and his weight.

When I've got a real rager going on, the slightest stimulation can shred me, but this—this is grounding me, sheltering me, as August's arms pull me against his chest.

I gasp, my eyes prickling with pain and frustration as I huddle against him.

The spell is broken.

I'm magically able to move again, now that I don't have to work so hard to hold myself up. The reprieve gives me that little bit of strength I have to lean into him and clutch the coat of his handsome black suit of fine-woven wool.

I bury my face in the whisper-soft linen of his dress shirt and gird my stomach.

It'd be just my luck to throw up on him right now.

Thank God his hold eases the nausea away.

I feel him bend over, and his breaths against my neck, my ear, my hair.

"I'm sorry," he says. It's not quite a whisper. I don't think a voice this deep *can* whisper. "Cover your ears, Elle. I need to be loud, and I don't want to hurt you."

I don't understand, but I obediently lift my shaking hands up and press them against my ears. The sound from outside mutes into a dull roar, while the ringing in my head amplifies, reverberating off my eardrums.

Even my palms can't stop me from hearing August clearly.

That dark, heady voice rises for the first time since I've met him.

Now it's a strong, ringing shout.

And maybe my senses are a little warped, but he sounds *pissed*.

He sounds protective.

He sounds like he's about to start chopping heads.

For me?

"Stop your goddamned cameras right now," August snaps. His tone says there will be hell to pay for anyone who disobeys. "Every last one of you. Shut them off and shut your yaps. Show me a single one of you has common sense, empathy, humanity." He's so condemning. Icicles stab every syllable, and I'm just glad he's not mad at *me*, when I might just find a reason to be nervous around him after all. "I just told you my fiancée suffers debilitating migraines that can be triggered by bright lights and loud noises—and you immediately bombard her?" His hold on me tightens, gathering me closer in his storming embrace. I think he's intentionally shielding me from their sight. "Don't make us regret wasting our time today. You've got your story. You have the truth to counterbalance the shit-eating rumors you vermin thrive on. We're done here, and you soulless assholes are dismissed."

Whoa.

I don't hear a single camera click now, though a few media hacks still have their phones on silent, quietly snapping shots.

The shouted questions have faded too. Now there's a vague murmur floating through the clasp of my fingers.

August's hand curls against the small of my back, grabbing a handful of my dress and cardigan, and that's when I realize it.

His fingers are shaking with fury.

No matter how sick I feel, my heart twists.

His voice quiets, speaking again in that thunder that soothes me.

"Lower your hands, Elle," he says. "I'll escort you through these hyenas, and we can sit in the car until you're well enough to leave."

I finally manage words, even if my voice sounds broken. ". . . thank you."

I can't help a bitter, awful smile, though I try to keep it to myself, wrinkling my lips and hiding my face against him a second longer.

So maybe I didn't fuck this up after all.

At least now they'll believe what happened at the airport, instead of the weird twisted story someone made up and ran with.

August holds me closer for a moment longer; then he slowly pulls away, shifting his grip to keep his arm firmly around my waist and drawing me against him.

I didn't know how desperately I needed that.

Just like I need his hold to keep me up and keep me moving when my legs are made of water and everything keeps swaying.

By the time I open my eyes, the number of reporters and camera crew has doubled, then tripled. The shifting and blurring are making me feel seasick.

Slowly, one baby step at a time, we venture out from under the overhang.

August is gentle, shortening his steps and making sure I always have him to cling to and lean on for support the entire way.

God.

I swear, if this man ever tells me he's not good again, I'm going to punch him for lying.

It's awkward, the mumbling stillness as we slowly push past them. It's worse when we hit the fullest patch of sunlight and I wince, slamming my eyes shut with a humiliating cry. I turn my face into August's side and dig my fingers into his coat.

I wish I could feel the cold right now.

But everything is this fountain of pain.

"Shh," August soothes. "Keep holding on, Elle. I'll be your eyes. We're almost there."

My only answer is a whimper. It's all I can grind out.

Still, I trust August to make sure my every step is sure and true.

But as we pass the loudest murmurs—I think where the thickest part of the crowd is, by the sound of it—a male voice calls out, loud and sharp enough to slice me in half.

"Mr. Marsha—"

I feel August go stone stiff against me.

He holds me tighter, both keeping me up and keeping me with him as he stops.

"Shut it," he snarls. The sudden, almost frightened stillness of the plaza carries his voice like a bullet. "Every last one of you should be ashamed of yourselves. If Elle ends up in the hospital from this, I promise your bosses will be speaking to my lawyers."

"August," I whisper, even though I don't fully know what I want to say to him.

Only Gran and Lena have ever protected me this way.

To have this man who barely knows me turn so strong and snarly for my sake . . .

It doesn't feel like an act anymore.

I curl my hand tighter in his jacket, even if I risk ruining the expensive fabric.

Stop, I think desperately. *Stop it, Jet Daddy, or I'll start to want you for real.*

But his hand against my back urges me forward.

The silence feels like another presence with us, hovering and oppressive, as he guides me across the plaza. I feel the shift in the light against my eyelids as we fall under the shade of the trees lining the property.

We're right at the gate now. Just the sidewalk, and I spot Rick waiting in the car on the curb and rejoice at the thought of lying down.

But August stops us just past the gate. I lift my head as much as I can.

He looks down at me with a strange expression before his jaw sets. I think there's something like determination in the knit of his brows and the firmness of his mouth.

What? I try to say, but all my wires are still scrambled.

Then his fingers graze my chin, gripping lightly yet with that sense of the thinnest leash holding back the strength of his touch.

All my wires burn out in a single explosive instant.

Ferocious blue eyes search mine.

"I'm sorry as hell," August whispers; only now the purr of it is deeper, this intimate, rough thing. "I do this for appearances. Don't have a choice, but fuck, I don't know how to stage a kiss. So this will have to suffice."

Stage a what?

My mind wobbles.

Then the full meaning catches up to me.

Not fast enough, as August bows over me and slams his lips into mine.

My mind screams for one last second of common sense.

Not real. Not real. Not real.

This man doesn't feel anything but irritation. It's not effing real!

My lips tingle with the soft graze of his mouth, the lush tease of his beard. Like every bristling touch peels away layers of armor until each time his mouth strokes mine, I just feel more.

More heat.

More texture, more touch.

Everything from the faint crease in his lips to their firmness, the way they feel just like the silk and velvet and dark chocolate of his voice, the tiny hint of dampness making our mouths cling to each other until we're like sweet sticky candy.

More, every time he draws back before another slow, tender collision of our lips connects us for just a moment longer before breaking apart with a soft slick sound.

More everything.

He kisses me like I mean the entire universe to him.

Like he's caught so deep in his need to protect me, to shield me, to love me, that he *has* to kiss me like I'm fragile and precious.

I can't even feel my headache anymore.

The reporters? Completely forgotten.

There's just me, just August, just this moment.

The breathless magic minute when his tongue parts my lips, hungry and claiming and teasing.

His kiss captures me so intensely I rise up on my toes with a sharp shock that starts at my lips and plunges down through my heart, through my stomach, to right between my legs, where it curls up there in a little pool of sharp heat.

Holy hell.

I've had boyfriends tease me with lips and tongue to take me to the brink, but it always fell just a little flat. It felt too contrived, too awkward.

But August takes me there with one kiss.

He tastes like clove smoke, though I've never seen him with a cigarette.

I can't feel anything but the space between us, the charged air between our bodies compressed and superheated until it slips under my dress and touches me like his tongue flowing over my naked skin, peaking my nipples, sliding between my legs to lick and tease and own.

I've never done drugs, but kissing August feels like a hit.

Everything bursts into vivid Technicolor sensation.

I can't help myself.

I part my lips and clutch at him, lean into him, begging him for more.

No matter how gently he kisses me, there's nothing soft about this.

There's a secret sensuality lingering, something that makes it dirty and needy and perfectly hot.

God help me, I want more.

I don't want to *stop*.

If we do, I'll go crashing back to reality, where I'm dizzy and sick while dozens of bystanders stare at us like we're zoo animals. Living reminders that I'm only doing this for his image.

Not because he wants me.

That thought isn't enough to smother this feeling, though.

It's like August could crawl inside me, deep in the darkest part of me, and ignite me from within so I burn in waves that pulse out through my whole body.

There's so much promise in such a barely there kiss that I can hardly hold back a moan, a sigh, a wanting whisper of his name.

But I can't.

Not with everyone watching.

Not when, to them, he's just comforting his distraught fiancée. Not when—

"Eleanor! Hey, Elle!"

I snap back from August, shock ripping through me. It's only been seconds, but I feel like we were locked together for hours, until someone called out my name. Our eyes lock in a hard, intense look before I turn toward the sound of my name without thinking.

Just in time for another atomic flash to melt my eyes.

Pain uppercuts me like it never left, driving an iron spike between my eyes.

Whimpering, I tilt forward.

August catches me with a snarl boiling up his throat.

I barely catch a glimpse of someone smirking, then disappearing into the trees along the sidewalk with a camera clutched in his hand, before my vision goes dark and murky.

From the vibrating tension in August's touch, he's about to charge after my camera ninja like a marine drill sergeant who's just caught some dumb boy climbing in through his daughter's window.

Only, he doesn't.

He stays, holding me tighter than ever, while I hear the car door open and a third set of footsteps, then another car door opening.

"This way, Mr. Marshall!" Rick urges softly.

"Thank you, Merrick," August answers. His hands guide me forward. "Just a few more steps, Elle. Fuck, I'm sorry. Old paparazzi trick to get you to turn for a good shot. I should've briefed you on their games."

"I-it's okay," I stammer.

But it's not okay.

It's worse being bitch-slapped from that wonderful kiss and back into this awful feeling than it was with the swelling migraine alone.

August ushers me into the car so carefully.

I still can't see beyond vague hints of things around the black-and-white flashers clouding my vision, but he coaxes me to sit, to draw my feet in, before Rick closes the door behind me and reclaims the driver's seat.

"Stay," August orders Rick. "Elle isn't well, and the motion could make it worse. Give her time." To me, he whispers, "Lie down. Just like before. We'll wait as long as it takes."

I let him guide me, stretching out gratefully across the plush back seat.

What I'm not expecting is that when he says *just like before*, he means—

Resting my head in his lap, apparently, instead of scrunching up to fit my head against the seat at his side.

I'm too tired to question it.

And I don't really want to when it's comforting and close, and that's exactly what I need right now without thinking too hard about it. So I settle with my head in his lap and close my eyes.

I don't mean to fall asleep.

I want to stay awake.

I want to talk to him.

I desperately want to wonder what that look was for after he kissed me, almost like he was angry at *me*, and not the photographer.

I want to hold on to the warmth still throbbing in my lips.

So many wants, but I can't.

My body takes over and drags me down a bottomless abyss.

Before I can think about what I want next, I'm gone.

VIII

SUNSHINE MADE FLESH

(AUGUST)

Strange how fast things have come full circle, landing me right back where I started.

Specifically in the back of my car, with Rick in the driver's seat and Elle sprawled across me, her head in my lap. She's so weak after her hellish migraine left her unable to stand.

She sleeps so quietly, so trustingly, her lips parted and her face at rest, not drawn into the lines of pain that shaped it so deeply before. When she's serene, she looks gracefully older.

There's a pensiveness haunting her that gives her this melancholy beauty, always longing and reaching for something just out of her grasp.

I wonder what she longs for so intently.

So deeply I can almost taste it on her lips.

That's the difference between the day I met her and now.

On the day after she collapsed at SeaTac, I didn't know how god-damned divine her lips would taste on mine.

Didn't know how easy it would be to devour her, to almost give in to the urge to explore, even if it would have made the front page of every rancid gossip blog tomorrow. I can imagine the headlines, journalist clowns shouting that the Black Widow Billionaire had just assaulted his future bride when she was in distress, unable to care for her pain when all that mattered was his lust.

A dark smile twists my lips as I glance out the window, watching cars ease past our parked G80. Many of them hold the reporters I rudely dismissed.

If only I were such a thoughtless fuck.

My life would be easier if I gave in to every whim, every impulse I have without a single thought for how it would affect others.

How does she do it?

Living so spontaneously and still being so kind.

I can't imagine being so hedonistic without being selfish too.

Yet Elle seems entirely selfless.

Especially the way she pushed herself today, knowing the cameras would set off her migraines if the reporters didn't honor the conditions of my agreement.

I'm a rumbling volcano of a man.

Furious at their disrespect and the way they hurt her. I'm tempted to make some calls that will sever heads, but I hold back for her sake only.

If I pull strings to make sure a dozen assholes wind up terminated and destitute, Elle might be disappointed.

Hell, why do I *care* if this little firecracker disapproves of my justice?

If anything, I should be angry with her.

I never meant to kiss her that way.

It was meant to be the lightest brush. Controlled and over in an instant.

Not this slow, fusing sizzle that made it damn near impossible for me to pull away.

There was an innocence and sensuality in the way she leaned against me that caught me off guard. I'm used to women who kiss with intent; whose every goal is to make me lose my head and get so swept up in sex that I'll drag them off to bed and let them weave their spell over me.

My ex-wife was like that in the end.

Only when she kissed me, she wasn't trying to ply my body.

She was toying with my emotions, hoping my love for her would make me surrender to her demands, even when they turned batshit insane.

Yeah. I'm accustomed to dealing with women who want something and who have zero qualms about aiming their wiles straight at my cock.

What I'm not accustomed to is a woman so skilled at it that she makes her response seem genuine, as if I somehow affect her so deeply that her cheeks flush honest pink, her breaths hitch a little too much, and her eyes flutter shut while her mouth becomes a soft, inviting strawberry, begging me to take everything.

Fuck, I almost did, losing my shit with a flirt of her honey on my tongue.

It's amazing how much just kissing this girl feels like straight filthy fucking.

I'm almost grateful to that sleaze for stopping me before I went too far.

Then Elle moves, and I remember why I'm not fucking grateful at all.

The slight weight in my lap exhales with a sleepy mumble. I flick a glare at her, holding on to my anger and suspicion. She's no different from any other woman. Her wiles are just a different sort from anything I know.

But as I watch her slowly waking up, holding on to that familiar resentment feels like trying to keep water in my fingers. I can't hold on as she shifts her shoulders sleepily, snuggling into me, her eyes slowly slipping open.

Nothing but gleams of gold through her lashes. The drowsy tiger kitten yawning.

Her tongue even curls like a cat's. I half expect to see a hand come up like a paw to rub at one cheek, or for her nose to twitch like she's moving her whiskers.

How is this maddening woman so damned cute?

Instead of playing the cat, she blinks her eyes open, looking up in confusion.

"August?" she asks with another yawn, rubbing her pink nose.

One thing she doesn't do is bolt out of my lap like she did last time. I suppose I'm losing any and all hope of preserving my intimidating mystique with her.

"How long was I out?" she asks, her voice still thick with sleep, giving it an enticing sigh.

I have to look away from her and take the excuse to glance at my watch. "About thirty-five minutes. Not long. How are you feeling?"

From the corner of my eye, I watch her smile faintly. "A little better. I can see, at least, and there's only one of you now instead of four or five."

"Thank fuck. Not sure the world could handle four or five of me, Elle."

She laughs loudly and then winces. "Wait. Did you just make a joke, Crankyface?"

"Believe it or not, I have a functioning sense of humor."

"Yeah? Prove it."

I toss her a look and change the subject. "Would ice water help? I made sure the cooler was stocked."

"You did? For me?" Elle blinks at me.

"Yes." Clearing my throat, I avoid looking at her—even if I must press far too close to her as I lean over her in my lap to reach the silver built-in cooler between the front seats. A press of a button and it slides out, ice cubes gleaming, several water bottles nestled among them, along with a few cans of my favorite sparkling water flavors. I pluck out a water, shake off the droplets, then lean back and offer it to her. "You had me worried, woman. Just thought it would be pragmatic to prepare ahead. Do you have your meds?"

For a moment, the only sound is the cooler automatically closing with a mechanical whirr, while Elle gives me a confused look.

Yet this time, that look makes my heart feel strange and my blood slow.

This time, she's the one who averts her eyes, gently taking the bottle from me and glancing at the sequined round shape of the violently colorful purse that's replaced her usual oversize bag. It's tucked into the pocket on the back of the front passenger seat.

"They're in my purse. The outside pocket."

She starts to reach for it, but I get there first with longer arms. I fumble with finding the zippers.

This thing looks like it was stitched together by a maniac, meaning it could only have been made by Elle herself.

I eventually find the right pocket and pluck out the small prescription bottle, scanning the label. *Take 1–2 by mouth as needed.* "One to two . . . how many do you want?"

"One should be enough."

"You sure?" I eye her.

She immediately looks away.

With a frustrated grumble, I set her purse aside next to her hip and catch her chin. I won't force her, but I nudge her to meet my eyes, searching her face for the lie. She must be able to lie so easily, to make me believe her response to that kiss.

"Do not lie to me, Elle Lark," I order firmly. "If you're feeling like a worn heel, you need a doctor."

But there's no trickery in that sweet expression she wears.

No deception in the gentle tremor of her eyelashes, or the startled part of her lips.

No manipulation in the way she colors, or the soft, confused stammer of her voice.

"I . . ." She stops, licking her lips. Her mouth glistens coral pink. The same color is probably still clinging to my mouth after the way our lips were pressed together. "I promise. It's not bad enough for more than one."

I shouldn't be grasping on to her like this.

I shouldn't be pressuring her and making demands.

To me, she's little more than an employee, a contractor filling specific needs.

So I let her go. Quickly, and yet it does no good when the softness of her skin stays imprinted on my fingertips.

Without a word, I shake out a pill from the bottle, put it away, and offer her the little capsule.

Elle hesitates.

Then she opens her mouth like a baby bird asking to be fed, a mischievous twinkle in her eyes.

"Are you serious?" I scowl, glaring down at her.

"My hands are full. And slippery. I might drop it." She holds the water bottle up with a grin.

Wide, innocent eyes.

Goddamn.

She's definitely faking it now.

It's annoying that it's so obvious. The girl couldn't lie if someone paid her, even if that's exactly what I'm doing. I need to believe that any attraction she might feel toward me is feigned for her own ends.

That's all.

But she's still looking up at me with that little smile, while Rick keeps pretending not to watch us in the rearview mirror.

I meet his eyes and stare.

"Just drive," I mutter. "We're taking Miss Lark home promptly."

Then, turning that glare on her, I pop the pill into her mouth.

My thumb accidentally brushes her lips—just barely—right where they're silkiest.

I jerk my hand back like she's a thousand degrees, folding my arms over my chest because I have nowhere else to put them with her in my lap.

"You're feeling better. Good," I growl.

Elle swallows what sounds like a giggle. "And you're sulking again."

"I am not—"

The moment I make eye contact, I realize she's trying to provoke me. Fuck.

I suppose I can't blame her.

She's trying to restore a little normalcy between us again—whatever passes as *normal* for us, when we barely know each other and we have to pretend we're engaged.

Still, there's a certain comfort in this too.

In knowing she doesn't want the memory of that kiss hanging awkwardly between us, no matter what latent things came to life the moment our lips touched.

I can't hold back my scowl.

Just like I can't bring myself to kick her out of my lap, either, especially when the car is coming to life with a rumble and moving forward when I'm not sure she should be sitting up.

Sighing, I watch her.

"Just rest, Elle," I say. "I'll have you home soon."

We didn't kiss again when I dropped her off, even if it wouldn't have been out of place.

For all I know, there were paparazzi hiding in Miss Jacqueline's hedges, but it felt prudent not to mix up my brain any further with this gal.

So I let her off on the curb with a polite farewell, watched to make sure she reached the door, and chose not to respond when she stopped and raised her hand in a little wave before ducking inside.

For some reason, missing a second kiss *bothers* the hell out of me.

Just logistics, I'm sure. Whatever helps keep this farce publicly visible and visibly believable.

Nothing more.

I have plenty of other worries—like the text waiting on my phone. Snarky. Cutting. *Angry.*

Oddly jumbled, like it always is.

Unknown: nice you gt the hole intentent buzzing laready

Unknown: tring to plafy for the sy mpthay points . . . SAD!

I frown.

"Merrick?" I ask pointedly.

"Yes, Mr. Marshall?" Merrick's eyes meet mine in the mirror.

"Has anyone requested my number lately?"

"No, Mr. Marshall."

He watches me strangely in the mirror as I text back.

I probably have the damnedest look on my face right now. Who the hell is this and how did you get my number?

Only, I already have a good idea, and I can almost hear the sneering laugh that comes back in the response.

Unknown: dnt you know hvingg ur contact is part of discverry???

I blink at the screen and wrinkle my nose before I send, Miss Sullivan?

Marissa Sullivan: shoudl I feell aspeiclah

Marissa Sullivan: fujkv

Marissa Sullivan: sent before I finishined

Marissa Sullivan: should I feeel like a special gril since u remembereed my name ??

What in the hell is going on here?

Why is the woman who's *suing* me texting like a drunken teenager?

I don't have the time or patience to decipher her cryptic messages. I slam the call button on the text window and lift the phone to my ear.

It picks up before the first ring finishes.

Miss Sullivan's voice slurs in my ear. "Ooh la la, you're callin' me now? You sure know how to woo a girl, Marshall."

I stare incredulously at—nothing, really.

When I'd thought *drunken teenager*, I wasn't expecting to be right.

"Miss Sullivan . . . are you drunk?"

"Issit your business?" She hiccups. "Whaddya want?"

"Nothing," I retort. "You texted me first. I thought this might be more convenient than interpreting your inebriated texts, but it seems you can't speak clearly either. Did you need something, or can it wait for the meeting with our lawyers present?"

An ugly little laugh comes over the line.

So different from Elle and her light laughter, it's like air versus mud.

"I'm just being gracious. God! Listen, I'm gonna offer you the chance to . . . to *consneed* before thissss goes to ker—cut—court. If you concede, I won't even shoe—*sue* for decades of damages. Asshole," she adds under her breath.

I almost roll my eyes out of my head.

"Absolutely not. There's nothing *to* concede, Miss Sullivan. Your frivolous lawsuit is a hostile takeover attempt, and I think you already know it won't succeed. It won't bleed my family's company dry, either, no matter how long you care to drag this misery out. I'll see you soon, though, and we can let our lawyers do the heavy lifting. Please be sober."

I hang up before she gets out more than a "Fu—" as a retort.

Then I mute my phone.

Talking to that wacko is a special kind of hell.

I suddenly wish Elle were here. Her brightness could clear up the sulfur stench Marissa Sullivan always leaves in the air.

Rick is still watching me in the rearview mirror.

"Should I turn us around, sir?" It's annoying how astute he is.

"*No*," I snarl, knowing I'm more aggravated with myself than him. "I need to be in the office. Our legal team is waiting, and I intend to be fully ready to deal with Marissa Sullivan come tomorrow."

◆ ◆ ◆

Come tomorrow, I'm not ready to deal with jack shit.

Did the woman who tumbled into my arms at the airport have to be a morning bird?

I know. I know most of the world wakes up before lunch. I know I'm a human oddity.

Still, I can't play the doting fiancé if I leave Elle to fend for herself on her first day in the office. Nor can I apologize to my aunt for dragging her into this fuss, though I hope she'll at least like Elle and be willing to work with her.

So here I am.

Slouched in the back seat of the car with my face buried in a bracing cup of hot gunpowder green tea, just inhaling the scent like it'll loan me the superpowers I'm lacking.

I watch Elle come flitting out into the grey morning light like she'll bring the sun with her through the Seattle gloom.

She's vivid enough in a yellow sweater and a knee-length pleated grey skirt with black kitten heels and black knit stockings. Smart, professional, but with her bright flourish in a rainbow-patterned scarf looped around her neck and matching colored clips peppered throughout her hair until it looks like a sunflower field dotted with butterflies.

Have I mentioned how much I hate how this girl makes me go poetic?

She waves at Miss Jacqueline over her shoulder as she strolls, then catches my eye through the car window with a knowing smile before she disappears.

Rick opens the back door for Elle, and she tumbles in—then stops short, blinking at me as she settles on the seat next to me, holding a paper cup of something steaming hot.

"Whoa," she says, eyes wide. "You look, uh. Not happy. Or awake."

"Not a morning person," I grunt into my cup. "Can only fake it for so long."

"What time do you normally wake up?"

"Noon," I mumble emphatically.

Elle just giggles when she realizes I mean it.

She reaches out to flick my hair off my brow, brushing aside the one unruly strand that never stays in place, defying every hair product known to science.

It tingles where she touches me.

Hell, it feels familiar.

We're acting, you jackass dolt. Keep it straight, I remind myself.

"You're so freaking adorable," she says brightly—and as Rick slides into the front seat after shutting us in, I catch a muffled snicker that tempts me to hire a new assistant-slash-driver. "If you're not a morning person, why are you up so early?"

I stare at her sourly over my cup.

She blinks and grins again before she slouches over, bumping her shoulder against mine. "You're too good to me, *fiancé.*"

"Give me a number," I grind out.

"Come again?" She blinks at me.

"How much more do I have to pay you not to be so damned peppy?"

Her smile widens. "How much are you worth again? There's not enough money in the world, my darling."

"Try me."

Elle laughs again.

I don't want to admit that the verbal jousting somewhat lifts my mood.

I wonder why the grouchier I am, the more pleased she gets.

Strange woman.

As Rick pulls into traffic, though, Elle tilts her head, studying me. "There's something else on your mind. What's up?"

"Lawyers," I mutter. "I hate meeting with them, but it's a necessity."

"Is this about that lawsuit your sister mentioned before I was ejected from the office?"

I at least have the good grace to wince at that. "Sorry. I tend to get tunnel vision when someone presents me with a problem. But yes, it's about that lawsuit."

Wrinkling her nose, Elle shakes her head.

"I don't understand. Why would anyone want to sue you?"

"It's the daughter of Aunt Clara's former coauthor. She owns her own publishing and media company." I sigh. I hate getting into this, but Elle deserves answers. "She claims that Inky the Penguin is her father's creation, not Aunt Clara's, and that she's owed the rights and all publication materials, plus decades of profits."

Elle just stares at me, horror draining the color from her face. "That's—no. No way. I didn't even know Clara Marshall ever *had* a coauthor. It can't be true . . . can it?"

"Of course not." I can't hide the disgust in my voice. "Aunt Clara would never steal. Inky was her labor of love from the start. I don't know what the fuck happened; she and Lester Sullivan had some sort of falling out early in their partnership. He left. Then the man tried to re-create her work and failed, while her ideas took off. Sullivan's daughter, Marissa, still blames us for her father's death. She says that losing his career made him an alcoholic and ruined him." That eats at me so harshly I pause. "So, she's out to ruin us, burying us in frivolous lawsuits."

Elle studies me, then leans in closer until we're shoulder to shoulder again, arm to warm, slender arm. She always looks at me like she's found some new treasure. I can't for the life of me understand why this bizarre woman would ever look at me that way, when all I'll ever give her are scowls and clipped words.

"You really care about your family," Elle murmurs, her lips curling up. "You're so loyal."

"Stop that," I snap. Why do my ears feel so hot?

"What?" Elle whispers.

"Complimenting me. You don't need to—"

Before I can utter another word, I have a face full of girl.

A face full of very gorgeous, wide-eyed sunshine made flesh.

Her nose almost touches mine, and her eyes are so wide and locked on mine with playful curiosity.

Her lips are too close.

"August Marshall," Elle says in an exaggerated whisper, touching her finger to the tip of my nose. "Are you *shy*?"

"Fuck no," I snarl.

Yes. Maybe. *Shut up.*

I pull my tumbler up as a shield between us so I won't do something reckless like kiss her again. "I'm trying to drink my damned tea, but there's someone in my way."

"You're *shyyy*." A coy smile teases at her lips. She pokes my ribs through my vest. "I bet you were that little boy who didn't know how to talk to people because no one understood you and you didn't have anything in common with them, so you didn't know how to relate. Instead, you just pretended you didn't want to have anything to do with people, and you got all grouchy about it and sat in the corner with your books, when really, you just wanted someone to come ask you to play video games."

I can't even growl at her.

My heart skips strangely as I stare at this annoying creature.

It *hurts*.

It hurts like the first time I tried to say hello to a group of bullies playing in the schoolyard sandbox.

"The orphan kid!" they screamed.

Depraved little monsters.

They laughed at my polished shoes and suspenders and threw rocks at me until I ran.

How did she know?

How the hell did she look at me and know the days I spent alone, learning to throw punches instead of running, then ignoring the other kids and being so formidable that they'd fear me too much to laugh behind my back?

How did she look at me and see the quiet afternoons spent with my aunt, sharpening her colored pencils and feeling like she understood me because she wrote books Debra and I loved?

Elle pulls back, concern darkening her brow.

"August? I'm sorry. Did I go too far?"

"No," I growl, forcing myself to sip my drink. Strong green tea with a splash of honey was always Aunt Clara's favorite growing up, and the habit rubbed off. It's a more regular morning go-to for me than coffee. "You just have excellent insights into how children behave."

Her concern melts away into another beaming smile. "I hope so! I like to draw things that make them happy. So I'd better know how the little squirmers think, right?"

"That makes sense."

I don't know what else to say.

I feel oddly shaken, tense, but also like something that's been binding me for a long time has loosened, and I don't know how not to fall apart without it holding me together.

Elle seems fine with silence.

She settles in next to me, humming occasionally to herself and keeping me company for the rest of the drive to the office.

After some time, I feel her gaze on me and glance toward her. She's watching me with a longing smile.

"Sorry," she says softly.

"For what?" I cock my head.

"I'm not very good at this fiancée thing. The faking it in public part, I mean. I couldn't even get one word out yesterday."

Shit, she was worried about *that*?

"You're doing fine, Elle. I promise you."

That brings her smile back brighter than ever.

She shines on for a little while longer before going back to reading her phone, with the air a little lighter between us.

I'm slightly more awake by the time the tea's caffeine has worked its way into my blood. From the scent of it, Elle's drinking hot cocoa.

She makes the goofiest happy little murmur every time she takes a sip.

I try to tell myself it's goofy, anyway, so I don't wonder if it's a noise she'd make in bed.

I also try not to be obvious about watching her as she flips through articles on her phone—mostly publishing industry news, but I catch her reading a few about us too.

It seems to be going well.

A few salacious headlines speculating about our age gap, a few trying to paint me as a villain robbing the cradle. Obvious clickbait sensationalized for maximum outrage, though the softer write-ups gush over how stylish and sweet we looked together.

Surprisingly, those kinder pieces have won more interest.

Gossip and scandal sells.

There's no stopping that.

But it's easy to forget that feel-good love stories have their own special hold on people looking for a little hope in a dark world. If they can't find their own happiness, they're content to gaze longingly at others'.

Even I know that.

I never expected to be starring in a feel-good story.

I just wish it wasn't one big lie.

Regardless, Rick parks and lets us out.

Elle seems more comfortable slipping her arm into mine today as we head for the lobby. We catch Deb just as she heads for the elevator, her hair swinging in a slick tail.

She stops in the middle of the lobby with a sharp *clank* of her heels and stares at me.

". . . you. I. What." Debra blinks repeatedly. "You're not turning to ash in the sun."

Elle snickers, then quickly covers her mouth. I eye them both. "You're not funny."

"And you're not my brother, if you're awake this early." Debra grins, sauntering closer, and flashes Elle a wink. "You stuck around, eh?"

Elle laughs and beams at Debra. "I do try to finish what I start."

Next thing I know, my sister's stolen my fiancée and dragged her away, leaning down to whisper in her ear—pointedly loud enough for me to hear.

"Listen. If you need to cut and run, I know this guy. Roland Osprey. He's this big-time media mogul in Chicago. He could make people believe the moon is made of tin foil and glue. He can spin a story that would get you away from this monster in a second."

"Debra, will you stop?" I fling my head back, staring up at the high arched lobby ceiling, swallowing a groan.

Goddamn, why are sisters such a torment?

Elle laughs. "I'm fine. I'm not here against my will." She squeezes Debra's hand. "It'll be okay. I'm just doing a favor for a friend, that's all."

That gives me pause.

Are we friends?

Just friends?

Just fucking friends?

Even if I have no real desire for a woman turning my life upside down and ruining everything, I suppose I could use that.

I could accept a friend—if only she didn't have to look like her.

Deb looks at Elle like she's just found a fun new puppy. "You're too nice to put up with my brother's crap."

She isn't wrong about that.

"If you're done harassing my fiancée," I say through my teeth, offering Elle my hand, "I'm taking her to see Aunt Clara before my meeting."

"Oh, your meeting's off the calendar," Debra answers.

"Sullivan canceled?"

"Maybe she chickened out." Deb shrugs. "Or she's got something else up her sleeve."

"We'll find out later. For now"—I incline my head toward the back of the lobby floor—"I believe someone wants to meet her childhood hero."

Elle's hand slips into mine eagerly. She's nearly bouncing on her heels.

"Let's go!"

Shaking my head with amusement, I lead her away.

I can feel Debra watching us the whole time, and I wonder what's on her mind.

When I lead her past the elevator, Elle hesitates. "We're not going upstairs?"

"Aunt Clara's office isn't upstairs."

I can almost feel her bristling with questions, but she holds her tongue and follows me dutifully as I lead her down a narrow corridor to a service door normally used by the building staff. The hallway we step into is dimly lit and utilitarian.

We've walked only a few feet down before another door opens up to let us back outside. It leads into the rear courtyard, which has been fenced in and turned into a private oasis.

Stepping stones wind their way across the grass, making a path that loops through trees, flowers, and bushes and ends around a small glimmering koi pond.

Elle sounds so delighted as we cross the stones, throwing glances everywhere. It makes me feel like I'm seeing this through her eyes—experiencing something I can't.

The wonder, the magic of finding this secret hidden away in the heart of the city.

When the little rose-colored studio hidden in the trees comes into view, she lets go of my hand and claps both of hers over her mouth. Her eyes sparkle as she takes it in.

It's little more than a cottage-style gardening shed, just large enough to share a workspace and a few conveniences with the living areas. Elle already seems enchanted.

"She works here?"

What is my mouth doing.

Why is it pointing up at the corners?

It feels strange. Very, *very* strange, especially since I didn't tell it to do that.

I ignore this goddamned smile and answer, "Yes. She's never done well in corporate spaces. She needed a private place she could make her sanctuary, so I purchased the rear courtyard from the building owners and let her design it as she pleased. Possibly doesn't jive with zoning laws, but no city councilor wants to be known as the hack who made Clara Marshall miserable."

"Amazing! I could sit out here and draw for hours." Elle looks at me. "Can we meet her now?"

"Only if you promise not to tackle her like a hyperactive puppy."

"I wouldn't dare!" Elle protests with a laugh, then pauses. "Um, I might do that."

"Don't," I groan, but I cut myself off as the white-painted door to the studio opens.

Aunt Clara steps out, and this time I don't have to ask myself why my mouth is doing that thing.

No matter how much other people irritate me, it always makes me smile to see her.

She's a tall woman—as most of the women in our family are—and she carries herself with a certain poise that evokes the Deep South and bygone class.

There's nothing superior or withdrawn about her. She carries herself with a welcoming warmth, and that warmth radiates off her as she comes closer and grips my hands, looking up at me, her blue eyes just a half shade off from mine creasing with her smile.

"August." No one says my name the way she does in that soft Georgia lilt that just screams motherly love. She pulls me down to kiss my cheeks, her half-greyed bun of black hair tickling my skin where it wisps around her face. "It's so lovely to have you back in town."

"Aunt Clara." I pull her into a brief hug.

She squeezes me back, then turns to Elle, looking her over thoughtfully with her smile never wavering. She folds her hands against the soft drapes of the gauzy, stylish wrap she wears over a well-cut silk suit.

"You must be the Elle I've heard so much about," she says. "Debra's spoken quite highly of you. And I do so appreciate you helping my nephew with his predicament."

Fuck.

I can't even get annoyed at the subtle sarcasm. I'm used to her good-natured teasing.

Elle's frozen in place, her eyes wide and her mouth slightly open.

I don't quite think it's a migraine this time.

"You . . . you're really her," Elle whispers. "Clara Marshall. You—oh my God!"

Clara's smile is sweet, understanding, kind.

I've never seen her react negatively to any fan, no matter how much they fawn all over her.

"I take it you've enjoyed my books, dear?"

"Yes! Oh, I wouldn't *be* here without your books," Elle breathes, flushing almost like she did when I kissed her. "You're . . . you're everything I've ever wanted to be, Miss Marshall. It's seriously an honor."

"Please, dear, call me Clara." My aunt pats Elle's hand, then nods at the bag she carries under her arm. "Is that your portfolio? I'd love to see it."

"Oh—no, it's just my purse—I mean, my portfolio's inside, but I never expected you'd—I—oh, I'm babbling, I just—"

Now it's my turn to hide a snicker that comes up so unexpectedly I can't stop it.

The layman's term for what Elle is doing is *fangirling*.

Damnably cute fangirling.

Aunt Clara laughs, and I realize why Elle's laugh makes me feel so at home.

Because it's how Aunt Clara used to laugh, before something I still don't understand broke her and she lost her art.

There's this delight I haven't heard in years, but somehow Elle's drawn it out of her.

I can't take my eyes off them as Clara coaxes Elle into calming down, into taking her hand, into going inside with her.

They're two completely different women, yet there's a kinship there, an affinity that makes it feel like Elle is already family, just from the way she fits with Aunt Clara.

I can't be having thoughts like that.

I can't be wondering what it would be like if Elle stuck around after our illusion ends.

And I shouldn't be lingering as Aunt Clara blows me a kiss and winks, like she knows she's just stolen "my" girl.

But I do stay.

As they slip inside the cottage, chattering like old friends, I sink down against the outside wall with my heart heavy.

I can't remember the last time anything felt this peaceful as I listen to them talking and laughing through the window.

IX

SUNNY DISPOSITION

(ELLE)

I think I'm bursting into confetti.

That's the only way to describe how I feel right now.

Like I'm going to explode everywhere like some kind of party favor, and the only reason I'm not is because if I do, then I won't get to spend another second with Clara Marshall.

She's so *cool*.

She's got this kind of classy southern reserve, and she dresses like she just fell out of a fashion catalog from the fifties, all poise and silk and flow. I can see the family resemblance to August, but where he exudes cool granite, she radiates warmth. The moment she meets you, she's already your friend.

Oh God, I'd love to be *her friend*.

The inside of Clara's studio is just as impressive as the outside.

The walls are a soft pastel blue and are covered in pinned-up sketch paper showing works in progress. There are shelves with Inky figurines—and they look handmade. I've seen a few of these as plush toys, but these look like originals Clara made herself.

Then there are shelves lined with original first-run prints of her books.

An easel, paints, sketchbooks everywhere, many left open across the U-shaped assortment of worktables, like she just stopped working a few minutes ago instead of years ago. There are even storyboards showing rough concepts for book plots, framed and hanging on the walls among the sketch paper.

It's pure magic, getting to see everything that's gone into a series that's shaped my whole life.

I stand below a print that's framed and labeled as the very first complete drawing of Inky. He's a chubby, cute little thing, a young penguin with a white coat and a black belly.

Most baby penguins are a sort of pale, floofy grey with no real contrast-color markings like adults, but Inky is the inverse of an adult penguin. He stands proudly with his signature backpack, tipping the little hat he wears when he hikes around the world and dipping his little fountain pen into the black blot on his stomach for more ink.

This is it.

The drawing that started it all.

I just can't seem to look away from its glory.

"The way you look at that drawing fills my heart." Clara's soft, ladylike voice at my shoulder startles me. "I wouldn't think someone as young as you would even know a series as old as this."

"People even younger than me love Inky!" I rush out. I turn to her, wishing so much to reach for her hands to impress this on her, but I have to remind myself that I've only just met her. "You have no idea, Miss Marsha—Clara. You really don't. Your books still fly off the shelves. I've seen kids now who play Inky with their friends, pretending to march all over the world delivering letters."

Her smile is sweet yet achingly sad.

Oh no. Why?

"Well, it's good to know I'm not a has-been yet. No one writes in anymore, so I've quite run out of things to do."

That strikes my heart terribly.

"They don't? I . . . oh. That's such a shame. I used to love sending letters to Inky when I was a kid. My friend Lena did too."

"Hmm . . ." Clara taps her lower lip. Despite the pensive air around her, her eyes brighten, looking almost playful. "What was your last name again, dear? And what year would this have been?"

"Oh—it's Eleanor Lark. Just like the bird. And I guess it would've been . . . sixteen or seventeen years ago? Maybe fifteen."

"Okay, yes. Let's see . . ."

Puzzled, I follow her as she turns away. In the small reading nook across from the work area, several huge trunks line the walls, crammed together until you couldn't fit another one in the small space. With one hand stretched out toward them, Clara turns in a slow arc, murmuring years under her breath—then stops at one of the middle ones.

"Aha. I bet it's right here."

She lifts the lid on the trunk. Inside it's bursting with—

Oh my God.

With letters slathered in childish scribbles, every last envelope opened and meticulously saved.

I'm going to faint.

"Yes, I do remember you, Elle Lark," Clara says as she flips through the envelopes, and I catch glimpses of those letters full of love right before she plucks out one with handwriting I recognize.

Mine.

My own scratchy, messy little-girl handwriting.

Holy shit, my eyes are burning.

Clara's smile is everything as she pulls out the letter on the special pink paper I begged my grandmother to get me just for that letter.

"You wrote to Inky over a dozen times, didn't you?" Clara asks with emotion, as if she's picking up everything vibrating through me. She unfolds the paper tenderly, then reads it over. "*Dear Inky, today my friend Lena and me went all the way to France! We told the French people we were Inky's friends and we came to bring them letters. But the mean Dodson kids next door were playing the French people and they ripped up the letters and laughed and said they were dumb. It's not dumb. I like writing letters! I just want a friend to write letters with from far away. Will you be my friend, no matter where you go?"*

Oh no.

Oh no, the waterworks are starting, and I press my face into my hands.

"And . . . and Inky wrote back. He said he would always be my friend. That I wasn't dumb and I wrote wonderful letters, and so did Lena, and anytime I wrote him, he'd always write me back." I suck in a shaking breath. I can't stop smiling, even as my eyes overflow. "Only August told me . . . he told me that was *you*. That letter was the one that made me want to draw things that made other kids as happy as Inky made me, and it was *you* the whole time. Not some assistant. Not a form letter. You, Clara Marshall."

"Oh, dear, let me get you a tissue. Perhaps one for me too." With a slightly embarrassed laugh and her eyes gleaming, Clara plucks a tissue from a box on the end table next to a cozy reading chair and offers it to me. "I didn't expect we'd both get so emotional. But yes, it was me. I do remember you wrote back and told me one day you'd draw books just like the ones Inky was in. So, my dear, have you?"

I take the tissue, sniffing and laughing at the same time.

"Um, not yet," I say, scrubbing at my eyes. "I've mostly been doing freelance illustration work to pay the bills and haven't been able to refine a concept yet. But with the whole thing with August . . . I'll be able to take plenty of time off to work on my own ideas, so he's really helping me out a lot. I'm not just helping him." I rub the tissue against my nose. "He's a really great guy. Better than I think he knows."

Clara's smile is radiant. "I do wish more people had your insight to know that. You must be quite a special girl to understand my August so quickly."

"Oh God. I don't know if I understand him. It's just really fun poking him." Then I groan. "I'm sorry. I'm being embarrassing. Crying and running my mouth . . ."

"No, darling. You're not embarrassing. You're honest, and I appreciate the honesty. It's needed in a world where people have forgotten how such things work." Clara folds my letter and tucks it almost reverently back into the envelope before she holds it up. "Would you like to keep this?"

I bite my lip, shaking my head. "It would mean more to me if you kept it, ma'am. I know it's just one of thousands, but . . . it's special, knowing that you've had it all this time."

"Oh, Elle—we're all one of thousands. Of millions. Of billions. But that's what makes us unique. We're the only ones who can be *that* one." She smiles gently, pressing my letter to her chest. "I'd be delighted to keep it. Every letter is unique to me."

My idol. My hero.

She's about to *kill* me.

I never imagined she could be so relatable. To think she'd remember a letter I wrote over a decade ago, when she must have been inundated, assuming all these wooden chests are stuffed with letters.

I want to be just like her.

Not just my career, but my life. I want to be this kind, this thoughtful, this warm.

Then it hits me so powerfully I actually stumble back.

I want to be someone August could love.

God, what's wrong with me?

Did one kiss mess me up this freaking much?

I've tried so hard to put it behind me.

It was an act, an instinct, and August went as mum as I did after it happened.

I didn't want to make things weird, so I just pretended it didn't happen. But that night when I lay in bed and touched my lips and felt him, plus the lingering thought of his scratchy stubble on my skin . . .

Oh God, did I misbehave.

But I can't be having those thoughts in front of his aunt.

Especially when I see so much of him in her now, and her mirrored in him.

That refined way of speaking—he got that from her, I think, even if Clara uses the elegant words of a southern lady, while August barks with the cold precision of a ruthless gentleman.

The careful, proper manners.

The kindness she wears like a second skin—while he tries oh so hard to bury his.

It makes me wonder who he was kind to in the past.

And who hurt him? Who made him throw it all away so he wouldn't get hurt again?

Aren't you making a lot of assumptions?

Yep. I need to get my mind off August ASAP.

So I pin on a smile for Clara.

"Thank you," I say. "Seriously, you've just made my day. My whole *life*. You know, they say 'Never meet your heroes,' but I'm glad I met you, Clara. I'm just . . . I'm sorry that you feel like you can't continue Inky."

Something remote flits across Clara's face for a split second.

A hint of pain.

She looks away, still holding my letter like it's a comfort somehow.

"Sometimes things happen. Unexpected things that drain the color from the world, dear," she says softly. "And I never did paint well in black and white."

I don't understand. But maybe I'm not meant to.

Maybe there's a bigger secret behind why she quit than losing her muse.

I just wish I could do something for her.

Right now, I feel like August hiring me as her assistant is just forcing something on her that could be a burden. But what if she needs a fresh face, a few new ideas?

"What if you weren't doing it for publication? Inky, I mean," I ask carefully. "August thought that maybe we could work together and I could help you somehow. Would you be willing to teach me just for the sake of it? Just to draw Inky again?"

Clara's smile is so kind, but her eyes are misty. "You're a darling to offer. However, I don't think I could, even for those reasons." She shakes her head. "I think it's time to let go. If that Sullivan girl truly wants the penguin badly enough to fight poor August for it in court, tooth and claw—well, I'm willing to let it go."

What?

Oh, hell no.

I freeze up.

I'm also deathly afraid I've just screwed up royally.

August is going to kill me if he finds out I had anything to do with his aunt throwing in the towel.

I try to find words—any words—to undo the horrible thought I've just put in her head, but my lips won't work.

Clara glances at me again and turns away quickly, evidently hoping she can hide the faint tremor in her lips. She crosses back to the chest to put my letter back inside.

"Could you give me a moment? I regret for you to see me out of sorts like this."

"Sure!" I manage.

I turn and walk stiffly out the door, and I close it gently behind me.

Then I thud my head against the wall next to it.

"Stupid, stupid, *stupid*," I mutter, pinching my eyes shut with a wince before I do a 180 to slide down the wall.

I'm definitely asking for another migraine, which I'd probably deserve this time.

The nausea climbing up my throat isn't that, though. It's just me feeling sick to the bone that I've just torn my idol's heart out with careless words and being pushy and—

Crap!

I have to fix this.

Before August finds out and possibly murders me.

But I don't know *how*.

So I turn where I always do when I need advice.

Fumbling my phone from my bag, I punch my grandmother's contact.

She picks up quickly, her pleasant warble instantly comforting. "Hello, my Elle. How's your first day at work?"

"That's Elle?" Before I can answer, Lena's voice echoes in the background.

Gran's voice pulls away from the phone. "Yes, don't shout in the house—and don't trim my English ivy too close!"

"Oh, I know how to trim an ivy, Grandma. Ask Elle if she fucked him yet!"

"I most certainly will *not* ask my granddaughter that, and you watch your mouth before I wash it out with soap!"

I can't help a tired laugh.

These two should take their act on the road.

"Lena's over helping with the houseplants, huh? Good. You shouldn't be up on that stepladder with your foot. For what it's worth, the answer is *no*."

"Thank you, but I didn't need to know that." Grandma clucks her tongue. "Now, you sound sad. Tell me what's wrong."

Lena butts in before I can answer.

"Hey, put her on speaker. If she's upset, I want to hear too." Her voice sounds closer.

"Glad to know my misery is a spectator sport," I mutter. But I can hear the echo of my voice, so I guess I've got an audience of two.

"Your whole life is a spectator sport right now, chica," Lena teases. "Now spill. What's got you upset?"

"Oh, I think I just pushed my idol into giving up not only her career, but the intellectual property rights to her most beloved creation. And the second her nephew finds out, he's going to string me up from the Space Needle," I say brightly. "No biggie. I'm just a walking disaster, like usual."

"Bull. You are not," August says at my side. "You are, however, about to witness me losing my temper."

I squeak and drop my phone.

My skin nearly leaps off my body.

"Shit!" Lena's voice drifts up from my phone.

"Language!" Gran hisses next.

Panting and still leaning away from August, even though I don't remember flinching, I stare up at him with my pulse going like a rocket. He's standing at the corner of the little shed, his mouth grim, his eyes sparking, his broad shoulders and agile body so taut he looks like a tightly strung bow ready to fire into the air.

"Where did you come from?" I hiss.

"I've been behind you the entire time," he rumbles, right before the door bursts open and Clara comes spilling out.

"Is everything all right? I heard a scream—"

"And you're about to hear shouting," August growls, rounding on her. "What do you mean, you're going to let Marissa have the rights?"

"Oh dear." Grandma's voice is faint from my phone, now sitting on the last flagstone before the studio. "I don't think we should be hearing this, Lena."

"Shhh!" Lena hisses. "We're getting to the juicy part!"

Oh my God, I'm living a circus.

Clara rests her hands on her hips, looking at August sternly. "I said what I said, and you will *not* take that tone with me, young man."

There he is.

The little boy I imagined when I thought of how August came to be this way, angry and isolated and scaring people off with his grumping and no-nonsense demeanor.

That boy is currently hanging his head, looking chastised as his mother figure stares him down with an iron will.

But apparently they have more in common than those penetrating blue eyes.

Because after a mumbled, painfully cute "Sorry, Auntie . . . ," August stiffens, his eyes narrowing. "I won't take a harsh tone with you, Aunt Clara, but I will say you're dead wrong about this."

"Ohhhh shit," Lena whispers from my phone.

"Shut up, shut up!" I snatch my phone up, whispering back into the speaker.

They don't even notice us.

"I'm not wrong about my feelings, August," Clara throws back. "I know what I want."

"What? To give up? Just like that, to abandon your life's work to a damn grifter who wants to steal everything you've created?"

Clara doesn't say anything. She only looks away, her mouth tightening as she glares mutinously toward the inside of the studio collage.

August recoils. "Tell me it wouldn't be stealing, Clara. Tell me she's right. I know you wouldn't. I know you better."

Clara's jaw trembles before she says, "There are complications at work here, and many of them are deeply personal. You don't know everything about my life, son. Nor do you need to."

"Tell that boy!" Gran shouts.

I glare at my phone.

"Gran, don't make me hang up on you too!"

August works his lips into a hard, angry battle line and folds his arms over his broad chest. "Aunt Clara, I'm about to face down a legal battle for the whole future of Little Key. The company built around *you*. If there's something that would affect the outcome, I need to know."

"What does it matter, if I'm willing to surrender the rights?" Clara demands.

"It *matters* because—" August throws his hands up. "Why are you so frustrating?"

"Because we both share the same cold blood," Clara retorts dryly. "But not so cold I don't think about the stakes. Our employees, Deb, you . . . If anyone has to lose their jobs over this, I'll work night and day to help send them off to better ones with glowing recommendation letters, pulling every string I've ever touched. We share enough guilt in our blood, too, I'm afraid."

August lets out a deep sigh.

"That's the problem, Aunt Clara. Because if I have to pull rank on you right now, I absolutely will."

Clara whips back to face him fully.

It's a war of cutting eyes and forbidding stares.

I can't even breathe.

I'm just caught between two demigods who are about to start throwing lightning bolts, razing half of Seattle with them.

"Excuse you, young man. In what world do you outrank me? I raised you. And I hate to remind you that I am almost twice your age. You're not too old to be taken over my knee, even if you're four times my size."

Lena's giggle leaps up from the phone.

I give up and mute them both.

August lifts his head haughtily, looking down his sharp nose at his aunt—but there's something there. Something behind his eyes that even I can see.

A flicker of pain that he has to speak to her this way.

He *really* loves her.

My eyes are stinging.

I want to hug him so much right now, I want to end this, but I don't dare move.

Especially when he bites off, "At the moment, Debra has stepped down as CEO, and I've taken over as interim. Which means I'm technically your employer. If I have to give you orders as your boss, I will. Don't make me, Aunt Clara."

She briefly bares her teeth like a cornered animal.

"You wouldn't dare."

"Try me."

My heart stops.

She tosses her head, her grey-streaked hair flaring briefly. "And what would your orders be, Mr. High and Mighty?"

Ohhhh *shit*.

Grandma and Lena would be screaming, if I could hear them.

August doesn't budge.

"My orders are for you to hold off on surrendering any damn rights until you hear what I propose. I want you to give it a fair shake with Inky, Aunt Clara. That's all. And that means—"

He stops and unfolds his arm, flinging one hand at me.

I freeze, pushing myself back with my feet until my shoulders hit the wall, my gut plummeting.

Guess he remembers I'm here after all.

"That means working with Elle," he commands. "That's all. Keep her as your assistant for the duration. However long she's willing to continue playing my fiancée, or until this lawsuit is fully settled, *or* until you're willing to tell me what the hell is so important that you can't share it with your own family to save everything you've ever worked for."

Clara's flinty stare is unwavering. "Haven't you drawn this girl into enough of your schemes? Why should I listen to you? If you're my employer, I can quit, can't I? I'll write up my resignation right now."

Oh no. Oh crap. Oh *God, no*.

I stare between them, panic rioting inside me like a scared jackrabbit.

I have to stop this.

Before the infamous Marshall temper is the death of me.

"But you won't," August retorts, his voice softening. "Because you know Deb and I are fighting like hell because we love you, Aunt Clara. And you love us too much to leave us flapping in the breeze."

Clara sighs.

"If you aren't the most stubborn—" Clara stops and throws her hands up in exasperation. I see my gran in the gesture, that moment when her pride won't let her back down, but she doesn't want to keep fighting with the child she loves either. Suddenly she turns to me, her voice softening. "Elle, I'm so sorry. Once August gets an idea in his head, he won't stop until he steamrolls everyone around him. Can you put up with me until this mess is sorted? You're welcome to use my studio to develop your own work. I'd actually love the company, and I make a lovely tea."

. . . put up with her?

My idol thinks I'd balk at *putting up with her* for months as her apprentice?

Holy hell.

I'm speechless.

This whole thing just came crashing down on my head, and now I'm getting wrecking-balled in the face by two obstinate Marshalls who've somehow made me the center of their mess.

Again.

I gulp. "I . . . I already agreed to be your assistant as part of the deal with August. I promise I don't mind. It's cool." I try a shaky smile. I don't know how to feel—elated that my apprenticeship is confirmed, upset that I'm a burden to Clara, or hopeful that maybe I can be of some help to her. "I'd be honored to work with you."

"There," August proclaims triumphantly. "You see? It's all fine."

Clara plants her hands on her hips, scowling at him. "It's not fine. I see I failed at raising you when you're still obstinate as a bull, and when this all blows up in your face—"

"Debra already said that," August interrupts dryly. "She's offered to take Elle for a drink. I'm sure they'd love to have you for cocktails."

What a mess.

But then August diverts his gaze to me. I can't help it—a shiver runs through me, his stare so intense that rather than being cold, it flushes me with heat as it rakes my body in a quick, sharp survey.

"Speaking of cocktails, after you clock out, Rick will be waiting to escort you."

I blink, recoiling. I feel like I've been turned upside down and shaken.

"What? Escort me where?"

"Wherever you like to shop. We'll be having dinner at the Loupe Lounge tonight."

I blink numbly. "You mean the one in the Space Needle?"

"Of course," he answers offhandedly.

Of course.

And he's chosen now to tell me this?

He couldn't have texted me yesterday and told me?

This must be revenge for poking the bear so many times.

Clara watches us with an eyebrow raised, her arms folded as I ask faintly, "What am I shopping for?"

"A dress," he replies irritably, like it should be obvious. I want to thwack him. "Dressy, but comfortable. It's not a black-tie location. Perhaps one step below cocktail dress."

"Oh. That's . . . helpful."

Despite my phone being muted, I swear I can hear Lena cackling.

"Good," August proclaims. Oh, he thought I was serious? "I'll be by to pick you up at seven sharp."

With that, he turns and storms away, leaving Clara and me looking after him in frozen stillness.

Before Clara sighs, her shoulders droop. She looks down at me with a rueful smile. "Well then," she says. "I suppose I'll put on some tea."

She turns and walks inside the cottage, but she leaves the door open for me.

I don't get up just yet.

I'm still sitting here, hunched on the grass and pressed against the wall next to the door, my knees drawn up like some demented goblin.

I finally remember to unmute my phone as my brain starts working again.

"—e mute us? I bet that little bitch muted us."

"Lena, I know you have a foul mouth, but could you refrain from calling my granddaughter a 'little bitch'?"

"You just said it!" Lena announces triumphantly. "Hey, I only say it affectionately. As in, that *lucky* little bitch."

"That little bitch can hear you," I groan. "Yes, I muted you. I don't even want to know what you guys were saying."

"Oh! There you are." Lena perks up, completely shameless. "There you are. So, what're you gonna wear?"

I stare down at my phone.

And then I instantly hang up, thunking my head back against the wall.

My God.

August Marshall has blown my life to bits in far more ways than I could ever imagine.

I've never had a day more awkward than this in my life.

Yes, that's counting the day in third-grade theater, when little Jimmy Schmitz pantsed me onstage in front of every parent, well-meaning aunt, and older sibling in my school district.

I made the best of that too.

I'm just glad I had on really cute floral panties that matched my bright sunflower costume, so, hey, technically I really wasn't that out of costume. It got a good laugh from the audience and Jimmy a week of detention, where every day as I passed by the classroom window during recess, I looked in, smiled at him, and waved as cheerfully as I could.

Look, I try to stay positive. But every now and then I can be positively petty.

Right now, though?

I'm positively *tired*.

I spent the whole day with Clara. If I thought I was going to work any miracles with her, I was wrong.

She didn't want to talk art. I didn't feel comfortable offering to show her my portfolio.

Instead, she had me sorting all the Inky originals, models, and merchandise so she could pack them up to hand them over to Marissa whenever a legal order shows up to do so.

She promised she'd keep the boxes until August made peace with the idea, but it didn't change the fact that her mind was made up. I wasn't about to get kicked out for starting an argument over this.

Depressing as hell.

Any joy I might've felt over getting to handle priceless one-of-a-kind artist originals was completely dampened.

Then there was the silent, strange ride in the car with Rick. He kept looking at me like he wanted to say something, these mournful little glances that made everything uncomfortable when he stayed silent except to mumble, *Yes, Miss Lark*, and *No, Miss Lark*.

The deference was weird. I know I'm supposed to expect a lot of butt-kissing as August's fiancée, but I'm still just me.

Not *Miss Lark*.

Except Angelique and the other girls at the boutique kept calling me that too. I didn't know anywhere else to go. I had August's Platinum Card in hand, about an hour to find a dress and get home to get dressed, and no time to wander from shop to shop.

At least they were nice about it.

Even if they exchanged pitying glances as they realized August wasn't with me this time.

Look at her. Poor girl. He's already tired of her.

Why do I care?

That question circles through my head, wearing frustrated ruts as I stare morosely at my reflection in my bedroom mirror. If anything, it's perfect.

Later, when the gossip rags spend one column on a third page on our breakup, these girls will pop up on Instagram saying, *You know, I helped them at the couture shop I work at. The first time I saw them he was already ignoring her on his phone, and every other time she came in alone. He'd just throw his card at her like it didn't matter.*

Believable, right?

So believable.

I rub my throat, right over the spot where a lump is forming, and smile at my own tired, pale face. Paler than normal, I should say.

Red lipstick with this dress was a terrible idea.

With an upset sound I rip a tissue out of the holder and scrub it off furiously, leaving red smears all over the paper.

I'm fine. *I'm fine.*

I look amazing. I really do.

This dress feels like an inverted white morning glory. A soft, shimmery sheath of sleeveless gossamer with a gently dipping neckline exposing a hint of cleavage.

Subtle ribs in the dress mirror flower petals as they form it to my body, flaring out over my hips into an A-skirt that skims down to midthigh. The subtle pearl dust of glitter in the ribs and at the hem matches the faint glittery body shine on my shoulders and arms, and the barely there shine of the simple white pearl-sheen pumps Angelique paired with the dress.

Again, I look like a little fairy dusted with moonlight.

So why can't I shake the gloom in my eyes and in my heart?

I paint on a smile—this time in a paler pearl pink that suits my complexion better.

I'm glowing tonight, from the pale shimmering pink of my eye shadow and darker glitter-pink liner to the subtle shades shifting in and out of my dress. It's a new look for me, honestly.

I usually go for bold, eclectic color combinations. I know I'm a wild mess, and I tend to dress to match.

But I don't mind this softer look either.

It feels like—

Never mind. It doesn't matter what it feels like.

Because I hear a car pulling up outside, and by now I know the sound of that engine. I glance through the curtains in my bedroom, and there it is. That deep-blue G80—such a flashy car for such a stiff man.

I wonder if he picked it himself.

His one splash of color, of boldness—whispering at secret urges inside?

Stop.

Stop romanticizing him.

He's your boss, and no matter what it looks like, this is a work dinner. Just play your role.

"Elle?" Grandma calls up the stairs. "August is here."

"I know, Gran," I call down. "Be there in a second."

I slide into a coat that's longer than the dress, thick and felted black, stylishly cut to flatter the feminine figure and keep me warm in such a thin, flimsy outfit. The little matching clutch purse to the dress fits right in the coat's pocket. Even with the thick coat on, I feel naked, maybe because I've pinned my hair up in a chignon again, leaving my neck bare except for a necklace of tiny seed pearls.

Right. No point in keeping Mr. Bossypants waiting.

I put on my smile and head downstairs.

Gran steals a quick hug as she catches me at the foot of the stairs.

"You look so lovely, darling," she whispers, patting my shoulder to scoot me toward the door.

When I open the door, I'm fully expecting to head down the walk and have Rick let me into the back seat of the car.

Instead, I jump back with a startled sound.

August himself waits silently on the front step, handsome as sin in a fine-cut steel button-down shirt and a pair of neatly pressed black slacks held up with a slim black leather belt dotted with a square gold buckle.

I don't think I've ever seen him this dressed down before.

His hair is a little messier, the same parted sweep but more disarrayed, softening the harshly handsome lines of his face into something more approachable and human.

The shirt is cuffed to his elbows and open at the throat. Enough that I can see the dip where his collarbones meet under smooth tanned skin.

I catch a faint wisp of chest hair, and everything goes tingly.

I'm suddenly so aware of that thousand-pound ring on my finger.

I've learned to ignore it, to forget it like I forget my earrings when I go to bed half the time, only to wake up with their imprint on my cheek.

But right now it's so heavy as I look at him with my heart in my throat and my head overflowing with crazy thoughts.

Like how nice it would be if he looked happy to see me.

But he's not looking at me at all.

He's on his phone *again*, and he finishes tapping out something that looks like an email before glancing up absently.

He's definitely playing the part of a man who's going to get dumped in the near future.

"Good evening, Elle—"

He stops short.

His lips remain parted, and he just *looks* at me, his blue eyes slightly widened.

Startled.

It's the same way he looked at me when I stepped out of the dressing room at the boutique. Like he's seeing something he never expected.

Like I've surprised him so much by not being a dumpster fire that he's actually seeing me for the first time.

It makes me feel naked, even in the thick coat. I bite my lip, failing to stop the smile creeping over my lips.

"Hi, August. You're early. Wanted to see me that much?"

It actually takes a second or two for him to speak. I hope that's flattering and not me looking so awful he's stunned into silence.

But then he flipping smiles, and I'm a total lost cause.

No amount of telling myself he's doing it for the paparazzi will make my heart believe it's not real and warm and just for me. A small, wry smile, devoid of that cynical bitterness or stiff formality.

Just a quiet thing that makes me think that boy who just wants someone to *want* him wasn't completely crushed to death under the weight of his life.

"You caught me," he mutters. His voice strokes me like I'm wrapped in raw silk and writhing against the texture. He takes a step closer, his sandalwood scent and heat overpowering. "Your suitor is impatient. Hope you can forgive me."

Faking it.

He's. Faking. It.

He's faking it too damn well.

I almost feel faint.

My skin steams, no matter the nippy chill in the evening, which is cloudless and bright with stars.

But I can barely see them, forced to tilt my head back to look up at him. He's all shadow, with the gold halo of the front step gilding him from behind, leaving his eyes like embers of cool blue fire.

They turn my heart into vibrant dust.

"You look nice," I manage. There's a thickness to my voice, like everything in me is slow and molten. "Um, I don't think I've ever seen you this dressed down before."

"If I can't relax with my fiancée, who the hell can I relax with?" But he stops, his brows pulling together. His expression sobers as he searches my face. "You're pale. Elle, if you're not feeling well, we'll do this another night."

This, I know, is definitely real.

For some unholy reason, this confusing, stubborn man actually cares about my health, about not pushing me too far.

That brings my smile back, even if it doesn't slow my heart. I curl my fingers in the front of my coat, drawing it tighter.

"It's just chilly. That's all," I say. I don't want to tell him I'm pale because I've been brooding and trying so, so hard not to want the reality behind the fiction.

I'm used to pretending to be happy until I really am.

I can do it now too.

August gives me a long look, like he can sense that something's not quite right.

But he lets it go and offers me his arm. "Dinner then?"

"Dinner," I agree, glancing back to wave at Gran, who's watching me with her eyes oddly misty before I shut the door and slip my arm into August's with increasing familiarity.

He escorts me down the walk, beneath the soft blue palette of a cloudy night sky. But when we reach the curb, instead of Rick stepping out from behind the wheel, August opens the front passenger-side door for me, giving me a peek into an empty car.

I blink.

"No Rick?"

"Not tonight," August answers, his lips quirking. It throws me off guard to see him like this. Being *human*, his guard down, his demeanor more relaxed, even if it's all for show. "If he was always shadowing us, people might grow suspicious that we never get any intimate time together."

Intimate time together.

This man is so freaking oblivious.

Just as he's oblivious to how being close to him makes my skin prickle as I slip past him and into the seat. He waits to make sure I'm settled and fully in, then closes the door gently behind me and strides around to the driver's seat.

As he settles in and starts the engine with the smooth, purring growl you'd expect from a car this expensive, I fasten my seat belt and settle to watch him as he steers the G80 into traffic with familiar ease. At least he's not one of those rich boys who can't drive because he's so used to someone else doing it for him.

"Hey, I've been meaning to ask," I say. "Did Rick pick this car out, or you?"

"Me," August answers, glancing at me with the same amusement that's messing with me so badly. "Surprised? Since I have such a stick up my ass."

I let out a startled laugh. "A little, yeah. I almost thought someone else bought this for you. Like Debra, maybe."

"I suppose it does suit my sister's flash." But it suits him, too, I realize. He looks casual and sexy behind the wheel, one arm draped against the window, pulling the muscles in his forearm taut. He scans the road in front of us, now and then glancing at me as he handles the wheel one handed with lazy ease, his legs rakishly spread and tight against his slacks. "Hot Wheels."

"Hm?"

"It wasn't video games," he murmurs. "The brats who shunned me were playing with Hot Wheels. I wanted to play too. Always did like fast cars."

. . . oh.

I realize what he's giving me.

A crumb of himself.

I don't even know what to say, but it warms me.

I smile as I settle in to watch the traffic in comfortable silence. It's scary how easy it is to just *be* with him, without needing to fill the space with sound, with noise, with anything but the quiet of us.

There is no us, I remind myself sharply.

And that's okay.

For now, this moment is enough.

That's why I'm not expecting it when August breaks the silence again. I almost don't notice.

He's so quiet tonight, his usual authoritativeness softened.

Intimate.

Close.

Inside me, every word.

"I don't expect you to singlehandedly save Little Key Publishing, you know," he says.

I glance over at him. The nightscape of Seattle and its traffic around us is dappling soft hints of color over his face, turning him into a portrait of pensive artistry, handsome and heart stopping in this weird grace where he doesn't seem so ice cold and unapproachable at all.

Not when those lights paint liquid color in his eyes, softening them from chips of ice into pools so clear and deep you can see all the way to the bottom.

I pull myself up from staring and this weird feeling like tonight could mean something.

"I don't understand," I whisper.

"Mmm." Again that little curl of his lips, subtle but captivating. I've never thought of men as beautiful before, but August Marshall is so darkly, devilishly sculpted that every expression on his face captivates me. "I know the burden I've dumped on you, no matter what benefits you might gain from it. Salvage my reputation to salvage the company. That's a big fucking ask. Let alone working with my aunt to see if her muse ever wakes up, just so we can keep her from surrendering her life's work to Marissa Sullivan and her little schemes. It's a hell of a lot to have dropped on your shoulders, I know. All because you fell into the wrong man's arms in a terminal."

I laugh. "I've been trying not to think too hard about it," I admit—and maybe, if I'm honest with myself, that's part of the reason for my jitters tonight.

Every step I take, I have to try not to screw things up for August and his family.

And actually falling for August, giving in to this magnetism that wants to draw me closer and closer to him?

That would definitely screw things up.

Fingering the delicate necklace against my throat, I look down at my lap.

"I just don't know how to do any of it," I say. "All I can do is be myself. I don't know how to be a billionaire's fiancée, let alone a struggling artist's inspiration."

"It's because you're you, Elle. That's why you're perfect," August says softly, his gaze fixed on the road ahead. My heart leaps so high it must touch the stars. But before I can ask him to explain, he continues. "You don't have to carry that alone. I know I've swept you along, but all I really need you to do is buy me time. I'll handle everything else. It's not your fight. Just bear with me through a few more date nights like this, and keep Aunt Clara distracted while I do what I need to." He glances at me sidelong, almost knowingly. "Instead of having to deal with everything on your own, consider us partners."

Yep.

Captain Oblivious.

He has no earthly idea what he's doing to me right now.

The tension in my chest.

The feeling like the walls that are usually closed up around him in mile-thick layers have thinned a little. I might even see a door starting to open as he lets me in just enough to reach a toe inside.

From the moment I met him, I've had this sense that somehow he sees me as the enemy—or at least another burden.

But now he's telling me we're partners.

He's starting to trust me.

That makes me ache so much worse.

If he only knew I was getting so emotionally messy and my breaths stop short every time he looks at me a second too long . . .

It'd be a betrayal of that trust.

So I just smile. Even if it takes all my heart, all my brightness, all my desperate need to find the good in everything.

I smile.

And I tease, "It's more fun if we call each other 'coconspirators.' Bonnie and Clyde? Like we're pulling off a heist."

August snorts, but that curl to his lips doesn't fade. "You are, as always, impossibly creative."

That's me.

Miss Impossible.

Except everything I'm creating tonight is the wrong feeling as I hold on to my smile and look out the window again, trying to drain these stupid thoughts into the night.

They can hang there like stars, shining and endless and so distant I won't be able to reach them again.

X

WALKING STORM CLOUD

(AUGUST)

Something's bothering Elle.

I noticed when she opened the door of her grandmother's cottage and I saw her pale, drawn face, tinted in shades of amber by the porch light.

I almost thought she was crying.

But her eyes were dry, not red. No telltale marks or swollen features. Yet something in her expression hinted at holding back tears.

What bothered me almost as much as the fact that she might have been unhappy was the fact that I cared at all.

She told me she was fine.

I don't have the right to pry when this is a business arrangement and nothing more. So I kept my foolish thoughts to myself, escorted her to the car, and tried not to watch her the entire time I drove.

She looks like pearl tonight.

Palest mother-of-pearl, a living glimmer of white, a hint of glitter that disappears the instant you try to stare at it too long. Even her hair carries a touch of glitter, and it's goddamned magnificent.

She looks like the moon fell into the sun and mixed together in a swirl of radiance.

I shouldn't notice her so much, but it's getting harder not to.

She's quiet on the drive there.

It's rare that Elle is ever this quiet, and the absence of her voice is—

Fuck, it shouldn't bother me.

Her chatter, her jokes, her teasing, her insufferable wickedness—they all drive me batshit insane. I should be grateful for a little peace and quiet.

Still, I watch her from the corner of my eye, and wonder.

Am I asking too much of her?

No matter what I might offer in return, it's nothing but money and a nudge up the career ladder. Material things, and I've had wealth for so long that I always remember how so much runs deeper than what can be bought.

I've bought Elle's presence and cooperation, yes.

But is she paying in misery?

The words we exchange on the drive do little to reassure me, even if the mood settles more companionably.

While I have no room for romance in my life, I wouldn't mind a friend.

Elle is everything that annoys me.

Too loud, too bright, too cheerful, too perky, *a fucking morning lark.*

She's also a good person.

Warm, effusive, gentle, kind.

Not the sort of person you look down on, even if their personality grates like splinters under your fingernails.

Does it, though?

Or does she only grate at your stuffy ass because she reminds you that you built these walls around yourself—and now you don't know how to tear them down?

As we find parking near the Space Needle, I pause, rubbing my temples and trying to push my worries away.

I'm supposed to be functional tonight. Whatever a waiting, eager public expects a man in love to look like.

Hell, I'm not sure if I was ever that in the past, before everything derailed.

Before the part of me that can belong in a relationship shattered forever.

I've never pretended to be anyone besides exactly who I am.

Somehow, my ex-wife put up with it for a few years, dragged me into her undertow, until the next thing I knew, I was wrapped up in her. I'm not sure if Charisma and I ever sincerely loved each other, but for a time we were enough in love with the *idea* of love.

Enough to get us down the aisle believing we'd make it despite the uncertainties.

Enough to buy a heaping pile of bullshit we fed ourselves.

And I still can't say it wasn't mostly my fault.

"August?"

Elle's soft voice dashes my thoughts like delicate fingers parting a curtain. I lift my head, opening my eyes.

"Yeah?"

Her hazel eyes search mine in the darkness. I wonder sometimes what she sees when she looks at me.

"You're brooding so loud I can't hear myself think," she says with a smile. "And not your usual stormy-storm. Or else I'd be giving you so much crap you'd pull over and leap out just to get away from me."

Despite myself, I smile slightly.

She just draws it out of me lately.

"Just thinking about the lawsuit," I lie. I think it would bother her to know I was worrying about her—never mind the fact that I'd be blurring the professional lines between us. "Also, whatever Aunt Clara isn't telling me that could affect its outcome."

"I do wonder what's up with her . . ." Elle reaches for the car door handle—then stops with this self-conscious movement that tells me she remembers she's supposed to be my fiancée and let me do publicly chivalrous things like opening doors for her. "When I spent the day with her, she seemed—I dunno—sad? Lost? But not guilty."

"Yeah. Hang on."

I slip outside and pull my long winter coat on against the wintry night. We had to park a few blocks down, and frankly I'm concerned about Elle's bare legs.

I'm too damned caught up on what those legs would feel like wrapped around me as I open her door and offer her my hand, gripping her slim fingers and lifting her out with a little too much force. It makes her clutch my arm as she finds her footing with a gasp.

My neck feels too warm.

"My bad." I clear my throat, looking away.

"Don't know your own strength?" she teases lightly, then pulls back. "Let me get my coat."

It's more that you're so light, I think. *Like the smallest breeze could blow you over.*

Like I could throw you around and make you bounce on my cock until you scream yourself hoarse, woman.

"Let me," I say quickly, dipping past her to fetch her coat from the car seat. "Here, you're shivering."

"Feels like winter lasts longer every year, though it's nothing like New York in February."

Elle turns her back to me and slips her arms into the coat.

I fold it around her. Drawing her into the fabric embrace feels like pulling her into my arms.

For a moment, I feel it.

What it would be like to be casual and relaxed enough to embrace her from behind, engulf her in my body heat to chase the cold from her bones.

Fuck, it's like she belongs there.

Like I *want* her to belong, and not just to keep this ruse chugging along.

I hurl those thoughts away, shaking my head.

I wish we had a stalker as attentive as the one who caught the photos in the airport right now. This moment would be picture perfect as I settle the coat on her shoulders and offer her my arm.

"It's not far," I say, as if she can't see the Space Needle's spire stabbing up into the night. "You'll warm up soon. Can you tell me more about Aunt Clara? What did she say earlier?"

"Hmm, let me think . . ."

Elle slips her arm into mine and cocks her head thoughtfully.

I'm caught up in the way the soft light of the lamps falls against her hair. I half expect to see light pooling at the tips like golden raindrops waiting to fall.

"She had me help her start packing up her things," Elle says finally. I don't miss how she subtly leans into me as we make our way down the sidewalk. "The old clay penguin models, the first-run figurines, her old concept sketches and original storyboards."

She stops me before I can open my mouth, her fingers squeezing my arm reassuringly.

"August, please don't lose your shit. Honestly, I think she was doing it more to spite you than anything else."

"She *is* my aunt," I grind out.

"She is." Elle's laugh is whisper sweet. "But it felt like she didn't really want to. The way she handled everything? She touched it all with love, August. Almost like she couldn't stand to part with it. I don't think she really wants to give up the Inky IP. And if she had lied, she'd be more angry, I think."

"More of your impeccable insights into human nature?"

"Psssh, I wish."

Sometimes, when Elle smiles, instead of seeming young and exuberant, she seems sad and ageless. Like she's some strange spirit who's only taken human form temporarily.

That melancholy timelessness is in her smile now as she lowers her lashes.

"You know, I don't think I understand people that well. But I might understand her a little. If she'd stolen that work from Lester Sullivan, then in her mind, the theft had to feel justified for some weird reason. So now if someone wants to take it from her, she'd feel angry and guilty. She'd be giving up the IP to avoid having to openly admit her guilt, but she'd still be angry about having to do it. And thanks to you, now I know what Clara Marshall looks like when she's angry." Elle laughs again. "It's a lot like you. And she definitely wasn't angry earlier. She was grieving—but I don't think she was just grieving Inky."

Damn.

That's a hell of a lot to think about.

I work through what's happened so far and where we go from here—and how to stop Marissa Sullivan from pulling the floor out from under us.

I don't want to think it's even possible that Clara *could* be guilty of intellectual property theft. That she's only faking her regret so people as trusting as Elle won't doubt her or believe she could possibly do something so reprehensible.

A light play of fingers up my arm draws my attention, and I look down at her.

"What?"

She flashes me a wicked smile. "Have I done my job as your informant?"

"I didn't mean—" I stop and sigh. "Fuck. I suppose I have put you in that position, haven't I?"

"If you were anyone else . . . I'd say something about you putting me in *other* positions."

"Eleanor Lark. You're really going to go there?" I growl—and she bursts into a laughing fit, the sound floating like fireflies over the night.

"My full name? I *really* scandalized His Lordship, huh?" Utterly shameless, she grins wider, looking up at me with her hazel eyes twinkling. The tilt of her head gives her lips a kissable pout, pink and plush.

"I'm sorry. I only said it to see the look on your face. Totally worth it, by the way."

"Incorrigible brat."

I look away, glaring across the street instead.

Only because if I don't scowl, my face might betray too much.

Like the thoughts that flashed through my mind the second those innuendo-charged words left her mouth. Hell, those thoughts were already there all night.

Everything no gentleman should ever think about a woman who's technically his employee.

Everything involving a dozen different naked positions in my office, straddled across my chair, banging her against the wall, the desk, the entire main floor of the company empty and dark, and solitary except for the sounds of panting, gasping, steaming bodies sliding together and her cries bounding off the textured ceilings—

Stop that.

Right the fuck now.

I draw a deep, slow breath.

Yeah, it's been a while.

Guess I'm a little repressed.

Possibly a little too suggestible, if the tightness of my slacks is any indication.

Clearing my throat, I fidget with my shirt collar as I stop at the street corner across from the Space Needle, waiting for the light.

"We're a few minutes early for our reservation," I say. "Still, they should be able to seat us."

Elle's only answer is an amused murmur and a gentle squeeze of my forearm.

I wonder if she knows exactly what I'm thinking.

I wonder, too, why suddenly I can smell her light, sweet apple scent so much, turned crisper and clearer by the sharp chill night air.

I escort her across the street as the light changes, and inside I get to see her shining with awe as the elevator brings us up in a stomach-dropping rush that leaves Seattle spread out beyond the glass, a bowl of stars and tinsel-gold lights ripe for the plucking.

As a city native, she must have seen this many times, yet she leans toward the window with her eyes as wide as if this were her first time.

Charming.

I take her coat at our table and pull her chair out, then settle her in before claiming my own seat.

The lounge melds classy and casual, a mixed bag of business wear and casual. People stop here for drinks after work, on dates, relaxing with friends, meeting with business partners.

We fit right in with our "date night" outfits. It startles me how well we fit, period, with Elle perched comfortably in her chair and me resting my arms on the table and watching her, even if I can't quite explain to myself why.

She's not looking at me, though.

She's soaking in the view as the Needle slowly rotates, giving us the entire sprawling expanse of this water-flanked city and the mountains beyond at night.

"All glitter and shadows," she says softly. "When you see it like this, it makes you believe in secret things. Hidden, beautiful things just waiting to be found."

"Spoken like a true artist." I prop my chin up on my fist, studying the view. "Don't you think they'd have been found by now if there were still secrets? People were here for at least four thousand years before this was ever Seattle."

"Maybe. Maybe not." She smiles with that wide-eyed enchantment that makes everything seem like a wonder. "Maybe there's this tiny little pocket of space nobody's ever found. A little hollow in the mountainside, buried under the snow, where there's magic. Just waiting for someone to go on an adventure to find it."

Damn her, she's doing it again.

Making my lips inch up against my will.

"No wonder you loved Inky," I say. "Wandering the world on his adventures, carrying letters and looking for secrets."

"I want to go on an adventure like that one day. Backpacking the Himalayas. Wandering the mountaintops of Tibet or Peru. That kind of thing."

"One day, you will."

Elle turns her gaze back to me, tilting her head with a little smile. "You really think so?"

For just a moment, I don't really know what the fuck to say.

She seems to honestly want my encouragement, while my tongue locks up.

We're not playacting right now.

We're just talking.

Being human.

Being together.

I don't know what to do with that.

Thankfully, I'm saved from finding words by the waiter arriving with water and menus. He offers us both a smile that threatens to out-perk even Elle.

I realize I haven't grown more tolerant of cheerful people in general.

Only more tolerant of *her*, because I immediately want to shut this chattering squirrel of a man in a cabinet somewhere and throw away the key.

I manage to grunt politely at him as he promises to be back soon to take our orders, offers us tonight's special cocktails, and accepts Elle's cheerful refusal that I suspect is for my sake.

I eye the smiling man as he bustles away with more energy than any human being should possess. Elle snickers and leans across the table.

"August, c'mon. You're supposed to look happy. You're out with your girl."

"This *is* happy," I growl, baring my teeth.

She covers her mouth with one hand to muffle her laughter.

"Oh, please. Was he that bad?"

"I'm not convinced he was human and not an overexcited golden retriever wearing a mask."

"Really." Elle gives me a canny look. "So if he's a golden retriever . . . what kind of animal do you think I am?"

"I don't." I glower at her.

It might as well have been a confession.

"Okay, now I *know* you do." Under the table, the toe of her heel gently nudges my calf. That shouldn't make me so painfully physically aware of her. Such an innocent, chaste touch, and yet it prickles my entire body with warmth. "C'mon, August. Spill it. What am I? A mouse? A dumpster raccoon? I bet you think I'm a trash panda. Admit it."

"You make me hate my life right now." I drop my face into my hand, groaning as I mutter under my breath. "Tiger."

"What? I couldn't *heeear* you," Elle lilts. She heard me just fine, damn her. "Say that again."

"Tiger cub, I said. Tiger kitten," I hiss through my teeth. My face is melting off. "And once you were like a—fuck this, never mind."

I can't say it out loud.

Only, it's too late.

She's already latched on, and she's not letting go.

"Tell me!" she insists, her voice ringing with laughter. I can't even look at her, but I know those tiger eyes are gleaming with wickedness without even seeing them. "I'll let you rub my belly, and I might even purr if you do."

I jerk my head up, scowling. "Why are you so terrible?"

"Because you get so huffy, and I love it," she throws back, nudging me with her foot again. Her smile is so bright it could blind the whole damn room. "Here, I'll trade you. You think of me as a little tiger? Fine. I think you're a moose."

"How elegant." I snort.

"No, hear me out. For one, you're big and scary. Temperamental. Protective. Maybe a little dangerous."

I blink.

If my face was hot before, it's on fire now.

I've never had a girl tell me what she likes about me so openly and matter-of-factly. It makes it harder to remember that this isn't serious.

That I shouldn't be getting attached, or even enjoying the way this hellion teases me.

Grumbling, I look away, watching the slowly rotating view instead. "You really have to know? A bunny," I snarl. "Only once. *Once.*"

I hold up my pointer finger.

"Oh my God! You are *so* cute." She snickers. "When? When was I a bunny?"

"The morning I came to your house and you made me eat muffins before you'd even speak to me," I force out. "You were in that fluffy robe, and you kept twitching your nose."

At this point, I think she's going to pass out from laughing.

I'm certainly going to crawl under this table and die.

Yet there's a bizarre pleasure in this banter too.

In being able to delight her, even if it comes at the cost of my own pride.

Again, I'm saved by the world's happiest waiter, even if not five minutes ago I was happy to see his back. He shows up at our table like he's just materialized from nowhere, and Elle jumps with a little squeak.

The waiter grins like he's used to that reaction.

"Glad to see the happy couple are already enjoying themselves!" His gaze drops to the engagement ring on her finger. Elle lowers her eyes with a blush and a smile, looking away—the perfect picture of the newly engaged beauty. "Have you decided what you'd like to order?"

"Oh, we haven't even looked at the menus," Elle says. "Sorry." She flips hers open, frowning and biting her lip as she scans it. "Wow. Oh, wow. I wouldn't even know what to get."

She looks dismayed.

And I can read between the lines.

She's actually worried about the prices.

"Elle, let me order for you," I say, hoping to smooth away her discomfort. "I've been here before. I know a few dishes I think you'll like. You like rich and savory, yes? High protein would be better for you."

Elle flashes me a startled look, then nods. "I—yes. Please."

"We'll share the charcuterie board," I tell the waiter. "For her, the Wagyu sliders, truffle fries, and marinated olives. I'll have the foie gras and the arancini. Elle, are you good with sharing a bottle of sparkling rosé? The lighter flavor should complement the food."

"Y-yes." Pure deer-in-headlights look, yet she manages to make *that* look cute. With a flustered smile, she closes her menu. "That all sounds great!"

The waiter was scribbling everything down on a pad, but now he leans toward Elle with a very *loud* conspiratorial whisper: "He knows what you like. That's a keeper."

Right when she'd been picking up her ice water to take a drink.

Elle sputters, trying not to choke while the waiter winks and swirls away with a "Be right baaack!"

"Well," I mutter, glancing after him. "That was obnoxious. You all right?"

"Um. Yes. Sorry." Elle sets her water down and quickly picks up a napkin, dabbing at her mouth and leaving a sultry pink imprint of her lips. "That was just a lot, you know? And don't think I didn't miss that you got me a burger and fries with fancy names."

I can't help smirking. "I also got you olives. Most of the food here is good; they just dress it up with a little five-star flare. Wagyu beef is tender and high protein." I eye her sternly. "You're too pale."

"How can you tell the difference?"

"I can tell," I insist. "Have you been eating enough? Taking your supplements?"

Elle rests her elbow on the table and props her chin in her hand, her pinkie finger toying at the edges of her slowly growing smile.

"August Marshall, are you worried about me?"

". . . of course." I blink at her. "I've brought a lot of hell into your life lately, not to mention that episode with the reporters. I don't want this entire ordeal straining your health. You haven't told me how severe your anemia is, so I can only hope I'm not subjecting you to undue stress."

Elle's smile flickers, and she sighs.

"You are *so* oblivious." She shakes her head. "I was a premature baby, that's all. Two months. I'm lucky I didn't have any other issues. Heart conditions, underdeveloped organs, that kind of thing. My blood just doesn't work quite right, but most of the time I manage with supplements. My blood pressure can drop really fast from malnutrition, rapid elevation changes, or stress, so that's what causes the migraines. Though if my hemoglobin levels drop below double digits, sometimes I need a quick iron infusion. Especially if it stays that way for so long that my red blood cells don't replenish right."

I frown, watching her—but she's not looking at me. She's turned her gaze to the view, watching the starry city pensively.

"You've dealt with that your entire life?"

"Since birth."

"It seems strange to me," I say, then cut myself off. This isn't my business.

But she glances at me, her brows rising curiously. "What does?"

Well, fuck.

I've stepped in it now, taking an interest, so there's no point in downplaying.

"I only ask because most parents of preemie kids get clingy. Helicopter parents. Especially those with chronic conditions affecting their health. The fear of almost losing their baby always remains with them, until they nearly smother that child in adulthood. Yet you mentioned that your parents were largely absent."

"Yeah. About that." There's a hurt curl to her lips I've never seen before and a wry cynicism in her voice. I briefly hate myself for causing it. "When I was first born, the doctors told my parents I was going to die. No ifs, ands, or buts. They prepared themselves to say their goodbyes . . . and they didn't really know what to do with me when I stuck around. They'd already emotionally let go, I guess. If they were ever there at all." She shrugs stiffly. "It's okay. I had Gran. She loves me enough for both of them. And she cared enough to protect me but knew me well enough not to smother me. I might not have turned out this way if my parents raised me."

I think about that too long, honestly.

What a pallid, timid girl she might have been under her parents' watchful eye, people who didn't know how to care for her but felt a responsibility to protect her to the point of caging her in and crushing her light.

My brows inch down, and I shake my head slightly.

"You wouldn't be you," I say absently, not fully aware of the words leaving my mouth. "They would have made you fearful and small, not bold and bright. I like this Elle."

"Do you?" she asks softly, a hint of vulnerability in her voice.

"I—"

Oh, where is that damned waiter?

I hadn't meant to say that out loud.

To admit such things to her, when I don't want to give her *ideas*—or give myself any, when there's something about this night, this moment, that feels too real.

I'm not falling into that trap ever again. But it would be a lie to take it back—a lie that would hurt her, and I have no desire to do that either.

I've put myself in quite a dilemma.

What can I do but face it and be honest?

"The fact that you stay so positive about life and you're resilient enough to handle anything thrown at you after the circumstances of your birth and your chronic illness?" I shake my head. "That alone is remarkable, Elle. But to live life like a ghost to your own parents and still turn into someone who can be so kind, so cheerful, and so gentle, that's nearly impossible. A rarity. And rare things are treasured for a reason. Once they're gone, you might never see such treasures again in your lifetime."

She finally looks at me again—startled, almost confused. There's a flush to her cheeks, but it's hardly flirtatious. Now she just seems lost.

"The only people who've ever tried to protect me are my grandmother and Lena," she whispers. "And lately—you."

Goddamn.

She keeps rendering me speechless.

This time, I want to deflect, but I can't.

I can't when I noticed her from the second she sat next to me on the plane.

I noticed her brightness. I noticed her paleness. I noticed how bravely she tried to hide the pain she was in.

I noticed how even when I was at my most off putting, she still smiled at me like nothing could ever dim her.

I noticed how restlessly she slept, with pain making cruel lines on her delicate face.

I noticed how shaky she was standing up.

I was already watching her even before she started passing out.

That was how I reached her to catch her so quickly, before she could hit the floor.

I just didn't want to admit it—and I refused to face it until now.

From the moment I met Elle Lark, I've been trying to protect her like she's the most fragile thing I've ever seen.

It's more than just general courtesy toward a stranger. More than simply doing what's right.

I think that light inside Elle is stronger than I'll ever be.

Every time she's near me, I can't rip my eyes off her.

And it's like she knows.

She looks past me toward the bar, giving me an escape as she smiles.

"Don't look now," she says teasingly, "but we're being watched."

I don't know if that's good news, even if the entire point of *being* here is to be seen. Still, I try not to be obvious about glancing over my shoulder, just to see what tabloid jackoff is ogling us with zero discretion.

Only to come two seconds short of scrambling under the table to hide.

"Shit," I snap.

That's *Marissa Sullivan* sitting at the bar.

It's easy to recognize her. At one point she was a model, and she used her looks as the face of her publishing brand to attract people in a rather business-savvy, Instagrammable move.

Dark hair, pale skin, and a refined face with a catlike—and catty—look. She's overdressed for the lounge in a sparkling deep-red floor-length evening dress.

She's nursing a highball and staring over her shoulder at us.

I sink down in my seat, trying to get my head below the level of the seat back, and search for a menu to hide behind—but the damn waiter already took them.

Damn. Shit. *Fuck.*

I casually run my hand through my hair, forming a shade with my hand.

"What?" Elle blinks, cocking her head, then gasps. "Oh my God, is that like your ex or something?"

"Worse. That's the woman who's suing us," I bite off.

Elle's eyes widen.

She glances past me, then back at me, lifting her brows. "August?"

"What?"

"You're too big to hide behind your hand. She already saw us." Her gaze flicks past me. "Aaand she's coming."

Shit, shit, shit.

I let out a few more curses under my breath, then drop my hand and straighten up.

When I glance back, Marissa has slid off her barstool. She saunters toward us with a sway that looks risky on her spike heels, her top nearly falling out of her dress.

The ball of ice in her highball clinks loudly as her hand wavers with the glass, sending the golden brown liquid inside sloshing back and forth.

Every time I've had direct contact with this woman, she's been piss drunk.

Considering how her father died, that almost concerns me.

It would, if she weren't trying to blow our lives to smithereens.

I try to let my concern outshine my irritation, if only so I won't tear her head off the moment she opens her mouth.

Which she does the instant she stops next to our table, looking down at us with a triumphant smirk. "Well, well, if it ishn't—isn't—Aughsht Marshall. You stalking me, big boy?"

My upper lip curls in disgust. "I'd ask you the same. It's an odd coincidence that you happen to be here the night we decide to eat out."

"My offersh—*office*—is two blocksh away. I wanted a drink after work." One of Marissa's heavily kohled eyes squints as she peels a finger away from her glass and points it at me. "Yer stressin' me out, man."

"I'm not the one filing a frivolous lawsuit," I say tightly. "You're free to withdraw your attack anytime, if it causes you such discomfort."

"What? Fuck no! Imma . . . Imma wring you dry." There's a lascivi-ous curl to those words that makes me shudder. Then she turns on Elle, squinting at her with a sneer. "So you the new dish?"

"Um." Elle just gawks at her for a few moments, but her character-istic sweetness is there. She just looks curious and pleasant. No judg-ment, perhaps a little concern. "Not sure about 'dish,' but my name's Elle Lark." She holds out her hand. "Marissa, right?"

Marissa eyes Elle's hand with clear disgust. "I don' wanna shake yer hand. Yer the *enema*." Then she blinks and laughs obnoxiously, her nasty tone turning girlish instantly as she covers her mouth. "En-e-mee."

Elle lets out a good-natured laugh, completely unfazed. "I've never been called an 'enema' before, though I've called a few guys 'douches.'"

"Well, *this* one's a huge dooshnozzle." Marissa jabs a wobbly finger at me. "You . . . you shoulda just settled out of court."

No.

This is not a conversation we should be having without legal counsel present. I pinch the bridge of my nose.

"Miss Sullivan." I sigh. "You're in no state for this conversation. Is there anyone here with you?"

Marissa smirks at me sloppily. Her bright-red lipstick is smeared, staining the edge of her glass in messy smudges. "Ashkin' if 'm single in front of yer fiancée? Shameless."

"Don't be crass," I bite off. "You are in no condition to drive home, and you're clearly at your limit." I pull my phone from the breast pocket of my shirt. "I'll call you an Uber."

Elle leans across the table toward me, stretching one hand out lightly to touch my wrist. The warmth of her fingertips soaks into me, soothing my irritation. "August, we could take her. It's okay. We don't have to stay for dinner."

Marissa turns her nose up. "Pfft. Like I want you to know where I live." She squints at me. "I don't wanna go."

"You're going," I snarl.

I summon a car, set a dummy address on Alki Beach, then signal across the restaurant to the bartender, mouthing to put her last tab on my card. As I stand, I reach down to cover Elle's hand with my own in a gesture that feels too natural. Her knuckles press lightly against my palm.

"It's all right," I say, turning a sterner look on Marissa. "Give the driver your real address *after* I'm out of earshot. Is that negotiable?"

She wrinkles her nose, thrusts her lower lip out, and tosses the rest of her highball back in a loud gulp before she slams the glass down on the table.

Right before pointedly turning her back and snubbing me.

All right, then.

"Marissa." I try to cut the irritation out of my voice. "Please. You've had too much to drink. I'm offering you a truce for tonight. Purely for your safety."

"Oh, fuck you and your white-knighting. You're not my dad!" she tosses over her shoulder.

I exchange a helpless look with a concerned Elle.

"No," I agree. "Definitely not."

I wait.

This stalemate can only go on for so long, especially when Miss Sullivan looks like she's struggling to hold her balance as the booze hits harder.

Finally, she relents with one more sour look over her shoulder.

"Whatever. Fine. Can't be an adult and just go have a drink anymore, huh?"

"I'd say you've had enough." I reach down to touch Elle's hand again. "Elle, I'm sorry for this shit. I'll be right back."

She turns her hand and catches mine, lacing our fingers together briefly in a squeeze that makes my heart jolt.

"Don't apologize. I'll wait so the waiter knows we didn't leave. Go deal with her."

I squeeze her hand back in genuine gratitude and pull away, gesturing to Marissa and sweeping my hand toward the elevator. "After you."

If only so I can catch her if she trips on those heels.

But she manages to wobble her way toward the elevator.

It's a tense ride down, both of us dead silent and looking anywhere but at each other.

I briefly worry I'm about to be vomited on when Marissa watches the view for a few frozen seconds, then turns away with a loud cough and covers her mouth.

Whiskey and high-speed vertigo don't mix.

But she holds it down.

I don't comment.

I also don't miss how, once we step out of the elevator and make our way outside in bristling quiet, she seems grateful for the bite of cool night air slapping us both in the face. She takes a deep breath, tilting her head back into the wind.

We reach the curb, stopping several feet apart from each other.

I check the app on my phone before extending my hand.

"Your keys."

"No!" Marissa scowls, clutching the little purse clamped against her elbow closer.

"Marissa," I repeat sternly. "I'll give them to the Uber driver. You can come back for your car tomorrow."

"*Fine*," she spits, digging through her purse before thrusting a jingling key ring at me.

I pluck them from her hand and pocket them for now.

"I'll wait with you until they arrive. Looks like they're three minutes away."

"Whatever," she huffs, folding her bare arms around her shoulders with a little shiver. I'd offer my jacket if I hadn't left it upstairs. After a sullen mumble, Marissa asks, "Why are you being so nice to me?" A suspicious look darts my way. She's speaking more clearly, at least; the cold air seems to be helping to clear her head, even if she's still not in her right mind. "I'm not gonna drop the suit just 'cause you called me a ride."

"That's not what this is about."

I'm not entirely sure what it's about myself, if I'm being honest.

Besides the fact that I wouldn't be able to live with myself if I sent her off drunk and then saw her name in the news the following morning, victim of a tragic accident.

"Just be safe, Miss Sullivan. Go home and sober up. I'll see you for the meeting on Monday." I arch a brow. "Don't cancel this time."

I can't read the look Marissa gives me. At once hostile and oddly broken. Vulnerable.

Like a little girl who's been hurt so deeply she can't comprehend it, and she hates it and wants to beg the person who did it to take it back.

I don't think that look is entirely for me.

But I wonder who she's thinking of right now—whoever it is, she seems like she might shatter.

I'm not surprised when she draws defensive armor around herself, shrugging and turning her back to me again.

"Go to hell, you prick."

I don't respond.

There's no point fencing words with someone in this condition when she won't even remember this in the morning.

There's little time for anything else, anyway.

The brand-new, sleek white Acura depicted in the app pulls up to the curb. I cross to the passenger window and lean in, offering Marissa's keys and giving the driver strict instructions.

The driver seems used to picking up drunk riders.

Once I've explained the situation and noted she'll provide her address, I lean back with a murmur of gratitude and open the rear door for Marissa in pointed silence.

She ignores me a second longer, but apparently she still has the sense not to embarrass herself in front of a stranger. After she's made her point, she steps over to the car, nearly misses the curb in her heels, grabs the car door with a squeal, and shoots me a look that reminds me of a cat telling me I didn't just see that.

"Asshole," she clips, like I'm the one who tripped her, before tucking herself into the back seat.

"You're welcome." I shut the door and wave them off.

The last I see of Marissa is a petulant glare as she flings herself against the car door and curls up in a surprisingly small, girlish bundle for someone so drunkenly pissed.

Fuck this.

Why am I so worried about her when she's half the reason I've had to turn my life and Elle's upside down?

I tilt my head back, looking up at the distinctive shape the Space Needle makes against Seattle's cloud-lit night sky.

Elle's still up there, waiting for me.

Her pull is stronger than it should be, this need for her company to ease this hollow ache inside me.

It's an old pain. A wound that never heals, but I never expected Marissa Sullivan to be the one to rip it open and leave me bleeding again.

I shake my thoughts off and head back inside, out of the cold.

The chill's worn off by the time the elevator lets me off at the top, and I make my way back to the lounge and our table.

Elle's settled quietly with her pretty legs crossed, resting her chin in her hand while she looks out over the city. Just seeing her there, with the overhead lights picking up the faint hint of shimmering dust on her bare shoulders and the matching gloss of her nails, solidifies something inside me.

She's always so self-deprecating.

Always hiding behind the splashy colors she wears, less like fashion and more like camouflage.

I don't think she realizes just how goddamned beautiful she is.

And it's the sort of beauty that's almost frightening because it seems so fragile.

Blink, and it could be gone.

Which just makes a man want to hold on even harder.

Yeah, I'm full of strange thoughts tonight. I try to rein them in as I slip back to my seat.

"I see the waiter hasn't brought our food yet," I say.

Elle turns her gaze to me, her hazel eyes less tiger orange tonight and more a shade of gold that could make a man stupid as hell.

A small smile flickers over her lips.

"She's suing you, and you're worried about her driving drunk." No BS, just straight to the point. I like that. "You actually paid for her Uber and her tab?"

I nod slowly.

It's embarrassing when it's all laid out.

I shrug. "She can pay for it out of the legal fees when we win the suit."

Elle's smile widens, her eyes glittering. "Another joke. That's two now."

"Mmm."

Was I joking? I don't even know.

I don't feel much like laughing right now.

Now it's my turn to look out over the broad expanse of the city.

Maybe searching the lights for something to hold on to, just so this feeling doesn't swallow me whole and ruin what could be a pleasant evening of make-believe.

Elle's soft voice chases me into the dark places my mind wants to occupy.

"August . . . ?" she asks, reaching across the table to touch my wrist. "Talk to me. Are you okay?"

When I make myself look back to her, she shakes her head, the few loose tendrils of her hair grazing her slender throat.

"I can't explain it," she says. "But that whole thing with Marissa—it seemed like it hurt you."

I sigh.

I don't understand how this woman reads me so easily when I've spent so long making sure no one can ever read me in detail.

"How is it," I deflect, "that you see the shit I can't stand to look at?"

"We're never objective about ourselves. Sometimes we look past the things we really need to deal with." Almost shyly, her fingers curl against my wrist, this anchor holding me to the light so I can't slide into the darkness. "Do you want to talk about what's on your mind?"

I shouldn't.

I should remind her that we're not even technically friends, barely even colleagues, strictly employer and employee playing our parts.

But I can't do that to her.

I can't be so cruel when she's offering her kindness.

Even if Elle were someone I loathed, my sense of fairness wouldn't allow it.

Still, I don't know how to say these words either. They're just feelings I've been holding on to for so long without ever unpacking them, laying them out, looking at them clearly so I can grind them to a pulp.

It's grief. It's resentment. It's confusion, frustration, an urge to lash out and punch the past until it's no longer a threat.

More than anything, it's *guilt*.

I stare into those golden brown eyes a minute longer, then look away.

Somehow, it's easier to be honest when I'm speaking to the glittery Seattle skyline, rather than to the lovely woman sitting across from me, asking for the tiniest sliver of my heart.

Where the fuck do I even start?

"I'm sure you know the rumors about my dead wife," I tell her.

"I don't. You asked me not to pry, remember? So I resisted every urge to google and practically taped Lena's mouth shut."

Those soft words almost force me to look back at her, surprise rippling through me.

"You did?"

"I mean . . . I wasn't going to hurt you that way. It seemed serious." Her mouth twists into a small, self-deprecating smile. "It's not a hard request to honor."

Is she even for real?

The girl has no clue how many people would disagree.

How many people who make a hobby, an art out of feasting on the delicacy of others' miseries.

Elle reaches across the table again, offering me her outstretched hand with her palm up and her fingers curled invitingly.

"Did you want to tell me about her, August?"

I don't know who I am right now.

Gone is the man who would have looked at that hand scornfully and rejected it outright in a crude attempt to deny any need for human comfort.

All I am right now is shattered ceramic, sharp and cold and broken.

I'll admit I might need that hand to hold what's left of me together. Still, it's damnably hard to reach for her.

Hard to cross my own boundaries and move, until my fingertips rest in her palm, leaving subtle indents in her soft flesh.

It hurts like hell when she smiles and curls her hand around mine, holding it so gently.

Fuck.

I'm the one who's supposed to be protecting her, dammit, not using her as a crutch.

"I should tell you about her," I say slowly, looking down at our hands. The pale cream of her skin contrasts against my darker tan. Her skin is moonlight, mine is sun, yet she's the one who shines so brilliantly, while I'm a pallid reflection of her light. "She's the reason why the tabloids were able to twist our interactions into this sordid scandal. The rumor mill was less than kind about the circumstances around her death. In fact, they were downright barbaric. They blamed me for everything." I swallow like I'm choking down glass. "Hell, some days I'm not sure they're wrong."

"Take your time," Elle urges softly. "You don't have to tell me if you don't want to, August. But if you need to . . . I'm listening. Say what you need to say."

What I need to say.

I look up from our joined hands, searching her warm, open face. She's so ready to take whatever agony I share.

I don't understand how she can be real.

I just hope the shadows inside me won't darken her, won't tarnish her light for letting them loose.

"Her name was Charisma," I start. "Like every relationship, I thought we were in love."

That's the bitter truth.

If we hadn't lied to ourselves—if we hadn't gotten as far as we had—maybe she would still be alive.

Once the words start, it's impossible to stop the avalanche.

"Truthfully, we were less in love and more suited for each other." I lower my eyes to our hands again. My fingers tighten on Elle's. "She was a rising actress. I was a high-powered executive. We looked good together on the red carpet. If not for me being on her arm for years, the tabloids wouldn't care what I do with my personal life. Billionaires only make headlines when they live flashy lives and send rocket ships to the moon, not spend half their time buried in supply chain indicators trying to figure out how to save a few million a year from the cost of shipping rebar. Drama aside, I'm a pretty boring man."

"Pfft." Elle clucks her tongue. "You're anything but boring. You're just very *focused*."

"That's a nice way of putting it." I smile, though it feels like a lead slug to the gut. "Unfortunately, my focus was a problem in our marriage. I thought we were alike. We were both so intensely focused on our careers. I thought her trips for filming and my long absences while working global contracts wouldn't be an issue. But even while we played at being in love, I missed how desperately Charisma wanted to be loved."

While I'm talking, our fingers shift. Lace together. Locking like we're sharing this story together, rather than me unburdening my faults and my crimes.

"What happened?" Elle's fingers fit between mine too perfectly.

"It started as blowout fights. Then stiff, wounded silences. Then longer, colder, angrier silences. She was lonely, and I was—fuck, I wasn't very good at recognizing that. Let alone giving her the attention she deserved. I wasn't innocent in this. I didn't recognize that her hostility and cruel words came from hurt, not hatred. It was such a habit to wall myself off that I walled off from her too. It's no surprise when she turned elsewhere."

"Elsewhere?" Elle's eyes widen, and her indrawn gasp tells me the conclusion she draws even without a single word. I shake my head.

"It's not what you're thinking," I counter. "She didn't cheat on me, though she easily could have. She was a beautiful woman with a charm that made her vibrant. Very few men would have refused her. But she didn't turn to another man." I stop and sigh. "First, she turned to drugs. It was the usual killing progression from the bottle and weed to the coke that runs through Hollywood like a live current. If I'd been around more, I would've seen the overdose coming."

My jaw pinches so tight it almost breaks.

"Oh no. Oh, August, I'm so sorry. You can't blame yourself, especially if you didn't know you had to be there to save her from—"

"Save her?" My eyes sharpen. "No, Elle. She didn't die from an overdose. Not even when she took too much of that crap, and it was laced with whatever the fuck it was that stopped her heart. They were at this resort in Arizona, and thank God her bombed-out friend woke up first, just in time to get EMTs over to restart her heart."

Elle shakes her head, clearly confused.

"Of course, I came rushing to the hospital as soon as I heard. Too little, too late, especially to stop what came next." I inhale slowly. "When she woke up, Charisma told me about going to a place with the prettiest flowers and magnificent birds and two blue moons. She said it was total serenity, a better high than any drug she'd ever had, and she vowed to sober up. She was certain she went somewhere special—the sort of place you only go when you die—and she'd do anything to get back there. Whether that's true or not, I don't think she ever lived totally in this world again."

Elle's eyes widen, desperate for more.

I hate this fucking part.

I swipe my hand over my face before I continue.

"She turned to New Age religion next. I'm told I shouldn't call it a cult." My mouth creases bitterly. "But it *was* a fucking cult. The sort that operates like a multilevel marketing scheme. Their whole goal is to suck in new members and indoctrinate them so they turn over all their funds to the higher-ups. Charisma needed so much to feel like a *part* of something, to get back to that special place she believed she saw, that she fell right into their clutches. It didn't matter how much I warned her, how many friends intervened, how many shrinks I hired to get through to her. She quit acting and exhausted her own substantial funds in no time, and then she tried to hide it from me."

Elle watches me with her eyes glimmering like she's hurting for a woman she's never met.

Her heart is big enough for that.

It makes mine feel like a shriveled prune.

"When I found out what she was doing while I was away, it was already too late," I say. The words taste like ash, but I need to finish what I started, and suddenly I'm holding on to Elle so tight my knuckles are bone white. "She was in too fucking deep to pull back. She believed in them more than she believed in us—more than anything. My anger only drove her closer to them, and I was still too blind to see this for what it really was—a cry for help."

"August—"

"No," I growl. "Let me finish." I take a deep breath and forge on. "I told her I wanted to file for divorce. She told me that if I did, she would ruin me by going to the papers with stories of how I'd abused her. How I stalked her, preyed on her, manipulated her, coerced her to marry me. All the ugly, fucked up shit that never happened. I swear it on my life. If I was guilty of anything, it was only neglect and ignorance. I lost my shit, told her to make her claims, and she did. In the middle of the scandal, she promised to retract her claims if I'd negotiate a settlement she could give to her new 'church.' I refused. We were set to go to court—her to seek her settlement, me to disprove her abuse claims."

I'm snarling so hard I have to catch myself.

That kindness in Elle's eyes is the only thing that keeps me going.

"Before our court date, she was set for a rite of passage with her faith. There's this cliff in Sedona, this sacred red rock supposedly surrounded by energy portals. It's the kind of place New Agey scammers love. Their initiates will jump off that cliff and drop over fifty feet down into a pool. Charisma's group call it their 'leap of faith,' a trial by air to prove their faith. With the deep pool, it's generally safe, even if there have been a few injuries over the years."

I wasn't there. I didn't see it. All I saw were the grisly photographs of the aftermath.

So why can I visualize the fall so clearly?

Why does it haunt me so fucking bad?

Elle's breaths are shallow and ragged. Even though we're surrounded by music, laughter, and the soft clink of glasses and absolute normalcy, we're both somewhere else.

All I can hear are the shaky breaths that tell me she's fighting to hold back tears.

"I still don't know how the hell Charisma ever missed the water," I whisper. "All I know is what they told me. A freak accident, they said. She tumbled too far. She hit the edge of the pool, and then the rocks below instead. No one could've survived. Her death was ruled an accidental suicide, but there are people even now who hint that I somehow drove her to it, just to avoid paying the settlement she demanded as compensation for shit I never did." I swallow hard, but I can't shift the heavy knot in my throat. "If I'd just understood her more, listened more, let my defenses down to see her—"

"August."

The rawness in Elle's voice forces me to stop and look.

I almost don't want to, when those tracks of wetness pouring down her cheeks are my fault.

Pain shared is not pain lessened, and now I've given this glowing girl my own pain, to let it multiply and spread.

But as I meet her eyes, she shakes her head.

"It wasn't your fault. Her choices aren't your responsibility. Maybe you weren't a great husband, but you can't save other people, August. All you can do is help them if they want to save themselves. If it wasn't the cult, I'm sure it would have been something else." Elle pauses to catch her breath. "She should have realized what she was looking for wasn't in your marriage and made the decision to end it and move on with her life. Not compensate with something like that and then try to extort you out of resentment that you weren't the husband she expected." She bites her lip, pink and glimmering and soft, her eyes glowing, tawny gold. "Whatever mistakes you made, you didn't kill her. You didn't make her die. You just fell out of love. You had a bad marriage, like half the US population. That should have ended in regret and divorce. The fact that it didn't is because of her, August. Not you."

I can't help but protest.

I've been carrying this cross with me for so long I—fuck, I don't know who I am without that guilt. Without that nagging warning that women and I are a catastrophic mix.

"If I'd been a better husband—"

"You wouldn't have been you," Elle cuts in. She's holding my hand so tight I'm sure it hurts her. "But whether you were an amazing husband or a terrible one, you didn't drive her to anything. She drove herself. I think you want to try to save Marissa because you can see the same desperation in her . . . but I told you. People can't save other people. Please don't hate yourself if you can't help Marissa Sullivan."

"I can't not try!" I flare before I even realize what I'm saying. Before I realize she's put her finger on a pain point I was blind to.

I look away sharply, breathing in deeply and lowering my voice.

"Elle, her father died from drinking. I have yet to have one encounter with her where she's not too fucking intoxicated to function. I don't know what's driving her into the gutter, but even if she's suing me for my family's legacy, I can't stand by and do nothing. Our families are—in their own way—hopelessly intertwined. Would you leave her to ruin herself with pointless lawsuits and booze if you were me?"

"No. I wouldn't. I'd do what I could for her, but . . ." Sniffing, Elle wipes at her eyes with her free hand and offers me the bravest smile. "You're not her favorite person, August. I don't know if she honestly believes Clara stole her father's work or not. But she definitely believes your family is responsible for his death. He made those choices, of course, just like your wife made hers. But Marissa won't be able to see that. And she won't be able to see help for what it is, coming from you."

"I know." I slump in my chair, sighing—then slip my hand into my pocket for a small cotton handkerchief and offer it to Elle. "She let me send her home tonight, at least. It's only a short-term solution, but it's something."

"I have a feeling you won't let it go until you find something more permanent. I've noticed that once you get fixated on a problem, you sink your teeth in. You won't let go."

I almost flinch at those words.

Charisma once threw them at me in a much more accusatory light.

My single-minded laser focus was why I couldn't see her as anything more than another problem to fix.

It may make me good at my job, yes.

It also makes me a shit human being.

Yet Elle said it fondly, still smiling as she took the handkerchief.

I watch her, puzzled. "You don't find it off putting, how I am?"

"No." No doubt, no uncertainty, her smile warmer than ever as she dabs her eyes. "It just means once you've set your mind to it, you won't quit until you do what's right."

How does this girl have more faith in me than I have in myself?

She laughs, looking down at the damp handkerchief. "This is the second one of yours I've ruined. I still need to give you back the first."

"I have too many. It's one of those things I picked up from my aunt and her southern upbringing. A gentleman always carries a handkerchief, especially in case a lady needs it."

The change of subject is almost welcome, easing the crushing weight on my mind.

I've never been able to talk about what happened with anyone like this.

Not even with Deb or Aunt Clara.

I never wanted them to feel obligated to comfort me. Yet I didn't feel like Elle was taking on a burden or an obligation. She genuinely wanted to know, and some part of me craved her acceptance.

Still, I think I've had enough honesty for one night. Especially when I realize that as I've been watching her, I've slowly been stroking my thumb over the engagement ring on her finger.

Goddamn, I need to get my head on straight.

Oblivious to my brooding, Elle squeezes my hand lightly and delicately folds the handkerchief on the table.

"Should I start calling you Rhett? I'd say Ashley, but he's way too mild mannered. You're a walking storm cloud." She grins teasingly. "And just as rude as Rhett too."

"And you're just as impetuous as Scarlett O'Hara," I counter. "You just put a brighter face on it."

"Hey!" She laughs, even though her eyes are still red rimmed, her lips swollen from crying. "C'mon. Scarlett O'Hara was an absolute *wildcat*. I thought you said I was a kitten."

"Kittens have claws too," I point out.

"Teeny claws!"

"Small claws still hurt. And before you say anything, bunnies also have claws." I arch a brow. "So if you call me Rhett, I will most certainly call you Scarlett."

Elle sticks her tongue out, a little pink barb.

It's suddenly like the spontaneous confession never happened.

We're back on even footing, except we were never on such even ground before. I kept myself close, while Elle was willing to let me into her world from day one.

The more she knows leaves us on a level field.

I do think, given time, I could call this woman a friend.

Friendship is why I'm lingering on the damp gleam to her lips, and the way the overhead lights gather in tiny galaxies against the hollow of her throat.

And *friendship* is why I hesitate to release her hand as the world's most annoying waiter chooses that moment to return with our food. He glances at both of us significantly as he sets our plates, wineglasses, and a chilled bottle of rosé on the table, lingering longer on Elle—and there's something in his voice as he asks, "Is everything all right?"

I bitterly wonder if my reputation precedes me now.

If this stranger thinks I've been such a colossal asshole that I've pushed Elle to tears in public.

If anything, it's the fact that she's been so kind to me that her empathy was too much for both of us.

"Everything's fine, except now I'm embarrassed. This big idiot told me he wants to elope," Elle answers seamlessly. "He *knows* I get emotional and cry in public when he says things like that."

Her laugh is totally on point.

The waiter lets out a sympathetic gasp, nearly fluttering.

With quick, capable hands, he uncorks the wine, fills our glasses, and leaves the bottle on the table for us. "Congratulations! I'll leave you two lovebirds alone. If you need anything else, please don't hesitate. Enjoy your meal."

"We will," I answer.

Somehow, I even force a smile that comes easier than trying to mold engineered steel with my bare hands.

The waiter twirls off, more obnoxiously cheerful than ever.

Elle flashes me the smile of a coconspirator and picks up one of her truffle fries. "Sorry. I ad-libbed. Shall we?"

Goddamn, what is happening?

Five minutes ago, I was carrying the weight of the world—a reluctant Atlas bowing under its pressure.

And now?

I find myself chuckling as I pick up my fork.

"Yeah, let's enjoy," I say.

I actually might.

Just like I might enjoy someone else's company for the first time in ages.

XI

CHASING THE STORM

(ELLE)

My head is way too full right now.

How did a dinner date turn into such a night?

It wasn't even a real date!

But somehow it turned into—something.

Something that felt real.

That felt like I was getting to see the real August.

It started even before we got to the restaurant. The way he was so worried about my health, the gentle way he spoke to me. The way he stepped in to order for me so I wouldn't feel out of my depth, and actually cared enough to worry about my nutritional needs and notice my taste preferences.

I've never had a man pay attention to me like August does.

What does it say about the guys I've dated before that my *fake* fiancé cares more than my real past boyfriends ever did?

There's been something almost lost about August all night, a guilt clearly weighing on him—but it came out sharply when I met Marissa Sullivan.

She wasn't what I'd expected.

I thought she'd be a sharp battle-axe of a businesswoman. Not this sleek former model who wears red better than I ever could in my dreams. Seeing her like that, drunk and trying to drown something that was weighing on her—

It hurt.

I couldn't blame August for wanting to help, despite the fact that she's made him her mortal enemy.

I was actually glad to let them go without me.

It gave me a few minutes to compose myself.

Otherwise, I might've said something really dumb that would have completely ruined the vibe between August and me.

God, I want him *so much*.

I want him to be mine so I can hold him, run my fingers through his hair, comfort him, tell him I'd be there for him through anything that was hurting him.

Stupid?

Yes.

How did I fall for a man like this? The one man I absolutely shouldn't?

It's so bad it hurts to be near him.

Hurts because he's gravity, and I'm trying so hard to stay in place. It takes all my strength to resist the force of his pull on every part of me.

I'm not good at impulse control—or resisting temptations with blue eyes that reach down to my soul.

If there's ice cream in the fridge, I'm going to eat it for dinner, because I'm an adult and I can do what I want.

But August is the ice cream I can't have.

Not even the tiniest taste, when every minute I look at him I just want to scarf him right up in so many wicked ways it steals my breath away and leaves my heart thrumming.

Just once.

Just flipping once, I'd like to taste him.

The story of his ex-wife shattered me.

The pain August has been carrying for so long.

The guilt, the shame, the *betrayal* he must have felt when she turned to a cult rather than an imperfect husband who still cared as a human being and who still wanted to solve their impossible problems. Even when she tried to extort from him instead of being honest that she just wanted his love.

Holy hell.

No wonder he's so dark all the time. So heavy.

He's a far more complicated man than I realized.

I just wish I could kiss away the pain he's engraved so deeply in himself it might never rub away.

I couldn't say any of that.

I couldn't hold back my tears, either, but I could at least try to listen, to support him, to tell him he's not the monster he thinks he is or the monster others have painted him as.

I'm so glad I kept my promise, now.

And I'm glad I heard August's story from his own lips before I heard it through someone else's warped need for slimy gossip.

Settling back into normal after that felt like a farce, but it felt nice too.

August offering me a bite of his foie gras and me recoiling when I found out what foie gras actually *is*.

He teased me with it like a little boy threatening to put a frog down a little girl's dress, menacing me with the forkful and smirking when I squeaked and tossed my head away.

He was too happy to steal a few of my truffle fries when I offered, though, nipping them right out of my fingers.

Even if tonight was a lot, he's more relaxed, too, since getting that secret off his chest.

I like that he can be that way with me.

That I can tease him and he'll tease me right back, and tell me what a brat I'm being when I pout and insist on dessert even though we're both stuffed.

A slightly tipsy brat, too, if I'm being honest.

I may have indulged in a little too much wine. It was sweet and fizzy and it tasted good, and it helped keep my brain from getting stuck to certain questions.

Like whether or not August still has feelings for his dead wife.

The way he talked about Charisma Marshall . . . he must, right?

Even if he didn't love her at the end, you see this with widowers.

The memory of their dead spouse becomes larger than life. Someone they can idolize and love as the deceased shapes every ideal in the imagination, no matter what the real person was like.

Worse, he just blames himself for Charisma's flaws.

Like he's the one who made her what she was, the person who would make the choices she did.

I don't know how to convince him otherwise.

I linger on that as I watch the city at night, twirling my fork through the remains of something called a Lunar Orbiter. It's a confection of dark chocolate ganache and vanilla meringue with macarons.

Well, the second one to be exact. I already finished mine.

This is the rest of August's. After he took one bite, he wrinkled his nose in the most adorably disgusted way and pushed it across the table for me.

But I don't have enough room in my belly to inhale a second whole plate, and the sparkling wine is settling in a little too deep. I'm thinking too hard as I watch the city rotate like we're up high in a lunar orbiter of our own, drifting gently among the stars and looking down at how peaceful the world is when you can't see all the small petty things up close.

. . . I think I'm trying to convince myself that August is still in love with his dead wife.

I *need* him to be.

Because as long as I tell myself he's in love with her, I can remind myself that he's completely off limits.

He's soft in the intimate shadows of the lounge, silently staring out the window with his legs crossed and a stem glass in one hand. He's somewhere else, and I wonder what stars he's seeing and wishing on.

Can he still wish on stars at all?

The shadows play over his face until I can pick out every small detail, from the way they kiss the space under his stark cheekbones to the way said cheekbones cut the light into a thin, gleaming sliver.

The way the sun has darkened his skin hints that he's not wholly a creature of the night or endlessly locked inside beneath corporate white lights.

That one unruly lock of hair.

His little bit of rebellion, curving over his decisive, worry-ridged forehead to tease at his right eyebrow.

What would happen in this strange air between us if I reached across the table, tucked that wild lock of hair back, and caressed his cheek?

What would he do if I kissed him again?

Wouldn't it be all right?

In public, we're meant to be intimate, to make people believe we have eyes for no one and nothing but each other.

Would he cradle my hand against his cheek, kiss my palm, let me feel the heat of his lips and the scratch of his beard?

My chest hurts.

This so isn't like me.

I always try to smile. I always look for the bright side of things.

I'm looking now, but it's so hard.

Maybe when this is over, I'll smile, because I'm realizing now that I've never actually been in love before.

In lust, sure.

But this feeling, this desperate desire for this one person, it's new.

It's definitely crazy.

Then again, this whole thing has been insane from the start.

"What are you smiling at this time?" August whispers, almost affectionately.

I blink, recoiling a little with a tiny thump of my heart.

He's very good at watching me without seeming to, and it hits me.

The entire time I've been looking at him, he's been looking at me.

I hadn't even realized I was smiling. That's how entranced I am.

But I look for a quick excuse and flick my gaze to his hair again. "I'm just wondering how much hair wax you used to try to get your hair to lie down, and it still doesn't listen."

It's not a lie.

I was thinking about that bit of hair.

August groans. There's a burr to his voice, raw and gritty, like the bubbles in the sparkling wine have gently sanded his voice down to give it the texture of crushed velvet.

He reaches up to flick the little arc of black hair aside with one blunt finger, only it sways right back to the same spot on his brow.

"It's been like this since I was a child," he grumbles. "I could use an entire tin of pomade, and in minutes it would pop right back out. It's terrible for my professional image. I look like Tom Sawyer."

I snicker. "It's cute. But if you really hate it that much, you could clip it. I have some little colored barrettes that would look adorable on you."

"You're not funny." His foul look doesn't have the usual force behind it.

"I think I am. You do too."

"Overconfident too." With a chuckle, he sets his wine down without finishing it, then leans across the table toward me. "You look like you've had enough." His gaze dips down toward the little plate of dessert. "Ready to go?"

"Mmm . . ."

I run my finger around the rim of my empty wineglass, pretending to consider it.

Honestly, I'm reluctant. I really am.

If this night has been one emotional gut punch after the next, it's also been really nice. Just a little magic and intimacy that will end when he drops me off at my door with one last kiss for the woman I'm playing for the tabloids, though I'll take it like it's for me.

But I can't hold on forever.

Still, I cling just a little bit longer, watching him. "Are you good to drive? We've polished off most of this bottle."

"*You've* polished it off," he points out with amusement. "I've been holding back, since I'm driving. A glass of water and I'll be fine." He arches a brow. "Will you?"

I laugh. "It's sparkling wine! Not straight whiskey. I'm just a little fuzzy. Not drunk."

"Good to know." August stands then, and with a dramatic flourish that's just playful enough to tell me he might be a tad more buzzed than he'll admit. But then he offers me his hand and says, "Shall we?"

I don't hesitate to slip my fingers into his.

His hand folds mine in pure heat, and he lifts me up with this effortless strength that makes my heart soar.

For an instant, it feels like he'll swirl me into his arms to dance, my body swaying closer to his, our eyes locking. But he lets go gracefully and slips my coat off the back of my chair, holding it open for me.

When I slip my arms into it, his chest briefly presses against my back.

I go hot and tingly.

Oof.

I need a second before I can face him again.

He stays a second longer than he needs to.

Then, holding my breath, I plaster on my smile, tuck my purse under my arm, slip my hand into his arm, and let him escort me to the elevator for one last stunning glimpse of the Seattle nightscape.

I hold on to that last view.

My last bit of magic before we're back to the mundane.

When the elevator doors open and I glance up at August, he's watching me.

The look on his face hints that he's as enthralled by me as I am by Seattle stretching to the horizon in a sea of lights like colored jewels.

No way.

I can't let myself believe that.

I'm tipsy and imagining things. That conversation climbed up in my bed.

So I glance away quickly, focusing on the icy nip of night air rushing over me, clearing my head as we step outside.

He leads me to the car, helps me inside, and slips into the driver's seat.

But when he starts the engine and pulls out into traffic, when we reach the next intersection, he doesn't turn toward Queen Anne.

I twist to look through the back window. "Um. This is a little déjà vu, but my house is that way."

"I know," August says quietly behind the wheel. "I thought you'd stay at my place tonight."

What?

I whip back to face him, every last nerve inside me seizing up in a hot flush rushing through me. I stare at him uncomprehendingly, a million things running through my head that definitely should *not* be.

Hot hands on my thighs, teasing them apart.

Bronzed skin against my paleness, making me feel so fragile as his fingers slide higher, higher.

His rough stubble, his mouth roaming my throat, tasting every moan that vibrates out of me as his fingers push between my legs, tease up against my—

Eleanor Jacqueline Lark, stop.

You stop that right now.

I can mentally see Gran wagging a finger at me, and she's right.

I'm being ridiculous.

August is so calm, he couldn't have meant—

Oh, but he glances at me, his brows knit sharply, before he jerks his gaze away with a guttural growl.

"I have a second bedroom," he says. "Sorry. I didn't mean to make you uncomfortable with any implications. I simply meant for appearances. Considering the paparazzi jackasses who've caught us by surprise before, we have to assume we have a very determined reporter stalking us. Someone who would notice that we sleep apart every night. We could be saving ourselves for marriage, yes. But most won't find that plausible."

"Oh," I squeak. I hope to God I sound embarrassed and flustered and a little uncomfortable, and not disappointed.

Totally not.

Of course, *of course* it's a practical thing from Mr. Practicality.

After a breathless moment, I groan and smack my face into my palm.

Calm down, my heart.

"For the record, we've got to work on your delivery," I mutter. "And your planning! You never tell me what we're doing until we're in it . . ."

"Sorry." August at least sounds genuinely chagrined. When I glance at him, his face is red and rigid, like he's trying to force his walls back into place. "You're right. I normally give my teams advanced notice. I should offer you the same courtesy."

"Just shoot me a text, tell me to pack a bag, let me know with more than an hour's warning what the dress code is, *something.*"

August smiles thinly—but there's something almost sad there too. "By the time I get in the habit, we'll be breaking up."

Oh.

Oh, that's a high kick right to the feels, and those feels aren't very good.

". . . yeah," I say, slouching against the door and looking outside. I find a smile somewhere because that's what I always do, even when it hurts. "I guess . . . I guess we will."

August says nothing. The silence in the car is strange.

I don't know how to feel, what to think.

I'm bouncing between this bizarre sensation of being completely alone, and this weirder desperation to ease the tingling that started the moment my imagination ran away and filled me with thoughts of August's hard body between my thighs.

I shift a little in my seat, restless, trying not to be obvious about pressing my thighs together.

It's embarrassing to desperately want a man who doesn't want anything to do with you.

But I can't make it stop, even if I know I'll be sleeping alone tonight.

Somehow I'm not surprised that August owns waterfront property in one of the most expensive cities in the country.

I am surprised, though, when he pulls to a stop outside a surprisingly modest house.

It's definitely not small, but it's also not a hulking, opulent billionaire castle like I'd expect.

Instead, his house is far out on the water, with a narrow bridge of weathered planks leading over Puget Sound to a big single-story ranch-like home of connected octagonal shapes. They're surrounded by sweeping decks that offer glimpses inside through enormous windows.

It's all shades of moody grey, peaceful as mist, right down to the sloping roof of slate tiles. The faint hints of dark-amber ambient light that seep past bamboo blinds cast their light over the wood and slate, coloring them like paint on a canvas.

"Wow! Not what I expected," I whisper. "I thought you'd own a home with a bajillion rooms or at least a utilitarian condo thing. All sleek glass and titanium everywhere."

"I want a home, woman, not another office." The G80 goes quiet as August pulls up a small concealed private drive through the curbside bank of grass that looks down on a small slope of sand coursing out to the waves. "I wanted somewhere I can still hear my own thoughts and the waves under my feet."

I cast him a startled glance.

It's not like him to admit something intimate so openly, but then tonight feels like it's changed so many things. I offer him a small smile.

"Hope I can see the sunrise from the guest room," I tease.

"You can," he answers. "I chose the bedroom facing west. I have no use for *sunrise* unless I'm on a trip, nursing jet lag."

"August Marshall. Was that a joke?"

He says it so stuffily I know he's teasing, and I laugh, reaching over to poke his arm.

"C'mon. Give me the grand tour so I can steal your guest room and sleep off this wine."

"I thought you said you weren't drunk?"

"I'm not! But I am buzzy. *Very* buzzy."

He fixes me with a skeptical look. "Will I have to carry you inside?"

"You cad!" I gasp, fluttering a hand playfully to my chest. "Why, Rhett, you're being positively scandalous!"

August rolls his eyes with an exaggerated sigh.

"That's *it*." He pushes the driver's door open pretty forcefully before getting out, slamming the door, and stalking around the rear of the car.

I blink, twisting to watch him through the windows.

What is he—

My door jerks open.

His body presses against mine in a sharp sizzle as he leans across me and unsnaps my seat belt. His arms fold around me, trapping me before I can catch a single startled, heart-tripping breath.

Then he picks me up against his chest and lifts me out of the car with a strength so undeniable it makes me feel like I'm nothing next to the powerhouse of granite muscles locked around me.

"You, Miss O'Hara-Lark," he says tightly, turning away from the car before kicking the door shut with his heel, "are clearly more drunk than you dare let on."

Oh God.

He's doing terrible things to me as I'm being held and carried this way, enveloped in his heat and smoldering power. Especially with that dark scowl on his face as he glares toward his house and marches across the half-buried planks embedded in the sand. They lead to the little boardwalk stretching out over the waves to his home.

That scowl is just a *tiny* bit intimidating.

That's what makes it meltingly sexy.

But I'm torn between sighing with pleasure and laughing my butt off as I push playfully at his chest. "*Me?* I'm sorry, which one of us is drunk again? Who is this man calling me Miss O'Hara-Lark and carrying me around? Do you actually sprout a sense of humor when you've had a few?"

"I am *not* drunk," August clips. But there's a twitch at the corners of his mouth that says if I push a little more, I might actually make this dour man laugh. He steps up onto the walk, his footfalls turning hollow with the space between the wood and the water. He looks down at me. "I'm just humoring the absolute madwoman I've invited into my life. Life is easier if I just don't fight you."

I grin, slipping my arms around his neck. "On the plus side, not fighting me means plenty more good photo ops. I bet someone's getting an eyeful of headline-worthy shots right now."

His sigh this time is more aggrieved. "There is that. I suppose you know that means I'll have to kiss you at the door before carrying you across the threshold, fiancée."

"*Hey.*" Just for that I catch a little hair at the nape of his neck and tug. "You don't have to make kissing me sound like a chore."

"Oh, that's not what I meant, and you—" He splutters. "Did you just pull my hair?"

My grin widens. "Pulling pigtails. That's what you do when you like a stubborn dumb boy, right?"

"I don't think little boys wear pigtails, Elle."

"I mean, it's the twenty-first century. Some might."

"You can stop pulling mine." Snorting, he halts on the deck, just before the front door. His scowl eases, and his dark-blue gaze searches mine. "You truly don't mind a moment of intimacy that should belong to a man you actually care for?"

If only I could be honest.

If only I could tell him I'm coming to care for him more and more every day, with every little detail I learn about him. Every kindness he shows me under that prickly exterior. Everything that makes him *August*, this grouchy idiot who doesn't know how good a man he actually is because he's been carrying someone else's guilt for too long.

So I just tug lightly at his hair again to bring that hint of an exasperated smile back.

"A little kiss between strangers never killed anyone," I tease, glancing over my shoulder toward the road. A few cars have passed, but I can't exactly see anyone hovering in the bushes across the street. "Doesn't it feel weird, though? Putting on an act for this unseen watcher. It's kind of creepy knowing there's someone looking at us right now. But it feels like a game too." I look back at August and lean in close to him. "We're spies," I whisper. "Trying to fool enemy agents. So we have to make it good."

August's eyes crease with amusement.

"Everything is a story with you, isn't it?" he whispers back, deliberately exaggerating the sound until I'm hard pressed not to giggle.

Even if we're playing at being in love, the game is exciting.

"Makes it more fun," I answer. "You going to kiss me, August?"

Please. Please kiss me, you lunk.

"You're the one talking."

I tell myself I'm imagining the husky, hot edge to his voice.

My smile fades.

Slipping one hand down his neck, I feel the beat of his pulse and press my fingertips to his lips. "So shut me up."

For once, I get a *real* smile out of him.

Soft, slow, and curving against my fingertips, like he's letting me feel how genuine and rare it is.

It melts his eyes until they're sky blue.

"Such a damn brat," he whispers.

Then, while my heart beats out of my chest, he shoves my fingers aside and bends to take my mouth with his.

It's hesitant, at first.

I can feel him questioning himself, feel him holding back, but me—I'm all impulse and fire.

I want this too badly to make it careful and performative.

Just one kiss, I tell myself.

Just one kiss, and then I'll make myself let this growing infatuation go.

I trace my fingers over his cheekbones, cradle his face in my palms, and lean up into him, turning that hesitant brush of mouths into something firmer and hotter, tilting my head until my lips fuse with his in perfect synchronicity.

Holy sparks.

For such a stern man, there's a sinful sweetness to his lips that makes my gut bottom out with the sheer sensuality of how divine it feels to kiss August Marshall.

How it feels when our mouths give and take and chase until they find the perfect collision, and everything just clicks.

And how it feels when he kisses me back.

He stiffens, a sound of surprise melting between us.

Then it's back and forth, trading the same sharp tension as the barbs we normally throw at each other. Only now they've turned from soft play into searing heat, all touch and wetness and wildness.

He kisses me so hard, so deep, like he's demanding my surrender.

Tongue slipping against my lips, darting and teasing, thrusting without giving me that full plunging feeling that would turn me inside out if he'd just *do it.*

His hands are hard on my body, pressing me against his chest.

I feel like he'll turn me to dust with the pressure.

His breaths are so hot, his beard dragging against my mouth. I'm close to breaking down and begging him to take me deeper. But I can't find the words, only more pleading with soft flicks of my tongue, then a single daring nip against his lower lip.

It's like flipping a switch.

His hold on me tenses, with a harsh growl exploding up his throat.

His lips turn feral, dragging against my mouth in unrelenting strokes.

His tongue plunges deeper, slipping into me hotly and tracing my mouth.

Intimate, melting, relentless.

I'm going down like a shooting star, barely able to breathe, digging my fingers into his hair and parting my lips to beg for more, *more, don't stop, please.*

It's like being kissed by summer lightning.

No warning before it's all flash and strike and burn.

I want him to burn me down.

And when I slide my tongue along his, arching and begging, pressing into the hardness of his body, he stops.

It's like someone's slapped him back to his senses and thrown him away.

There it is again—that almost *angry* look as he stares down, like I've done something to him. He's certainly done something to *me* when I can't stop panting.

My mouth aches with raw, fiery need.

He's breathing just as hard, his chest heaving against me.

His mouth is red, not just with my lipstick, but with the rough pressure of our lips.

Though he's giving me that look that makes my heart turn inside out with confusion and hurt and wanting . . .

His hands still clutch so damn hard, digging into my flesh with delicious pressure and making me wish I was naked against him so I could feel his roughness *everywhere.*

I'm flipping dying.

The way he molds me against his chest forces my thighs together, and all I want to do is wrap them around him.

"I should hope," he rasps, breaking the charged silence, "that will be sufficient for any Peeping Toms."

I'm so dead.

The thorns in his voice alone rip me apart.

I almost can't speak when his voice does things it's never done to me before, and I feel like those thorns are wrapping around me now, digging in, injecting this poison of lust into my veins.

"Y-yeah," I manage, pulling my hands back to wipe at my mouth, trying to pull myself together. To keep this professional, when it's anything but. "I think it'll . . . it'll be enough. You can put me down now."

A spastic jerk only pulls me closer. I almost moan when it's just making the torture worse.

Then August bends without a word to set me on my feet, and if not for the fact that I'm clutching at his shoulders, I'd tumble right to the deck with how wobbly my legs are. There's another quick look between us as the heat of his hand falls to the small of my back, spanning from hip to hip and making another hot surge rush through me to weaken my knees.

I'm combusting.

Just swimming in this liquid heat, this dark and molten tropical sea of desire.

Even though he gives me another almost harsh look, the burn in it tears at me even more.

With slow breaths, I try to steady myself, while August turns away, fishes out his keys, and pushes the glass front door open, making the blinds over the inset rattle in a whisper like rain.

When he reaches back for my hand to draw me inside the dimly lit house after him, I know it's just for anyone who's watching. Making it look like after that steamy kiss, he's leading me inside to his bedroom to finish what we started.

If only.

His hand is so coarse against mine, and that sensation consumes me as I step over the threshold behind him.

It's hard for me to drag my focus off him enough to take in the house around me. I get faint impressions of dark-polished bamboo walls, green-black slate flooring, tasteful minimalist decorations with subtle lighting thoughtfully placed to highlight an earthenware piece of pottery here, a painting there, a plant over there.

The furniture is sparse and masculine in dark fabric, well matched but also clearly full and chosen for comfort.

Hints of moonlight stream in everywhere. The whole house was designed so at least one wall is all windows facing the water, complete with those bamboo blinds for privacy.

All around us is a faint echo of the waves, captured by the open spaces and wooden walls. They make the entire house feel like it's slowly moving with the tide.

August lets go of my hand the moment we're inside—but he turns to close the door behind me, reaching over my head to press his palm against the wooden frame before pushing it shut.

It leaves him leaning over me with one arm stretched overhead, practically pinning me back against the door.

Eep.

I'm suddenly so painfully aware of how *tall* August is, how much larger than me he is. His shadow looms over me, and his eyes strip me raw as I fall back against the door with a gasp.

He's so deliciously ominous right now.

Dangerously sexy.

That hard glare fixed on me in the same silent accusation I still don't understand—and the mystery is thrilling.

Don't do it.

I have to fight myself when I want to be bold.

I want to feel the adrenaline of almost-fear as I reach for him and drag him down to kiss him, beg him, make him admit that this is *real* and that I wasn't misreading the smolder in his eyes.

I can't.

I can't.

He's still infatuated with the idea of his dead wife. He's not interested in me beyond our sham; it was just an uncontrollable physical reaction. It was just—

A lost moment.

August drops his arm and pulls back, then turns away from me and releases me from the paralyzing spell of his eyes.

So cold.

Like frostbite, stinging so deeply it burns.

"This way," he says. "I'm having one bathroom reworked and another guest room shower's out of commission this week, so there's only one other bathroom, unfortunately—the master bedroom en suite. You're welcome to use it first if you'd like to shower and sober up before bed. Assuming you prefer to wake up without a hangover."

I start to insist that I'm *not drunk* again, but right now I'm not sure I'd believe it, when I'm reacting to every little thing about him so powerfully, my body so sensitive and hungry.

So I keep my mouth shut and trail after him, keeping enough distance so I won't lose any sense of pride and beg him to fuck me until I can't stand it.

But I still notice the way his shoulders tense, making his shirt draw tailored tight up against his chest and down to the taper of his waist.

Or how his hands clench and unclench, big knuckles knotting into powerful ridges against his skin, silent agitation in rhythmic motion that matches my racing pulse and the wanting throb between my thighs.

He takes me through a few corridors lit with gold and cloaked in shadows.

The hallways have an almost spiral layout, branching off to the three interconnected octagons that allow every room to face the water. The last octagon is his bedroom—all windows on six sides, facing away from the shore so it's just water and sky.

Absolutely beautiful.

The room is just like August—utilitarian but elegant, decorated in warm wood tones and countering neutral greys. The walls are diagonal interlaced slats of varnished gold brown bamboo, the bed wide and pillowy with a bookshelf headboard of weathered wood.

I want to look at the books, to know what he reads late at night until he passes out at some ungodly hour. But if I get an inch closer to that bed, I'm going to do something impossible to take back.

The tension chokes me.

And it almost snuffs the life out of me as he gestures to a door on one of the two interior walls, its seams almost hidden in the paneling.

"Bathroom," he says tersely. He's not looking at me at all. Pointedly. "Everything you need should be there; feel free to use anything you like. I'll prep you a guest room. Call for me when you're done."

Come with me, I want to say. *Half an hour under the steaming spray together.*

Just come with me.

Before this thing between us cuts me to pieces, while you stay whole.

For once, I can't be bold.

I can't be brave.

I can't be bright.

All I do is lower my eyes and whisper, "Thanks."

He doesn't say anything.

He just turns away and walks out like I'm not even there, his steps a little too sharp, his fingers still balled in a fist.

I'm only standing there for a minute, but it feels like I'm losing hours.

I can't even tell if he's actually angry at me for something he doesn't understand—or if he's angrily trying to deny that this feeling building between us is mutual.

Whatever.

I can't think about it.

I won't *let* myself think about it.

So I let myself into the bathroom instead—an expansive space of black-veined granite counters, sinks in dark-matte metal, a ridiculously large mirror, bamboo walls that match the bedroom's diagonal pattern.

The floor is still that same rough slate without a single seam, tile, or crack.

It feels cooler in here somehow, misted with the scent of the tall fronded fern plants potted in the corners. There's a massive rainfall shower with seating surrounded by glass and multiple showerheads, plus a skylight letting in a hint of the moon. The bathtub is separate, an enormous sunken thing that's practically a small pool.

I'm so tempted to take a dip.

But I'm suddenly dead tired.

I just want to wash the glitter off my skin and go to sleep and try to forget where I am—stuck with a man who makes me want him so much I feel depraved.

I strip down quickly, then pile my clothes on the edge of the counter, hang my coat from the hook on the back of the door, and drop my purse on the crumpled stack of my clothing.

When I turn the water on, it takes a little fiddling to not *drown* myself in the deluge cascading down. I realize it's running down the sides of the walls, too, pouring from insets high up near slits of windows to create a decorative glassy sheen.

Dang.

He may not be about McMansions, but August still has plenty of that fancy billionaire flash.

I snag a towel from the laid-out stack, step in, and let myself melt under the soothing downpour. It's honestly just what I need right now—shutting my brain off to let the heat take over and make me think about *nothing*.

Not August.

Not the way I'm getting all up in my feelings in the most hopeless way.

Not anything except that maybe I was a little drunk.

The hot water pulls me back to my senses, calming me down.

Everything's going to be fine.

I'll say good night, curl up in the guest room, try not to wonder about the thread count on the sheets, and sleep. I'm making up all this tension in my head, imagining scenarios that are completely one sided.

Just let it go, because if I don't, if I just keep brooding . . .

Well. We know what happens when I end up in migraine land, don't we?

And I don't think August wants to peel a limp squid of a girl off his shower floor with a gash across her head.

That's almost a porno setup, anyway.

The damsel in distress faints, the hunky guy comes to save her, they get hot and heavy because suddenly once she sees his rippling biceps, she's completely fine and doesn't need 911 at all.

I smirk as I scrub myself off using August's shower gel—*that's what his crisp scent is*—and wash my hair with a little dollop of his shampoo.

August is hot. Migraine-forgetting hot, but he's not migraine-curing hot.

I don't think he could fuck me out of one of those whoppers.

Or could he?

I kind of wouldn't mind finding out.

Surely, he wouldn't turn down a girl in medical distress, would he?

I can't help laughing, my mood clearing like the clouds after a storm.

He's also right. I've got the oddest imagination, but at least I entertain myself.

With a pleased sigh, I give myself one more rinse, then wring my hair out and wrap it up in a lush, fluffy dark-grey towel that feels just as much like heaven as the one I cinch around me from my boobs to my thighs. Loose and lazy, I step out, rolling my shoulders.

I just want to put on something clean and slee—

Oh, god*dammit.*

See, this is why August needs to learn how to text a girl.

I didn't pack an overnight bag. I had no idea I'd be spending the night here—even as an unwanted guest.

I eye my clothes.

Definitely not putting those panties back on.

They're ruined, considering how he had me wound up earlier.

Okay, I could put the dress back on, but my skin's still a bit damp too. That sheer fabric will cling to me and make it look like I'm naked, and sleeping in it might ruin something that expensive.

"Damn it, August," I mutter, smacking my face into my palm.

After I make sure the towel is wrapped tight and everything is fully covered, I crack the door open and peek out.

No sign of him anywhere.

"August?" I call. "Could I, um, borrow a shirt to sleep in?"

No answer.

He must still be prepping the guest room.

I duck back into the bathroom and gather up my things, clutching my clothes and coat against my chest until it's like I'm not mostly naked at all. After shouldering the bathroom door open, I step out, raising my voice to call his name again.

"Augu—*oop!*"

I go smashing right into him.

Face first into his chest.

Guess he heard me after all.

Everything I'm holding drops on impact. I make an undignified scramble to catch it.

Maybe that's how real life turns into an X-rated setup.

Dear God.

How I don't realize my towel's come loose and it's slipping down.

Until suddenly I'm standing there, naked and damp and shivering.

Completely exposed, with the towel and my clothes scattered around my feet.

August stands so rigidly in front of me, staring down with his eyes livid, stars of blue fire burning through the shadows.

I'm too frozen to even cover myself with my arms.

Pure mortification washes through me until I'm numb.

He must think I'm making a play for him, pulling some kind of contrived—

But no.

August's mouth tightens into a forbidding line, his jaw a knot of hard steel.

I lower my eyes, humiliation fuming through me, and just wait for him to walk away so we can pretend this didn't happen. I hear the faint scuff of his feet and brace myself for the hurt of something I didn't even offer being rejected.

But he's coming *closer*, not falling away.

I lift my head sharply, feeling my lungs turning to stone.

There's barely half a second to register the storm lashing in his eyes.

Then that storm crashes over me, sweeping me up in his hold and his kiss and his everything.

His rough fingers curl around my arms, jerking me against him.

His mouth captures mine like a predator, injecting me with *heat*.

He slams me back against the bathroom door, the wood rattling in its frame as my body presses against it—cold on one side, hot on the other, as his frame molds to mine.

I'm so lost.

But maybe I don't want to be found.

There's no way to explain how this feels.

It's like the moment when a small ship gets caught up in a violent storm, cataclysmic waves standing ten times higher, swirling with the sheer power of an ocean gone mad while the clouds and wind and rain whip the boat with one force of nature and then another.

August is the sea and the storm.

I'm defenseless, unguarded, his pressure molding every inch of me with nothing to save me from the sheer rush of his heat.

The scrape of his shirt against my breasts and nipples.

The thrust of his hips against mine.

The hardness against his slacks.

He's so *thick* as it prods between my legs and rips a startled gasp out of me, pushing me up on my toes with the thrill, bleeding the sound from my lips to his to be devoured.

I don't even remember dropping my arms.

But they're around his shoulders now, fingers buried in his hair, strain pouring down the backs of my calves to the tips of my toes as I stretch up to reach him, to meet him, to give every inch of myself over as I let my lips fall slack and let him take, take, take.

And God, does he *take*.

Growling, grasping, his harsh breaths drag against my lips.

His mouth brands me with the sweetest pressure and the savagery of his tongue.

He's already *in* me, every licking thrust searching, invading, touching me in impossible ways with phantom echoes deep inside.

It's like I'm riding those furious waves in imaginary thrusts that make me want the real thing so bad I can't take it.

I bite him, begging and tasting the firmness of his mouth.

He bites me right back.

Animal.

Pure animal teeth and the perfect bloom of pain.

His fingers slide up my arms, curling against my neck for that extra little spark of danger.

Then they rip the towel away from my hair and bury themselves in my damp locks with a touch so blazing he could practically steam my hair dry.

But it's nothing compared to the moment when he drags my head back by his grip, my scalp burning with pleasure-pain and the sheer dominance, opening me until I'm powerless against the onslaught of the most vicious erotic kiss I've ever had in my life.

His hands slip down with thunder spilling up his throat.

His growl vibrates through me like I'm a ringing vessel.

Molding over my back, pulling me away from the shocking coolness of the wooden door until it's just heat everywhere.

His touch melds me to his muscle inescapably until I'm wet, so *wet*, just from how he feels, moaning against his lips, squirming in his grip, begging for more of that touch, those long fingers spanning me, and then—

Digging into my ass.

Broad palms cupping either side, kneading me, spreading me open from behind.

Every time he drags his fingers against soft flesh, it pulls on inner muscles, drawing my pussy open, making me throb, exposing an aching emptiness that desperately needs his cock *now*.

"August," I whimper against his mouth, the sound dripping like honey.

All I can manage is his name.

What I really mean is *Fuck me.*

Fuck me before I lose my mind.

I can't take it anymore.

I've held back so much, and now I need to feel you.

He doesn't answer.

He doesn't say a word.

But his fingers gouge my ass as he claims handfuls, forcing needy sounds from my throat as the pulse at each pressure point heightens into a rhythm inside my needy pussy.

This time, his grip doesn't loosen as he lifts me up off my feet, dragging me against his body as he sucks my lower lip into his mouth and teases me with those cruel teeth.

My toes leave the ground.

My legs open wider.

I can't help myself.

I *have* to wrap myself around him right now.

Even as sleek and elegant as his build is, even with the sharp taper from his broad shoulders down to a narrow waist and punishing hips, he's still too wide for me.

I have to strain to wrap my thighs around him, locking my ankles against his back, and oh *God*, now I'm ruining his slacks because I'm so open.

That thick, angry ridge of his cock pushes against his slacks, rubbing against my dripping opening.

"Elle, fuck," he whispers.

I'm panting.

I know he can't stand the anticipation either.

He almost fucks me right through the fabric, taunting my naked flesh, soaking me as I throw myself into it, practically riding me as his hold throws me up and down in rhythm.

Tossed by the storm, I throw my head back, clinging to him and arching my back and letting myself swirl into this whirlpool of mad pleasure.

I can't stop my moans, my whimpers.

They're louder as his mouth descends on mine and then finds new targets.

My neck. He covers my racing pulse in sucking kisses and sharp bites.

My collarbones.

My breasts.

His mouth closes ravenously over my nipples, and he sucks them one at a time with such obsessive intensity they swell in seconds.

I grit my teeth, fighting for control, because all I want to do is scream.

Every draw of his mouth hits the sweet spots that make me flutter, hurling me straight to the edge.

Can you come from just this?

God, this feels so dirty, and I love it.

Arching in his grip, my breasts go tender hot with the sensation.

I grind against him while his cock pushes into me even with the fabric still in the way, this weird but wonderful sensation of wet cloth and braising heat.

Growling, he spreads me open, dipping inside like a flirting kiss, strangling every word on my lips until there's nothing left but *wanting*.

I want him so bad, and I can't flipping wait.

Pulling myself back, I let go of him with one hand and slide it down between us, taking a moment to savor the delicious strain of his muscles against his shirt before I find his zipper and drag it down.

His thick, musky maleness wafts out, a scent so earthy it immediately overwhelms me in the best way.

Past the slit of his boxers, I find hot flesh—if only my fingers weren't shaking so much.

August shudders against me, silent and electrified.

I regain enough control to wrap my fingers around him, telling him with my touch what I can't find the words to say.

This.

I want this inside me, hard and pounding and splitting me open.

Fuck me raw, August.

Rip me to pieces.

Without fear.

Without regret.

Without mercy.

He's so huge against my palm, all thick veins and a flared, angry head.

Just touching his cock makes me shudder, feeling his pulse thumping through his fullness. Every beat of his heart feels like a war drum.

Just gripping it makes my mouth water. I don't know if I want to taste it or ride it more.

But August makes the decision for me.

The more I touch his cock, the tenser he grows, until he rips his mouth from my aching nipple and rests his brow to my shoulder. His lungs are heaving and his hips rake me with tiny thrusts toward my hand.

He hasn't said a word.

It's almost eerie in his worn silence, yet somehow that only makes him more intense, even more enthralling.

Definitely more demanding, as he suddenly pulls me away from the bathroom door and tumbles me against the foot of the bed.

The next thing I know, I'm down on my back, my arms falling to my sides.

August looms over me, his gaze all lightning, striking and searing everywhere it touches.

He's in a fury of desire, with rage, frustration, and lust written all over his face. I don't understand, but there's not even a second to think, to question.

He catches my hands, laces our fingers together, and pins them to the bed.

He locks eyes with me.

Then that hot flesh I'd touched so greedily nudges back between my legs.

No fabric in the way this time.

Just the thick swell of his cock and the wet, pulsing flutter of folds that part for him too eagerly.

I'm already acting like his whore, and I don't care.

I'll beg, offer myself up on a plate, anything—*but I don't have to.*

There's just one more moment where he holds back, fire crackling between us in the silence.

Then he slams into me, so wild and hot and hard it's like he's punishing me for making him want me so bad.

I can't hold back my cry, the way I arch, pulling against his hands, but he won't let go.

He has me now.

He owns me, taking my body until I have no will, no thought, no self. Not when I'm drowning in the rough sensation of his cock plunging into me.

I don't know if I can hold it, but there's more, more, *more*, surging into forbidden places, touching me inside in ways that feel so good it must be wrong.

I feel like I'm doing something dirty. Filthy. Taboo.

And I'm going to need it again and again.

As he starts to pull out, I wrap my legs around his hips and pull him in.

"Not yet," I plead, finding words at last. "Just let me feel it a second longer."

August's brows darken.

He watches me with his jaw fixed in that tight, angry iron.

And he moves, a rippling shudder of power pouring down his tightly sculpted body until I can see every muscle straining against his disarrayed clothing.

A single short, savage jerk.

Burying in me so deep he's practically grinding into me, forcing into deeper depths, and then—

He hits that one perfect spot.

I scream, completely losing my flipping mind, clenching my thighs against his hips and clutching him so tight.

My fingers dig between his knuckles, and my body thrashes.

And he's still not done—not by half—because even as I lose it, he keeps perfect control over his movements, twisting and grinding his hips so that instead of pulling out of me, he just teases that spot against my inner walls until there's something deep within that shivers and trembles and quakes, this pleasure that feels so *naked*, stripped and exposed.

I don't know how I'm not coming already.

I don't want to yet.

I want to hold on to this, to the feeling of August lowering himself down, the feeling of him letting my hands go and wrapping his arms around me, burying his face in my throat, biting cruelly as he fills me with piston thrusts.

Slow.

Slow but violent, gathering his entire strength, pounding me so vengefully but so perfectly.

I'm nearly sobbing at how good this is, riding every deep, rolling thrust, digging my heels into his ass, completely incoherent as I make up for his silence with my cries.

Holy shit, I'm going to—I'm going crazy.

No one's cock should feel this good.

No one's cock has any business being this *thick*, stirring and twisting up my insides until he's remaking me, I—I—

I thought it was just me, falling apart.

But August drives in harder still.

His teeth sink into my shoulder and *hold*.

Still no sound, so obsessively silent, and yet he feels so intensely focused on me that it's unnerving and wonderful. This monster storms halls of pleasure, intent on looting everything from my body.

There's this wicked swelling inside me, thicker, *thicker*, and the warm hot jet of molten fire as he comes.

Ruined.

I'm overflowing with him, so thick and hot and filthy that I love it, want it, need it—

Oh God.

I go blind as he growls again.

Just another helpless animal in heat, a captured bunny shrieking to the moon.

I'm petrified with white-hot pleasure, crashing into myself, pouring out everywhere, coming with him.

Coming!

I think I bite him in the frenzy.

I'm not quite sure.

Because the next thing I know, darkness falls like a curtain, pulling me into an ecstasy so deep and perfect it brands me to my core.

I'm not out long.

I don't think I really passed out; it's more like I just went dark for a few seconds from sensory overload. But when I come to, August has already let me go.

I open my eyes, blinking up at the ceiling.

I'm sore everywhere, wet and sticky between my thighs.

Still shamelessly naked, sprawled on my back in a pretty awkward position, with my legs flopped over the side of his bed.

That was easily the most magnificent orgasm of my life.

And I wonder if it was a magnificent mistake.

From the corner of my eye, I see August sitting on the foot of the bed next to me, his elbows resting on his thighs as he rubs his temples. He's tucked himself away and tidied himself up a bit.

Watching him carefully, I slowly sit up, wishing more than anything I had something to shield myself with.

When I move, he lifts his head, looking at me.

It's a careful look. Guarded.

Every semblance of easy friendship we've built between us gone in one night.

It hurts.

It hurts like I'm being flayed open from heart to gut.

But before I can say anything, he asks sharply, "You on birth control?"

All I can do is nod slowly.

My lips tremble, and I press them together tightly.

I won't fall apart.

My feelings are just raw after getting fucked blind, that's all.

This was just . . . it wasn't a thing.

It was confused people out for a good time giving in to reckless urges.

August only accepts my answer with a tight nod and stands.

He moves like he's walking a tightrope, tense and controlled. He crosses the room to a tall chest of drawers next to the door and yanks the second drawer open, speaking as he reaches inside.

"I'll text you a copy of my most recent STD tests. Obviously, I'm clean." Mechanical. Practical. "I'd thank you to do the same."

Anger boils up inside me, hateful words needling my tongue.

Not even "Thanks for the ass, Elle"? Maybe even "Nice pussy, now get out?" Or "Hey, hope I didn't hurt you piledriving you like a wildebeest?"

But I can't bring myself to say it.

I don't know how to deal with this.

And I don't know how to handle it when he turns back to me with a white dress shirt in hand, folded and clearly soft-worn enough that it's been retired from everyday use.

He offers me the shirt at arm's length. The storm in his eyes has gone flat, leaving nothing but his usual glacial ice.

"You can clean up in the bathroom. Turn left where the hall splits," he says. "The guest bedroom is the door on the right."

I feel like I've been punched in the heart.

I have about sixty seconds at best to get away from him.

Forget the bathroom.

I wobble to my feet and reach for the shirt, clutching it against me for some cover. I don't even have the presence of mind to go back for my dress, my purse, everything else I dropped.

I just stare down at my feet, wanting to scream at him.

We could have kept this casual, dammit.

At least he didn't have to be *cruel*.

But all I can manage is a small, mortified "Thanks" before I brush past him and try to walk—not run—out of his bedroom.

I make it around the curve of the hallway before I break.

First the painful sniffle, the burning tears, and then I'm pelting away with a sob until I dive into the guest bedroom, shut the door, and fling myself down on the bed.

I don't feel like getting dressed right now, so I just curl around the crumpled mess of his oversize shirt and bury my face in the pillow to muffle my cries.

Why the hell did I have to fall for a rhino dick like August Marshall?

I wish I wasn't right about sleeping alone tonight.

Not like this.

But hey, there's a bright side in this too.

Now I know for sure to never, ever get my hopes up.

XII

MORNING GLOOM

(AUGUST)

I am the worst human being alive.

I'm not sure I deserve to be called *human* anyway.

Filth.

That works just fine.

Absolute fucking gutter trash.

I slump onto my bed, staring at what Elle left behind when she fled the room.

No—fled from *me*.

I drove her away like the absolute blackhearted bastard I am.

I'd ask what the hell I was thinking—except I already know.

I wasn't thinking at all.

I ravaged her as soon as she bumped into me and I saw the moonlight pouring over her skin, turning it to pale perfection, highlighting every irresistible curve.

She glowed so much she barely looked human, so radiant, her skin kissed with strawberry pink on her nipples and between her thighs and across her enticing lips.

I snapped.

Everything I'd been ignoring erupted out of me.

Elle met me halfway, yes.

I certainly didn't take her by force, without her consent.

But the second the red sex haze lifted and I realized what I'd done, panic took over.

Every rotten fuckup with Charisma came flooding back. Every mistake I ever made. Every moment when I was selfish and thought of what I wanted and not what she needed.

I shut the fuck down.

I shut Elle out the same way I shut Charisma out once.

I smothered her warmth, her brightness, and even if she barely said a word, I know, goddammit.

I know I hurt her.

I force myself up, knowing I'll have to face it tonight.

I have to stuff my ego in a box and apologize.

Call Rick to take her home, as I doubt she'll want me to drive her anywhere. I won't force her to stay here tonight for appearances when she'd undoubtedly like to be anywhere else.

I pick up her coat, her dress, her purse, and fold everything into a neat stack before taking it with me as I step out into the hall. But the moment I stop outside the guest room, I know.

I won't be going in there tonight.

I can hear her now.

Crying like her heart's been torn out and stomped with hooves.

My own heart twists violently.

You did that, you miserable fuck.

You did that to her, and you're the last person she'll ever want to see again.

I've never hated my malfunction—my disconnect with others—more than I do right now.

All I want is to comfort her, to make up for this bullshit somehow.

But I don't know how that's possible.

So all I do is touch my fingers lightly to the door, pretending I can somehow reach her through it.

"I'm sorry," I mutter.

I leave her things next to the door where she can easily find them, whenever she's ready.

Before retreating to my room, I peel off my clothes and settle into the chair next to one of the glass walls with a tumbler of bourbon and all the self-loathing I've earned a thousand times over.

I never should have sucked Elle Lark into my black hole of a life.

All I can ever do is devour the goodness in everyone around me and send them spinning away, broken.

◆ ◆ ◆

I must have passed out in the chair.

I didn't quite get piss drunk last night, but I came close.

Now I'm waking up with a terrible crick in my neck and my entire body knotted up from being slumped in the chair all night. At first, I think I must have knocked myself out until evening from the grey-dark tint to the sky, but no.

It's sunrise.

Something I almost never see, coming up over the horizon in splashes of spreading gold.

I linger on it with my mouth feeling dry and scummy. It's not sour with the booze, rather the bitterness dwelling inside me.

The morning makes me wonder if Elle's light will be dimmer, her sunlit eyes less radiant.

No. Not her.

She might burn less fiercely for a little while, but my shit could never snuff her out.

She's too strong for that.

One fine day, I'll just be one more bad memory she hardly thinks about at all.

"It can't come soon enough," I mutter.

I stand, rolling my shoulders and drifting to the window. If I'm up, I might as well take in this bizarre novelty.

Yet I'm not the only one awake.

When I hear footsteps, I almost retreat.

Elle's up.

Standing outside, where I can just barely see her from my vantage point facing the sound.

She's dressed in that pretty sleeveless dress again.

The morning wind blows it against her and breezes her hair back from her fine-featured face. Her coat and purse are piled on the shore, while she stands in the shallows with her shoes dangling from her hand, her face tilted to the rising sun.

The dawn paints her pink and gold.

Again, I'm struck by that crazy feeling that she isn't fully human.

She's an angel of light captured straight from a fairy tale, and as the sunrise thins the barrier between worlds, she'll fade away like she was never here slumming it in flesh and blood at all.

Ridiculous, I know.

The image punches me so painfully that it wrenches me with longing. I unconsciously reach for her—then catch myself as my fingers hit the glass and remind me she's too far away.

Forever out of reach.

That's for the best.

I pull back with a scorched breath and snatch my phone from the nightstand. I need to let her be free from me, so I dial Rick's number.

Even if I'm not usually up at this hour, he always is, and he's quick to answer.

"Mr. Marshall?" he says, a bit of a rush in his voice. "What's wrong?"

I pause with my eyes still on Elle. "Why do you think something's wrong?"

"It's only seven a.m., sir . . ."

A dark, heavy smirk tugs at my lips. "Fair enough. It's simply a practical matter."

"Ah, sure. What can I do for you?"

"Miss Lark stayed the night at my place for appearances. She'd like to go home now to prepare herself before office hours." It comes out so smoothly, this lie, like I'm not asking Rick to bring her a getaway car. I don't expect to see her at the office today either. "She'll be waiting for you outside."

"Understood," Rick answers. "You took the G80 last night, so should I take her in my car or yours?"

"Mine, please. If you leave your keys, I'll take yours to the office and trade with you there."

"Of course, sir." There's a hesitant pause. "Are you all right?"

Damn.

I'm not as good at suppressing my feelings as I thought, if he can sense it.

Once again, my gaze gravitates to that beautiful fairy girl on the shore, soaking up the sun like a morning flower.

"I've been worse," I answer faintly. "But I've been better too."

"Very sorry to hear that, sir. I'll be there as soon as I can."

"Thanks."

I hang up and leave my phone on the nightstand, then push the door open on the spray-dampened deck. I don't know why I'm going outside, stepping into the chill morning air, the rising sun blazing against my eyes.

Maybe because it feels like being close to her.

If we can both soak in the sunlight, then in some small way, we'll still be touching each other.

I walk to the deck railing and let myself watch her. I almost never see her without a smile, but right now she's quiet, her lips parted, as much as I can make it out at this distance.

Fuck, I just want her to smile again.

The same way she did with Aunt Clara.

The same way she made Aunt Clara light up.

That's Elle's gift.

I hope she keeps it for the rest of her life.

I don't know how long I watch her.

Rick lives just outside the city, but traffic at this time of morning typically isn't that bad. It can't be too long before I hear an approaching car. Elle doesn't move, even as the grey dart of Rick's sedan slides past and turns into my place.

When Rick steps out and calls out, "Miss Lark!" Elle turns.

She looks back over her shoulder and slowly raises a hand to him before bending to pick up her things.

Then she tilts her head up and punches me square in the chin with one glance.

She knows I'm here, watching her like the emotionally stunted creeper fuck I am.

My heart squeezes into a lump of coal as she stares at me, and the sloshing waves and the crying gulls become part of a hollow silence.

I'm definitely not expecting her to smile, thin and sad.

I don't know how the fuck she can stand it, but she smiles at me for the briefest second, right before she ducks her head and walks barefoot across the sand to meet Rick.

I want to call out for her, but I don't have the faintest clue what the fuck to say.

I'm left alone with my brain spinning, watching helplessly as she disappears from my life and into the waiting car.

XIII

SUNSHINE STATE OF MIND

(ELLE)

You know that meme with the stuffed monkey in the light-green shirt?

You know, the one people trot out when someone says or does something that deserves serious side-eye. And the monkey is just looking at the person, then away, like, "I'm gonna mind my business, but *yikes.*"

That's how I felt, like everyone was looking at me, when I showed up at the office this morning—the morning after that night.

That night.

I felt like that was how Rick looked at me when he took me home. I'm sure he came because August called him.

August, who clearly didn't want to talk to me or even see me. Despite spending God only knows how long watching me while I stood in the morning light, trying to pull my head together.

If I had any common sense, I'd quit this whole thing.

Crossing that red line with August was an epic mistake. Whatever silly infatuation I'd gotten into, August is so unreachable that he'll just call that one quick crashing torrent of desire and wild sex a momentary lapse in judgment.

Maybe it was for both of us.

But what sucks the most is that we'd just started becoming actual friends, trusting each other with personal secrets.

That's ruined now.

So hey. It would be really easy to let this bleed into our publicly advertised breakup moment, right? It'll just happen sooner than planned.

That's what I told myself on the drive home.

It's what I told myself when I asked Gran to go back to bed, lied that everything was fine, and said that I'd see her at breakfast.

It's what I told myself through a cold shower, curling up in bed to lick my wounds and cry a little more and fight off another creeping migraine.

How could I have been so *wrong* about him?

I thought August was a good man who just didn't see the goodness in himself.

That thought falls out of my head when my alarm goes off, the one that tells me it's time to get up and get dressed and go spend the day worshipping my childhood idol, trying to learn everything I can from her.

That alarm is the reminder I need.

I'm not just doing this for August.

I'm doing it for Clara Marshall, too, and I can't bear the thought of abandoning her.

No, maybe I can't salvage her lost love for Inky the Penguin. Maybe I can't convince her to keep plugging away, or to weather the court fight either.

But that doesn't mean I won't try.

A story about the night the *Titanic* sank comes to mind. We mostly hear about the people who died on that ship.

The tragedy, the horror.

Kate Winslet telling Leonardo DiCaprio to draw her like one of his French girls.

What we don't hear about is the heart-wrenching story of bravery behind the ship that picked up the survivors, the *Carpathia*.

The *Carpathia* was fifty-eight miles away when it got a distress signal. Too far to help. Too far to get there in time to save people as the massive ship sank, broke apart, and doomed over a thousand people to their icy graves.

But over seven hundred people lived.

All thanks to the *Carpathia*'s captain, Arthur Rostron, who saw that impossible chance to reach the *Titanic* in time. He thought he couldn't do it.

He did anyway.

Everyone on board stepped up to help, prepping the ship to receive survivors while Captain Rostron shut off everything to divert power to the steam engines. Hot water, central heating. All of it. The engineers, stokers, and firemen pushed the engines beyond their capacity.

For hours, the RMS *Carpathia* surged through the night, through icebergs and fear and desperation.

They made it to the site of the *Titanic*'s sinking in just over three hours.

How, no one is honestly even sure. Even with their superhuman efforts, what they did shouldn't have been physically possible.

The first time I read the post summarizing it on Tumblr, I cried like a baby because it felt like it could only have been the sheer *need* to save those people that moved the *Carpathia* so fast, pushed by the hopes of everyone on board. We may never know how they did it.

But we know that far more people would have died that night if Captain Rostron hadn't decided he couldn't just let the survivors go.

I'm not Captain Rostron. Maybe it's arrogant of me to even think I could push past impossible odds to succeed.

But if there's even the tiniest chance to be the *Carpathia* to Clara's *Titanic* . . .

I have to try, don't I?

And August and I, well, we don't have to see each other for that.

That's what I tell myself, anyway, when I walk into the office and feel everyone staring at me.

They're not. I know they're not.

August may have been a ginormous dick last night, but he wouldn't humiliate me by telling everyone what happened. He wouldn't even breathe a word.

But I step off the elevator just as he steps out of his office, deep in conversation with Deb and awake far earlier than he has any right to be, considering his sleeping habits.

I freeze.

That sick hurt churns in my gut again, even though I told myself to ignore it and treat it just like a one-night stand between strangers.

He stops, absently glancing up and going stiff. His eyes widen briefly.

Right before his face shutters again and he looks down swiftly, focusing on the stack of pages held between him and Deb.

It hurts.

I knew it would happen, but the reality is still heart shredding, digging its claws just under my ribs.

Deb looks between us in confusion, with her brows tight. The resemblance between brother and sister is suddenly very sharp—I can see the thundercloud brewing and almost hear her demanding to know what August *did*, and why he's ignoring me in front of the staff, while I'm standing here blank and miserable and paralyzed.

I don't give her a chance.

I force the same smile I always do.

I wave and cheerfully call, "Hey, Deb! I just wanted to let you know I'll be down with Clara today."

Then I turn and walk back into the elevator, frantically pushing the *down* button to cut off the sight of August lifting his head and watching me with the most haunted look on his face.

I nearly race to Clara's little studio cottage, where I find her pouring tea when I burst in. She gasps softly, almost spilling it before she catches herself and tips the delicate porcelain pot upright, then switches over to pouring into the second cup.

"Elle?" she whispers. Her soft southern lilt is automatically comforting. "What's happened, dear?"

"Bee," I deflect, taking a shaky breath. "Guess spring's coming after all. It chased me all the way here."

What?

You think I'm going to tell her *I fucked your nephew last night, and he threw a shirt at me and kicked me out, and now every time I look at him I want to cry because I think I might be in love with who I thought he was?*

Nah, I think I'll keep that bit to myself.

Instead, I ask her to show me how to draw Inky again, hoping that teaching me might rekindle her love. Hoping that the joy of drawing her most beloved creation will ignite something fresh in her.

It's a strange day, honestly.

Heartbreak weighs heavily in the pit of my stomach, but also elation at getting to watch Clara trace those familiar round shapes and flippers with so much precision and—dare I say it?—fondness. She shows me all the base shapes she uses, watches me sketch them myself, offers gentle corrections, and then draws for me again.

Pure bliss.

It's amazing, learning from a total legend, fulfilling in ways I never thought it would be.

It's just not enough to stop me from feeling sad.

Every day becomes like this. I make myself come in to work to keep up the facade.

Grandma watches me go to the door with a worried look that says she knows something is wrong but she'll let me come to her when I'm ready. I try to avoid August at work, but he keeps coming in *early* like he's a pod person or something. We keep bumping into each other in the parking lot, in the lobby, the little espresso bar downstairs.

It's always awkward.

Frozen moments.

Haunted looks.

A few times, he parts his lips and then just stops and turns away.

I've come so close to texting him and demanding that he just stop holding back and say whatever he's going to say.

But I don't think I'm ready to smile through that hurt just yet.

By Friday, though?

I am *absolutely* sick of it.

So we're going to hash this out, make a decision, and figure out just how long we're going to keep this farce up so we're not dancing around each other for weeks at a time.

I pack a basket with food and some comfy blankets and tuck it in the back seat of my grandmother's cute little light-green Audi. I've been stealing it for the commute every day, since it's pretty much a given that August isn't picking me up anymore, and I won't put Rick out picking me up.

Then I drive to the office.

I march—well, glide, I guess, in the elevator—upstairs, then walk to his office door.

I knock firmly and walk in without waiting for permission.

August glances up, his mouth opening sharply—only to shutter over again. He gives me another mournful puppy dog look that makes me seethe before he looks away, staring glassily at the wall.

I'm almost mad that he looks so *good* when he's being broody.

That little curl of hair over his wrinkled brow, his full lips just slightly parted and pensive.

And of course his suit—steel grey today, with a black tie and a dark-grey shirt—looks impeccable on him, framing the perfect lines of his well-built body.

He's not allowed to be this hot when I'm pissed at him.

"Miss Lark." His tone is empty when he finally speaks. "Is there something I can do for you?"

"Oh, fuck off," I throw back. Not exactly how I wanted to start this, but my temper's just as explosive as the rest of me. I stalk across the room, my heels clicking, and steal his hand from his laptop keyboard, tugging as hard as I can. "And come with me."

My tugging isn't even enough to make his desk chair swivel. But August flinches and pulls back on his hand.

"Miss Lark, I have to work—"

"Nope! You have to stop being a coward first." I yank on him again. "You're coming now. I'm not giving up, even if you pick me up and chuck me out of here."

This time I manage to pull him off balance, more by sheer luck than anything.

He slides forward in his seat and rises to his feet to get his bearings in a flex of his muscular thighs against his slacks. It gives me a little more leverage to brace my heels and really *pull* as I turn to drag him toward the door.

"Miss Lark!" he protests. "Where are you—"

"Stop calling me Miss Lark, and I'm taking you to eat a picnic." I whirl back to face him, letting go of his hand and bracing my own on my hips. "Look, you can sit here and sulk, or you can come eat with me. Somehow, I don't think you want to sulk *that* badly."

August gives me an odd look, but his gaze flits away again, avoiding eye contact. He gives me a weary sigh and reaches up to brush that wild lock of hair back, but it just falls over again, dangling in front of one glassy blue eye.

"If I agree to this, will you let me finish my damned work?"

"Sure," I say, suddenly feeling sour. "You can do whatever you want."

His lips purse. It's like the old August I met on the plane all over again.

"Whatever."

Yep.

I could kick him right now.

This has been building up for a solid week, but even I wasn't expecting that I'd end up bullying him into coming with me.

It feels so awkward as I compose myself so I don't look like a tiny red ragey monster, then turn to lead him out of his office. It's so weird, when before we'd been leaning on each other in front of the staff, walking arm in arm or hand in hand, but now I'm leading, with him trailing behind.

As I pass one of the sales guys at his workstation, I catch a little whisper I probably wasn't supposed to hear.

"*Somebody's* gone and pissed off the little missus . . ."

"Can you blame her?" the woman next to him whispers back. "Marshall's a cold fish."

I flush with embarrassment.

I hate that even after the way he's treated me, the instinct rises up to jump to his defense.

But I pretend not to hear their shit-talk.

The ride down the elevator is *painful*, both of us on opposite ends and staring up at the numbers. Getting in the Audi is worse. It's small and cramped, and August has to adjust his seat to slide it all the way back so he's not eating his knees with every speed bump.

As I pull out onto the street, I try to smile for my own sake—but it feels like it's stitched on my face in rigid seams. The silence could choke a rattler, as Gran would say.

Good thing we're not going far.

It's midmorning, and there's less traffic as we head to Alki Beach.

I park and reach into the back to snag the picnic basket. I try to pretend I'm alone instead of with a stiff wooden blockhead shadowing me as I march onto the sand in pumps that do not like sinking into the loosely shifting granules with every forceful step.

Look, I didn't think parts of this through, okay?

But I've started this, so I'll finish it.

I find a good spot where we can see the waves and the sea lions playing in the tide—but not too close that we might get chased off by one of the more aggressive beasties.

Determined, I set the basket down, rip the blanket off the top, and spread it on the sand before plunking down with the basket at my hip.

Honestly, it's a barrier. So we can keep a little space from each other.

August stands at the edge of the blanket, looking down at it skeptically.

I point at the free space.

"Sit," I command. "Eat."

With another long sigh, August steps on the blanket and sinks down slowly to sit cross-legged. He keeps his eyes on his hands as he pulls off his polished dress shoes and shakes sand out over the side of the blanket.

"We're here. You want to explain what the hell's going on?"

I mutter under my breath, then dig out one of the wrapped sandwiches inside and thrust it at him. "We're going to sit and eat lunch. That's all. Capisce?"

He doesn't say anything or take the sandwich.

He just sets his shoes down on the blanket, his long feet angular inside black dress socks, and looks at me strangely.

Eep.

I can't do this if he's just going to stare at me like I've got two heads, and not even let me use the pretense of eating to work my way up to what I want to say.

My hand on the sandwich trembles, and my outstretched arm starts to dip a bit.

Just take it, I plead silently, making myself watch him. *Take it so we can pretend everything is fine for a few seconds. Just eat and relax and take the olive branch, call a truce.*

But all he does is look at me.

Until he says, "I'm sorry."

I blink.

It's so abrupt my hand drops, the sandwich wrap crinkling as it lands on the blanket.

"Huh?" I don't understand.

This time, August's sigh is more patient. He's still giving me that hangdog look, but at least he's *looking at me.*

"I said I'm fucking sorry," he repeats. "We did something without thinking. And then, instead of talking to you about it, I shut you out and left you flapping in the breeze for days." There's a hint of scorn and disgust in his voice, and I think it's directed at himself. "I shouldn't have treated you that way."

My mouth opens and shuts.

My heart does that weird compacting thing again, but I don't know if it's relief or fresh hurt coming up as I remember that night, or—

"Why *did* you?" I ask.

"Because I'm an idiot, Elle. I panicked," August retorts bluntly. "When I don't know what to do, I shut people out."

"Asshole move," I quip.

"Yes, I'm aware. I've been trying to figure out how to address it all week."

I blink at him again.

Then I throw the sandwich at him. "*Not* by ignoring me, dude!"

"Hey!" August's arms come up. The sandwich bounces off them and lands next to the basket. "I deserved that, but why waste good food?"

"*Asshole,*" I repeat. "Stupid, awkward asshole."

"Yeah," he grunts, hanging his head. "The kids would say, 'I never figured out how to people.'"

"I've kinda figured that out by now," I huff, folding my arms over my chest and looking away. *"Asshole."*

"You don't have to forgive me, Elle. That's not what I'm asking for."

I shrug one shoulder, turning my nose up. "It's not like we're really dating. You can't exactly break my heart."

I'm such a bad liar.

"I suppose that's good news," he says, sounding dejected.

God, I really wasn't far off the mark when I compared him to an angry outcast boy.

Grown-ass man can handle global billion-dollar business matters but can't handle *talking* about his emotions.

. . . but I guess I'm not being much better, huffing and puffing at him, all up in my wounded feels. He *did* apologize before I had to ask for an apology. That's more than most men give.

I try to relent a little.

"August?" Exhaling, I glance back at him.

"Yeah?" There's the puppy dog again. Head coming up, ears practically pricking. Never would have imagined this the first time I met him.

Dammit. I can't stay mad at this absolute grumpy *goober* of a man.

But I will not let him make my heart flutter.

I won't.

"We can be friends, you know," I say. Maybe that will be the olive branch that smooths this out so we can go back to pretending. And so I can forget how he felt inside me, practically hollowing me out and making me burn in ways I felt the next day. "We can talk about things without making something formal about it. It's okay to just talk to me about what you're thinking. And . . ." I swallow. Yeah, I'm a bit nervous. "And we can talk about what we did."

August tilts his head, considering it, before he says, "I appreciate that. More than I can tell you." There's a way he talks when I know he's sincere, bringing that panther purr back to his voice. "I do like you, Elle. I respect you."

Ugh, I said no fluttering.

Make my heart stop.

I look away from him again. My face burns.

I don't want him to see me blushing when I don't want to stop being mad at him just yet.

"I don't know that I've done anything to earn your respect," I say.

"Then you aren't aware of your own admirable qualities," he points out, blunt as ever.

See? Tactless flipping goober.

"Flattery won't make me forgive you," I say loftily. Mostly to the sea lions, because I'm still not looking at August. "But if my *friend* wants to flatter me, I won't complain."

Yeah.

Because friends totally attack each other like animals in heat.

Stop thinking about it, or you're just going to want it again.

Too late.

My thighs are already tense, my insides clenching.

Am I ready to let that whole thing go just because he makes me so horny?

A soft snort erupts at my side. "Now you're just fishing."

"A little." I peek back at him and pinch my fingers together.

I expect him to roll his eyes. Instead, he regards me with sincerity. "Elle. Are you all right?"

I flinch. That peek turns into closing my eyes, then turning my face away again. "Why wouldn't I be?" I throw it out as casually as a wedding crasher, smiling.

"You always smile," August says softly. "You don't always mean it."

Yikes.

When he throws one down, it's a heavy hitter.

My smile fades, and my stomach sinks.

I'd started to open my eyes, but now I keep them closed.

"I know," I say softly. "But I keep smiling until I do. Mean it, that is. Eventually it gets easier, and then it becomes real."

His voice is a little closer when he speaks.

A little heavier.

A little warmer.

"If we're friends, you don't have to do that," he points out. "You can talk to me too. You can tell me if I hurt you."

You have no idea how much.

I have to screw my lids together, or my eyes are going to start stinging. The punch from that night is a bruise that's still tender.

I draw a shaky breath, force my eyes open, and make myself look at him. He's shifted to lean on his hand—and he leans closer to me across the basket, watching me so intently I almost melt into the beach.

"Being rejected by someone after having sex like that would hurt anyone, August." I force myself to be honest, but here I am, deflecting the same way I smile and trying to distance myself from the bad feelings. "I know it's not about me. It's not personal. You'd have done that with anyone."

I don't know if I want him to deny it.

I don't know if I want him to say it's personal, because that would mean there's something about *me* that's wrong—or maybe there isn't, and that's what it was about.

I don't know.

I don't want my heart lodged in my throat while he taps his knuckles against his lips, thinking hard.

"It was still unforgivably cruel. I'm still sorry. You deserved more respect *then*, not later. Also, you didn't need to force me to say what I've been wanting to say all this time. My piss-poor communication shouldn't cost your feelings. You deserve better than my bullshit, Elle."

This time my smile is small but genuine.

Sometimes August's honesty hurts.

But sometimes it's the balm I need, especially when I know he means every word.

"I forgive you anyway," I say, pulling my legs up to wrap my arms around my knees and watching the waves. The sun shines so brightly along the shore, turning the water silver, with the scent so sharp and cool. "Thank you, though."

"You shouldn't be thanking me. I fucked with your head."

"But you said something important. Maybe I had to drag you out here and make you face me to hear it, but you didn't make me bring it up. Most men would. They know they were assholes, but they'll ignore it and hope you won't say anything because if you do, you're the one who looks like she's starting fights just to be a shrill bitch. And suddenly you feel bad for being upset and end up letting it go. All because he's looking at you in that special way that makes you feel like you're the problem."

Oops.

I hadn't meant to say all that. It leaves my throat tight.

I'm not sure what I'm expecting him to say in response, but I definitely don't anticipate the tanned hand slipping across my vision to touch the back of my wrist.

No fire, no sparks this time.

Just companionship, one caring human being to another.

"Sounds like you've known some shitty men," August whispers as his hand withdraws.

"Yeah. I guess I didn't realize just how shitty until now."

"Anyone specific?"

"No, not really." I tuck a lock of hair behind my ear, stealing it back before the wind throws it across my cheek. "Just the usual parade of high school boys, college boyfriends, postcollege dudes who date like they're still in college . . ." I lace my hands together over my calves, bare in a bright blue-and-white checker-print dress with long sleeves, a tight bodice, and a ruffled A-line flare. "They all kind of blur together after a while." I realize how that sounds and clear my throat, darting him a look. "Not that I've dated like fifty guys or anything. It's only been about . . . five? Some of them I wouldn't even call boyfriends. Just bad first dates."

August just *watches* me now with that gentleness back in his eyes, that warmth—and a hint of amusement. When I realize he's been watching me that way the whole time, I recoil and look away, huffing.

"Elle," he says—soft but pointed.

"Stop looking at me."

"*Elle.*"

"What?" I slide a look his way.

August's brows arch. "You don't have to apologize for the life you've lived. Those mistakes brought you here, didn't they?"

Here, with him.

It hits me what he's saying.

In his life, no matter how messy and confusing that may be.

When I look at the water again, my lips curl and don't stop.

"Yeah. I guess they did."

"There you are," he says appreciatively. "Now you're smiling."

And blushing. And failing horribly at keeping my heart intact.

I laugh quietly. "You're kind of sweet sometimes, Auggie."

Desired effect: achieved.

Now he's scowling, and I've got the upper hand.

"Never say that shit again," he growls.

I grin. "Sweet. *Sweet.* Mr. Adorable Gruffykins."

August throws me a flat, disgusted stare completely undercut by the breeze playfully tossing that one loose lock against his brow. "Are you having a heat stroke? Those are not English words."

"Very funny, Gruffykins."

"Stop," he snarls.

"Why, Gruffyki—oop!"

That noise?

That was me jerking back as the sandwich on the blanket bonks me in the nose.

He threw it back at me!

I narrow my eyes, smirking, and dive for the basket.

I come right up with the pot of chocolate fondue.

"You wanna have a food fight?" I challenge, pulling the lid off. "'Cause I can throw *down.*"

August blanches. "Do you have any idea how much this suit cost?"

"Do I care?" I dip my finger in the fondue pot, coating it in sticky chocolate.

I stretch my dripping finger toward him. His eyes widen in sheer horror, and he tumbles back on his hands.

"Elle, what are you—Elle. No. *No.* Bad kitten. Bunny. Whatever you are, don't you fucking dare! I have meetings today and no time to change!"

"Aw, that's just begging me to do it," I tease, darting toward him.

He throws his hands up. "Oh God—"

I stop.

Just a micron short of touching his face.

Then I dab a tiny dollop of chocolate on the tip of his nose before pulling back with a laugh. "Boop."

August blinks and lowers his arms, setting me off in peals of laughter.

Glowering, he swipes the chocolate off his nose with one finger, then licks it.

"You are *impossible*."

"I know, but the look on your face—oh no."

August dips into the basket and comes up with an entire Tupperware container of coleslaw. He less smiles and more bares his teeth in warning as he eyes me.

"I know *exactly* how much that dress cost, and I'm not afraid to ruin it."

Oh, I am *not* losing this playground fight.

I lift my chin and square my shoulders, making myself a target. "Dare you. In public. Heck, let's make it fun. Chase me around. I *dare you* to chase me around with a plastic bin of shredded cabbage in runny mayo. Triple-dog dare you."

That gets me *multiple* blinks. I already know I've won.

August just laughs.

Any attempt to stop my heart from fluttering away dies as it beats so hard the velvety sound rolls through me.

"Another day." August sets the coleslaw down on the blanket and reaches into the basket to lift out the plates and utensils. "We should cut the schoolyard shit, eat, and get back to the office. Being the temporary CEO only gives me so many luxuries, and being the creative assistant gives you even fewer."

I giggle and accept the plate he offers before stealing the sandwich we've been using to score points for my plate. I dig out a second, less battered sandwich and offer it to him.

"If a black mark shows up in my employee file, I'm blaming you."

August actually looks regretful. "I really have tangled you up in my affairs pretty terribly, haven't I? Fiancée. Employee. Coconspirator. Aunt wrangler."

"I don't mind. Do you?" I tilt my head, offering him a chilled can of sparkling water.

His fingers brush mine warmly, lingering as he takes the can and leans back to look out over the water, his lips still curled up at the corners.

"No. Truth be told, woman, I don't mind it at all."

XIV

RIDE THE STORM

(AUGUST)

I have no fucking clue what to do with Miss Eleanor Lark.

For once, I'm not ready to pull my hair out when I say that.

I lean back in my office chair, looking out at the late-afternoon skyline.

Seattle is always strange this time of day. The sky wants to be bright and grey at the same time, until an odd smoky haze clings to the horizon and outlines the taller buildings and the tops of the trees. Right before it all melts up into a cool, deep blue that looks almost backlit.

Behind me, my laptop sits ignored. A minute ago I was engrossed in a project proposal Elle posted to the company intranet.

Her proposal was simple—adding a few more new characters to Inky's collection of friends to help bring him into modern times. The concept art is very similar to my aunt's, but not quite on point.

While Elle's great at adopting another artist's style, there are differences.

The penguin looks softer in her hand, a tad more whimsical.

I see her loving hand in every line with her Inky drawings. I can imagine her style as I read about her koala bear called Kiki, this sweet-as-pie creature who's always smiling and wearing a giant sun hat as she harvests tea leaves. Her own imagination gives Inky's new pals a fresh cheerfulness.

Honestly, I can't believe she's still here.

Putting all this work in with Aunt Clara.

Showing up bravely with a smile on her face that rivals her cartoons—especially after the way I curb-stomped her heart.

Facing me down.

Infecting me with her courage to say the shit I need to say, when I've been fighting myself for days to figure out how to make peace and give her the apology she deserves.

I never expected that we'd find a way to carry on.

If she'd taken my apology and told me where to shove it, putting an end to our bizarre entanglement, I wouldn't have blamed her one bit.

Somehow, though, she's still a part of my life.

And I can't deny just how much that eases the tension in my chest, freeing me to breathe again.

Fuck, why can't I stop?

Why is she always first, second, and third on my mind?

Why can't I forget how she looked straining under me, unafraid to show her pleasure, and every time she screamed, I just wanted to hear her louder, *louder*—

"Hey." A pencil bounces off the side of my skull. "Earth to asshole."

I jerk up, blinking.

My eyes are slightly sore after staring at the sunlight for so long.

When I swivel my chair, Deb is standing over my desk. She's trim in a navy blue sheath dress with short sleeves and a chunky black vinyl belt. She props her hands on her hips, eyeing me.

"Oh, *now* you notice I'm here?"

"You did try to blind me with a pencil." I kick the pencil away from my chair and send it skittering across the floor. "How long have you been here glowering?"

"Oh, I've been saying your name for like three minutes, nerd. You've been on Mars."

"Pardon me for being lost in thought. Someone has to do the thinking around here."

Deb bares her teeth, clearly not amused.

"Makes me wonder what you were thinking *about*." She smirks.

I roll my eyes. "Did you want something, or did you just come here to gab?"

"Yeah, stupid brother. Your *fiancée*"—she stresses the word, taunting but not cruel—"is waiting in the lobby. You forgot you were going to go out straight from work, didn't you? Since Elle's too polite to text you the kick in the head you need, I'll do it for her."

I blink and glance at the clock on my laptop screen.

6:07 p.m.

Fuck.

"I didn't forget," I snarl, standing quickly and throwing my suit coat over my arm. "I just lost track of time."

If I haul ass, we can still make our ticket time.

If we miss it, we can go out to eat until the next showing.

"Someone's in a hurry." Deb keeps smirking as her gaze trails after me toward the door.

"I'm *late*," I growl.

"Sure, sure, that's all it is," Deb says mockingly.

I stop before the door, impatience vibrating through me as I turn back to her. "Why are you being so smug?"

Deb whips out a folded paper she had under her arm and shakes it out so she can hold it up.

It's a tabloid magazine.

Elle and I are on the cover, sitting next to each other on the beach, passing a container of strawberries and another one with cold chocolate fondue back and forth. She laughs brightly with her hair in tangles across her face from the wind.

I just start swearing.

"How the fuck is someone *following* us this closely without being noticed?"

"Dunno," Deb answers too cheerfully. She taps her manicured green nails against the headline. *BAREFOOT BILLIONAIRE'S BEACH BOUDOIR!* "But you look like you're having fun for once, Mr. Barefoot Billionaire."

I grit my teeth.

The image stops me cold.

I don't recognize myself on that cover.

I'd taken my suit coat off. My socks, too, because Elle insisted that the sand would be warm under the surface if I just dug my toes in.

She was wrong—it was goddamned arctic—but I kept my toes buried in the silky-soft sand anyway while the wind flipped my hair. My vest was half-unbuttoned because she'd stuffed me so full of sandwiches it was getting uncomfortable.

And I'm laughing.

She's pointing toward the shore. A sea lion pup was doing barrel rolls in the shallows until it hit a deeper pool and sank with a splash, only to pop back up with a comically confused look on its face.

Even I couldn't help it.

The little pup almost reminded me of one of Aunt Clara's characters.

But that man in the photo—

I don't know him.

I only see myself in the mirror when I'm shaving and styling my hair, or in press photos.

I never smile.

I'm always serious, thinking about anything besides how I look, beyond making sure I'm professional and clean and respectable.

Yet around Elle, I turn into someone different.

Apparently, I become a functioning human being.

"What's that, big brother?" Deb teases. "Did you say something? Oh? You're stunned silent, is that it? Embarrassed someone caught you *smiling?*"

I just flash my sister a disgusted look.

Then I turn and stalk right out the door.

After a quick ride down the elevator, I stalk into the lobby. Elle's right there, staring at something on her phone, stifling a laugh with her fingers pressed over her mouth. I know that look, and I shake my head as I step closer.

"What terrible thing has Miss Joly said now?"

Elle starts and glances up at me with wide eyes.

She's sweetly casual today. The more time she spends with my aunt, the less she wears office attire and instead shows up in whatever's comfortable—and most fitting.

Today it's high-waisted jeans that hug her hips in lickable flows, clinging tightly to her legs, ripped in artful slashes over her creamy-soft thighs. Plus, a thin white long-sleeved crop top that exposes a dick-teasing flash of her belly. Her navel flirts in and out of the ragged holes in what used to be a long-sleeved black Cure concert shirt, now stretched thin with just a hint of screen print paint still showing here and there.

Her hair is up in a messy twist, secured with colored pencils. It falls in sprays into her face, a few tips kissing her eyelashes and the wings of color lining her eyes. Shades of pale green and blue match the remnants of paint on the shirt, making the tawny color of her irises flash like gold.

Her mouth is a rich rose pink, dotted with a subtle blue liner the same shade as her shadow, fading toward the kissable part of her lips in hues of blended purple. Paired with her chunky, strappy blue heeled pleather sandals.

She looks fun and flirty, while I'm the same stuffy overdressed ass-hole I always am.

". . . August?" Elle laughs, and I realize she's been talking to me this whole time. "Are you even listening?"

I shake myself. How does she make me lose my head just looking at her?

"Sorry, it's been a long day," I deflect. "What did you say?"

"I asked how you knew it was Lena."

"Because you always laugh a certain way when she says something inappropriate, and then you try to hide it." I arch a brow. "That girl never grew a brain-to-mouth filter."

"Aw! Aren't you the cutest fiancé, noticing how I look when I talk to my friends?" She hooks her arm in mine, bracing up on her toes to kiss my cheek.

She makes it look so natural, the way she leans into me with her scent wafting and the plush warmth of her mouth against my skin, my beard.

For a second, I give in and kiss her back, barely keeping a growl from exploding into her mouth.

"C'mon. If we drive fast, we'll just make our showtime," she whispers.

"If we're late, it's my fault." I let her tug me toward the parking garage exit. "I was wrapped up in reviewing your proposal."

Even as we step out into the dimness of the garage, she brightens, lightening the shade of the day. "Did you like it?"

"If we could get Aunt Clara to return to the series, it would be an excellent way to relaunch it for a new generation." I take the lead, drawing her toward the waiting car. I see Merrick already stepping out of the driver's seat to meet us. "I can see your personal touch, though. Will you let me see your portfolio sometime?"

The way she flushes so prettily, it's clear her portfolio is very damn personal.

"I—sure," she says, ducking her head before she quickly changes the subject. "Rick's driving today? It's not just us?" She glances at him as we draw closer. "No offense."

"None taken, Miss Lark," Rick answers politely, bowing as he opens the door for her. "Trust that I won't be accompanying you into the theater. You'll have each other all to yourselves."

I clear my throat, avoiding his eyes, while Elle's blush deepens.

She doesn't say another word as she ducks into the back seat, while I round to the other side and let myself in. Since we've cleared that hurdle, things between us have been at once easier—and far more difficult.

That day on the beach made this insanity too real.

We forged an intangible bond.

Whether it's friendship or something more, we weathered the storm I created and came out of it on the other side with a new understanding, a new trust.

That only leaves me more self-conscious than ever about the employees in the office whispering a little too loudly behind our backs. I can already imagine their comments, blabbing about how the girl with the magic touch finally revived the dead fish—*fish, really?*—and about how I am, apparently, quite fucking whipped.

First, I'm no one's simp. Not even Elle's.

Second, I shouldn't react, when this is all still pretend.

It leaves me feeling embarrassed nonetheless, and Elle's blushes and body language have made it clear she feels the same.

She still looks flustered as Merrick starts the car.

I offer an olive branch to the silence.

"Are you really making me watch a film called *Winnie-the-Pooh: Blood and Honey*? Hardly sounds appropriate for a children's franchise."

She snickers. "That's the point! It's awful but it's also pure camp. And since *Winnie-the-Pooh* is now public domain, people can do anything they want with the brand. I'm not watching it because I'm a big horror buff. I'm interested in the artistic freedom when copyright laws get loosened up." She flashes me a wickedly amused look. "Plus, a lot of people go to bad movies just to have an excuse to make out in the dark without missing anything important."

The copyright mention sobers my dick up, thinking of the case with Marissa.

Not enough.

Every time her hand touches my arm, her shoulder brushes me, her apple-sweet hair teases me, I remember how her mouth surrendered to mine.

Her heels digging into the small of my back.

How burning hot she was inside—so tight, so wet, gripping on me like she never wanted me to pull out.

I keep those thoughts to myself, letting Elle tease me as she pleases on the ride to the Thornton Place theater, just twenty minutes from the Space Needle and with a clear view of the spire jutting up to the dark, reddening sky.

She's still fucking impossible.

I'm just not sure when I stopped minding.

At the theater, I help Elle out while Rick pulls away to park. Elle slips her hand into mine so easily, not even seeming to notice that she's done it—or the way my fingers reflexively tighten on hers.

She looks over her shoulder, watching the car pull away. "So he's just going to wait in the car while we watch a movie?"

"He'll likely run a few errands, or enjoy dinner somewhere. I don't police what he does with his time while he's waiting to pick us up again. Let the man enjoy himself."

"You billionaires are so weird."

Damn it, I smile and look down at the top of her head. More butterflies, this time little paper-craft things woven into her hair.

"You don't like to wear the same look twice, do you?"

Elle tilts her head up to me with a soft, startled sound and shrugs. "I like trying different things. It's fun. And if I look awful one day, who'll notice?"

Me.

Very much me.

I really do need to stop.

Right fucking now.

Before this spins too far out of control to ever rein it in.

We join the crowds streaming into the theater but skip the line. I pass my phone over a QR code scanner, and we're waved through.

A question about concessions gets a wrinkled nose about syrupy Coke and greasy movie theater butter, so we skip it. As we make our way down for what promises to be a ghastly film I cannot *believe* I let this woman talk me into, I ask, "How did things go with Aunt Clara today?"

"She stopped packing up the studio," Elle answers. "Progress—I think? Though I bet she realizes I'm stalling for time by getting her to teach me how to draw Inky." Elle sighs. "Today she suggested I'm getting good enough to take over the line. I don't want that. It would be an honor, yeah, but it would just feel . . . wrong."

I glance at her, my chest going tight.

She doesn't just admire my aunt, does she?

Elle genuinely cares about her, and what's best for her.

She wouldn't even dream of accepting what could be a career-making opportunity, if it means taking anything away from Aunt Clara.

"The fact that you have her drawing again, even if it's only to teach you, is something no one else has managed. You're goddamned brilliant," I tell her.

Blinking, she casts me a startled glance before looking away with a blush that's so enticing I want to shove her against the nearest wall and kiss her breathless.

For someone so brazen, she can be surprisingly soft.

"It's nothing," Elle whispers. "If anything, I'm getting the good end of this. She seems to enjoy drawing again, but I know I'm a pest."

"You're no such thing," I toss back firmly. "She's not faking it, Elle. It's easy to tell she enjoys your company."

I don't expect the frank question that follows.

"Do you?"

"I—"

Fuck.

I certainly don't mind it.

How could I? I'm paying you well enough to not be too disagreeable.

But the way she looks at me—the near innocence with which she asked that question, that strange childlike wisdom that demands honesty—has only one answer.

"Yes," I say firmly.

Of course, she lights up like Christmas.

For such a complex, intelligent young woman, she's remarkably easy to please at times.

"Why the pause, *Gruffykins?*"

"Don't start." I roll my eyes. She hasn't let up on that Gruffykins crap at all. "I had to stop myself from demurring, if you must know. Honesty is the best policy with you."

"With me? Not with others?"

"Not for a long time." I sigh. The damnable thing about being honest is that once you start, you have to continue. "I don't outright lie if I can help it, obviously."

"But you deflect and close off," she finishes with a small smile like she plucked the words right from my mind.

"Guess those were the words I was looking for. Damn." I eye her. "You're starting to get me a little too well, Miss Lark."

Her lips shine with a mischievous grin. "You mean like how you only call me *Miss Lark* when you're trying to create distance."

"Not this time."

"Huh? Then were you"—she mock-gasps, fluttering her fingertips to her lips—"teasing me?"

"Now she catches on." I smirk.

With a delighted laugh, Elle turns to walk backward, pulling me along by my hand. "There may be hope for you yet." She dances away, dragging me toward the door to our assigned theater. "C'mon! The best seats are in the middle."

I let her drag me along like my arm is a leash.

She bounces into the low-lit theater. The previews haven't started yet, and we have our pick of seats in the sparse crowd.

True to her word, she plunks us right down in the middle, wiggling into the seat at my side and leaning against me.

Dutiful "fiancé" that I am, I stretch my arm along the back of her seat.

She fits against me so well, the curve of her shoulder tucking into my body.

My nostrils flare as I inhale her.

Of course, she smells divine.

Still not as good as that night with sweat and the fresh-washed shower smell, with the scent of my shampoo, *my* body wash on her, the smell of our sex clinging to the sheets and—

Enough.

I clear my throat, adjusting my seat so my slacks fit a bit looser around the hard-on from hell, and eye the blank white screen. "I hope you know I'm docking your pay for making me watch this."

"I hope you know being a freelancer for years means I probably know labor laws better than you do," she throws back without missing a beat.

"Nothing ever fazes you, does it?"

"Well, a few things," she admits. The hurt on her face as she ran away flashes in my memory. But she's still smiling, looking at me like I never did something so terrible, and it was all just a bad dream. "But I know you're all empty threats, Gruffykins."

I thud my head back against the seat. "You're never going to stop with that Gruffykins shit, are you?"

"Nope!"

Only, at some point she will.

At some point we'll "break up," and I'll never have to hear *Gruffykins* again.

We're not really together.

Even if we're together in the moment.

I'm saved from sinking into one of my ridiculous brooding spells by the lights going down and the screen lighting up with the usual green ratings screen for the first trailer. Elle makes an excited sound and burrows deeper into her seat, catching my wrist. She pulls my arm closer around her.

"*Cold,*" she whispers. "Keep me warm, Gruffykins."

It *is* chilly.

Dutifully, I wrap my arm around her slender body, pulling that delectable scent and delicious warmth closer.

I resign myself to seeing horrors beyond human comprehension as we watch the trailers. If the film itself is as campy as the previews, I've just condemned myself to new circles of hell.

As one clip blends into another, Elle stiffens, her eyes widening, before she turns her head subtly, her eyes cutting to the side.

"Um, I think I just heard a camera go off behind us," she whispers.

"You *cannot* be serious." I don't turn around. I trust her judgment, and I don't want to give us away.

She turns a little more, her gaze searching, before she faces forward again, slumping against me. "Maybe someone's just making a bootleg of the movie."

"Why? It's going to be terrible. Plus, this is the age of digital leaks."

"Hey. This is going to be a cult classic. Pure grindhouse masterpiece."

I frown. "Grind-what? What does coffee have to do with it?"

Elle stares at me. "Oh my God, you are an alien. So adorable."

"Stop using that word," I growl.

"'Cute'?" she ventures.

"Not that one either," I bite off.

Elle just grins unrepentantly. "'Sweet'—"

"Shh!" erupts from the row behind us.

"Oops," Elle whispers, dropping her voice—and herself, sinking down in the seat and wiggling closer. "Well . . . just in case they're watching us, should we put on a show?"

It takes a moment to get what she means.

I arch a brow.

"You're enjoying this part too much," I whisper back.

"Oh, don't flatter yourself, Gruffykins." She lets out a suppressed laugh and twists to face me, pushing up the seat rest that's been the only barrier between us. "C'mere. I'll show you how to do a stage kiss."

"How do you know how to do a stage kiss?"

"Theater kid. Duh. Are you really surprised?"

"Not in the slightest."

She grins and reaches up to stroke my cheek, my jaw. I don't realize how cold it truly is in here until the warmth of her slender fingers burns into me with their slight pressure.

"Tilt your head that way," she says. "I'll tilt mine the other, and then . . ."

As I oblige, she pushes up, her mouth coming close to mine, offering her sweet-scented breath. When her lips touch me, it's below my bottom lip.

A warm imprint of a kiss. Not the heated lock and pressure and slick caresses I suddenly ache for more deeply than I have any right to.

"See?" she whispers, her lips moving against my skin in caresses that rouse a shudder against me. "Easy."

Whispering back like this is awkward, to say the least. "I know it's dark, but can they not see our lips aren't touching?"

"Not with my head tilted this way," she answers. "My face blocks where our mouths would tou—mmn!"

I shouldn't have tilted my head to ease the slight strain on my neck.

Because suddenly those syllables are pressing into my mouth.

And I lose all sense.

All reason.

All control.

Her strawberry mouth fits mine like we were made for each other.

The whole damn movie becomes a blur.

The sounds of screaming, hacking blades, and sinister voices fade away until I can hear only our mated breaths. It's like no matter how we pretend, some part of us knows and draws us back to each other again and again.

Our dueling lips meld until there's no room to breathe between us.

Nothing left but the air sizzling between this kiss as my lungs grow tight.

I don't care.

Tonight, I'll indulge, even if I can't be the man Elle needs me to be.

I can't risk hurting her again, but for now I need to taste her more than I need to breathe.

Heat. Velvety skin. Lust.

The dark lusciousness of her mouth, so soft and reminiscent of the feeling of plunging into yielding flesh and feeling her arch against me. Her inner depths open to let my tongue probe and seek and claim within her. I feel every taste of her like I'm thrusting into her all over again, the cold of the theater vanishing when I'm just a thin shell over a dark roaring fire.

The way she submits to me.

The way she leans in and clutches at my shirt like she'll take everything I have, if only I just give it all up.

Give.

Some warped, deep part of me wants to.

Some devil part of me wants to break myself into pieces until I can be just as open as her, meet her halfway, feel this thing unrestrained as I groan and sink deeper into her mouth.

Mine, goddammit.

Mine.

Just for tonight.

I capture her lips, biting them hard enough to leave my mark, loving how her sweet flesh gives and plumps and rises for me.

Elle spills a whispered moan and goes trembling against me, her mouth so ripe and waiting.

"*August . . . ,*" she breathes, and I taste my own name in her mouth. It's never tasted this warm, this vibrant.

I'm definitely neither of those things.

That stark reminder of who I am—a stunted, broken thing who can only hurt her—dashes that heat and leaves me ice cold.

I break back sharply.

Fuck.

I feel like a human knife, all frigid edges, as she looks up with confusion. Then with a flicker of hurt, like a small animal hoping the carnivore won't sink its teeth in.

"Elle." I swallow hard. "I'm sorry."

There it is.

Her smile.

Lovely as always, and yet now I know it's not real.

"For what?" she asks brightly, turning to face the screen again. She nestles against me comfortably like nothing's happened, her head resting against my arm. "At least now we can be sure it was convincing." She glances at me from the corner of her eye curiously. "Do you think I should stay over tonight? Since we're clearly still being followed."

I look at her helplessly. I want to say something to bridge this distance, but what can I say?

So I only shake my head. "Not tonight. I'll be on the phone all night with the legal team. It'll just keep you awake."

"From the guest room?" Her lips curl in wry amusement.

"You've never heard me shouting at Little Key's lawyers."

"That's fair."

I turn my gaze to the screen as the previews fade, the screen goes dark, and then the flicker of the opening credits and music rises.

This disquiet feels wrong.

"Tomorrow night," I say impulsively.

Me, impulsive? Ha.

This little brat is scrambling my wires.

"Would you like to go ballroom dancing?"

A stunned look flies at me. "Wait. You're actually *asking* me instead of telling me five minutes before I have to be ready?"

Teasing. It restores some of the ease between us, and I smile slightly.

"I said I'd try." I snort.

"*Shh!*" rises from behind us again, more irritable than ever.

We both slouch down guiltily in our seats.

She stifles a giggle behind her hand, waiting before whispering, "You'd better get me a nice dress."

I can only hold my smile as I sigh and settle in to find out what kind of atrocity the rest of this film will be.

"I will," I promise, dragging her hand to my lips. "I won't have my woman looking anything less than fucking magnificent."

◆ ◆ ◆

For all that Elle insisted I buy her a nice dress, she's been cagey about letting me actually see it.

I hadn't even meant to go to the political fundraiser tonight.

I've already made my donations, and I'm not a fan of rubbing elbows with politicians or their orbiters, especially when anyone who shows their face is assumed to be currying favor for their own interests.

I have no need for that shit.

I make my own way, and I've staked my career on my good reputation alone.

Still, when I remembered the event had ballroom dancing, and I thought she might enjoy it, how could I resist?

We'll treat it as another publicly staged event. The wealthy donor introducing his fiancée to high-society movers and shakers.

Really, I just want to see her light up again.

I haven't seen her at all since Rick dropped her off yesterday with my credit card tucked in her purse.

I had to assume she went back to that same couture boutique where the staff know her, which is becoming her favorite store.

So I'm a little surprised when my bank alerts ping me with a four-figure purchase at a shop called Luly Yang.

Isn't that a bridal store?

I frown, racking my memory.

My thoughts start spinning, and I shut them down sharply.

Elle's just being Elle.

She'll probably show up in a wedding gown she's torn to shreds and covered in punk swatches of color in a tribute to mideighties Cyndi Lauper.

When Rick brings me to her grandmother's cottage, though, I think she can't find a new way to take my breath away.

Every fucking time, I'm hilariously wrong.

The door to the house opens before Rick turns off the engine on the G80.

I catch a glimmer of light like there's a small sun shining in the entryway of the Lark cottage. One glimpse builds so much breathless anticipation.

I'm barely aware of moving forward until my chest bumps the gate.

Until I behold the sunrise, captured in the shape of a woman.

Her dress is empress waisted, gathered at her ribs in a thin gold band. Her pale skin shines softly above a straight bodice, sheer layers of cream-colored fabric crusted in swirls of glittering gold.

It flares out into gold-embroidery sleeves so small they're almost straps, making celestial patterns down the front of the dress.

From the gathered waist, the dress sheets outward, a subtle flare falling to the floor and trailing around her. Despite its flare, the thin layers of fabric cling to her, offering hints of her thighs, her hips.

The hem of the dress is dyed in a soft rose gold ombré, fading up into the ivory of the fabric. The color draws out the whiteness in her skin, accenting her red lips.

Fuck me senseless.

Her hair is pulled up in a loose bun, her neck circled with a delicate golden chain dotted with tiny moons. There's a matching bracelet swinging from her right wrist.

Her makeup is fresh faced, dewy, and instead of her usual boldness, she's painted her lids in a pink-and-gold gradient.

This woman is the entire dawn.

I can't fucking breathe as I look at her.

I don't know—I just know if she kisses me tonight, I might be trapped in her spell forever.

Ever since Charisma's death, I've sworn I'll never love again—if you could even call what we had *love*. I swore I'd definitely never trust again. Never let anyone else past the walls and barbed wire that keep me safe from more agony.

Now I, August Marshall, am a damn liar.

I can't deny how much my heart drums for Elle Lark.

Thankfully, she breaks the silence with a shy sound, ducking her head. She lingers in the doorway, fingering her skirt.

"It's dragging on the floor," she murmurs, giving it a small swirl that shows off her glittering heels in pale rose gold straps. "I'm afraid of getting it dirty."

I pull the gate open immediately.

"Let me." Wild horses couldn't stop me from going to her.

Rick leans out the driver's side window of the vehicle. "Sir, I can—"

"I've got it," I snap. I don't even look back at him.

I'm not letting another man touch her.

Only me.

I'm staring like an adolescent kid as I hasten up the walk to the front step.

I'm an awestruck fool, but tonight I'll suck it up and be foolish if I must.

And I feel wonderfully stupid as I adjust my tuxedo to sink down on one knee, gathering her skirt carefully. I layer the trailing end over my arm like a bridal train.

Just a glimpse of her legs, slender and enticing.

My heart drums harder, teasing my dick to full attention, before I stand and make myself look away from her legs, instead meeting those tiger-gold eyes.

"There," I say, careful not to lift her skirt too high, holding the fabric delicately. "I'll try not to walk too quickly."

"Thank you." There's something softer about her tonight. She looks at me through long lashes dusted in gold and smiles. "You look really nice in a tux."

"I'm just another penguin now." I grin at the irony. "Perhaps I would've been more striking if I'd mirrored Inky's patterns." I turn to escort her down the walk, where Merrick waits with the rear door open. "No one will even look at me, Elle. Not standing next to you."

Shit, I can't let myself look at her, but her airy gasp catches, perfectly timed with the erratic rhythm of my heart.

I'm so damned tangled up inside, and for once, I'm glad.

It's hard to remember she isn't truly mine tonight.

That this is all just a game.

Not when her warmth walks so close to me, and I want to feel her skin so badly.

Soon we're at the car, shut up inside. The silence as Rick pulls into traffic is less awkward and more anticipatory.

Elle laughs, leaning against the door.

Her skirt fills the space between us, stretched along the seat to keep from dragging on the floor.

"We're not looking at each other. Don't tell me we got all dressed up in our fanciest clothes to ignore each other? Is that a rich people thing?"

It's an August thing, I think, but I don't say it.

I glance at her, quirking my lips. "You have a point. We're acting like high school kids on their way to prom."

"Ugh, we are." She bounces to face me, drawing one leg up under her dress and leaning toward me. "Isn't it fun, though? To feel all jittery again. To feel a little shy to look at each other just because we're wearing such nice stuff."

"I am not *shy*," I grumble.

But damn her, she's right.

It's hard to look at her because every time I do my entire body pulses, and I don't just mean my cock.

"You're shy," she teases, poking my cheek.

I turn toward her quickly and snap my teeth at her fingertip.

Elle jerks back, her eyes widening before she erupts into laughter. "God, you really are a wild animal!"

"I am no such thing."

She parts her lips—but if she's started to say something, she stops. I don't need to hear it.

We're both thinking it.

I was an animal that night, wasn't I?

Heat roars through me, and I have to look away from her again.

"Hate these things." I clear my throat, tugging at the band around the neck of my tuxedo.

"Then why wear it?"

"It's a must for these stuffy-ass events. Full black-tie formal."

Elle makes an odd sound that's half scoff, half giggle. "Sounds like you don't want to go."

"I don't." At least, not for the reasons that have anything to do with more political BS.

"Huh."

I feel something prodding my arm and look down.

Elle pokes the crook of my elbow.

Over and over again, like she can't keep her hands still and has to occupy them doing something.

Pretty little weirdo.

"If you don't want to go," she asks, cocking her head and still poking me, "why are we going?"

"I thought—" With a growl, I stop and catch her hand, holding her fingers firmly. "I thought you might enjoy it more than annoying me."

Elle's grin says I've played right into her hands. Or played her hand right into mine.

Whatever.

"I won't have any fun if you're miserable, August. Can't say I'm much for big speeches either."

"So what? That's every day of the week that ends in *y*."

"Liar." Laughing, she twists in the seat, but somehow she has her back against my side, my arm wrapped around her, my hand still her prize. She tilts her head back against my shoulder, looking at me upside down.

Again, I'm awestruck by both her frailty and her warmth—and the way my body burns everywhere for her slender, sleek curves. "Where would you rather be tonight? If it was just you, and you'd skipped the fundraiser . . . what would you be doing?"

"Hm." I run my thumb idly along the side of her hand as I think.

"Reading at home," I conclude. "Watching the moon over the waves."

"Then let's go do that! We'll watch the waves all dressed up, and you can read to me."

I cock my head. She can't be serious.

"That does sound like a better way to spend a beautiful evening," I admit slowly.

"So what's stopping you?"

"An overdeveloped sense of responsibility, for one."

The kitten's eyes glitter with mischief.

"Dude, live a little. Play hooky with me."

I tilt my head. "You really don't mind putting on that dress just to sit in my living room and read a book?"

"I really don't," Elle answers with frank sincerity. "I don't fit in with your fancy crowd anyway. I just thought you wanted to go, so I did. Plus, I got to see you dressed up." Her eyes crease at the corners. "I also made you blush, so in my opinion the night's already peaked."

Instant scowl.

The girl knows how to push my buttons.

"I did not *blush*," I grind out.

"Oh? You took one look at me and turned into a human raspberry." Her smile softens and she sighs. "I know you think I'm pretty, August. It's okay. It doesn't have to be a *thing*. It's just one friend flattering another, and I'm all about the flattery."

I exhale deeply, annoyed that she's already won me over.

"You have absolutely no shame, do you?"

"Teeny bit." She squeezes my hand and lifts the other to pinch her fingers together, barely a micron apart.

This woman is going to drive me out of my ever-loving mind.

I lift my head and look at the privacy divider. It's open just a crack, so he can hear when I call, "Merrick?"

"Yes, sir?"

"Turn at the next light. Take us home."

"Are we dropping Miss Lark off along the way?" Merrick reaches back to push the divider open enough to meet my eyes in the rearview mirror.

"No," I answer, looking down at the little wretch still tucked cozily in the crook of my arm, as if she does this every day. "No, we're not."

Elle grins with a pleased wiggle, burrowing against me.

I have no idea what's going on here.

Still, I don't push her away as Rick changes lanes and takes a sharp turn back toward my little hidden slice of Alki Beach.

The quiet is different then.

Peaceful.

It shouldn't feel so comfortable sitting with Elle like this, but it is.

It's easy to slip into idle thoughts, watching the streetlights pass and cars flowing past us, casually aware of how well she fits against me.

She'll make a place for herself no matter where she goes, and suddenly it's like she's belonged there this whole time.

When Merrick pulls into the small paved lot just off the street in front of my house, I'm almost reluctant to let her go.

He waits patiently while I guide Elle out of the car—and instead of trying to navigate carrying the train of her dress, I just sweep her up in my arms, looping the hem of the dress over my shoulder.

Elle yelps, then laughs, clutching at my jacket.

"You are getting *way* too used to carrying me around."

"You hardly weigh more than a feather. It's easy." I exchange a brief nod with Merrick and turn to carry her down to the beach and the scattered path of planks leading to my walkway over the water. "You'd have sunk right into the sand in these heels anyway."

"Fair point." Elle pauses, lifting her head and looking up at the night sky. Her eyes close, and an expression of guilty pleasure settles over her face. Soft gold wisps blow loosely over her brow. "Hey, just stay here a minute. It smells nice."

I stop, standing there awkwardly, until her expression draws me back.

Watching her experience the night like she's never smelled the Pacific breeze before. I wonder how long it's been since I stopped to notice it myself.

Yes. I smell that coolness, that crispness, that hint of something like mint and spice, brine and sweet night air.

More than anything, I smell apples.

Her.

Her scent radiates through me like I could cradle her inside me.

Yet I can't even cradle her in my arms for long because I blink, and there's a wriggling bundle against my chest. Knocked out of my reverie, I open my eyes to find Elle squirming forward to hike her dress up and pull at her heels.

I should be used to how spontaneous she is by now.

"What are you doing?" I ask.

"Taking my shoes off. You're right. They'll sink in the sand." She flashes me a wicked smile. "Put me down and come on."

I know better than to question her at this point.

I wait until she's done yanking her strappy heels off, then set her down on her feet. She immediately drops her shoes and gathers the skirt of her dress up like she's stuffing a load of laundry into her grip, ungainly and eager.

Somehow she goes from ethereal to adorable in two seconds flat.

"Take your shoes off," she orders. The night is in her eyes until blue and hazel war with each other like candles in the sea. "Let's go!"

I have no idea what she's planning.

Not until she goes racing across the pale, gritty sand toward the rolling waves. Her slender feet leave prints behind her.

I stare after her. "Elle, hold up, that's freezing—"

Wasted breath.

With a shake of my head and a sigh, I bend down to pry my dress shoes and socks off, leaving them next to hers. Just for good measure I take off my jacket, cummerbund, and the neck band as well, dropping them in a pile.

Then I do something I've never imagined I'd do in my life.

I follow this wild, reckless woman across the sand, my footprints melding into hers, and go tumbling into the icy waves after her.

It's like sticking my feet into a vat of ice.

I let out a shocked gasp and almost stumble to a halt, while Elle patters a few more steps into the shallows before squealing, her laughter rising up over the night.

"Oh my God, that's *cold!*" she cries.

"I could've told you that." I take a few steps toward her into calf-deep water that soaks the hems of my slacks, making them cling to my legs like a frigid film. "It's Puget Sound in February. Were you expecting a sauna?"

"Okay, smart-ass." Visibly shivering, Elle takes a few dancing steps backward, the water swirling around her ankles. "Keep being sarcastic and I'll dunk you."

"You will not." I lunge toward her and catch her waist, pulling her against me.

Our warmth collides, two opposing storm fronts swirling around us—body heat and winter waves.

"And you will not go a step more in the dark," I say. "You know what the riptides can be like out there."

"Yeah, I know." Undaunted, she leans into me. She's still holding her dress above the waves, her pretty, slender calves speckled in the dewdrop spatter of sea spray, her curves lush against me. She tilts her head up, asking for a kiss, and I want so much to answer that unspoken request. "But I got you out here, minus the stick up your butt, didn't I?"

That insolent little mouth, pink and full.

Her tits rise in pale arcs above her bodice.

The flicker of her pulse against the thin skin of her throat.

The way I feel her hips so close to mine, our clothing not nearly thick enough to mask that raw heat.

The sound is freezing right now.

And I can't feel a damned thing but fire.

My fingers clench convulsively against her back. The dip of her spine glides against my knuckles. She inhales, her smile fading into confusion, her eyes searching mine.

"August?"

I can't.

But it still kills me to let her go, step back, and take a deep breath of the cutting air to clear my head.

"Apologies," I deflect. "I was worried you'd fall."

A lingering look tells me she doesn't believe me. But she doesn't press, either, letting her smile return as she steps back, spreading her arms and pretending to wobble. Her dress trails into the shallows, swirling around her gracefully and soaking up to the knees, turning almost fully transparent and offering the silhouette of her slim, enticing legs.

"I might," she teases, her eyes wide. "Oh no, whatever would happen if I fell into the murky darkness of these treacherous inch-deep waters?"

I roll my eyes, folding my arms. "You'd be very wet, and I'd have to haul you inside before you wound up with hypothermia."

"Oh no." She feigns pure drama.

Brat.

She tilts a bit more, and the breeze pulls several locks of hair loose, licking the strawberry-gold strands against her neck.

"I'm losing my balance, Rhett. Whatever shall I do? Someone save me—save me! Where is my brave hero?"

This wretched child.

I'm not laughing.

I'm *not*.

I'm not smiling either.

That feeling pulling at my mouth is purely phantom.

Imaginary.

And I'm most definitely not uncrossing my arms to sweep my hands through the water. My fingers go numb as I splash her.

"I'm not your hero," I say. "I'm the kraken, and you're going under."

Elle shrieks, bursting into laughter as she dances back. Her movements slow with the drag of her wet dress. Her *extremely* wet dress, the splatters of water hitting her chest and stomach in splotches that offer tempting views.

Pale skin.

Lacy underthings.

Apparently, I'm the architect of my own doom because it's damned impossible to look away from her.

"You *jerk*," she sputters, tugging where her dress sticks to her skin. "Don't you dare do that again."

"Miss Eleanor Lark," I say, stalking closer, "you should know by now that I don't take well to being ordered around."

She freezes. "Oh shit."

"'Oh shit,' indeed."

There's a frozen moment when we hold still like we're hunter and prey. Then with another yelping laugh she turns and sprints along the shore, flitting in and out of the rolling waves and kicking up arcs of spray, her fingers fumbling with her dress to hike it up and free her legs.

I give her a second's head start before I dart after her.

There's no hope for her to outpace me. Not with my longer legs and that dress tangling her up and weighing her down.

I let her stay ahead of me anyway.

I can't believe I'm enjoying this.

I'm fucking laughing, unrestrained, until I'm winded whenever she glances over her shoulder to see how close I am, yelps, then sprints faster with laughter trailing behind her.

The back of her dress is scooped enough for the delicate lines of her shoulder blades to entice me, the channel of her spine glittering with kicked-up spray like clear pearls. Her hair comes looser from its pins until it's a banner, begging me to reach out and wrap that sunset gold in my fingers.

I'm almost on her.

Ready to catch her.

When her foot catches on something, and this time her yelp isn't so playful.

It's panicked as she goes tumbling forward, her arms flailing out.

I'm there in a heartbeat, one last lunge of speed.

Diving, I catch Elle around the waist and pull her up—but her momentum has us both, and I can only twist, using my body as a cushion for her as we spill down on the sand.

I land on my back hard, but not painfully, the damp sand absorbing much of the blow.

Elle comes crashing down on top of me, her elbow catching a glancing blow against my ribs before she goes sprawling.

We're soaked in an instant—lying in the waves, with the water rushing up to our waists and then receding.

All I can feel is *her*.

She molds wetly to me like we're melting into each other. Dissolving in the water, caramelizing in the heat of our flesh, and as she inhales sharply and pushes herself up with her hands braced against my chest, I know she feels it too.

Nicole Snow

Her skin is spangled in diamonds—wet spray drenching everywhere, turning her into a pale sugar jewel. Her soaked dress looks clinging and completely transparent now, offering me a mouthwatering view of everything I've been craving since I found out what she tastes like, what she feels like, what I've been struggling to pretend means nothing all fucking night.

Her mouth glistens as her lips part.

Her eyes are golden witchfire.

And her flesh is so damn soft in my hands, where I instinctively gripped her hips—and now I have zero intention of letting go.

I try to be practical.

Try to rein myself in, when there's nothing stopping my cock from taking what's mine.

"You all right?" I manage. The words scorch my breath into sparks.

"Uh-huh," she answers—dazed, raspy.

There's a trembling silence.

She should get off me. I should lift her away.

But our eyes lock.

And then there's no hope left for us.

I don't know if I kiss her first or she kisses me.

I just know my hands are tangled in her wet hair, stroking it back from her face, pulling her against me as I seize her mouth.

"Elle," I whisper.

She answers with a needy moan, wrapping her arms around my neck, pulling herself against me until we're all friction and burning skin and wildness that could steam the ocean dry.

Her hunger is a challenge, baiting me to meet her ferocity as she kisses me hard, her tongue sliding against my mouth and inside to tangle and twine with mine—until she gasps as I tumble her over on her back, pinning her down and taking the upper hand.

Her mouth is mine.

Soon, all of her.

No more banter tonight.

No more defiance.

No more play.

I'm serious as hell as I subdue her with slow thrusts and firm strokes of my tongue, nipping her bottom lip just to feel its ripeness.

I taunt her with long, lingering licks and swift flicks against the tender flesh inside her mouth.

Until she goes soft underneath me, whimpering with delight.

Until she arches up, and *fuck*, I can almost fit between her thighs. The wet fabric clings to us both, this simulation of fucking that tortures us with denial.

It hurts.

It *hurts* that every time I thrust my tongue inside her mouth, I'm not thrusting in her, and I need something to take the edge off.

My fingers catch her dress.

I curse how long it is as I hike it up, *up*, peeling the wetness away from her skin until I can touch her naked waist.

Her ribs.

Her breasts, peeling the damp bra away to knead them against my palms.

I groan with every liquid roll of flesh spilling over my fingers.

And I nearly burst when her sounds turn high and needy, sugar drops of her pleasure poured between our crushing kisses.

Everything is slick.

Her.

Me.

Everywhere our flesh glides together, where our need meets.

I flick her nipples with my thumbs and she bites me, begging my name in a ragged groan and bruising my lip. I rock my hips against hers, and her body meets mine, pleading with her legs spreading and her thighs flanking my hips.

I can't fucking stand it anymore.

It's too much sensation, the sand and the waves, the night breeze and the burn of her skin, the taste of her and the desire flaming through me to leave nothing but ashes behind.

I feel like I'm dying and coming back to life.

I don't know.

I don't care—

I just need her.

So I plunge deeper into her mouth, chasing every taste of her, then pull back as I feather one hand down over her smooth stomach and find the line of her panties. When my fingers brush between her legs, I know it's not just the ocean water leaving her soaked.

"Elle," I whisper, almost begging.

Begging her to let me off my leash.

Her eyes slip open.

She's intensely beautiful beneath the starlight, disheveled against the sand, this wild creature of the night.

No one's ever looked at me with her softness before.

Like she sees past my issues, past my rough edges, and she'd pull them in and dull their sharpness until I can't hurt her anymore.

She curls her fingers against the back of my neck, making me shudder with her delicate touch stroking against my skin.

"Please," she whispers. "Even if it's the only time . . ."

It can't be.

I won't let it be.

But I can't make that promise in stone either.

I can only steal the plea from her lips in another fierce kiss.

I can only glide my palm down her thigh, pulling it against me, spreading her open.

I can only slip her panties aside, rip my slacks open, fit flesh to flesh.

As she inhales, tensing, holding herself against me with her mouth liquid and her flesh squeezing the head of my cock, I do it.

I surge.

It feels like I'm one with the waves as I thrust deep inside her, needing her so much that I can't wait.

Can't hold back.

Can't build up to it.

Can't go slow.

Not when I need to feel her wrapped around every inch of me, taking me in, taking me home.

Elle cries against my lips, clutching me tighter, digging her nails in my neck. I let out a growl as I pull her into me, moving her body, drawing her into my rhythm.

The rhythm of the tide and the stars spinning overhead, the rhythm of my beating heart, the rhythm of desire.

This is more than pleasure now.

More than crude lust.

More than sex, when I feel her in my bones and she fills the cavities inside me.

I can't rip my eyes off her to save my life.

Her pleasure is incandescent—the way she writhes, reaches for me, gasping with every deep-rolling thrust that brings us together in this fiercest way.

We are the night.

We are the waves.

We are the lashing wind, caught in this primal dance and thrashing wildness.

Her tight, gripping body is sheer heat, sheer madness.

A dark fire inside her that I chase to feel again and again, plunging into her, searching, *needing* to find and grasp something that I can keep for my own.

I'm so close.

So fucking close and almost reaching, almost there, almost—

Fuck!

She lets out a cry as I fuck her over the edge.

That tightness squeezing my cock is crushing; the heat is scorching, and the wetness makes me glide so sweetly inside her—

Goddamn!

I find that dark fire—or it finds me.

With one more savage thrust, I push to her depths, everything swelling as my spine ignites.

Then Elle Lark consumes me with the ocean.

I'm still growling and kissing the sweetness from her lips when I come, making her *mine* this once.

Just for tonight.

And I fall with her.

I fall apart with the violent rip of pleasure tearing us in half. Mating with pure fire, unafraid of the consequences.

I give in and let myself be utterly consumed by the burn.

XV

THE SUN AT NIGHT

(ELLE)

I wonder if my tits are going to be all over the tabloid rack in the Walmart checkout lane in the morning.

I can't believe we just had sex on the beach, barely a few hundred feet away from hills where anyone could have looked out and seen us down here rolling around in the spray.

I don't know if I want to hide my face in mortification and stretch as languidly as a sated cat—or run away from August before he sticks the knife in me again.

We're still sprawled next to the waves washing against the shore.

I've probably got hypothermia at this point, but I can't feel it when he's got his arm draped around me and he's soft and lazy and quiet, his chin resting on the top of my head. My soaked dress weighs a thousand pounds, and even if August hadn't just fucked my legs to jelly, I think I'd have trouble getting up and walking to either go inside his place or run away and never come back.

Except I don't want to run.

I don't want it to hurt this time when it felt so good to have August inside me, to taste him on my lips, all while the stars spun overhead like they were binding us together.

But I don't know what to do in the silence either.

After a hesitant moment, I peek up at him. He's relaxed and calm, with his eyes closed and his breathing heavy. His hair is a mess, slick with sand everywhere except for that one untamable strand.

It still falls over his brow like it's as stubborn as August himself.

I bite my lip and make myself break the silence, tensing to push away if I have to.

"So is this . . . okay?"

I'm expecting him to shove me back. Go stiff and cold.

But the only tension is the tightening of his arm around me, pulling me against the warmth that beats back the freeze of the ocean mist rolling over my calves.

"It is." A lazy rumble, sex in his voice. Sex and a warmth that my needy heart wants to believe is *affection*.

August's eyes open. They're no longer glacial blue, but a clear, welcoming summer sky.

His lips are softer, thawed from their forbidding line.

My heart skips as he gives me a searching look.

"Frankly, I don't know what the hell I'm doing with you, Elle. Something just started moving like a freight train out of control the moment I saw you tonight. I had no prayer of stopping it, even if I wanted to—and I didn't."

My teeth sink into my lower lip.

My heart trembles, unsure if it wants to rise high in a joyous trill or plunge low in despair.

"But you wanted to," I say.

I know he's going to say it. That he doesn't want this, or me. That it's a mistake he never should have made.

Instead, all he says is, "Only because I don't want to hurt you again."

"Then don't." My hand rests against his chest, tangling my fingers in his wet dress shirt. It's transparent against his sleek lines of sculpted muscle. "The only way you could hurt me right now is by pushing me away."

"Come the hell here," August coaxes, his hand spreading against the small of my back.

My heart makes its choice and leaps high as his mouth descends on mine for a kiss.

A slow, tender, gritty kiss.

I can't even taste him.

He's all sand and brine, and I suddenly remember a horrible little bit of trivia—that a lot of white sand on many beaches worldwide is actually parrotfish poop.

I try to spit without spitting in his face, scrunching my nose and mouth.

"Ptheh. Pfft. Sand!"

August lets out a half-exasperated laugh. "I have sand in other places and would prefer not to."

"Race you to the shower?" I pull my hand back and scrub it against my mouth, grinning up at him.

August only looks at me skeptically.

His eyes skip down to my legs, still mummified in the waterlogged dress.

He doesn't need to say a word when his eyes return to my face.

I'm still gonna kick him just as soon as I'm untangled.

"Fine." I pout. "Carry me to the shower. I only wore this stupid dress for you, anyway."

"Did you, now?" he whispers with that subtle humor I'm starting to catch on to more and more.

"Well, I wanted you to think I was pretty." I huff. Hopefully the cold keeps me from blushing. "Now *carry me inside*. I want naked skin and hot water. I won't be nearly as pretty if I lose my feet to frostbite."

"Yes, we can't endanger such pretty feet." August pulls away—but only to rise and dust himself off, sending sand showering everywhere. He steps away and fetches his jacket and our shoes, then comes back and slips his arms under me. I squeak as he lifts me up, but it turns into a growl as he strains. "Did you gain weight?"

"I'll kill you," I bite off. "In your sleep. Kill you dead."

He *knows* it's my waterlogged dress.

Jerkwad.

And said jerkwad nearly kills me with a quick boyish grin, there and gone again, fast as lightning and striking harder.

I didn't think he knew how to smile like that.

He's surprising me every day.

And I'm falling harder every minute.

After last time, I wanted to get over this so bad. Just because a guy's dick wants you doesn't mean *he* does. But every "fake" kiss, every idle touch that came so easy has left some tiny part of me holding on.

That tiny part is never going to be able to let go now.

Not when my thighs still ache and I'm sore and full inside. Every part of me is still tender from his touch.

I'm content to lean against him and let my eyes close as he carries me across the sand to the wooden walkway leading across the water to his house. Now that I'm not burning up inside with desire, the cool breeze and icy water are really sinking in, and I huddle closer to August's warmth, shivering as my skin pricks with goose bumps.

"Almost there," he whispers gently. "We'll get you warm."

It's already working.

The promise in his voice ignites new heat in my core.

I press my lips to his neck and hold on tight as he carries me inside to the bathroom.

This time, it's slow as we strip each other out of our soggy cloths. I suddenly want to cover myself, when I've never been truly, visibly naked with him before. Never seen his body completely when he's tall and hard and subtly scarred with old marks that make me want to know every story, every old hurt, every place I can kiss to learn the hard, tapered power of his body.

His skin feels as cold as mine as our arms slip around each other and lips find lips.

Every kiss leads us back to warmth.

With lips, with touch, with the heat of the shower spray. With the way we slide together, the way we fit so perfectly.

The soft whispers, the lazy sighs, the groans.

The deep, languid thrusts that could stretch on until morning.

All the unspoken things build higher, hotter and hotter, until I feel like as long as August holds me, takes me, finds his way so deep inside me, I'll be home.

With him, I'll never be cold or lonely again.

XVI

WASH US CLEAN

(AUGUST)

I'm making a colossal mistake.

If this were a corporate contract, I would halt it immediately, figure out where things derailed, and correct course.

But Elle isn't a damned project.

I can't rewind time.

And I still can't call this something that went *wrong*.

Rather, it's the setup for something terrible later on, when Elle either betrays me—or I betray her warmth and trust when I can't accept the honest sweetness she gives me.

Right now, though, my mind is somewhere else as I lick the water away from her skin and she wraps her legs around my waist and buries her face in my throat with soft cries of *August, August, August*.

How can a mistake feel like it's the only truth I've ever known?

This feels more right than anything I've ever known in my life.

Like *she's* the only good, true thing I've ever known.

When we come down from our high, we stay silent under the shower spray with my lips pressed to her brow. It's hard as hell to pull away from her.

Hard to want to move at all, but we can't stay like this forever.

Slow kisses and light touches become murmurs, soap, all warmth and lazy caresses with warm towels until I'm not sure if this is bathing or foreplay.

Later, when we're clean and tired and sated, I wrap her in my robe and carry her to bed.

Not the guest room tonight.

I can't stand more space between us.

Tonight, I need to hold on to this messy thing of ours like it's something I want to cherish for the rest of my life.

Elle forms a small bundle against me, sleepy and soft and just right, her head pillowed against my stomach as I turn on the bedside lamp and open an old leatherbound copy of *Robinson Crusoe*.

I barely manage to read *I was born in the year 1632, in the city of York* before she's gone.

This strange, quiet angel rests against me with her starry lashes trembling against her cheeks and her lips parted.

I turn the light off, but I don't sleep.

I'm still a nocturnal animal, and tonight I've captured the sun.

I just watch Elle dream, clasping her tight until the hours run long and the morning comes to steal her away.

◆ ◆ ◆

Unfortunately, morning *does* come.

And with it, an absolute brat of a morning lark that's been cursed upon my life.

I don't have to open my eyes to know it's too bright, and I'm not just talking about the sun for once.

I mean the fucking madwoman who's been poking me in the head for the last five minutes despite my dogged attempts to ignore her and keep sleeping.

"Gruffykiiins," Elle sings for what must be the fifth time. "Wake u—EEP!"

That's it.

I've had it.

I drag one eye open and snap my teeth at her finger.

This time, I catch it.

She freezes, staring at me with wide eyes, while I hold her finger prisoner between my teeth, biting down just hard enough to taste the warm salt of her skin and keep her from escaping.

"Go back to sleep," I mutter incoherently around her finger.

Elle smirks. "You have to let go if you want me to understand what you're saying."

I do let go—just long enough to speak.

"No. Mine," I say, barely giving her a second to realize she's free before I capture her finger again and flick the tip of my tongue against it.

Her face goes crimson.

Even if her cheerfulness annoys me, she's adorably sexy this morning, shamelessly nude and sitting cross-legged with her hair a mess of gold falling down her shoulders. The red undertones in her hair almost match the warm, well-loved pink of her nipples.

Blushing up to the tips of her ears, she's still grinning. "Don't stick it out if you're not going to use it—*oh God*."

That *oh God* is my fault.

Because the moment she chastises me to *use it*, I do.

Pushing myself up, I capture her mouth in a kiss.

Just a glimpse of her wide eyes before they sink closed and she sways into me, catapulting me into heaven.

She tastes like everything made to ruin a man.

Submissive and sweet and so damned needy.

Even when she melts against me, she's never shy about demanding what she wants. Her lush little mouth begs me to slip deeper inside her, to take more, to storm her with a pleasure that could keep me here all day.

It's too easy to ignore the entire world when I'm this addicted to the way her lips give every time I gently sink my teeth against them for slow, teasing bites that coax small moans from the back of her throat.

She's easy to fall into.

She could almost make me stop caring that it's not noon yet.

I'm still drowsy as I slip my tongue slowly inside her mouth to glide against hers, savoring every moment before I draw back to take in the stunned, confused look on her flushed face with as much satisfaction for her dazed eyes as for the wet, plumped gleam of her lips.

"Now, what's that face for?" I ask softly.

Elle blinks rapidly and shakes herself. "I just . . . I wasn't expecting you to . . ."

So brazen, most of the time.

Yet so shy when she has to admit how she really feels around me.

"I know." I catch a lock of her sleep-wild hair and tuck it behind her ear. "I don't know what we're doing, Elle. I wanted to kiss you, so I did."

Her smile peeks out slowly like the sun finding its way past the clouds.

"Well, I could be okay with that."

I smile and kiss her forehead—then sprawl back against the bed again, draping an arm over my eyes to block out the damnable light. "Could you be okay with turning off the sun and letting me go back to sleep?"

"Nope!" she chirps—and this time she pokes me in the ribs. "If you get up, I'll make breakfast."

"You can cook?" I lift my arm, just enough to peer at her.

"Hey!" Elle folds her arms over her chest. Pity. I was enjoying the sway of her naked tits. "What makes you think I can't?"

"You're a chaos monster." Grumbling, I push myself up on one arm. "I don't trust you not to burn down my kitchen."

Her delectable lower lip thrusts out. "Oh, please. I've never burned down anyone's kitchen. Only set one on fire *once*. Singed a little. A lot. A little a lot. Gran only had to replace three cabinets, I think?"

I stare at her flatly.

Elle lets out a dramatic sigh, slumping forward.

"Fine. *You* cook breakfast."

With another look, I drag myself out of bed.

My entire body feels heavier before noon, slow and dull and sluggish. Sunlight is my kryptonite.

"Looks like I may have to if I want my house to survive intact."

Elle grins and bounces out of bed, splendidly naked in the morning light.

The sunlight isn't so terrible after all when it highlights her ass.

"Got you out of bed," she gloats.

I'm torn between watching her peach curves and reaching for my dresser and something to cover my own nudity when the reality of this little monster's manipulative ways truly sinks in.

Narrowing my eyes, I yank the drawer open and pull out a soft-worn button-down that's been retired to housework, and I fling it at her head.

"Wretched girl."

"Eee!" Elle squeals, flailing at the shirt. She ends up with it draped over her head and giggles, yanking it down. "You're twice the asshole in the mornings, you know."

"Just mornings?"

"You're *slightly* more tolerable at night." A sly smile tells me exactly how tolerable I am when she knows I sent at least six orgasms crashing through her last night. She wriggles into the shirt, then turns and sprints toward the door, the unbuttoned shirt flapping around her. "First one to the kitchen gets to cook!"

"Elle, you're not—"

Too late.

She's gone.

Thank God I've got excellent homeowner's insurance.

I stare after her for a moment, then chuckle helplessly and pull a pair of pants out of the drawer.

This girl.

Life hasn't been the same since she literally crashed into it—and I wonder if it ever will be again.

◆ ◆ ◆

Right about now, I'd kill for a little normalcy.

Or perhaps I'm just feeling extra homicidal today.

You'll never force me to admit aloud that I enjoyed frittatas and coffee with Elle this Monday morning, while she flicked through—cartoons.

Of course.

Coming in to work was actually pleasant with her excited chatter stealing my attention, one eye on my laptop and the other on her throughout the drive.

She was thrilled. Aunt Clara asked to see her pitch portfolio, which features her original characters, versus her work portfolio, which has a variety of styles and mediums tailored to win over new clients. Before I could express my curiosity to see it myself, Rick let us off at the office.

Where my lawyers are waiting.

With Marissa Sullivan and *her* lawyers.

I've been so wrapped up in Elle Lark that I half forgot we're meeting this morning. The moment I walk into the office and see Marissa sitting in the reception area, impatiently tapping her heels, I know she's bombed out again.

Piss-donkey drunk.

Her eyes are dilated, her lips slack, and her scowl is comically childish. The two men flanking her on both sides look uncomfortable. She's every bit the spoiled Mafia princess with her handlers, minus the street wars and bloodshed.

Too bad she still raises enough corporate hell to count.

The moment Elle and I step off the elevator, her head comes up sharply. Marissa's sharp glare hits me first before she turns it on Elle.

"You," she slurs, pointing a manicured nail at Elle, "are wh-*whey* too perky."

Elle smiles.

Perkily, I might add.

"Hello to you too, Marissa," she says. "You're looking nice this morning."

"Don't you try to sheet-talk me!" Marissa snaps. The two men with her look uncomfortable, stirring in their seats. She flicks her glare back to me. "You guys are *late*."

"I am perfectly on time," I counter cooly, glancing at the receptionist.

She offers a nervous smile of agreement. "The legal team is already waiting in the conference room with refreshments, Mr. Marshall."

"Very good, thank you." I catch Elle's arm lightly and lean in to kiss her cheek. "Go see Aunt Clara. I'll see you at lunch."

"Gotcha." She winks, and I have to fight not to smile as she bounces back into the elevator, her pretty bright-blue skirt swirling around her.

"Bitch. Way too *perky*." Marissa aims a disgusted look after Elle.

I pinch the bridge of my nose and turn to push the door to the main office open. "If you'll come this way, please. We can make this quick."

I have no damn intention of entertaining what will no doubt be an insultingly low buyout offer to prevent this from going to court.

I wouldn't listen even if she offered up her entire company for a dime.

It's tense and silent, save for the click of Marissa's heels as she stalks after me.

I can feel every eye in the room on us and low murmurs in our wake.

"Get off me!" Marissa hisses at her lawyers every now and then. I suppose it's when they reach out to steady her.

Holding in a sigh, I deliberately thread a path through the open-plan workspace so she has more space to wobble around without crashing into anything.

I won't be liable for damages if she falls and breaks something.

My legal team—Mr. Oxford, Miss de Silva, and Mr. Tanden—are already seated at the long, glossy walnut table in the window-studded conference room. They're crisp and professional with their heads bowed together as they pore over briefs and whisper conspiratorially.

The murmurs stop as soon as we enter. With smooth precision, the three rise, smiling coolly.

Smiles that falter as Marissa staggers in and slams her purse down on the table with a loud *slap!* Just walking, her stylish grey pantsuit has come half-unbuttoned at the waist and looks completely wrinkled.

"What firm you with?" she demands harshly, glaring at my lawyers. "Bet've never heard of 'em." She plants her hands on her hips with a triumphant smile, while her own embarrassed team takes tense flanking positions again. "*I* came prebeared. The besht lawyers in Sheetle."

Sheetle?

God help us.

Thankfully, Miss de Silva shakes from her frozen, thin-lipped smile and says, "Our private practice exclusively serves Mr. Marshall. We aren't publicly advertised, although I'm sure your lawyers are all skilled *professionals*." The way she stresses *professionals* leaves no doubt about her opinion of Marissa's behavior. "If you'll all take a seat, we can begin. Would anyone like coffee?"

No one wants coffee.

I don't think anyone wants to be here a second longer than they have to be.

Marissa's lawyers settle down stiffly across the table.

I take a seat next to my team, while Marissa stumbles into a chair opposite me like a petulant child and glares.

She was the one who called this meeting, dammit.

I'm simply obliging her stupid request.

And I refuse to let this situation get out of control again, so I take the lead, steepling my fingers over the glossy wood.

"Miss Sullivan," I begin. "I believe I can offer you an acceptable agreement. Your intellectual property claim has no merit. However, I can understand the pain and suffering that your father endured after his partnership with my aunt ended, and the subsequent addiction that resulted. While the statute of limitations on an emotional distress case wouldn't extend this far, I'm willing to overlook that to offer you a generous posthumous settlement on his behalf. Drop the copyright case today, and I'll gladly negotiate a number with you."

My lawyers offer affirmative murmurs.

This is the best strategy we came up with to stop the circus. A reasonable sum to solve a very big problem.

Marissa's lawyers look relieved. I don't doubt they'll advise her to take the deal and scram.

Only, Marissa Sullivan is smirking.

An ugly, lopsided smirk that ruins her magazine-perfect beauty and turns it into a caricature. "You think that's it? You think I want your *money?*"

She's still intoxicated, but suddenly she's speaking clearly. Determination gives her words clarity and force. She practically rips her purse open and pulls something out.

A battered sketchbook, its cover worn and its pages tattered.

She flings it down on the table so hard the resulting *smack* makes Miss de Silva jump.

"What's this?" I stay motionless, eyeballing Marissa.

"My father's sketchbooks," she announces. "Proving a copyright claim."

She flicks the pages open. The sketchbook stops on a page full of concept drawings, clearly showing iterations working up to—Inky the Penguin.

It's all there.

Motion sketches, base geometry, various phases of the big magic ink spot on his belly. It's clearly developmental work refining the ideas into the finished chubby character we know today.

Only years of practice keep me expressionless.

The fury boiling inside me feels like an unsheathed sword.

Fury, and pain.

This can't be real.

I refuse to fucking believe it.

"And you can prove that these sketches predate Clara's . . . how?" I ask sharply. "None of these are dated. Do you intend to carbon-date Lester Sullivan's sketches versus hers right down to the day of creation?"

Marissa's expression falls, then tightens into a sneer. "Oh, I don't need to. This is enough that even if I lose the case, I'll create a big shit-pile. I'll ruin you, Marshall. I'll ruin *her*. Tear her shitty fucking legacy down brick by brick till there's *nothing* left. Your precious IP—your stupid fucking penguin—will be worthlessh then!" Her voice descends into another snarling slur as she snatches the sketchbook back, holding it protectively. "Save yourself the trouble. Sell Little Key to me and sh-sail away."

My lawyers look troubled.

Her lawyers look pained and embarrassed.

I don't know how the hell I look.

But I know I feel like a chainsaw-wielding maniac.

I keep myself contained—barely—as I meet Marissa's eyes without blinking.

"Leave," I clip.

She recoils. "Excuse me?"

"I said *leave*," I repeat firmly. "This meeting is done. You're once again not in possession of your full senses, and I won't talk deals when you're under the influence and unable to consent to anything legally binding. Leave, Miss Sullivan. I will ignore the insult of you appearing for this discussion drunk, and hope that this time you can make your way home with assistance." I can't resist the pointed reminder. "Perhaps we'll have a more civil discussion another time."

She gapes at me.

Her lawyers shift uncomfortably.

I narrow my eyes.

"I am not above having you escorted off the premises, Miss Sullivan," I growl.

Marissa makes a flustered, angry sound and jumps to her feet.

"You'll regrets this!" she snaps. "I *will* ruin you, you preppy fuck. Tear your fucking aunt apart! She took *everything* from my family—you understand? From *me*!"

Her voice cracks.

Real emotion.

Genuine grief.

I hate this shit.

Hate the complicated history that makes her feelings valid even while her actions are unconscionable.

Or are they?

I damned well intend to find out.

All I say is "Good day, Miss Sullivan."

She stares at me for another bitter moment, trembling with rage.

Then she turns and storms out on unsteady steps, her hair whipping behind her with the toss of her head.

Her lawyers stand. One sighs wearily and nods.

"Mr. Marshall," he says. "Thank you for your patience and your time."

He turns to follow his colleague and client out, then leaves us alone.

As the door to the conference room closes, Mr. Tanden sighs. "That went well."

Oxford shakes his head. "I expected a disaster. She's been publicly falling apart for months."

"Indeed," I answer. "I just wonder what's triggered her downward spiral." I swivel my chair toward my team. "Would you be able to contact a private investigator without that information becoming public?"

Miss de Silva winces. "That . . . I don't know what you're thinking, Mr. Marshall, but stalking your opponent in a civil suit for damages usually doesn't look good in front of the judge."

"Then it's best if the judge doesn't find out." I stand, barely able to contain my movements, my teeth grinding hard enough to make my jaw hurt. "Make it happen discreetly. Get me in contact with someone who can find out what the hell's driving Marissa Sullivan to an early grave."

I turn to walk out.

"Mr. Marshall? Where are you going?" Mr. Tanden calls after me.

"To find out the truth," I fling back, right before I slam the door open and step out onto the office floor. I beeline for the elevator, ignoring a voice trailing in my wake.

There's something Aunt Clara isn't telling me, and I have to find out what it is.

XVII

BREAK IN THE CLOUDS

(ELLE)

I think I've died and gone to heaven.

My idol, *the* Clara Marshall, is looking at my concept sketchbook.

I've never shown *anyone* this. Not even Lena or Grandma.

I haven't had time to look at this work in years: I pushed it to the back of my mind, told myself it was impossible to ever go anywhere with my silly little characters, Kiki the Koala and her cast of friends.

Before art school, I wanted to make her the star of my own series.

After art school, after learning about the freelance life, I tucked my sketches away and told myself I'd go back to them one day when the time was right.

Even as *one day* faded further and further into the back of my mind while everyday life took over, and eventually I stopped thinking about Kiki and her cozy evening cups of eucalyptus tea at all.

Until I mentioned Kiki to August.

Until the other day, when I was working on refining my lines as I sketched Inky over and over again, only for Clara to rest her hand over mine and stop me.

Elle, dear. I can feel your love for this darling penguin of mine.

But don't you have anything you love of your own? Isn't there anything you want to show me?

I'd never have presumed to offer.

But after she asked, I went home last night and dug out the presentation portfolio I swore I'd always present to a publisher but never did.

I've been bubbling out of my skin this morning, and not even seeing Marissa Sullivan seething as she waited for August could stop it.

But now, I'm about to *explode*.

Clara and I sit in the little reading nook under the window while she slowly pages through my sketches, her touch on the paper almost tender. A small smile curls her lips.

It almost seems like she approves.

My heart is so messed up right now.

As if August hasn't already got me popping like crazy, now Clara Marshall has me breathless.

I suddenly wish I hadn't ever put Kiki and her sunny smiles away.

Why did I stop thinking about her? Why did I give up?

Why did you start smiling even when you didn't mean it? And why didn't you realize it until August noticed?

Clara reaches the last page and lets out a satisfied sigh.

"So much personality in these lines," she says. "Kiki nearly leaps off the page with this sweet joy. Kids would love her. Have you ever pitched her to a publisher?"

I shake my head. "No, ma'am. I . . ." I shrug. "A few of my art instructors tried to push me toward modern art. They said I had a better eye for it, and I should try to develop a passion there instead. I tried—I even had an exhibit once—but . . ."

"It wasn't where your heart is," Clara finishes with an understanding that nearly breaks me. I can tell her heart is still with Inky. So why is she giving up? "Your heart is in these drawings. I can tell."

I smile weakly. "I think so. I—"

I stop and scream.

Because the door to the studio slams open, banging off the wall so hard it rattles the framed pictures.

My heart stops like I've been shot in the chest as I whip around.

August stands in the door, looming and dark with the light from outside cast against his back. He glowers into the room, hot fury simmering off him like smoke.

"Clara Marshall," he growls, his voice deeper than I've ever heard it. "We need to *talk*."

Oh shit.

Did something happen?

Even if August scares me out of my skin, Clara doesn't react with more than a thinning of her lips as she carefully closes my sketchbook and sets it on the table between us.

"Not in that tone, young man," she bites off with a coolness that's as much of a warning as a rattlesnake's shaking tail. "You will calm down this instant and lower your voice. You will not ruin the pleasant tea we were just having."

"Tea? *Tea?*" August snarls. "I don't care about tea, Aunt Clara. I care that I just met with Marissa Sullivan, and she showed me Lester's fu—"

"Finish that foul word, August Tristan Marshall," Clara lilts calmly, standing and fetching another tea mug, "and it will be your last. Sit down and get your dastardly temper under control. Have some tea and apologize to Elle. *Then* you can tell me what's wrong."

August bares his teeth, clearly seething.

Whatever's wrong, it must be bad.

My heart remembers how to beat again, but it's sluggish with worry.

If being chastised like a moody teenager by the aunt he loves so much can't defuse him . . .

Oh, this is going to suck.

I shake my head, smiling and standing hastily, then gather my sketchbook and portfolio. "I don't need an apology. You guys clearly need some privacy. I'll make tracks."

"Absolutely not, young lady," Clara says, and despite August still bristling, that tone plunks me right back down in the chair like someone's pushed me. "You were here first. August, sit."

Her sharpness is just enough to cut through August's tension. He sighs and steps into the room, closing the door more delicately.

"Marshall women," he mutters. "Bossy as hell."

"You're no better," I point out. "You give orders like you own the place."

"Because I do," he answers pointedly, trudging across the room and dropping down into the third chair at the table, folding his hands. His blue eyes crackle, but at least he seems a smidge calmer. "I have a twenty-five percent share. Deb has another twenty-five. Aunt Clara has the fifty percent controlling stake."

"Which is why all your blustering about firing me was absolute nonsense," Clara says, setting a teacup in front of him before reclaiming her seat. "Do be careful with that. Don't spill anything on Elle's sketchbook."

August starts to open his mouth but stops, looking at my battered book on the table and ignoring his tea. His expression eases, but the lines around his eyes are concerningly deep. He flashes me a glance, that unruly lock of hair drifting across his eyes.

"May I?"

"O-oh." I don't know why I'm suddenly embarrassed, but I clear my throat and look away, tucking my hair back. "S-sure."

"Thank you."

I don't say anything. I *can't*. I'm suddenly more nervous than I was when Clara was looking at them. I don't know what I'll do if August laughs, or something worse.

But there's only silence, except for the soft sounds of paper against paper.

Chest tight, I glance back shyly. I can't look at him directly.

But then I stop.

Because he's really *looking* at the pages.

He has the intense concentration I've seen on his face before that says whatever he's looking at has his full attention.

He's staring at my drawings, absorbing them, taking time to appreciate them.

To appreciate something I created, like my silly little doodles are actually worthy of a focus so intense.

I really am about to blow to smithereens.

Fireworks everywhere, bright and hot and bursting.

While August looks at my sketchbook and I look at him, I realize Clara's looking at me.

Her smile is small and thoughtful, her eyes glittering with warmth.

I clear my throat, looking away again. That seems to break August's focus, and he murmurs, "Hello, Kiki."

My heart goes to pieces right there.

"Kiki the Koala," he says again. A touch of rumbling approval, softening the anger that roughened his voice only a minute ago. "How did you come up with her?"

"Oh, well . . ." No one's ever asked me that before. It takes a second to find my voice, and I breathe deeply. "Gran," I say. "Gran and Lena. When we were little, Lena and I fought like wet cats in a bag. We'd be best friends one second and hate on each other the next. Sometimes we didn't mean it. Sometimes we did. We were both really headstrong. And when we swore we'd never talk or play again, Gran would call us inside and sit us down with tea for everyone." The memory warms something inside me, like holding my heart in front of a crackling fire. "She'd always ask us to try to figure out what was in today's cup. Anise, lavender, vanilla, honeysuckle, jasmine, mint. We'd get so distracted guessing, we'd forget what we were even fighting about. And then she'd bring us cookies, and we'd all enjoy the rest of the afternoon." I smile, ducking my head. "So I turned that into Kiki. There's no problem she can't fix by sitting people down with a cup of eucalyptus tea and getting them to talk."

"Teaching children conflict resolution and love for a good cup of tea," August says, his lips curling. I fizz like champagne, breathless and bright. He turns to the last page, closes the back cover, and gives me those stark blue eyes again. "I like it. It's a damn good concept. There's a warmth to her that creates an immediate connection to the page."

Oh no. Am I about to start crying just because August gets my drawings?

I smile, trying to hold it back. "Don't embarrass me like this. I can't cry in front of your aunt."

"Of course you can, dear," Clara says. "It's always better to cry with joy."

I shake my head. I need to divert the subject quickly, or I *will* start bawling.

I glance back to August, biting my lip.

"Hey, are you okay? You look tired."

"I'm worn out," August answers slowly, before his mouth creases and he turns a dire look on Clara. "I'm tired of being lied to."

Oh crud.

Wrong direction.

Clara draws herself up, lifting her chin. "If you have something to say, young man, be direct. I don't appreciate insinuations."

"I don't appreciate deception," August throws back. "She had Lester's sketches, Aunt Clara. His developmental work. She's going to use it to prove he created Inky first. Did he? Is there merit to the claim? Can she date the sketches to before your own?"

Say no, say no, I plead. I know it can't be true. My idol wouldn't do that. Clara's such a kindhearted, thoughtful woman—she has integrity, a good heart.

Tell me everything I believed in as a little girl wasn't a lie.

But she doesn't say anything.

Her eyes lid and she looks at the window, her expression blanking into stubborn, glassy emptiness.

August slams a fist against the table.

The teacups bounce, clatter, splash.

With a muffled squeak, I scramble to pull my sketchbook and portfolio away.

"Damn it, Clara!" he snarls. "You can't stay silent on this. This is the whole future of Little Key—your life's work!"

"Yes, yes," she says icily. "It *was* my life's work, son. Now that work is done. What does it matter who owns or publishes the Inky books? They won't disappear just because Miss Sullivan has taken over."

"It matters to *me*!" August roars. "I won't have her ruining your reputation, besmirching your good name, shitting on everything you built over all the years! Where's your spine? Where's your love? Where's your pride? What happened to the woman who raised me?"

Clara turns a slow, heartbreakingly sad smile on August. "She realized some things are more important than owning an idea."

I don't understand.

There's something weird there, like something haunting her, some terrible secret even deeper than this.

August must realize it too.

He goes silent, slumping back in his chair and staring at her in a silence that stretches on longer and longer, until I can't take it anymore.

"If you win the case, I had an idea," I venture slowly. Breaking the silence feels mortifying, especially when they're still looking at each other and not me. "Maybe to keep Little Key afloat and revive interest in the brand, we could relaunch the pen pal program."

"Pointless," August mutters, crushing the idea and my heart as carelessly as he'd pulverize a dazed wasp under his heel. "Children these days text. Send DMs. They don't write letters by hand."

"Oh," I say faintly, forcing a smile. "Yeah, I guess you're right. The novelty probably would wear off pretty fast . . ."

"Oh, don't be stupid," Clara snaps. There's a *thud* under the table. August squints one eye and jerks his leg back, wincing.

"Ow!"

"I'll kick you again if you ever speak to Elle so dismissively again," Clara bites off, and I flush. "Apologize. And listen to her *properly*."

To his credit, August looks a little shamed.

He glances at me, offering his hand. "I apologize. I shouldn't be taking my temper out on you. We can discuss your idea another time."

"It's hereditary," Clara mutters.

August rolls his eyes, but when I place my hand in his, he gives it a squeeze.

"I'll think about it, all right? I'll need to do a little market research. Retro is in. There may be a way to spin it to make the idea viable. It's a good one. We just need to find an angle and crunch the numbers."

That *we* warms me a bit. Making me a part of it, telling me he's taking it seriously. I squeeze his hand back, but that apology isn't enough for me.

"I don't think so," I say. "You want an angle? I'm going to give you one firsthand."

He blinks blankly. "I don't know what you're talking about."

"Block some time off tomorrow," I say with a smirk, "and I'll show you."

XVIII

STORM OF DESIRE

(AUGUST)

Hell is a real place, and I am in it.

I stand frozen in the doorway of a kindergarten classroom—Elle on one side of me, hot as hell in a red paisley print pair of capris and a sleeveless pink blouse with her hair in a ponytail with a matching paisley scarf, Miss Joly on my other, wearing an almost sadistic smirk.

When Elle said she would show me, I had no idea she meant *this*.

A room full of screaming kindergarteners, their teacher calling for them to calm down because Miss Joly has brought new friends to see them.

Surprise: they don't calm down.

They erupt into pure chaos, screeching, *The puppy lady! I wanna pet the puppies! Where are the doggos?*

They swarm the door.

I immediately duck out of the room, stepping back into the hall and flattening myself against the wall like there's a raging river bearing down on me.

Snickering, Lena Joly steps through the door to hold back the wave while I stare at Elle with my nostrils flared.

"What is this insanity?" I demand. "Have I mentioned I'm not good with children?"

"Isn't that part of the problem with Little Key?" Elle smiles.

Miss Joly leans back out the door, giving me a skeptical look. "Dude. How are you bad with kids? You publish children's books, don't you?"

"I do no such thing," I bite off. "I'm the temporary executive of a children's publisher. I'm focused on business strategy and long-term market planning—not audience engagement. My aunt enjoys those squirming little *things*. I do not."

That just makes Elle grin wider, and now I understand why she and Miss Joly get along like bandits.

Because behind that sweet, pretty smile, there's *definitely* a sadistic streak.

"You'd better learn faaast," Elle teases, catching my hand.

She pulls me along after her as she turns to walk into the room.

"Elle—Elle, *no*—"

Too late.

She marches me right into the gaggle of tiny creatures.

Goddamn, they're bright. They're loud.

They're a churning sea of pastels and ruffles and primary colors, sticky fingers and dirty knees and pigtails and freckles and gap teeth. They swarm me like ants crawling over an apple.

I freeze, holding my hands up to keep from touching any of them.

The teacher claps her hands together.

"All right, guys! Settle down," she says. "Miss Joly brought her friends today instead of the puppies. Say hello to Mr. Marshall and Miss Lark. They're going to lead craft time today."

"Craft time. We are?" I ask weakly.

"We sure are." Elle hefts her enormous bag with a grin.

I can't quite call the screams that follow cheers.

Or words, even if I catch hints of my name and enthusiastic *hellos*.

Or even human language.

What they are is piercing, hitting that special ear-breaking decibel level that only kids this age can reach. I wince with a knuckle in one ear.

"Admit it," I mutter, pitching my voice under the chatter. "You're still angry with me, and this is revenge."

"Little bit," Elle teases as she rummages around in her bag and pitches something cylindrical at me. "Now grab some glitter glue, and let's get to work."

I instinctively snap the little container of glitter glue out of the air, staring after her as she saunters across the room.

The subtle sway of her hips looks as enticing as ever. The gaggle of hairless rats trailing after us is infinitely less so.

How are they so loud?

And why do they smell like . . . *children*?

Something bumps my arm—and I realize it's Miss Joly's elbow.

"Tuck your tongue in and quit staring at her, hound dog," she says dryly. "We're writing pen pal letters today. So sit your butt down and help out."

I'm not—

I don't know how—

Ah, *fuck*.

At least I don't shy away from hard work.

I look down at the tube of glitter glue and roll up the sleeves of my dress shirt.

Then I move, wading carefully through the tiny munchkins pulling at my legs, careful not to step on them as I work my way toward one of the activity tables.

Before I can even sit down, small sticky fingers catch mine. I frown down at a little brown-haired girl with her hair up in a blue bow and a giant googly-eyed hippo on her T-shirt. "You can sit with me, mister," she lisps.

"Yes. Yes, thank you?"

She just beams and drags me over to the low tables.

I have to nearly fold myself in half to fit on the end of the child-size bench, bowing my legs over both sides.

The teacher goes around the room, passing out stacks of cardboard, crayons, markers. I watch as Elle settles at another table and starts passing out the things to the kids.

Okay.

Okay, I should be doing that, too, right?

I lean over the little girl's head as she plunks down next to me and pick up the stack of colored paper. "Here you go," I say, passing her a sheet.

"No!" she exclaims in a squeal. "That one's green! I always get the *purple* one!"

". . . purple. Right. Purple." I really don't want to set off the tears, so I quickly take the green sheet back and fish out a purple one before handing it to her.

And so it goes, down the entire table, giving them each the color they want.

"Don't start writing or drawing yet," the teacher says as little hands scramble greedily for markers and crayons. She claps her hands together. "We're going to fold them first. Remember when we made Valentine's cards? Do what Miss Joly, Miss Lark, and Mr. Marshall show you."

Shit, I'm supposed to be teaching them?

I glance desperately at Elle again for help.

She catches my eye with a sweet little smile and pointedly creases her sheet of bright-blue paper in half along the long side, folding it into a card shape.

Right.

"Like this," I say. Why am I so anxious? I have my own sheet in green—the sheet the little girl rejected—and I set it down and smooth it against the table.

The children mimic me solemnly, *very* seriously focusing on creasing their pages in half. The little girl's so intent on it she practically has her nose on the page, but she's making a mess.

"Careful," I say, gently nudging her hand. "You're bending the corners."

"Oh no!" she gasps, then pouts up at me. "Will you show me again?"

"Of course, Miss—what's your name?"

"Sara!" she says happily.

"All right, Miss Sara. Watch me."

I fold her paper for her carefully, showing her with slow movements until it makes a perfect crease. She claps her hands together with that ear-splitting squeal again.

"It's so *good*!"

"You can be that good with practice," I say, right before the teacher's voice rises again.

"All right, everyone, we're writing to our pen pals today," she says. "Pair up with the people next to you and start writing letters. Say nice things. When you're finished, you can decorate your letters and give them to each other."

Sara bares her teeth up at me in a wickedly joyous smile.

Goddamn, children are terrifying.

"You're my pen pal, mister!"

"I guess that makes you mine. Do you know how to write a letter, Sara?" I look down the rest of the table. "Do all of you know how to write letters?"

I have no idea what their answers are.

It's all just a blur of noise from the few who are listening.

"Slow down," I say desperately. "Okay—okay, let's just listen, okay? You should start the letter with 'Dear' and then the name of the recipient. So I'm going to write 'Dear Sara,' and then I'm going to write what I want to say to her. At the end, I'll sign it. 'Yours, August.' That's how you write a letter to your friends."

I have no idea if any of that got through.

They just all blink at me, writing utensils poised up, their mouths open, before chatter erupts happily again as they start scribbling on their construction paper.

Well, fuck.

I tried.

Sara looks up at me quizzically. "What's your name again?"

"August," I say.

She frowns. "That's a month."

"It's a month, but it's also my name. Do you know how to spell it?"

She shakes her head, her eyes wide.

"All right. Why don't you get that white marker? It'll look nice on the purple."

She grabs the last marker from the center of the table, wrestles the cap off, and stares up at me, and I realize she's waiting.

"A," I say, watching her draw an enormous, scraggly *A* that takes up half the inside of the folded paper. "U . . . G . . ."

It takes almost five minutes to spell my name.

By then she's made a mess all over the page.

But she seems to be having fun, at least.

I steal the last marker, a red one, and write *Dear Sara* at the top of my page.

"I'm going to write something nice about you," I say. "You can just tell me hello, if you want."

"Okay!"

Sara sets busily to work. I'm not sure if she's writing in any known language; it mostly looks to be squiggles and a few random stick figures.

Still, she's enjoying herself, and that's the important thing.

They all seem happy.

I shake my head slightly and set my marker to the page, the red bleeding in fuzzy lines on the soft green paper.

Thank you for being my friend, I write. That's a good thing to say to a little girl who's claimed you, isn't it? *Sincerely, August.*

After I finish, I glance up and find Elle watching me, even as she stops a little girl from putting a glitter glue stick into her mouth, handling her with a gentle touch.

A touch that turns into a little tap of her lips as she blows me a kiss.

I clear my throat, looking away quickly.

I hope like hell my face isn't turning red in front of all these little devils.

Not that they'd notice, anyway.

They're having a grand time, slashing messages onto their construction paper, trading off glitter glue sticks and, worse, loose glitter.

Glitter that gets puffed in my face as Sara tries to get a canister open.

The can pops, pouring glitter everywhere in a silvery eruption.

Closing my eyes, I jerk back and try to swat it off with my hand—but it's useless.

Glitter showers me.

From behind, I hear Miss Joly's raucous laughter and Elle's giggles. Spitting a little, shaking my head, I swipe at my eyes, carefully opening them and then looking down at myself.

I'm *painted* in glitter.

There's a wall of it down my front, all over my shirt.

All over my slacks.

It's even in my mouth, and when I shake my head it showers down from my hair.

Sara clutches the near-empty canister, looking up at me sheepishly.

"Sowwy," she mumbles. "Sowwy, Auggie."

"It's okay," I manage, though just talking makes me nearly choke on more hell-glitter. "No one got hurt. I'll clean it up."

"But who's going to clean *you* up?" comes from over my shoulder, light with sweet laughter as Elle catches my arm. "Here. There's a wash station this way. I'm going to steal *Auggie* for a minute, okay?"

"Okay!"

306

Nearly blind with glitter, I let Elle pull me to my feet and nudge me toward the wash station. It's not hard to tell she's struggling not to bust out laughing again as she wets a paper towel in the sink and starts swiping at my face.

"Wow," she murmurs. "Didn't think you'd get this into it."

"You're not funny, brat."

"Liar." She flashes that adorable smile up at me. "You want to laugh. Admit it."

"If I inhale too hard," I say through my teeth, "I'll be digesting glitter for a solid week."

Elle giggles and gently draws the paper towel across my brows, cleaning delicately around my eyes. "Sara's taken a liking to you."

"She has the charm of a jackal cub. Cute. Scruffy. Unsettling."

"Oh, please, you aren't scared of that little thing."

"Her voice could crack glass."

"That's just how kids are. *I* think you like it."

I give Elle a sour look. "You've made your point. Yes, they're enjoying themselves." I glance over at the table I left. Sara's happily trading a glue stick back and forth with another little girl, both of them spackling their cards with streaks of shimmery stickiness. "I think our target market might be slightly older for actual pen pal activities, but we can certainly create a vertical of secondary merchandise for this age group."

The next thing that touches my face isn't the paper towel, but Elle's lips—brushing a light, chaste kiss to the corner of my mouth before pulling back. I glance back to her, her pink lips shining with traces of silver.

"Thank you," she murmurs with a sweet smile. "But we're not done yet. Brush yourself off and go give your little friend her card."

"You've got glitter on your lips." I brush my thumb to the corner of her mouth. "It's a good look on you."

"If you're nice here, you can do something a little more hands-on about that later." She grins.

"Does that mean I'm forgiven? And you have no further intention of torturing me?"

"For now," she says airily—then flings the wet, glitter-crusted paper towel at my chest as she spins on her heel and flits away. "But I have every intention of torturing you."

I stare after her, catching the paper towel.

That woman.

If we weren't in a kindergarten class . . .

Let's just say I'd make her regret tugging my leash.

I finish wiping my face off, brush my clothing off over the trash can, and return to my seat.

I suppose I can't give Sara an undecorated letter, so I draw a heart on the front in glitter glue and shake my hair out over it before it dries, filling it in almost completely in silver.

"Done!" Sara crows, holding her card up triumphantly. "All done! It's for you!"

She thrusts it at me like a weapon.

The thing is soaked in glue, covered in so much glitter it bends in half, but I take it anyway and open it.

The only part that's legible is my name, and even that's questionable.

The rest is all squiggles, the number 3, a few hearts, a stick figure, and I think that letter might be an *F*.

"Great work," I say, forcing a smile. "What does it say? It's pretty. You did a good job."

"It says we're gonna be friends always, Mr. Auggie!"

She flings herself at me in a hug that almost crumples her card.

I pat her back gently, holding the card away from her so she doesn't get glue in her hair, but the glitter was a lost cause the moment she hugged me.

She pulls back spangled. Her parents are going to murder me when she goes home like that and infects their house with the silver plague.

"Here you go." Shaking my head, I pick up my card and offer it to her.

Another shrill, ecstatic squeal. She actually hugs the letter, crumpling it, then pets the glitter heart like she's petting a cat. "Pretty!"

"Can you read the inside?" I ask.

She opens it sharply and shakes her head.

"I see my name," she declares. "I know my name!"

"It's good that you can read your name." Even if I'm still worried about asphyxiating on glitter, I chuckle. "It says 'Thank you for being my friend.'"

Her eyes grow round and wide.

"You really mean it?" she whispers. "You mean it, we're friends?"

"Friends," I answer firmly, glancing over to watch the other children.

Elle was right, I think.

She has good instincts, and she knew better than I did.

Not only are the kids trading their letters and happily interpreting their squiggles, but they're happily tottering around to show off their letters to other friends. There might even be new friendships forming.

Writing letters really does bring people together.

Maybe Inky's time really isn't past just yet.

It must be an hour before they're done shouting around and laughing—and clearly very sleepy. The teacher, Elle, Miss Joly, and I help marshal the munchkins into the washroom to get the worst of the glitter, glue, and marker streaks off them.

As if this is common routine, as soon as they're done in the washroom, they toddle out to blankets and folded mats taken from cubbies in the wall, claiming a spot on the floor and rolling their mats out to curl up.

As I help Sara scrub her fingers off, I glance at Elle. "Nap time?"

"Story time," she answers, teasing a glob of glue out of a little boy's hair. "And you're going to read to them."

I sigh, but without much exasperation this time. "You're really grinding this in."

"Mm-hmm."

Smug little wretch.

"All clean!" Sara proclaims, and holds her hands out for me to dry.

I wipe her fingers off one at a time with a towel and lightly pat her shoulder. "Go get your mat and find a good spot."

With a bobbleheaded little nod, she darts off, bouncing toward the wall cubbies. I wipe a little more glitter off my hands, watching her while Elle shoos off the little boy with clean hair.

"You're better with them than I expected," Elle says.

"I said I'm not good with children. I didn't say I'm a complete imbecile with no common sense. It's not that difficult to make them happy. Just be nice to them."

Her lips curl.

"Seems like a good rule with just about anyone." Her smile widens. "I thought you said being nice was pointless?"

"They're *children*, Elle. What kind of monster do you think I am?" I toss the towel at her. "No, don't answer that."

Her grin says it all.

I just shake my head as I let her drag me out into the classroom to an actual adult-size plush chair.

The children have arranged their mats around it like sunflower petals. Elle pushes me down into the chair, then steals a book from the top of the stack the teacher offers her and slaps it into my hands.

"You're up, Shakespeare."

"You are enjoying this *far* too much," I grumble, but then I look down to see what she's given me.

It's something about a puppy that pokes.

It's a very ugly puppy.

Well, I suppose puppies don't need to be show winners to poke things.

I crack the book open, looking inside at the illustrations, then at the sleepy faces watching me expectantly.

This suddenly feels strange—all these trusting little things looking up at me, fully believing that somehow I have the magic power to soothe them to sleep with just a few words.

I don't think of myself as a calming presence, as someone safe enough for children to look at with such innocence.

But they clearly don't see me like I see myself.

Sort of like Elle never has either.

The thought softens my voice as I begin reading slowly about the five little puppies digging under a fence. I'm careful not to let my tone jar the children out of their sleepiness.

The book's longer than I expect.

A silly story about a group of five puppies, and how one of them always seems to find his own way, and the things the other four puppies find as they search for the poky little puppy, then pick up the smell of rice pudding.

It makes me think of the stories Aunt Clara used to read to Deb and me on the nights when we remembered Mom and Dad were gone, when the world felt large and frightening and very alone.

Those stories made us feel like we were all together in a safe bubble. They always eased us right to sleep.

By the time I turn to the last page, they're all out cold.

Sara chews on the neck of her shirt in her sleep. The little boy who had glue in his hair has one foot sticking out of his blanket.

Elle sits on one of the craft tables, watching me with her eyes soft and a look on her face that makes my heart twist with yearning.

I close the cover and stand, then make my way quietly through the room to offer her the book.

"Here. You win."

"I knew I would," she whispers, sliding off the table to take my hand. "We should go. If we're here when they wake up, they'll never let us leave."

I nod and turn the book over to the teacher.

We thank her before slipping out into the hall. The door closes carefully behind us and latches.

Miss Joly gives me an amused look the second we're free.

"Silver. I'm calling you the Terminator from now on."

"You're not as funny as you think, Miss Joly."

She flashes cunning teeth at me.

"Yes, I am." Then she pokes Elle's shoulder. "You owe me one."

Elle rolls her eyes in amusement. "*Thank you*, Lena."

Lena just snorts and waves us off, sauntering down the hall toward the exit. "We're well past my lunch break. I gotta get back to work. We've got six neuters and spays on the docket today at the clinic, and I'm itching to cut something's balls off."

The warning is clear.

She's picked up on something undeniable between us.

If I hurt Elle, Miss Joly will neuter *me* next.

Elle chuckles, leaning against my arm. "Don't pay attention to her. She threatens everyone."

"Glad to know I'm not special."

"Oh, you're special. You're just . . . a different kind of special." Elle snickers and reaches up to flick my hair off my brow. "I should help you get out of those glittery clothes."

There's a sudden ache between my ribs and between my legs.

The implication. The memory of the taste of her flesh. The *wanting*.

Yeah, I wouldn't mind letting her strip me naked and inspect to make sure there's not a single grain of glitter left on me.

Before I return the favor with my tongue, searching every inch of her body.

Only, that warning lingers.

I remind myself I'm no good for her. I can't be.

But it's hard to say no.

Harder to shake my head and force a smile, squeezing her hand.

"I couldn't get the whole day off," I say. "Not when I've got a strategy meeting with a few new investors this afternoon. I have to go straight home, shower, change, and get back. Rick can take you home. I'll take an Uber."

Disappointment flashes across her face before her smile returns.

I almost can't stand it.

The way she smiles at *everything*, when what I want most is her.

I want her whole heart, all her feelings, no matter how intense.

For now, all I can do is accept, when I created this situation—and nod as she teases, "You asshole. You're taking an Uber so you don't get your own car dirty."

"Guilty," I admit. "You've never seen Merrick angry. Glitter on the upholstery, though?"

I wince.

"Well, in the interests of saving your fancy car . . ." She rises up on her toes and kisses my cheek—and comes away with more glitter on her lips. My beard must be foul. "I'll follow the game plan. You'd better tip the Uber driver a week's worth of pay for this mess."

"I will." I shake a little more glitter out of my hair before turning to follow her outside.

I'm almost walking unsteadily from the madness rattling around my head.

All I want to do is pull her too close to breathe.

Pull her close and lay claim and take everything, every soft inch of her, until she's entirely mine forever.

XIX

WALKING ON SUNSHINE

(ELLE)

I can't stop thinking about the way August looked at me.

Standing there with the sunlight pouring through the hallway windows of that school, looking like he just lost a fight with a can of silver spray paint, telling me *no*.

He'd made an excuse, but I knew what he was really doing.

Drawing a line between us.

Being careful.

Because even if we kiss and touch so casually, neither of us knows what we're doing, and he's made his doubts clear about whether we should be doing anything at all.

So he told me no.

Reminded me of my place.

And he looked at me with such longing it nearly cut my heart into a thousand tiny slivers of want.

God.

How can a man look at you like you're water in a desert? Like he wants you more than life itself?

And how can that wanting make me feel *lonely*?

It's because I'm not with him, I realize.

Because I'm falling so hard for the man behind the defensive walls and knee-jerk reactions, and every time we're apart it's like this hole opens and eats me up inside, swallowing more and more of me up without August there to anchor me in place.

I curl up in my bed in my pajamas, a little rose pink silk cami and shorts set with lace embroidery on the edges. I eye my phone.

My notifications are still popping at a good clip, but I can't even look.

Some of it's nice, some of it's ugly, some of it's dick pics, and after considering for a moment I just tap and uninstall the Twitter and Instagram apps.

They're not what I'm thinking about, though.

I pluck my lower lip with two fingers, eyeing Google.

I shouldn't.

I *shouldn't*, but . . .

He already told me about Charisma, didn't he?

Is it really that bad for me to look up how long ago she died?

It couldn't have been too many years.

If it happened before I left for college, I'm sure I would've heard about it. The whole city would have talked about little else for at least a week.

I just can't help thinking that's part of why he puts that wall up.

I still worry that deep down, he's still in love with his dead ex-wife.

And I need to know the truth.

I need to know where the lines really are.

Just like I need to crush this ridiculous hope inside me that maybe, *maybe* he could feel something for me, when I know he can't.

Just because he didn't push me away after sex the last two times— just because he held me and read me to sleep as tenderly as he read to those kids—it doesn't mean anything.

It just means he was humoring me. Being nice.

The same gentle niceness he showed today at the school.

I had to call in a favor with Lena to make that happen. Just showing up at a random school and asking to play with the kids is begging to end up on a federal list somewhere. But the veterinary practice Lena works at does puppy days with the kids every so often, especially when they've got a new litter on the shelter side and want to socialize the dogs so they'll get used to being around noisy kids with no concept of personal space. She's friends with several of the teachers, so she talked Mrs. Morris into letting us weasel in for the day.

I just did it to make a point.

I hadn't expected my ovaries to implode as I watched August bond with that little girl and patiently let her glitterbomb him.

He's going to be pulling that stuff out of his teeth for a *week*.

And I'm stalling.

Why am I even having a crisis of conscience about this?

Do it. *Do it.*

charisma marshall date of death, I search.

Oh.

I don't know why I'm surprised she's got a Wikipedia page. She was an actress, after all.

My Gawd, she was stunning.

Seriously more beautiful than model-pretty Marissa Sullivan. I guess August has a thing for brunettes. She was smoky and smoldering and lived up to her name, with large green-brown eyes and a mouth so gorgeous I might start questioning which way I swing just looking at her.

I wryly tweak a strand of my own hair.

Definitely not his type.

I could never pull off her presence and elegance.

She looks like she'd have fit with him perfectly, though.

Meanwhile, in every tabloid pic I see of August and me . . .

I look like someone cut me out of a photo of someone's tacky back-yard barbecue and photoshopped me in with him.

Totally out of place.

I skim the details. They started to divorce seven years ago, and the article cites it as a bitter, drawn-out one, contested by insane alimony demands. The article says they were part of her attempts to funnel his fortune into her newfound religion. It's no different from what August told me, but hearing it described this way feels so cold and clinical, draining the reality and depth from it.

Never mind the loss.

Soon, she was dead, before anything was finalized. Not leaving him a widower, technically, but it definitely left him with some heavy things to carry.

Five years.

It's only been five years, even if they officially split seven years ago. But grief has no timeline.

When you have so much unresolved guilt, maybe you can handle a fling, a little pleasure, but someone prying at your feelings? Your heart? Trying to insinuate her way into your life like a spoiled child? Wanting to selfishly pry up those feelings you've held so close to your heart?

I close my eyes, curling over my phone as I press it to my chest.

I've been such an *asshole*.

Sinking my teeth into my lower lip, I straighten as I look down at my phone and swipe to August's contact.

You up? I text.

He's probably buried in work, phone muted or even dead—

But my phone buzzes back.

August: Yes.

I stare down at the blinking cursor.

I don't know how to say I'm sorry.

How to explain everything swirling in my head.

How to tell him I've been a jerk and that I shouldn't have needed to look up that information to respect the clear lines he's laid down, even if I'm not the only one who's been blurring them again and again.

I don't think I can just type it all out.

It makes me think too much of those cold, clinical words describing Charisma's downward spiral.

Screw it.

I stand and stuff my feet into my slippers, then grab my long, fuzzy robe.

I'll just tell him to his face.

It's only eleven.

I can be there and back in an hour and a half. Say what I need to say, let him send me packing, and then go home and get a good night's sleep before it's back to wrangling this strange situation I'm in with Clara tomorrow.

I go flapping down the stairs in my robe and slippers.

Pants? Who needs them?

As I swing past the kitchen, though, Gran blinks up at me, looking up from rolling her dough into a lump for morning. Dusting her hands off, she leans out the kitchen door.

"Elle, dear? You're going out this late?"

"Just running over to August's," I call back, belting my robe shut as I head for the door. "You know. Have to keep up the game."

After picking up a damp rag and wiping her fingers off, Gran follows me.

"Is it just a game, love?" she asks, watching me with concern. "Or is he playing games with you?"

I stop with my hand on the doorknob and slowly let it fall, turning to face her with a smile.

I don't know why I suddenly need to see August *now*, but it can wait a few more minutes when Grandma Jackie's looking at me that way.

"He's not. I promise you he's not."

"Good." She reaches up to cup my cheek with damp fingers. "Be careful with your heart, dear. It's a shiny thing, but enough dirt can dull its light."

"Poetic, Gran." Smiling, I lean into her touch. "Actually, I don't know what I'm doing. But I'll be a little careful."

"And a lot reckless, because you live your life out loud, and I wouldn't have you any other way." Her eyes glitter with good humor. "I love you, my dearest granddaughter."

"Love you so much, Gran." I pull her into a hug, squeezing her tight before letting go. "If I'm lucky, I'll drag him back here for breakfast in the morning." I swipe her keys from the hook by the door. "I'm taking the Audi!" I call as I pull the door open and race outside.

"Drive safe!" drifts after me before she pulls the door shut, laughing.

I tuck myself behind the wheel and back out into the road, pointing the Audi toward Alki Beach and August's house. Suddenly, I'm not in such a hurry, and not just because I'm going for my Safe Driver merit badge.

I still don't know just what to say.

But since I'm on the way, I might as well go through with this crazy impulse.

I try practicing on the drive, muttering to myself beneath the flicker of golden streetlights. "I'm sorry," I say. "I'm not trying to come between you and, uh . . . Charisma's ghost?" No—crap, that sounds dumb. Um. "I'm sorry I made too much out of casual sex? I know you don't really like me, you're just paying"—ah, crap. Now I sound like a hooker. Wait. Am I a hooker?

My reflection in the rearview mirror doesn't answer.

Anyway.

Before I know it, I'm turning onto the quiet private street running parallel with the beach. I'm way too close to his comfy house with my brain blanking, but I'm here and parking and now I've got to face this.

We'll start with *I'm sorry* and see what happens next.

The cold hits me as I step out of the car. I linger next to his G80 for a moment, shivering in my robe.

Would a pair of jeans have killed me?

My slippers make slapping sounds on the planks as I cross the water to his house. The lights in the house are dim. It's possible he isn't even home, and maybe Rick left the car here while August stayed late at the office. It'd be just like him.

Still.

Stomach twisting, I stop in front of the door and knock.

No footsteps. But then—

"Out here, Elle."

August's voice.

He's outside, and it's coming from around the side of the house. He sounds off.

Thicker, heavier somehow.

Frowning, I hug my arms around myself and make my way carefully along the deck ringing the house, my footsteps treading carefully on planks wet from sea spray.

It's not until I'm all the way around the back of the house that I find him. He's sitting on the deck outside his bedroom, with the sliding glass doors open.

August perches on the edge of the deck, with one leg drawn up and the other hanging over the side, dangling over the water. He's shirtless in a pair of dark-grey sleep pants, the thin fabric clinging to his narrow hips and riding down low enough to bare the dimples above his ass, his thighs tightly outlined against the fabric.

His back is taut, his spine a deep canyon framed by steep muscle. The wind ruffles his hair, making it fan out in dark arcs.

One arm is draped over the railing, with a half-full tumbler of golden liquid dangling from it.

I stop where I am, watching him and biting my lip.

I'm all knots inside, confused and scared and wanting.

He looks back, one pale eye over his shoulder. Unreadable.

The moonlight gives the light-blue color impossible depths, like trying to see the bottom of a glacier.

"Nice outfit," he says dryly.

The heat in my cheeks tries to beat back the wind blowing off the water.

"I didn't think I'd need formal wear tonight." I sink my teeth deeper into my lip. "Um, you're drinking."

He gives back a soft, cynical snort.

He unloops his arm from the railing and tilts his head back to take a deep drink, his throat working before he exhales roughly and drops the half-drained tumbler to the deck at his hip. He looks away again to where the moonlight flirts over the water.

"You drive me to it," he says.

I flinch. That spears deep, hurting and colder than any late-winter night.

"I'm sorry." It comes out thick, hard.

Well, here we go.

Start with *I'm sorry*.

Then what?

I press my knuckles to my lips. There are words building, but I don't know what they'll be until they tumble out.

"I shouldn't . . . I shouldn't be so pushy with you. Always flirting and wanting more." I shake my head. "I know nothing can ever ease the pain Charisma left behind. I know you're still in love with her. Or maybe the idea of her. That can happen after a death, and you said you weren't right for each other, but once someone turns into a memory, it's easy to—mmf!"

Faster and faster.

I'd been talking like a chipmunk because the moment I said *I'm sorry*, August stood, kicking the tumbler over the edge of the deck, followed by a faint sound of glass shattering against the wooden piles. He's stalking toward me now, head lowered like a panther, this predator prowling closer with dark intent.

My pulse quickens.

God, if I don't talk fast, he's going to pick me up and haul me up and put me out on my ass in the sand and—

He cuts me off with a kiss.

Savage.

Deep.

Rough.

He tastes like whiskey and frustration and darkness.

His mouth is so hard on mine, almost accusatory.

Confusion swamps me, dizzying heat as he nearly tears at my mouth with a probing tongue, seeking harshly like he's searching for something I *haven't* said yet to steal it from my lips.

His fingers grip my chin, tilting my head up, forcing me open to take more of that bruising kiss, until I'm overwhelmed and my knees are shaking.

He leaves me whirling, my heart racing ten thousand miles a minute.

With an irritated sound, he rips back, still holding my chin with his thumb and stroking the line of my jaw.

"For someone so perceptive," August says bluntly, "you're incredibly stupid."

"*Hey!* What's wrong with you tonight?" I scowl at him. If only he wasn't so flipping hot, the moonlight turning his tanned skin silver at the edges. "I'm going to let that go because you're drunk, but I am *not* stupid."

"No. You're definitely not. You're too smart for your own good, and I'm sorry." He almost snarls it, this odd mix of cynical humor and anger tangled in every word. "You can be oblivious, though. But smart. So smart. So bright. So beautiful. So batshit insane. You're out of your fucking mind, Miss Eleanor Lark, and you're driving me out of mine."

. . . I'm so lost.

And I can't catch my breath when his eyes are blue fire and he's so close and he smells like that stark stony scent of his aftershave.

The roughness of his thumb glides over my lip until it feels sensitized again.

"A-August?" I manage. "I don't get what you're trying to say."

"I'm saying I'm not in love with Charisma, or her memory, or whatever the fuck my guilt has made her," he snarls. "I'm—"

He cuts off sharply, looking away.

His hand falls.

"I'm not fucking drunk enough for this conversation," he mutters. "Or maybe too drunk. I don't know. I just know that drunk or sober, you're turning me upside down, and I don't know what to do about it. I can't stop thinking about you, woman. Can't stop *wanting* you. It's confusing as hell."

"I don't mean to be." And August isn't the only one who's confused, but more than anything, what I'm feeling is . . . hope?

Yes, that's it.

Selfish, guilty hope.

I came here to apologize, to stop pushing at him, but all he's done is make me want even more.

Tentatively, I step closer. I touch my fingers to his stomach, tracing the sleek, hard ripple of his abs.

"Does it have to be confusing?" I whisper. My voice trembles, matching my fingertips. He feels so good under my touch. "Can't we just make this simple?"

His haggard breaths echo over the night.

He steps closer, his heat invading me, his looming presence nearly enveloping me, this menacing beast, and yet to me he's never been dangerous.

He's the wounded beast with a thorn in his paw.

Just begging for a gentle touch to pry it out and soothe the pain.

With my eyes lowered, I can see how stark his knuckles are as his hands hang at his side, clenching and unclenching restlessly.

Touch me, I beg silently. *Touch me with those brutal hands.*

"Do you know what you're asking me, Elle?" August growls.

I look up at him.

Anyone who didn't know him would think he was furious right now—his eyes livid and hot, his lips slightly peeled back from clenched teeth, his jaw steel.

But I *do* know him.

Right now, he's not angry.

He's desperate.

"I know," I whisper, sliding my hands up his chest, curling my fingers against his neck. His pulse beats so hard against my palm, furious and powerful. "I'm asking you for everything."

I don't have the power to force him, to demand anything.

But I can still ask.

And I do, asking in the sway of my body toward his. In the stroke of my fingers against his throat and the subtle pull against his bulk.

He answers.

The night may be silent, but together we're the rumble of an approaching storm.

His hands are hard against my arms.

His mouth is violent against mine.

And I wouldn't have him any other way—passionate, needy, telling me that no matter what he says or how he fights it, there's something inside him that's honest and raw and *wants me* as much as I want him.

His mouth slants hard against mine, stealing my breath, stealing my will, until I'm a molten wreck.

I rise up on my toes to meet him.

We're two storm fronts colliding to make lightning with every touch.

"Please," I whisper against his mouth. "August, *please.*"

I still remember the first time.

The silent, devouring intensity when August locks onto me and shuts out the world.

So locked on there are no words, only desire, and desire is what pours into me as his tongue lashes my lips until they burn.

His teeth nip and play until I quiver with every sharp taste of him, his body leaning into mine and backing me across the deck until suddenly we're inside.

The shadow of his bedroom falls over me, and my calves hit the edge of his bed.

Gravity and his strength tilt me down, spilling me irresistibly onto his bed.

He's a titan hovering over me, a silent shadow in the darkness, the shape of his body sculpted for perfect sin.

For a moment, I can only look up, totally breathless. So overcome by his blue eyes, completely helpless to resist as he rips my robe away.

I kick my slippers off next, and there's nothing left to shield me from his roving touch as hot fingers slide over my silky camisole, my shorts, shaping me like his burning touch could melt my flesh into any shape he wants.

I feel naked already.

Not just my skin, but my soul.

The all-consuming way he's watching me: it's the same way he looked at my sketches earlier.

Seeing nothing else.

He takes in every detail, like he's trying to brand me on himself.

I don't know when I started shaking. But when he coaxes my legs apart, when he brings himself down against me to rest our bodies together, I'm a trembling wreck as I touch my fingers to his lips.

They're so hot, so full, and I want their taste so bad.

"Kiss me," I whisper. "Kiss me and don't stop."

Still no words.

Still only obsessed eyes and those possessive hands raking my thighs until my skin burns with his touch.

God, I'm so wet for him I could die.

Not a sound.

I'm expecting another onslaught. But when he bends over me, when he presses his mouth to mine, it's lighter.

It's sweet.

Somehow, that strips me more naked as his mouth strokes mine tenderly.

He kisses me like I *matter*—and that's going to rip me apart even more if morning comes and it turns out I mean nothing.

Right now, it feels like I mean everything.

Like this is everything as our mouths and bodies twine and with every second our hands explore each other.

There's more skin—more than touch—more than clothes falling, until there's nothing but our bodies and the hiss of sheets and this perfect rhythm that feels like *us*.

Every inch of me shivers as I feel his roughness, his masculinity, his strength moving over me.

Holy hell.

"Elle, fuck," he whispers.

It's like he's caressing me with his entire body, lighting me on fire with friction.

Everywhere he's hard, I'm soft.

Everywhere he's rough, I'm smooth.

Everywhere he's hot—

Oh my God, I'm *hotter*.

As his angry cock rubs my stomach and thighs, as the dusting of dark hair on his chest teases my nipples, I become a writhing mess from the gentle torture of it.

I stroke over his back, dipping my tongue against the heat of his mouth, tracing the stark muscles surrounding his spine with fascination, drawing on him like I could pull him into me, merge us together, match the racing beat of my heart to his.

I feel too vulnerable right now.

Yet his strength over me holds me safe, holds me close.

Holds me deep as we fit together oh so right, and then his mouth soothes mine slowly and deeply.

On the next thrust of his tongue, he's inside me.

A long, punishing stroke that takes forever to fill me, forcing me to feel every inch until I arch my back and dig my nails into him.

But he won't let me break this silence.

Not when he drinks every sound from my lips, locking us in this thing like a sacrament, binding us together.

I can't think.

I can't breathe.

I don't know anything but *him* as his cock plunges deep, and I feel him in my darkest place where everything trembles and the lightest touch makes light explode behind my eyes.

Again and again.

Taking his sweet time, driving me mad.

I want it to stop and never end, everything swirling around me. I'm lost.

Nothing has ever felt as good as August Marshall filling me now, stretching me open, making my thighs clench and every inch of me quake.

Even going slow, he's no less powerful.

He sweeps me away like a fifty-foot wave, taking me over until I can only hold on for dear life and let myself be pulled under.

I'm drowning in this man.

Sinking.

Into his darkness, his need, and every time he fills me, every time he reaches that *place*, my entire body convulses with pleasure and this trembling, heart-singing emotion I don't dare name.

I don't dare name it, but it feels like it's not just mine.

It can't only be mine.

As the shivering ecstasy pitches me higher and higher, racing through me in waves with every thrust that leaves me dripping and clenching, gasping and writhing, raking my nails down his back, *I feel him.*

He's in the storm with me.

Kissing me, taking me, shaping my body and emotions in the dark sweet calm between our chaos, letting us taste it like melting chocolate shared between our tongues.

More. *More.*

I can't take it.

I'm a raw nerve, my thighs around his hips, my nails deep in his back, silent but screaming with my touch and the rake of my nails, with the grip of my knees and the arch of my body.

Too sensitive.

Too good.

Too much, too hot, too hard, too *large*.

I can't contain this man to save my life, and he can't contain *me*.

And when I burst with my pussy tightening around him, greedily drawing his pleasure out, quaking until I can't, I'm more than combusting fireworks.

I'm an entire supernova, washing brightly over the sky.

And he's my entire night that makes my light shine that much brighter, clutching me against him as I burn without mercy.

His heat locks my entire body up in throes of pleasure like nothing else I've ever had.

He's tense against me, breathing hard, his darkness chasing me, and then he throws his head back with a roar.

I feel his cock swell, right before he turns into that shudder, that animal growl, that eruption that tells me he's breaking and marking me from the inside out.

We burn together all night long, only stopping to catch our breath, an entire galaxy of hearts and flesh on fire.

◆ ◆ ◆

In the wee hours of the morning, I can barely move.

The first time was rougher, but this wore me out so much more when it was so emotional, so sweetly draining.

I'm a limp dishrag draped against him, idly drawing patterns on his chest with my fingertip, making his chest hair swirl.

Until his arm tightens around my waist—he's *holding* me, instead of pushing me away, at ease and lazy and so wonderfully relaxed—and his other hand comes up to catch mine, stopping me.

"Don't make me bite you again," he rumbles, and I love to hear it. No tension or doubt because yeah, I'm still scared he'll realize his mistake any moment now and turn on the deep freeze. "Stop that. It tickles."

"I'm not sorry." I snicker and curl my fingers in his, nuzzling his shoulder.

"No, you wouldn't be. Wretch." August yawns, cracking one eye open, watching me before he kisses the top of my head. "Go to sleep. We still have work. And I know you'll try to drag me out of bed with the sunrise."

I giggle because it's true, almost giddy with *happiness.*

I'd never expected to find this happy place with August.

A place where he can relax, tease me, accept me.

Where he tells me I drive him crazy and because I do—and where maybe we can have a chance.

Maybe these giddy feelings don't have to die with the sunrise.

I turn my face into his shoulder to hide my smile. "Fine, fine. Good night, Gruffykins."

"*Good night*, brat."

I snicker, fumbling for the covers and dragging them up.

Now that the sweat is cooling, it's cold with the doors still open. But after a moment I crack one eye open, peeking at him.

"August?"

"Hm?"

"You've still got glitter on your nipple," I point out.

I shiver with pleasure as he blinks in confusion.

Then his deep, rolling laughter fills the night as he wraps both arms around me and pulls me in for a final good night kiss.

XX

STOLEN THUNDER

(AUGUST)

I'm having a dream.

I'm a fireman, sleeping in my bunk at the station during my shift. An alarm's blaring, waking me up with a start and calling me to action.

There's a big fire to be put out, the chief bellowing, and I'm supposed to throw on my gear and slide down the pole to hop on the candy-red truck so we can go tearing out into the street to save people's lives.

Only, it's a very strange fire station. Everything around me—from the walls to my bunk to the pole across the room—is drawn in clumsy crayon lines.

I think this might be a drawing from when I was a little boy, when I idolized firefighters.

Still, I need to get up, or the crayon-and-paper truck won't be able to roll to save the crayon-and-paper town—but I can't.

There's a cold, wet nose poking me in the forehead over and over as the station dalmatian nudges me. It's a weird dalmatian, slender and feminine, with golden spots instead of black, and hazel-colored eyes.

Instead of barking, it grins and pokes me with its paw, teasing, "Gruffykiiiiiiins. Wake up. Your phone won't stop ringing!"

My . . . phone?

My phone.

That's not my normal ringtone.

That's—fuck.

That's the shrill alarm of Rick's Black Box emergency phone.

The dream clears in an instant, and I bolt upright in bed.

Then my entire home erupts into chaos.

Even as the blasting ringtone ends and starts again with a new incoming call, Elle yelps as my sudden movement tilts her off balance. All I see is a blur of ivory skin and bright-blonde hair tumbling to the floor, dragging the duvet with her.

I lunge for my phone while another ringtone starts screaming from the fuzzy peach bathrobe on the floor. Meanwhile, my doorbell starts dinging like mad.

Shit, what now?

Is there a missile heading for Seattle, or what?

I'm going to get one of Elle's whopper migraines at this rate.

Tensing, I snatch my phone and swipe the call. Elle wobbles to her knees and presents a distracting view as she crawls across the floor bare assed to work her phone out of her robe.

"Merrick?" I growl into the phone. "What's happened?"

"Oh my God," Elle mumbles from the phone, plunking to sit on top of her bathrobe and staring at her screen. "Jesus, not even TikTok's safe. Why is everyone calling me a 'gold digger whore'? I'm . . . using kids to get to you? Who's Duetting my migraine at the press conference?"

Shit, shit, and also, *shit.*

I don't think it's even eight o'clock in the morning, and everything is on fire.

This is *not* fine.

As I stagger out of bed and hoist my pajama pants up to head for the bedroom door with a light touch for Elle's shoulder, Rick babbles in my ear.

"Mr. Marshall?" he says breathlessly. "You need to get down here. Right now."

"Where the fuck is *here*?" I demand, heading down the hall to make that damnable ringing stop. Who the hell would show up at my door instead of just sending a text?

"The office. Not ours, but Marissa Sullivan's office—"

I yank the door open while Rick keeps talking.

I almost don't recognize the man on my doorstep.

I've only met him once via video call.

Mr. Carlton, the private detective.

He's a slim man in a suit, neat and precise. Not at all the image of the grizzled PI you'd expect. He glances at the phone against my ear and smiles thinly, keeping silent as he mouths, *Good morning, Mr. Marshall.*

He offers me a manila envelope under his arm.

I nod tersely, take it and pry the prongs open, and spill a stack of pages and photographs into my hand.

Then I stop cold.

What Rick just said clicks in my brain through the chaos swirling around me.

"She did *what*?" I snarl into the phone. "Repeat that."

Even as I'm talking, I'm leaning into my office next to the front door, fumbling around with a hidden pocket safe to find my checkbook.

My heart is fucking pounding hard enough to drive nails. I need something to keep my hands busy, *anything*, so I rip off a check for probably three times the amount we agreed on, thrust it at Carlton, and slam the door in his face.

I don't have time for niceties right now. Not after what Merrick's just said.

"Miss Marshall. Clara," Rick repeats breathlessly. "She left on her own to meet Miss Sullivan. She asked me to drive her, and I said you wouldn't be happy about that, so she took an Uber."

"Shit." That bullheaded, impetuous woman. We're too much alike, my aunt and I. I slump against the wall, holding the phone against my

ear with my shoulder, rifling through the pages. "Call Deb. Her apartment's closer to Marissa's office. Get her over there ASAP. I'll be there soon. We need to do damage control—"

I freeze.

While I'm talking, I've been flicking through the pages of the PI's report, absorbing his summary.

Marissa developing a drinking habit after her father's death. Her drinking affecting her publishing operations, sending everything into decline. It's clear now why she blames Little Key and wants to absorb it, taking what she feels is her birthright to compensate for the failures she feels drove her father to his early death.

More about her surviving mother, Yvette Sullivan, Lester's widow. She's apparently estranged from Marissa. No contact in years, not since before the drinking started. Yvette currently lives in a rural town in Minnesota, retired and raising chickens, according to her Instagram bio.

But that's not what makes me stop cold.

It's a fuzzy photo taken in what looks like Bainbridge. Marissa would live somewhere like Bainbridge, I suppose.

Which is where Rick is meeting her.

In *my* car.

It's a rainy night. Probably right after he dropped Elle and me off for our movie date.

God fucking damn.

So this is what he does with his free time, while waiting to chauffeur us around.

He's leaning against the car with Marissa next to him, and she's passing him a thick envelope bulging with what has to be cash.

Cash.

Untraceable.

No bank records.

Now, I fucking know exactly how those candid photos keep appearing, caught by some mysterious stalker who always knows just where we'll be to catch us in our most private moments.

Nicole Snow

You might think I shouldn't be angry when that was the entire point of this illusion.

But the fury, the betrayal inside me turns black, burning like a volcano.

"I trusted you," I bite off, the only words I can think of, but they stop Rick short.

". . . sir? I'm . . . I'm sorry, what?"

"I *trusted* you! How long have you been my right hand, Merrick? How long have you been more involved in my life than anyone else? My shadow. Always there. And you took advantage of that."

"I . . . I . . . ," he stammers, but I can hear the guilt in his voice, clear as day. "I don't know what you're talking about, Mr. Marshall—"

"Cut the shit. Fuck yes, you do. And I'm entirely out of patience for your backstabbing." I turn to stalk into the bedroom. I do not have *time* for this. I need to get dressed and get downtown ASAP before Aunt Clara makes a hideous mistake. "How much was she paying you to spy on me? On *us*? Was it worth it, you asshole?"

Dead silence.

His next breath sounds almost like a sob.

As I step back into the bedroom, Elle glances up from the floor, then recoils, blinking as she looks at me.

What's wrong? she mouths.

Fucking everything.

I can only shake the lump of solid fury masquerading as my head. There's nothing I can explain while Rick is whining in my ear.

"It's not about the money," he says weakly. "It's—it's my grand-daughter, sir. You don't understand, I—I didn't know she was in trouble with money. She started doing these adult films to pay for medical school, and Miss Sullivan found out. She threatened me—she said she'd make sure the whole world knew, and Emily would never get a job in her field. I couldn't let that happen—"

"You could have told me the truth, Merrick. You could have turned to me for *help*. I could have protected you, and her. Instead, you ratfucked me. Don't bother coming to collect your last paycheck. It'll come in the mail from corporate."

I don't wait for his response.

I hang up and rip my closet door open, dragging out a pair of slacks from the dry cleaning bag.

"August, what's going on?" Elle's on her feet, padding over to touch my arm.

"Rick was the shithead taking photos of us. He's fired," I snap, turning to kiss the top of her head. "Grab a shirt and see if you can turn it into something presentable. We've got to go now."

"Go?" Her wide, worried eyes track me as I kick my track pants off and step into my slacks. "Go where?"

"Marissa Sullivan's office," I growl. "Before Aunt Clara does something we'll all regret."

◆ ◆ ◆

It's a miracle I don't get pulled over for traffic violations.

The G80 was made to speed, and I push it to its limits, weaving in and out of traffic, while Elle clutches the oh-shit handle and tries not to say anything, her jaw clenched tight.

She's somehow managed to turn one of my button-downs into a pale-blue shirt dress that looks like it was designed for her. She's pressed back in her seat, sick with worry and possibly a little fear over the razor-sharp turns I'm taking.

I'll apologize later.

Something tells me things are about to get very, very bad.

Clara won't answer her phone.

Not for me, not for Elle, busying herself in the passenger's seat, calling over and over, leaving worried voice mails.

I take the next turn like the car is on rails—and almost come bumper to bumper with Deb's car, lunging ahead of mine through traffic.

Shit, shit.

I hoped she'd beat me to the office, but luck isn't on my side today.

I know it's too late by the time we both go skidding into the parking lot.

I spike the G80 to a halt at an angle to Deb's fishtailing Mazda. Deb, Elle, and I all go spilling out into the front lot just as the door to the tall high-rise building opens.

Aunt Clara steps out, deep in conversation with Marissa and one of the lawyers we met the other day.

Suddenly, there's no one for me but Clara.

Everyone else fades into the background.

Even the ridiculous flap of Elle's fuzzy slippers trails me as I stalk across the concrete. There was no time to change her shoes.

"What did you do?" I demand. "What is this?"

Clara freezes the second she sees me.

There's a painful flash of guilt on her face before her lips thin with determination and she lifts her chin proudly.

"What's in my right to do," she says woodenly. "I love you, August, but you don't get to make that choice for me."

"What choice, Aunt Clara?" Deb stumbles to a breathless halt next to me. "Auntie, what did you *do*?"

It's not Aunt Clara who answers.

It's Marissa Sullivan.

Crowing triumphantly, she holds up a small USB recording device.

"Lookie here," she says, and this time she's quite sober, her eyes glinting with evil joy. "Clara Marshall's confession. She's admitted everything. You lost, Marshall. Clara stole Inky the Penguin from my father, and the entire world is going to hear about it. Once I submit this evidence—everything you have is mine."

XXI

DIMMING THE LIGHT

(ELLE)

It's official.

I've never witnessed anything go to hell in a handbasket faster than this—and to think it all started with one innocent phone call.

I'm still reeling from this morning.

Private eye photographs.

Rick, stalking us and taking intimate photos.

Clara going to Marissa to confess her *guilt*.

And now we're just standing here, unable to breathe, the sky torn open and falling down.

August could scare off a whole pride of lions. He's so deathly still I wonder if he's turned to granite, staring at his aunt with a terrible look I've never seen before on any human face.

This hard, ugly mix of betrayal, hurt, agony, and loathing.

It's like he's looking at a stranger, an intruder in his house, in his life.

A look so visceral it hurts even *me*—almost as much as realizing the woman I've looked up to all this time is a fraud.

No. No, I can't believe it.

She must be doing this for some reason, right? My instincts can't be this wrong; this whole thing feels off, and I just can't—

"You lied," August clips. His voice is a contradiction, brittle titanium. "Either you lied my whole fucking life—or you're lying right now to Sullivan. So, which one is it, Clara? Which lie?"

Clara.

Oh my God.

Not *Aunt Clara.*

Just this cold, impersonal thing, like he's divorced himself from his feelings for her entirely.

Clara's eyes glimmer as she shakes her head. "Don't press this, August. I told you, some things are more important than money and copyrights."

August's fists clench slowly.

I watch helplessly.

I hate Marissa right now. She's just watching with a smug smile like she's *enjoying* this, like she's relishing breaking a family apart and ruining the trust and love they had.

Deb shakes her head, covering her mouth with one hand. "Auntie, why? None of this makes sense—"

"It doesn't need to, sweetheart." Clara smiles sadly. "One day you'll understand."

"Make me understand right now," August bites off. Forceful. Deadly. "Make me understand why you would go behind my back, just like everyone else."

Oh God.

That's what it's about, isn't it?

Charisma went behind his back, trying to take everything he had for her crazy cult. It's no wonder he's been so standoffish with women—prickly with me.

And then Rick, his right hand, the closest thing I think August had to a friend . . .

Tears sting my eyes.

But I'm not going to cry. There's no time for selfish tears.

I can't sit by and let this happen. It's breaking my heart.

I step closer and touch August's arm.

"August. Not here," I whisper. Not in front of Marissa. Not over enemy territory. "We should go somewhere more neutral to talk—"

"We? There is no 'we'!" he thunders, whipping around to face me. His eyes blaze as he flings my hand off him. "You aren't a part of this. You don't need to intrude, inserting yourself into goddamned everything. This isn't *your* family, Elle, and it's not your damn business."

He might as well have struck me across the face.

Punched me in the chest.

Ripped my heart out and punted it.

I stumble back like I've been shot, pain clogging my throat, my vision blurring.

I can't even speak.

Not when he's just torn the veil from my eyes. Forced me to stop pretending we could ever be anything more than a lie—or that I have any place in his life that isn't bought and paid for as a matter of convenience.

Because he's right.

I'm not a part of this world.

It's not my business.

I don't belong here.

I don't belong with *him*.

My chest feels like it's caving in.

I can't breathe.

I can't be here.

Shaking my head, I falter back a step.

Deb steps forward, reaching for me. "Elle, Elle, he didn't mean it—"

"No," I sob out, shaking my head again and twisting away from her touch.

I can't stand it right now.

Worse, I can't stand to look at August because she's the one saying he doesn't mean it. Not him.

"H-he . . . he does," I stammer until I can't.

God, I can't do this.

I trip, my loose slippers tumbling off, leaving me barefoot against the concrete.

And I am the worst broken Cinderella imitation ever as I spin away from this soul-killing mess and *run* like I'm being chased by the cutting fragments of my own broken heart.

◆ ◆ ◆

There's probably something more humiliating than standing barefoot on a street corner in an oversized shirt from a man you hate, waiting for an Uber with tears running down my face, but right now I can't think of it.

I haven't run far.

Just far enough to get out of sight before a little common sense took over. I realized if I kept up like this, I was going to step on a nail or a little glass, and then it'd be just my luck to get tetanus on top of everything else going straight to hell.

So I took a side street where they wouldn't see me and dug my phone out of the breast pocket of the shirt to summon a ride.

At least I don't have to wait long, standing here like some kind of messed-up Victorian orphan child on the street corner.

When the dark-grey sedan pulls up, the driver leans out the window. "Elle?"

"Y-yeah. Sahib, right?"

He nods with a friendly smile and unlocks the doors. "Come on. Let's get you home."

I must look like the ugliest mess to get this much sympathy from a total stranger.

But I do want home.

I want Gran. My childhood bedroom. Lena's shit-talk. Everything that comforts me.

So with a miserable nod and a sniffle, I climb in the back seat, dusting my feet off before getting in fully and curling up in the corner to wait.

Sahib watches me in the mirror as he pulls into traffic. "Walk of shame, or too much partying last night?"

"Neither," I answer, huddling the shirt around me and hating that it still smells so much like August. "I think I just got dumped."

"Oh, ma'am." He clucks his tongue with sympathy. "You're young. You'll find the one who deserves you. He obviously didn't."

I smile gratefully. It's sweet of him, but it rings hollow.

Because now all I can think of is what an intrusion I've been on August's life.

Always poking my nose everywhere.

Yeah. I guess I really am that pushy and obnoxious.

I remain silent on the drive home, and the Uber driver is nice enough to let me curl up and lick my wounds quietly. But I've never seen anything more welcoming than Gran's pretty blue cottage, and it's a relief when I get out of the Uber and thank the driver.

He leans out the window and flashes a peace sign.

"You'll be all right," he says. "I know it doesn't feel like it today, but give it time."

"Thank you," I say again.

I know he's right.

It just doesn't feel like it right now.

I straggle up the walk. Just as I reach the front step, the door opens. Lena steps out carrying a basket of lemon poppyseed muffins under her arm, her head turned back to talk to my grandmother.

"Hey! Mom was hoping you had some tips for the mold in her roses. It's in the roots and—"

Gran cuts her off with a startled gasp, jolting forward and already reaching for me. "Elle? Elle, dear, what happened?"

Just like that, the waterworks switch on again.

"August" is all I can say, my voice rattling like shattered glass.

Lena and Grandma barely catch me as I tumble into them and break down, sobbing in the arms of the only people who've ever loved me and wanted me around.

Thank God they're still here, and they still love me, no matter how much of an *intrusion* I really am.

XXII

EYE OF THE STORM

(AUGUST)

Aunt Clara has never hit me in my life.

Right now, I wish she would.

What I'd done failed to sink in for a full damning minute as Elle ran away.

Not when I was so wrapped up in my head with my anger and my betrayal.

Not when I'd just taken an entire lifetime of resentment out on the one person who deserved it the least.

By the time it caught up to me, she was gone.

Despair eats through me like acid, melting my heart into slag.

I pick up one of the pink fuzzy slippers that went flying off her foot, just staring at it before I let it fall limply to the ground.

Everything's gone to shit faster than I can comprehend.

My PA and driver spying on me.

Aunt Clara confessing—*fucking confessing*—to stealing Inky the Penguin from Lester Sullivan.

The grim fact that we're going to lose Little Key and everything she's ever built because the Inky IP was either built on a lie, or else it was all thrown away with a lie—either way, it's going, going, gone.

And the ugly truth is that I just ran off Elle like a total savage.

I shoved her away when all I want is her in my life, more than anything.

She's not an intrusion.

She never was.

Hell, she opened doors I shut so long ago that I forgot there was still a living man behind them, and not the lifeless workaholic asshole I've mutated into.

I am a heartless fuck of the highest order.

"Way to go, Casanova," Marissa mocks, lifting her chin with a sneer. "Y'know, I just wanted to destroy the bitch who killed my father . . . but getting to watch your life come crashing down has been a fun bonus."

Aunt Clara looks sick. Ready to faint.

Despite the anger boiling my veins, concern swamps me.

I throw Marissa a sharp look.

"Don't," I say. "You got what you wanted. Learn to savor your win with a little class."

Aunt Clara shakes her head, giving Marissa a long, strange look.

"I never meant to hurt Lester," she whispers. There's something odd in her voice. Something distant and detached that tells me I'm missing a major piece of her puzzle. "I never meant to hurt you. I was simply trying to protect you in my own way, Marissa. I can't explain—I can't—but believe me, I was. Please believe that. I only hope this can help set things right."

Marissa looks confused, silent as she cocks her head at my aunt.

Aunt Clara smiles faintly and turns to me, touching my arm.

"Please take me home, son," she says. "You can rage at me all you like . . . but I can't handle one more sip of this day."

No rage left.

I can't will myself to stay furious.

I don't even know what's happening right now.

We're all just standing here like someone called *Cut!* on filming, and now we don't know what to do when we don't have our parts to play. Even Marissa looks like a puppet with her strings cut.

The worst part is, Elle would know what to do right now.

She'd know how to smooth things over and move everything forward again.

Of course Elle's not here anymore, thanks to my dumb ass.

All this time, I've been so angry at what my ex-wife did, expecting each and every last woman in my life to hurt me the same way Charisma did.

Only, I was the one who hurt the one woman who was trying her very best not to.

I knew I would.

I *knew* I'd hurt her again.

For a few bright minutes, I fooled myself into believing I could behave like a civilized human being.

Like the man she truly deserves.

It's the stiff, silent lawyer who finally breaks the awkward scene. He clears his throat, adjusts his tie, and plucks the recorder from Marissa's hand. "I'll just add this to our evidence and make sure it's entered into the record before the case."

Marissa shakes herself, giving him a lost look before her face tightens into a scowl.

"Right." She sweeps us with a look. "The only Marshall who was invited here was Clara. The rest of you can get off my property. Unless you want me to have security escort you out." Her eyes flick to me like glinting knives.

Very fucking funny, throwing my words back at me.

"Let's go." Aunt Clara touches my arm lightly.

Deb catches my eye over her head. She doesn't have to mouth any words at me for me to know what she's saying.

I've known her my whole life, and despite our teasing and bickering, she's still my sister.

We'll talk later, she says silently.

Still dazed, I start moving, feeling like the entire world's been ripped out from under me.

I escort Clara to my car and tuck her into the passenger seat, then climb in and wait for Deb to drive through the roundabout before I follow her car like we're in a funeral procession.

It's dead silent, though now and then I'm painfully aware of little things like Rick's sunglasses clipped to the visor, a bottle cap from one of his lemon Italian sodas in the cup holder, all those reminders that—*fuck.*

I can't even sort my feelings there.

Why? Why didn't he just trust me enough to come for help, instead of letting Marissa goddamned Sullivan blackmail him against me?

Then again, when I refuse to trust anyone else—

Have I really been someone who *anyone* could turn to for help in their darkest hour? Even my driver?

Goddammit.

Fine.

Maybe after this is over, we'll sort this out and we'll talk. But it'll be a long damned time before I trust Rick to do anything more than pick up my dry cleaning.

I'll definitely hire someone to get that compromising info Marissa has, even if it's by less-than-legal methods.

Aunt Clara sits silently next to me, staring out the window, her expression ghostly. It's like she's deflated.

Everything that makes her Aunt Clara has drained out, now that she's given up the core of her life.

It's not right.

None of this is fucking right.

And I don't know what to do about it, as long as she's keeping her lips so stubbornly sealed about why this is even happening.

I cast a few frustrated glances at her, start to say something, and stop.

I don't know if I want to yell, beg, accuse, cry, or just fucking give up and let it be.

So I'm not expecting her to abruptly say, "You're still angry at Charisma."

"What?" I blink at her before turning back to traffic. "Of course I'm angry at Charisma. She tried to—"

"That's not why you're angry." Clara smiles sadly.

"The hell it isn't."

"August." She watches me knowingly. "You hate liars. Please don't lie to yourself."

"I . . ."

I recoil, my fingers tightening on the steering wheel as I stare at the taillights ahead of us. I've been so out of it I didn't even realize we were no longer behind Deb. She must have merged into the turn back to Little Key a few blocks back.

Why am I so angry at my dead ex-wife?

There's no point in it. I can't even tell her if I knew—

Oh.

Well, that's it, isn't it?

"I'm angry at her for dying," I admit. I feel like I'm spitting words at my reflection in the windshield. "There was no reason. No *reason*. We could have been normal divorced people. We could've said we were sorry it went wrong and gone our separate ways. I know I wasn't husband of the year. I *know*. I know we weren't right for each other. But instead of talking about it, she had to fucking go and get sucked in with those lunatics, and then—"

I cut myself off, pounding my fist on the steering wheel.

"I wish she was alive." Why is there a knot in my throat? "I wish I'd handled it *right*. I wish we'd settled our shit and gotten on with our lives, but we didn't. And I've been blaming myself for that, and that's wrong. All because I blame her. I blame her for what she did, and she'll never be here again for me to tell her to her face."

It comes out in a snarling rush, leaving me winded.

Clara watches me with her usual patience.

I'm reminded of when I was a little boy and she'd watch me screw up my face, trying like hell not to cry when I was hurt and angry. And she'd always coax my feelings out until I was an angry little mess, ranting about how mean the kids at school were, when all I wanted was a friend.

"No, she's not," Clara agrees gently. "But you're still here. You're alive. You're here to admit that to yourself. To heal, now that you've acknowledged your real feelings."

"I don't know if I'm capable of healing." My lips twist bitterly.

"I know someone who thinks you are," Clara points out. Just the softest reminder of Elle is a knife to the gut—hurt, longing, regret. "You don't have to forgive me, August. I did what I did for my own reasons, and I know it hurt you. I'm sorry for that. You have no idea how much. But there's still a chance *she* might forgive you."

The vehicle goes quiet as I pull up outside her modest little two-story house in Laurelhurst. The same place I used to call home.

For some reason, I vaguely remember when I ran a background check on Elle. Before she moved to her grandmother's cottage on Queen Anne Hill, her parents had owned a home in Laurelhurst.

If life hadn't taken us on wildly different paths, we might have grown up practically next to each other.

"Is there?" I ask. "Would you forgive a man who told you that you were nothing but an intrusion?"

"Give her a chance," Clara urges. "Not everyone holds grudges like you do."

"Very funny. I'm glad this day hasn't trashed your sterling sense of humor." I roll my eyes.

She smiles, but it's a shallow imitation of her old warmth.

"I have my moments."

I let myself look at her. Really look at her, but I can't muster any anger. Not even resentment at her bizarre betrayal.

Mostly, I'm just tired, but more than anything, I'm worried about the woman who raised me like a mother. Worried about what's going on inside her that would drive her to do something so drastic, despite knowing how it would hurt Deb and me.

It must be something terribly important.

I refuse to believe the woman I love and admire this much has spent my entire life deceiving me.

Wouldn't Elle be proud of me now?

Putting all my faith in a woman who more than deserves it, instead of cutting her off and rejecting her out of mistrust and my own selfish feelings of betrayal.

If only I'd had the sense to treat Elle the same way.

"What will you do now?"

"I'm going to have a cup of tea and read a book," Clara announces pragmatically as she pushes the door open, stepping out. She leans in, giving me a long look full of love that I know isn't a lie. She didn't have to take on Deb and me after our parents died, but she was always willingly, happily here for us. "Take care of yourself, August. Regardless of what you think of me, even if you despise me now—I do love you, and I always will."

I thunk my head back against the car seat.

"I can't stop loving you, Auntie." I sigh. "Even if I can't shake the feeling that you're hiding something important. I'll never believe you stole Inky from Lester Sullivan."

"Well . . . that's something you'll have to wrestle with in your own way." She straightens, pressing a hand to the small of her back with a groan. "For now, I need to grapple with getting these old bones inside. I'll talk to you later, dearest heart."

"Later," I say as she pushes the car door closed.

I watch her make her way slowly up the walk.

Just another reminder that this isn't fucking *right*, and I desperately want to fix it, but I don't know how.

It's only after Clara's safely inside that I pull back out into traffic, pointing the G80 toward home.

◆ ◆ ◆

My house feels too empty now.

Elle's barely been here enough to leave a mark, even if her silky pajamas and her bathrobe are still on my bedroom floor. I pick up the soft rose-colored top, breathing in her scent.

Then I fling it away, leaving it crumpled on the bed.

I can't stand the heartache right now.

Instead, I pick up the sheaf of papers, the report I tossed aside when I threw on my clothes and went dashing out earlier. I take them out to the deck and sink down in one of the high-backed chairs, slouching forward and paging through what the private detective uncovered.

Isn't there anything here I can use?

Some evidence that Marissa fabricated the sketchbook, or—

Wait.

I stop and flip back a page. Clara's name jumped out just now, but it was about Marissa's mother and not Marissa herself, so I'd skimmed past it before.

Now, I read carefully.

Lester and Yvette Sullivan never had a happy marriage, but it was rather peaceful until his partnership with Clara Marshall. Clara and Yvette became close friends. So close it sparked rumors that their friendship was shattered by infidelity between Lester and Clara.

There were other rumors too. Even more scandalous ones for the time. You know how people were about certain things back then.

And those women certainly were very, very, close.

"Thick as thieves," you might say.

But hey. People do love to gossip, and gossip isn't always true.

I lean back, staring across the water. Cold calculations flick through my head.

I'm catching on too slowly, but now it hits me like a train.

There's never been an *uncle* with Aunt Clara.

Hell, I don't recall her ever dating anyone, or talking about a love life at all.

Of course, Deb and I always chalked that up to her being too busy with Inky, and then unexpectedly saddled with two young brats on top of a full-time career dedicated to her art.

On the other hand, she's never expressed much interest in men at all.

It's not something I've ever thought about. You tend not to think too hard about your parental figure's love life for the sake of your own sanity.

It's not that she hates men.

She just seems oblivious to them, minus the stubborn little bastard she's sculpted into some semblance of a man.

Fuck.

Did she and Yvette Sullivan . . . ?

She won't tell me, but I know who might.

I grab my phone and tap Deb's number.

"Well, that was a complete shit show." She answers without a hello. "How're you holding up?"

"A particularly smelly one, but that's not why I'm calling. I need you to take over operations for a bit. I'm going out of town for a couple of days."

"What? Why? The trial's coming up! Even if it seems kind of fucking pointless now. We should still be there, shouldn't we?"

"I'll be back in time, Deb," I promise. "I don't think it's pointless."

"Oh no. Idiot brother, what are you planning? Where are you going?"

"Minnesota."

Long silence.

"What the *fuck* is in Minnesota?" Deb hisses.

I smile for the first time all day. "I'm not sure yet, but I'm about to find out."

XXIII

THE SUNNY SIDE OF GLOOM

(ELLE)

We've come full circle.

Me, sitting with Lena and Gran at the kitchen table, sipping cups of hot tea and watching the rain come down outside while I nurse my broken heart.

They're here for me the same way they always are.

I'm so glad I have them.

I couldn't handle being alone right now.

Not even after getting out of August's shirt and scrubbing off his scent so it wouldn't make me burst into fiery tears all over again.

There is no "we"!

You aren't a part of this.

You don't need to intrude, inserting yourself into goddamned everything.

My lips quiver.

I pinch them together hard and take another long, burning sip of my tea.

Orange blossom with honey today.

Comfort tea.

She always knows exactly what I need.

I rub my thumb against the warm ceramic cup and look up at my grandmother with a thousand-pound heart.

"Gran? Do . . . do you ever resent looking after me?"

Lena rolls her eyes like it's the dumbest question she's ever heard. It probably is, but sometimes I just need to *hear* it.

Gran reaches over and lays her paper-thin hand over mine gently. "Never, dear. Not once. You've brought so much light into my life. You always will." She squeezes my hand. "Having you here has made my life happier than I can describe."

"So I wasn't an intrusion?"

I know I sound like a needy little girl right now.

And I feel like one too.

"No." She shakes her head firmly. "You were right where you belonged." Her brows crease with concern. "Is that what he called you? An 'intrusion'?"

Lena bares her teeth. "Oh God, I really am going to cut his balls off."

"Now don't be vulgar, Lena." Gran purses her lips.

"Nope. Not this time. Not listening. Balls go poof!" She slides her finger across her throat. *"Shhk!"*

Sighing, Gran says, "Well, I can't fault your motives, at least. Do use a sharp knife, if you must be so uncivilized."

"Do I look like an amateur, Grams?" Lena smiles viciously.

I don't know how they do it, but I'm laughing.

It doesn't fix the heartbreak, no; it just makes it tolerable for a few minutes.

"You two are awful," I whisper.

Lena grins at me. "We love you anyway, you dinkus."

"'Dinkus'? Is that a word?" I laugh—but between one breath and the next I start crying again.

Again.

God, why?

Why do I care so much?

I know August is a hollowed-out grouch with a heart smaller than a peanut. But I also know that when his temper snaps, sometimes he says things he doesn't mean.

Why am I so upset then?

Because he did *mean it.*

Because you're a loud, annoying, chaotic intrusion, and you think if you just act like you don't care, then the people who find you annoying and obnoxious won't hurt you.

He's struck one of my deepest insecurities, the one that I've never been able to face myself.

All shoved at me by the one man I wanted to like me more than anything.

With a panicked sound, Lena jumps to her feet, her chair scraping. "Hey—hey, okay, we're out of tissues, hold on." She dips into the kitchen and snatches a wad of paper, thrusting it at me. "There we go. Paper towel time."

I take the paper towels and scrub my face.

They're scratchy, but I don't care.

"Sorry, guys—sorry I'm such a mess, I just—"

Lena snorts.

"Stop apologizing, girl." Her voice is harsh, but her touch soothes as she squeezes my shoulder. "That man bought himself a fiancée, and you had to go and be dumb enough to fall in love with him for real."

She says it with such certainty.

And it echoes inside me with an awful clarity, something that should feel wonderful and beautiful, but right now it's chokingly bittersweet.

God help me.

I love August Marshall.

I love his angry, grumpy, heart-thieving butt, when I'm nothing to him but a minuscule fly in his orbit.

"Well, when you put it that way . . ." I give Lena a lopsided smile.

"Was the sex worth it, at least?" She plunks back down in her chair.

"Lena!" Gran gasps.

I wrinkle my nose. "I mean, it was good . . ."

Gran looks faint, a hand fluttering to her chest. "I *cannot* know this about my granddaughter. While I know you two impertinent kids are just riling me up, let's change the subject."

My smile is a little more rueful as I wipe the last tears away with the paper towel. "I actually think I'm going to go up and lie down. I'm starting to get a headache behind my eyes. I think I have a date with my meds and the blackout blinds if I want to stave off another attack."

"Of course, dear." Gran reaches over to squeeze my hand again. "I meant to send *this* one home, anyway." She swats Lena's shoulder lightly. "Go take those muffins to your mother, you vulgar child."

"I just say the things you won't." Lena grins unrepentantly.

"The two of you should take your act on the road." I shake my head, rising with an amused sigh.

"Hey, not a bad idea, huh, Grams?"

"It's a terrible idea. Those comedy clubs smell, and you'd make me tell rather *blue* jokes."

I love them so much.

And that love gives me just enough energy to trudge upstairs, where I plunk down on my bed and stare for a solid minute.

I feel like my entire life has just fallen apart.

I won't be going to work tomorrow, or seeing August. Or Clara.

Which reminds me of the sketchbook on my nightstand.

I pull it over, slide the pages open, run my fingers over the little Inky doodles.

The new product line to revive the pen pal program. We were planning it all out—stationery, labels, stickers, pen wraps and toppers, erasers and pencils and collectible toys. A young guy in accounting even had a cool pitch for an Inky app.

August promised he'd look into everything.

And that night I'd gone home and curled up and sketched ideas for product designs in a frenzy, too excited to sleep.

But I guess it doesn't matter now.

Whatever we had is toast, and so is the entire brand.

That lump in my throat rises, so large it nearly chokes me. When I was a little girl and I used to feel this rudderless, I'd write Inky a letter, never knowing it wasn't Inky answering at all, but Clara Marshall herself.

I wish I could talk to her.

I wish I could understand.

I wish I could tell her I love her nephew, just so *someone* knows *it*, even if it's not August himself.

But now I can't.

Maybe writing will make me feel better, though, just like it used to.

I turn to a blank page in my sketchbook and curl up against the headboard of my bed.

I snag a pen from my nightstand.

Then, with all my gnarled feelings, I begin to write.

Dear Inky . . .

XXIV

BREAK IN THE CLOUDS

(AUGUST)

I'm almost crawling out of my skin by the time I disembark at Minneapolis–Saint Paul International and plow through the busy terminal to the rental pickup area.

For a last-minute same-day flight, all that was available was a rental van that looks like it should have **FREE CANDY** painted on the side in creepy serial killer script.

Beggars really can't be choosers.

Still, I wish I'd been a little choosier as I wrestle the boxy van onto the road and set out for a small town of only twenty thousand people called Northfield. It's only a forty-five-minute drive, but I nearly chip a tooth as the van rattles over potholes left behind by another grueling Minnesota winter.

I don't know how people live in this state.

I also don't know if it's the shocks or the suspension, but this thing needs service.

Only Aunt Clara would drive me to this.

Clara—and yes, dammit, Elle.

All so I can try to fix this. So I can save Little Key.

So I can prove I can get over my bullshit.

Enough to tell the truth when I tell Elle I love her and I trust her.

And I'm sorry as hell for exiling her from my life the way I did, when she's all that's worth holding on to.

The address the investigator found leads me to a small brick house on a cozy lane with a tidy fenced yard. In the back is a chicken coop, true to the PI's word.

The chickens roam contently, a mundane backdrop to my frantic pulse as I park, get out, and walk to the gate.

I don't have her phone number, so I couldn't call to let her know I was coming.

This might be a very unpleasant surprise.

I scrub my hands against my thighs and step up the walk to knock on the door.

"Just a minute!" a woman calls ahead of footsteps pattering toward me to answer.

As the door opens, I'm struck by a memory.

The same face, petite with silvery red hair in the same braid.

Only, back then she was younger.

Dinner over Aunt Clara's sketches.

Me, organizing her colored pencils, and this friendly face helping Clara in the kitchen. Deb underfoot wanting to help, too, but just banging giant spoons everywhere.

Me, thinking they were so noisy, but it was the kind of noise I loved, and when this woman laughed, Aunt Clara laughed too.

They looked at each other so warmly—warmer than Mom and Dad ever did before the accident.

Their secret smiles made everything feel like home.

I stare at her with my heart stalling.

"I remember you," I say weakly.

Yvette Sullivan shakes her head, smoothing her hands over her flower-patterned blue cotton dress. "I'm sorry, who?" She stops, her eyes widening. She looks at me hard, her fingers fluttering to her mouth. "August? Little August Marshall? Is that you, all grown up?"

How had I forgotten?

Back then, I'd been too young to understand.

I just thought she was another old friend of Aunt Clara's who came over to help.

"Miss Yvette." I find myself smiling. "It's been a long damned time, hasn't it?"

"Too long!" she says, then steps back. "Come in, come in, please. It's so good to see you." She casts me a nervous look, licking her lips as she leads me into a cozy home decorated with paintings and sketches, some of which have a distinctively familiar hand. She looks back again uncertainly. "Wow! I never expected—wait, Clara's not—is she?"

I suck in a breath as I realize what she must think.

That I've come to tell her Aunt Clara has passed away after a death-bed confession, or something equally terrible.

"No, no," I assure her. "Aunt Clara's still alive and making trouble. That's why I'm here. I need your help—and frankly, I think your daughter needs it too."

She stops cold at the entrance to her living room, decorated in soft earth tones and plush cushioning. Hurt flashes in her eyes.

"Marissa? How do you know her? I never brought her over when—well . . ."

"She's suing me, for one," I say dryly. "And Aunt Clara too. Marissa wants Little Key, and ownership of the Inky intellectual property."

Shock flashes across her face.

"What? *Why?*"

"Because she claims that her father—your late husband—came up with the idea first. She thinks Clara stole it and ran with it, and that's why he drank himself into an early grave. Because she took everything from him."

"Oh, my . . ." Yvette clenches her fingers in her skirt, frowning, trying to understand. "But that's an outright lie. Inky was always Clara's. Lester never could duplicate her work, though he tried like mad."

I didn't realize how tense I was until I hear those words.

Even though I wasn't invited, I sink down in the closest chair, burying my face in my hands with a heavy sigh that turns into a crazed laugh.

"Oh shit. Thank God," I say. "No, thank you, Yvette."

I get it now.

I understand everything.

I know why Aunt Clara gave in. Why she lied.

The secrets she was keeping, that she's been keeping bottled up for an eternity.

What she was running from and trying to protect.

Apparently, I'm not the only idiot Marshall who does stupid shit to run away from love.

But I might be the only idiot Marshall who can fix it.

I pull my hands down from my face and look up at Yvette, who watches me with confusion.

I can't blame her.

For the first time in a long time, there's hope.

"Please," I whisper. "Clara needs you. Marissa needs you. *I* need you. Will you come back to Seattle with me? To save Clara's legacy? You're the only one who can help me set many wrongs right."

XXV

ONE LAST RAY

(ELLE)

August's pocket square.

I forgot I still had this.

I've been sorting through my things. He left me in such a tizzy that I've less unpacked and more just lived out of boxes, with stuff flung everywhere and falling out of the cardboard.

August's pocket square from weeks ago was one of those things.

I found it when I went digging around for one of my older sketchbooks, hoping to recover some of my ancient ideas from high school. No matter what happens to Little Key, I'd like to round out Kiki's friends with an owl named Gruffykins before I try to *do* something with these characters instead of just flailing around.

The pocket square goes tumbling to the floor.

Just like that, I'm demolished all over again.

Yes, it's been a few days.

Brutally long days where I've dehydrated myself crying, now and then checking my phone and *hoping*.

But of course there's nothing from the real Gruffykins.

I won't mortify myself by texting him first.

I'm so not begging.

I can only be so bold before I get the message, and he made his message loud and clear.

I feel stupid, really.

One moment I'll be fine; the next I'll try to force a smile because it's what I always do. I'll remember how August was one of the only people who could tell when it wasn't real.

He cared enough to notice, and that breaks me again.

Usually, the tears don't stop until the migraine hits. Then I just hide in my room, pressing a cold cloth to my face and sulking until I feel like Ophelia, wasting away.

I pick up the little silk square, running my thumb over it.

My mouth tries to do that quivery pucker that warns more tears are imminent.

God, I'm confused.

He's a walking contradiction.

The man shut me out, let me in, pulled me close, pushed me away, until I think even he didn't know what he wanted, so there was no hope for me.

But if he doesn't want me, that's the end of it.

I'll just have to let it hurt until it doesn't, and then eventually I'll—

Ugh.

One day, I'll fall out of love with August Marshall.

That shouldn't feel so soul crushing.

But real-life love stories don't work like they do in movies.

I set the pocket square aside and go back to rummaging around in the box.

When I hear the doorbell ring, I don't think much of it. Probably just a delivery person wanting Gran to sign for one of her special-order heirloom seed packets or something similar.

So I'm surprised when I hear the door creak open, followed by a familiar voice.

My head jerks up. My stomach drops.

Is that . . . ?

"Ellie?" Grandma calls up. "You have company."

I straighten up, dust off my clothes, then pad out into the hall and peer over the banister. Clara Marshall looks up at me with a smile, holding up my fuzzy slippers.

She's as stylish as ever in a blue-fringed drape over a shimmery white silk top, loose, embroidered chiffon ivory pants, and slim blue strappy heels.

"I washed these for you, Elle," she says warmly. "I thought you'd need them back."

I could burst into tears at the sight of her.

Despite everything, I still respect Clara Marshall so much, and it's good to just *see* her and know she's okay.

But it also stings that she's the one who's brought my slippers.

Not August.

I smile anyway and head downstairs, taking them gratefully.

"Thank you. How are you . . ." I fumble awkwardly. "Are you okay?"

"Oh, you know how these things go," she deflects. There's something troubled behind her eyes. "I've been very busy. I've certainly missed your help."

"Oh—I'm so sorry, I just—you know, I thought after everything . . ." I scuff my feet, looking down. "I thought I was sorta fired."

There's an awkward pause that Gran fills with a clap of her hands. "Well now! This is tea conversation."

I smile.

Clara hesitates. "I'm afraid I don't have much time . . ."

"Nonsense. There's always time for tea." Gran taps Clara's arm lightly. "Do come with me. I'm so delighted to finally meet you, Miss Marshall. Elle talks about you nonstop."

"Grandma!" I hiss.

Clara gives me a patiently amused look and follows Gran inside.

"Well, I'm quite flattered, but I must say I can't stop talking about this wonderful young lady too. She's a darling—kind, lovely to be around, and such a help to me. Not to mention how brilliantly talented she is."

"Clara!" I gasp, going red up to my ears.

Oh my God, are the older women in my life all trying to kill me today?

Gran and Clara trade wickedly amused looks.

"My," Gran says mildly. "That's a lovely shade of pink on her, isn't it? Really complements her complexion."

"Absolutely," Clara answers. "She should wear that color more often."

Mortifying.

I glower at them both while they descend into casual chatter like they've known each other their whole lives. Clara compliments the vines and ferns that have practically taken over the house.

Gran enthusiastically explains how she cultivates outdoor flowering vines to thrive inside. It saves me from more embarrassment, at least, as I set my slippers aside and help Gran to put tea on.

It's jasmine today. The weather's getting a little warmer, and jasmine tea is always good in spring.

The atmosphere feels relaxed and light by the time we settle at the table in the atrium with our teacups.

Clara breaks off from exclaiming over the delicate lace of the table doilies and looks at me, smiling over a sip of her tea before setting the cup down.

"The truth is, Elle, I had an ulterior motive for coming here. Don't look so frightened—I'm not here to make things worse."

She doesn't have to say what *things* she means.

But if I think about August, I'm going to break.

She only shakes her head with another smile. "Actually, I'm here for me. I'm selfish enough to prevail on your support, if you wouldn't mind. You see . . ." She looks uncomfortable. "The trial is in a few hours."

I frown, warming my hands on my teacup. "There shouldn't be a trial. Sorry, but you've basically surrendered and agreed to Marissa's demands. It's a civil case, not criminal. A settlement doesn't need a court date, does it?"

"Yes, well . . ." She sighs heavily. "Marissa wants a spectacle. She wants it trotted out in front of a judge with all of us there—not you, no, but at least myself and my niece and nephew. A private settlement isn't enough. She wants a full court circus."

Gran scoffs. "How tacky. She wants to drive the final nail in. Make it as humiliating as possible."

"Apparently so. I've tried to be graceful, considering the situation, but this really is rather tasteless." Clara shakes her head. "Deb's very distraught. She has enough work on her plate. August, he's nowhere to be found—he's turned his phone off. I haven't seen him for days. He's likely run off to Taos or Ketchikan or some other far-flung place to find his perfect brooding nest."

Despite myself, I snicker.

Yeah, that's Gruffykins, all right.

"So you see," Clara finishes, "I'm on my own, without a friend in my corner. And if I'm about to go through with this, I would be eternally grateful for your company, Elle. That is, if you wouldn't mind coming."

I don't know if I can do that.

I don't know if I can stand there passively while this woman gives up her life's work, all for an idea that means so much to her *and* me. And all to this greedy mess of a woman who's only doing this because she needs to hurt someone to make her own pain better.

But I can't leave Clara to face hell alone.

I stare down into my tea. My reflection looks up at me, the tea trembling like it shares the nerves I'm trying not to show.

August won't be there, I tell myself.

I won't have to see him and hurt quietly in the courtroom while he looks anywhere but at me.

So I smile, lifting my head.

"Sure," I say, pushing my chair back. "Just let me get dressed."

◆ ◆ ◆

Twenty minutes later, and I match with Clara.

I've picked out a bright-blue A-skirt in almost the same shade as her drape, with a short-sleeved white silk blouse and a small blue scarf at the neck to pair with it. It's fine for court attire—professional but bright. The wings of my eyeliner match, with their accent of pearl shimmer.

I kiss Gran on the way out after she turns down the invitation to join us, then ride with Clara to the courthouse in an Uber.

We're quiet in the car. Our nerves speak volumes.

She looks so anxious, the sorrow hovering over her like a cloak.

It still doesn't add up.

If she really meant that confession, she'd either be feeling guilt or regret. Maybe even shame.

She'd be carrying the weight of getting *caught*, of feeling awful for what she'd stolen across decades of cruel deception. And even if her emotions had the appropriate chagrin, she still wouldn't act like she's almost in mourning.

You only grieve something lost when it's really yours.

That's why this doesn't make any freaking sense.

What am I still missing?

The car drops us at the courthouse. It's not that busy, people streaming in and out, handling their own business or standing around with busy-looking lawyers.

I give Clara my arm to lean on for comfort as we check which courtroom we're assigned to; then we make our way through the halls to the wood-paneled room.

There's hardly anyone inside.

Just a few lawyers settled at tables on opposing sides. I see Marissa with her team, and Deb with the Little Key defense. Her eyes are red, but her face is cold and composed.

There's an empty chair waiting for Clara.

A few reporters scroll their phones in the seating area, looking either anxious or disinterested.

The judge is an older man, balding and with a monk's crown around the back of his head. The overhead lights reflect off the dark-brown skin of his skull and his narrow rimless glasses.

As we enter, the Little Key lawyers glance back at us. One lawyer catches the judge's eye and nods. He straightens, shuffling through some pages on his desk.

"Everyone's here?" the judge asks, his voice echoing in the solemn chamber.

I pat Clara's hand and give her a gentle nudge. She looks petrified, but I know she'll get through this, no matter what happens.

She's tied with Gran as the strongest woman I've ever met.

"I'm here if you need me," I whisper.

"I know. Thank you, dear."

She pulls away and drifts to her seat, settling in next to Deb.

I claim a place in the row behind her, making sure to stay as close as I can.

Marissa looks so smug I wonder if she's drunk again.

An ugly thought inside me says she didn't deserve the kindness August showed her that night he helped her home. But even I can't help but hurt for her too.

This crusade of hers is horribly misguided. I know she's trying to take from Clara to make up for what she's lost.

Pain makes us do crazy things.

Sometimes it makes us merciless.

"All present, Your Honor," the lawyer on our side says.

The judge bangs his gavel once, quick and perfunctory.

"Calling to order, Judge Harris presiding. We're here for the case of *Sullivan v. Marshall*, regarding intellectual property rights for creative copyright over a series of children's book characters and all associated trademarked merchandise, branding, and properties." He frowns at the pages. "It looks like you've reached an agreement regarding a settlement. That means we can dismiss this case in favor of the plaintiff, with the defendant surrendering all rights voluntarily. So, why are we here again?"

Marissa opens her mouth, but she doesn't get to finish.

The courtroom door slams open.

"Because," August says, his voice projecting authority and determination, all dark fire. He steps inside with a slim older woman behind him, still pretty with her long greying red hair in a braid and a matching grey dress. "The defendant's confession was forced under duress, and the entire premise of this case is a lie."

XXVI

STRUCK BY LIGHTNING

(AUGUST)

I've never made a bigger mess from just walking into a room.

The moment I enter, the entire courtroom erupts into chaos.

"Objection!" shouts one of Marissa's lawyers, flying to his feet.

Marissa stands, too, cupping her hands over her mouth as she screams, "What the fuck, asshole?"

Aunt Clara pops up next.

"Yvette?!" she cries.

And promptly starts to faint, with Deb struggling to catch her.

"Clara!" Yvette screams.

And so does—

Elle?

Why is Elle here?

Bright as a new-bloomed flower, her blonde hair flying behind her as she rushes around the wooden barrier and drops to Aunt Clara's side. She sinks down in a crouch with Deb as they both help Clara up.

She's already coming to, shaking off her daze, her eyes blinking open.

Marissa whirls on us.

Yvette had started to rush forward, but now she freezes as Marissa points a stern finger at her.

"What's *she* doing here? Get her out of here!"

"If everyone would kindly shut up," the judge demands, his voice booming as he slams his gavel several times. He throws me a fierce look over his glasses. "Sir, this is a private case. Unless you have business here, you're asking for contempt of court—"

"I'm sorry for barging in late," I cut in. "I have a quarter share in Little Key. My name is August Marshall, acting CEO. Clara Marshall is my aunt. This case pertains to me as well. And this"—I gently nudge a shy, faltering Yvette forward—"is the plaintiff's mother, Yvette Sullivan. Also, Clara's long-separated lover."

Everyone in the room gasps except Clara and Yvette.

They just stare at each other in disbelief.

They watch each other the same way I can't help but look at Elle.

Like they've been blind all this time, but now they can finally see, and their first restored vision is the glory of lost love.

Everything they've craved through the darkness for all this time.

It's definitely a moment.

Intense and heart wrenching and beautiful to see.

Clara can't take her eyes off Yvette, even while Elle and Deb help her up on shaky feet, her lips mouthing, *Yvette, Yvette, Yvette . . .*

Elle looks up then.

Her eyes meet mine, that soft hazel gold—my tiger kitten, my jewel, my insane bright summer flower.

Yes, I know.

I fucking know I'm just staring at her like I've been lobotomized, while she's looking back at me with such confusion and hurt in her eyes and something else.

Longing.

Hand to God, I'll make this right.

But first, I have to correct another massive mistake.

I jerk my attention back to the judge as he lets out an exasperated sigh. "Mr. Marshall, while this is an entertaining soap opera, how does this pertain to the case? Make it brief, or get the hell out of my courtroom."

"Your Honor, the entire case is predicated on a lie Marissa Sullivan was led to believe to salvage a dead man's pride," I say. A little dramatic, yes, but it's true. "Surrendering these rights is a grave miscarriage of justice. If you'll allow Yvette Sullivan to take the stand, she can tell you that this case is false—and provide proof."

"Mom, don't you dare!" Marissa hisses. "That woman is my mother in blood only. She cheated on my father!"

"No," Yvette says, shaking her head. "I never cheated, love. I would never do that to you. Not even to Lester. But I admit, I didn't love him. He wasn't the man he led you to believe he was. It's true I loved someone else while we were married . . . but we never did anything about it. For your sake."

"My sake . . . ?" Marissa staggers back, wrinkling her nose.

Yvette looks at the judge pleadingly.

He sighs, adjusting his glasses. "I'll agree, if everyone will *sit down* already—and if Mr. Marshall will stop turning my courtroom into a zoo."

"Absolutely," I answer. "I apologize again, Your Honor."

I glance around for somewhere to sit. I want to go to Elle as she reclaims her seat, but sitting next to each other, unable to talk, to hold her, to apologize, would feel like pure torture.

So I steal an extra chair and join Clara, Deb, and the lawyers at the table.

Clara wears a dozen emotions on her face.

Screaming. Crying. Laughing.

I was more than right, then.

All this time, she's never stopped loving Yvette.

Yvette nods slowly, giving Clara a nervous look and a shy smile before she lets the bailiff guide her to the stand. She clasps her hands together and looks up at the judge. He nods, not unkindly.

"Go on," he says.

Then he shoots a stern look at a frozen Marissa.

"*Sit*, Miss Sullivan."

Marissa plunks down in her chair so hard the legs scrape.

In the silence, Yvette takes a shaky breath.

"I'm . . . well, I'm not quite sure how to start," she says.

The beginning, I mouth to her.

"Right. So, Lester, Clara, and I met in art school. We were fast friends. Lester and I were already dating. Frankly, I think Lester originally had notions of . . ." She blushes. "Of having both of us. But Clara was indifferent, though I don't think he noticed. He *did* eventually notice how close we were, though."

Her flush deepens as her eyes lock on Clara with such yearning. Like she speaks only for her and there's no one else in the room.

"I was in denial for so long. You didn't feel those kinds of things back then. You certainly didn't talk about them. By the time I let myself acknowledge the way my heart beat and my body yearned—"

"Mom!" Marissa hisses.

"—every time Clara so much as brushed my hand, I fell a little deeper. But I was pregnant. Lester and I were married. And suddenly, I was a wife and mother, and Clara had two kids to raise after her brother and his wife died. All I could be was backdrop while my ambitious husband and best friend started talking about publishing together."

"You were never a backdrop to me," Clara whispers, so low I think only our table hears her. "Never."

Yvette shakes her head with a sad yet beautiful smile.

"I couldn't stay away. Always hovering, trying to be helpful. Back in college, Clara and I had gotten in the habit of sending each other letters, and we still did. Those letters were where she first told me about the idea she had. About a penguin who didn't fit in because he was different from everyone else. I knew what she was really saying with that. I wanted her to tell that story so much, about that penguin who was accepted and loved by the friends he made all over the world and the people he brought together. Loved *because* of his difference."

There's a soft sniff behind me.

Elle.

I know how she feels.

I don't show it, but my own throat is burning, raw.

"I was there the day Clara showed Lester her first sketches," Yvette confesses. "He hated the idea at first. *Hated it.* But she slowly won him over, and they started plotting the first Inky books, refining the base illustrations together. During that time, I . . . we never said a word to each other. But I think we were obvious. The nights I would go over without Lester to help with Deb and August, bringing Clara dinner after she'd worked herself dizzy all day in the studio and was too tired to cook for the kids. The times I'd stay over. I'd sleep on the couch, but we'd wind up talking late into the night. And sometimes—well, sometimes we'd just look at each other, and I'd want to say it so much. 'I love you. I love you, and I don't know what to do about it.'"

She says those words to Clara and Clara alone.

Tears stream silently down Aunt Clara's face, curving her lips in the most painfully sweet smile that makes her look thirty years younger. The bright, hopeful woman Yvette had fallen for all over again.

"But I never could," Yvette continues, shaking her head. "I had a husband and a daughter. I wouldn't be unfaithful. I wouldn't break apart my family and take my daughter away from her father. And if society knew, they would hate us. So I only craved her from afar, but eventually, Lester started to notice. All these years he still looked at Clara a certain way, and I think he even tried to make me jealous with their solitary studio sessions. But he finally started noticing the way we smiled at each other. The way we touched. Chaste, but there was something about it, something we couldn't hide." She draws a shaky breath. "Lester confronted us. Accused us of cheating. Said the most hateful words. We denied it, but that was the end. The partnership was over. Lester moved us away and said he wanted nothing to do with Inky the Penguin. He was controlling, monitored my letters, my phone calls. And when Inky blew up and became so famous, that's when he started drinking. That's when he started trying to re-create it, claiming it was his idea all along, venting his bitterness to Marissa."

Her gaze flicks to her daughter.

"I know you loved him, sweetheart," she says. "And he was good to you. He was a decent father. I won't pretend he wasn't. He loved you too. But even though he was good to you, he wasn't a good husband. He lied so you'd think he was an amazing man who'd just been cheated, when he was so selfish. So cruel. He never created Inky, and I never cheated on him. But I did hurt him by falling in love with someone else. That's my fault, I know. If you hate me for it, I understand. Everything else, those were his choices, my darling. I only wish you'd accept that instead of trying to punish Clara for Lester's mistakes."

Click.

Just like that, the last puzzle piece falls into place.

Marissa always knew about her mother and Clara, and that's what she's really been trying to punish Clara for.

Not for being a lesbian, no.

But for being the lost love that tore her family apart.

"Please," Yvette pleads. "You have your father's stubbornness, and sometimes it's admirable. But please don't follow his path. Don't go down that long, dark road he walked. I know about your drinking, Marissa. Please, I can't lose you that way too."

Marissa recoils, her face blanking.

"Who told y—" She gasps, turning a vicious glare on me. *"You."*

"Guilty." I raise my hand and wave.

There's a choked snicker behind me.

A little of Elle's sense of humor might be rubbing off.

"You called my *mommy* on me?" Marissa flares.

"Also guilty," I say.

"You fucking—"

"Order!" Judge Harris snarls, slamming his gavel again. With an exasperated sigh, he points it at Yvette. "You. Go sit." Then he points it at Clara. "You, testify. Is any of this true?"

Clara rises slowly as Yvette gets up and exits the stand.

For a moment, they pass each other, trading places.

For the briefest second, they stop.

A long, deep look passes between them.

Their hands brush, and my heart aches so deeply for the love denied, and for the touch of Elle's hand. What Clara and Yvette had, what was torn away from them . . .

Goddamn, I really am stupid for waiting so long.

I want that with Elle Lark.

I want to reclaim it before I'm grizzled with denial, looking back on years of regrets, wishing like hell I'd never let her go.

Aunt Clara takes the stand and tucks her hair back, drawing a deep breath.

"It's true," she says plainly. Marissa almost screeches, but Aunt Clara continues: "I'm sorry. I lied, Marissa. I lied because . . . because I felt like I owed you something. Because of our secrets, your father became bitter, and he lost himself. I felt responsible for his death, so much that I slowly lost my will to draw the gentle bird that caused us so much trouble. But I've always loved your mother. There's never been a day I haven't missed her. But I felt like I didn't have the right—not after the pain we'd caused. The only thing I could do was stay away, trying to protect her, and keep her from getting dragged into this legal battle." Her blue eyes lock on Yvette. "An attempt that I know now was misguided. I should have told you I loved you years ago. So I'm telling you now. I love you, Yvette Sullivan."

Gasps.

Even our lawyers are wiping their eyes now, and dammit, I'm losing my dignity and pushing a cactus of emotion down my throat.

At my side, Yvette falters, swaying faintly.

I clasp her elbow to steady her.

"Clara," she whispers. "Oh, Clara, I never—I could never *not* love you. You've been my whole heart. I've missed you so much . . ."

"Yvette . . ." Clara's trembling smile is so full of joy it could blind the whole room.

Judge Harris clears his throat. His eyes are suspiciously soft.

"Yes. Well. That's all very touching, but it's not legal proof. You said you had *proof.*"

"Oh—um, yes." Yvette fumbles around in her dress pockets, then walks toward the judge quickly and passes over a crumbled sheet of paper. The handwriting on it looks blurred by time and repeated handling. "That's it. That's the letter where Clara Marshall first told me about what eventually became Inky. It's dated years before the publication of the first Inky book."

"Oh my. You kept that?" Clara lights up.

"I kept everything," Yvette admits with a shy grin.

Damn.

They're like schoolgirls with each other, sweet and hesitant.

Judge Harris scans the letter while the entire courtroom holds on to silent, bated breaths.

"Thank you for letting me read something so heartfelt and personal, but technically, this isn't admissible because it was never entered into evidence," Judge Harris says flatly, passing the letter back to Yvette.

The entire room deflates with a groan.

Marissa smirks.

"However . . ." Harris raises his voice to be heard. "If you'll pardon me, this entire case is a cluster. The dates on this mean nothing when they could have been added after the fact, and it would require extensive forensic analysis that we don't have on hand, do we? No. No, we don't. Therefore, it's all down to a case of 'he said, she said,' and I can't pass a judgment based on that kind of testimony." Another bang of the gavel before he points it at Marissa. "I'm throwing your case out without judgment and dismissing your claim." Snorting, he leans back in his

seat, adjusting his robes. "Jesus Christ. Sort your goddamned lives out, people. Case dismissed. Everyone *out* of my courtroom."

I sit stunned for a moment.

Relief sweeps through me in a rush.

Deb shoots up at my side with a fist-pumping shout. *"Yes!"*

"No!" Marissa slams her hands down on the table.

"Eee!" Yvette and Clara tumble toward each other with loud squeals.

Marissa stares at them like she can't decide if she wants to laugh or scream.

Clara and Yvette collide—and then they're kissing—deeply, passionately, frantically.

My eyes widen and I clear my throat, looking away politely.

"Not fair," I mutter. "How the hell does she get to kiss her girl before I do?"

"Because she wasn't a dick to her girl," Deb mutters back with a smirk. "By the way, your girl is right behind you, doofus. I think you have some things to say to her."

Shit.

I finally let myself look back at Elle.

If I'd done it during the case, I'd have lost my shit in a heartbeat, gone to her, begged for her forgiveness.

For her love.

But Elle's not looking at me now.

She's watching Clara and Yvette, her eyes streaming with happy tears. Her hands are clasped over her mouth, but it's not hard to tell she's smiling, laughing, crying all at once.

Yvette breaks away from Clara, smiling so wide, leaning into her to nuzzle their noses together tenderly before she pulls back enough to look at her daughter.

"Marissa," Yvette says softly. "I'm sorry I never told you the truth, but I'm still your mother. I never stopped loving you. I want to be here for you, no matter what you're going through. Please . . . please, can we start over?"

Start over.

That's what I want so badly.

To start again with Elle, this time being together for real.

Which means I have to man the fuck up and be honest about how I feel.

"Elle," I say softly.

Her breath sucks in.

For a moment, she doesn't look at me, her shoulders tensing.

"I'm sorry," she chokes. "Clara asked me to come. I know I shouldn't be here, but—"

"No—no, I'm glad you came, to be there for her, especially when I was preoccupied."

"I see that." She blinks. Despite the tension, she laughs, shaking her head. "I can't believe you figured all this out. You found her, August. You brought them back together. It's amazing!"

"It is," I agree, when all I want to say is, *I want that. I want that with you. I fucking want what they have, and I'm not afraid to admit it.* "I hope they're happy now. Hope they can make up for lost time."

She's watching me intently.

Why is this so difficult?

Deep breath.

"Elle, I can't lose more time making things right with you," I grind out, my heart tumbling out in the open.

She falters, her smile fading as she looks at me with wide, confused eyes.

"What?"

"Elle, I—goddammit, woman. You know I'm bad at this." Muttering to myself, I lift up enough to fish around in my pockets and pull out a folded piece of paper. "Just read it."

Puzzled, Elle reaches out carefully to take the folded page.

"I feel like I'm back in sixth grade," she murmurs, unfolding the paper.

Now *I* have to look away.

I can't stand to look while she reads my clumsy words.

Miss Eleanor Lark—

I wanted to start this with "My everything." Because on paper I get to cheese it up, and you are my all, Elle Lark.

I should have told you that the second I realized it.

I should have told you every damned day.

I should have shut my yap instead of screaming and been honest—as bright and honest as you've always been with me.

When I was a little boy, I loved Inky because he was different. The kind of different that makes children feel less alone.

The same way Inky found acceptance because he was unique, you made me feel accepted. Like I can be myself—rude, blunt, and strange as ever.

You let me be me without complaints, without trying to change me.

You still care for me just as I am.

But I didn't make you feel the same, did I?

I called you crazy, chaotic and disruptive. I treated you like an intrusion on my life, when you were anything but.

You were—you are—what I never knew I needed to make my life complete.

Screw chaos.

You bring joy.

You light up everything you touch.

I'm so accustomed to remaining untouched that I mistook change for destruction and love for intrusions. Your joy is not destructive. Your care is not invasive.

It makes me whole and it's part of what makes you so beautiful.

If you're insane, then I'm fucking pathological.

I'm insane for everything about you.

All the things you think I couldn't possibly like about you—your brightness, your impulsiveness, your whims, your goofy pet names.

I'd rather wake up to "Gruffykins" a thousand mornings than breathe another minute without you.

I love them all.

Just like I love you.

I think I've loved you since the day you fell into my arms in an airport terminal. I've just had to wrestle myself to face the truth, and in the process, I wound up fighting you.

I'm sincerely sorry for that.

So sorry I made it difficult to be with me.

And I'm sorry I made you walk on eggshells around me. That's a sin when you should be free to be as wild as you are with me.

I want you, Elle.

Don't care about the name on what that means.

Girlfriend, fiancée, whatever.

Just give me what's real.

Because now I know that I love you, I can't stop, Elle Lark.

I know you love Inky. Can you ever love another awkward penguin?

August

Go ahead and laugh.

I don't give a damn.

If I'd tried to say any of that shit out loud, I'd have tripped all over it until I gave up and stormed away chewing my tongue. But waiting for Elle to finish reading it, dead silent except for her sniffles, is *agony*.

I've never felt my heart split before, cracking and lining and vulnerable.

Vulnerable.

That's not something I ever am.

But with her, I'm willing to face the pain.

I trust her not to ever take advantage of my openness.

"You love me," she whispers.

My head snaps up sharply to find her watching me with those brightly lit eyes.

"August, you . . . you really love me?"

"More than humanly possible," I whisper. "More than I can stand."

There it is—her smile creeping back.

I can't take my eyes off her gorgeous lips to save my life.

"Say it," she breathes. "Let me hear you say it out loud."

"I love you," I say immediately. It's like an anvil lifting off my shoulders. "I *love* you, Elle."

"*August,*" she cries—and suddenly she's flying across the barrier.

Into my arms.

Into my kiss.

Into the rest of my life.

"I love you," she answers—kissing me again and again, pressing the words into my lips, elating me with her light until I could shatter the stars. "I *love* you, you stupid man. Oh, you're such a dick, and I still love you—"

I laugh like mad, wrapping my arms around her waist and nipping her lips. "Insult me again. Just so I know you really mean it."

She loves me, and I can't hold back anymore.

Right there in front of my aunt, her beloved, my sister, Marissa, the lawyers, the judge—fuck, everyone—I do it.

I sweep Elle closer and kiss her until I touch her soul.

I kiss her the way I should have that day I broke us, healing the wound before it grew any deeper. Kiss her like I can never kiss anyone else again, and dammit, I don't want to.

Not when her mouth fits mine this perfectly.

Not when our lips lock, and we meet like our mouths and minds and souls were made for each other.

I finally feel whole.

For the first time, that searching feeling inside me gets filled by a woman who's become my everything.

Everything I need.

Everything that could ever make me happy.

I want so badly to make her as happy as she makes me.

God willing, I'll try.

With every day of my life, I'll try to be a better man. A man who deserves her, who's worthy of standing in the light of her sun.

Maybe even worthy enough to be her *Gruffykins*.

No matter how bright she shines, I'll always love the burn.

But suddenly, somehow, everyone in the courtroom is kissing.

Clara and Yvette.

"Oh, fuck it," Deb says, grabbing one of our lawyers by the tie. She pulls him in and kisses him hard in a sexual harassment lawsuit waiting to happen.

Even Marissa throws her hands up.

"Not fair," she says. "Not fair!"

So she rises up on her toes.

Grabs the judge's robe.

And drags him down, planting a big wet one on his lips.

I break back from Elle, looking around the room with a laugh as I hold her tight. "See that? We've started a trend."

"That's a trend I could follow forever," she says, laying her head on my chest, right over the pounding tumble of my heart. "If we can spread this much love with a kiss, I think you'd better kiss me again, Gruffykins."

Goddamn.

Until now, I never thought I'd understand that phrase about lightning striking twice.

Sometimes it does, and sometimes you need the shock and awe.

"Darling brat," I say, bending to take her mouth again with laughter rolling through me, "you only need to ask once."

XXVII

DOUBLE RAINBOW DAY

(ELLE)

You'd think going from fiancée to girlfriend would be a downgrade.

But fake fiancée to real girlfriend?

That's not so bad at all.

It's been an exhausting day.

An enormous family lunch where we dragged Lena and Grandma along to the restaurant after stopping by Grandma's house on our way from the courthouse. Marissa bristled and sulked like a little girl but slowly warmed up to her mother again. Clara and Yvette stuck to each other like glue.

Ditto for August and me.

We can't get enough of each other after kissing and making up.

Touching, looking, stealing little kisses every chance we get.

It was chaotic while we all talked, found our vibe as a group, hit it off, started a few small fights, put them out, and stopped Deb from punching Marissa in the face for dragging us through all this.

But even Marissa eventually conceded.

She actually apologized.

Better yet, she agreed to let her mother be her AA sponsor, and Yvette swore she wouldn't let Marissa slip away like her father did.

It was well after dark, lunch blending into dinner and a second dessert course, before we finally slipped away. Transportation has been a mess, shuffling between different cars, dropping each other off, but now it's just August and me in the G80.

I don't get out at the house with Gran.

I want to be with him tonight—and every night going forward.

But I'm exhausted, leaning against his arm while he drives, dozing off like the passing lights are hypnotizing me to sleep.

It feels nice to be tired with him, to share the silence with his relaxed body language.

I think I've seen August laugh more today than I have since the day we met. Though I love stuffy August too. Serious August. Broody August. Angry August. Sarcastic August. Kind August. Sexy August.

Best of all, happy August.

Especially when I can be the reason he smiles.

"You never took it off," he says.

"Mm?" I startle awake with a little mumble.

Smiling, he takes one hand off the wheel to clasp my hand, running his thumb over the engagement ring.

"This."

". . . oh." I look down at our hands, my face heating. "I actually forgot it was there. It feels so much like it belongs that I never thought about taking it off."

"Good," he growls softly, and my heart flips over. "Don't."

I hide my face against his arm and stay there for the rest of the drive to his house.

As he pulls in, though, I ask, "Are you happier now?"

A warm look slides over me. "I'm happy now you're mine again. I'm sorry I fought it so hard, Elle."

"I forgave you the second you handed me that letter. Your drawing *sucks*, by the way. It took me an hour to realize that blob was Inky in the margins."

He snorts. "You're the talent in this relationship, no question."

"I'm glad you recognize my superiority." I kiss his shoulder. "But that's not what I meant. You've been carrying Charisma with you for so long. The fact that you couldn't save her. But you saved Yvette and Clara's relationship, and you just might have saved Marissa from herself."

He goes quiet, thoughtful.

"Sometimes you really do see me too well," he whispers, killing the engine until we're silent outside the moonlit house. "I don't think it's so much about saving people. I'm no one's white knight. It's about letting go of my ego to recognize someone crying for help, even when they're hurting others, and not ignoring it. It's choosing to help, instead. I'm glad that I made that choice this time, instead of having regrets later, when it's too damn late." He looks down at me again, his eyes softening. "So, yes. I'm happy. And I'm grateful to you for knocking me out of my head enough for me to recognize that."

I laugh in embarrassment, hiding against him again. "I didn't do anything. Well, besides turning your life into complete chaos."

"Needed chaos." He kisses the top of my head. "But you're about to pass out. Let's go to bed."

"You're the boss."

Honestly, I'm so tired after all the big emotions and catharsis of today that when he says *bed*, the only thing I'm thinking is sleep.

Sweet, glorious sleep.

Leaning against him, I walk in a half drowse as he lets us into the house, then trail him down the hall to the bedroom.

But the second I see his bed, I flush.

It's still disarrayed from that night—and I realize he hasn't been here, instead traveling and making arrangements with Yvette. My camisole is even still on the sheets.

I drift to the bed and pick it up. "I still can't believe I came running over here in my nightie."

"I can," August says dryly, pulling at his tie. "It's what you do best. You're impulsive, Elle. You chase your every whim." He smiles slightly. "Always brave as can be."

I duck my head, blushing, my fingers curling around the camisole. "I don't feel very brave."

"Bull." I hear the sound of his tie pulling away, and then he steps up behind me, wrapping his arms around my waist. "You're confident, even when you're insecure. You know your own heart. You know what you want. That's admirable as hell."

Blushing, I reach back to swat him. "Enough flattery. I'm not getting naked for you tonight."

"Who said I need you naked?" His lips graze my neck. "In fact, I've had thoughts about you in my office, straddling my lap, riding me while we're still clothed."

My breath catches.

My body immediately heats, no matter how tired I am.

I look at him over my shoulder, biting my lip.

"I bet that violates half the HR code."

"Yeah. But we're not at work now, are we?" His fingers curl against my stomach, pulling me back tighter against him. I can feel exactly what he wants, pressing against my ass. "And I wouldn't mind you on your hands and knees while I fuck you in that cute little skirt."

I groan, but he's already got me.

"Do you ever turn *off*?"

Then again, do *I* ever turn off, when all he has to do is say something dirty, and I can feel my panties melting?

"Not with you," August growls, pushing lightly at my back. "Do it, Elle. Hands and knees. Now."

The command in his voice makes me shiver with pleasure.

I know if I really didn't want to, he'd leave me be.

But I want this.

I want him.

And I want him to not take no for an answer.

My stomach still twists as I slide on my hands and knees on the bed.

It's a tad embarrassing, presenting myself like this—but the self-consciousness is part of what feels so good, making it different, making me deliciously nervous.

Especially when I can't see what he's going to do to me. I can only *feel* as his hands glide over my ass, down my thighs, taking me down with one rough touch at a time.

He flips my skirt up, leaving my spread thighs exposed. The cool air licks the damp fabric of my panties, ass up and ready to be mounted.

He lets out a soft rumble, running his fingertips along my slit.

I jerk with a faint sound, thighs tightening, body fully on fire.

That touch flits away—then returns in a sharp slap against my ass.

Just a sting that makes my hips jerk forward with a cry while a sudden wetness erupts between my legs.

Oh God.

He's in a mood tonight.

And suddenly his hands are on my hips, dragging me against him. My spread-open pussy is assaulted as he grinds his cock against me, his slacks hissing against my panties, lace against wool as he rubs deep, teases me, torments me, makes me feel helpless.

Hard and fast he taunts me, every once in a while coming back for another crisp *smack* that makes me clench and shudder and whimper his name.

It shouldn't feel this good.

But there's something intensely erotic about it.

Even more so when he stops, and I hear his zipper dragging down.

His fingers hook my panties, dragging them aside.

His fingertips scrape naked flesh until I keen softly, biting the inside of my cheek.

"August!" I whisper-scream as he drives into me sharply, brutally, sinking home in a single hard stroke.

It's like he's punishing me for making him miss me.

It's harsh, desperate, *fast*, plunging hard and deep, fucking me like a wild animal.

His thrusts catch me up in it until I'm losing my mind.

I'm so wet, squirming my ass back into him like a madwoman.

So good.

Every single slash of his hips electrifies me when he's so thick; the flare of his cockhead teases me just right and rips cries from my body.

God, I want more.

More.

I spread my legs wider, clawing at the sheets, writhing to meet him and trying to take him so much deeper.

So deep I'll feel the veins of his cock for days.

When I walk, when I sit, even when I move.

I want to feel used by this gorgeous man.

I want to pulse with the memory of him pounding me until I'm sore in all the best ways.

Thankfully, he's relentless.

Taking me harder, *harder*, forcing me down on the bed and still keeping my ass up and presented to him, but he pushes my head down on the sheets in utter dominance.

The change in position makes his cock hit different, deeper, hammering delicious friction in this one spot that acts like a detonator.

When he hits it again—

Foly huck!

I can't tell where the lightning ends and my orgasm begins, leaving me thrashing, gasping, coming so hard, so much.

I'm completely flooded, and I still want more.

I want to be full.

I want him.

I want his lust.

I want his love.

I want him, knowing that loving me means he can feel safe enough to let me know his deepest, truest savagery.

Knowing he'll fuck me like a depraved beast and then hold me tenderly when it's over. After he's done.

After he's used my body to sweet perfection.

And I realize I won't be sleeping tonight.

Because he's not ready to come.

Not for a few more sheet-ripping minutes.

While his manic thrusts are already quickening, pushing me past the edge again, his cruel hands slip between my legs to pinch my clit and taunt me and make me realize what he's doing.

He's going to string me along all night.

Make me come again and again before he finally gives me himself.

He'll make me feel cherished—and then he'll destroy me with his love.

He'll leave me craving more of this addiction, this man who's all gruffness when his head rears back, when his gaze drills mine, when he fists my hair with a single command.

"Fucking come with me, Elle. *Come.*"

And I do.

God help me, I obey, blinded while white-hot pleasure rips up his throat and he pours himself into me.

He empties his balls inside me with his teeth clenched, grinding my name between his teeth like an animal.

We share it all.

This strange, perfect moment that says he belongs to me.

After tonight, I belong to him forever.

Months later

Let's get one thing straight—I do not have that much stuff.

So why is moving in with August such a pain?

His house—oh, it's ours now, isn't it?—*our* house is nice. Tons of open, airy space.

And very little storage.

I might not have that much stuff, but I do have a lot of art supplies.

I stand against the window in the guest bedroom, which doubles as my newly converted studio. I've already hung my framed original sketches of Kiki the Koala, plus a special original Inky print Clara gifted me.

I'm so insanely glad she never surrendered it to Marissa Sullivan.

Well, Marissa would have had to give it back anyway.

Just last week, August finalized the acquisition and merger of her company. A sobered-up Marissa is now a junior executive at Little Key, managing her own line of children's books, with her flagship product being—

Me.

Villain to boss. What a twist.

Then again, my whole life has been bonkers for the past six months.

I went from only being on the cover of tabloids as August's fiancée, famous by proxy, to making headlines as Little Key announced a new coauthor on the newly expanded Inky line.

Never, in my wildest dreams, did I ever imagine such a thing, but when Clara Marshall asks, you answer.

I'm barely her apprentice anymore, but her partner. We put her name and Inky back in the headlines, and together we worked up the new product line, new books, the revived and smashingly successful pen pal program.

Then people started asking when I'd put out my own books.

Suddenly, I had shiny new social media shouts. Instead of jealous women calling me the *gold-digging whore*, I now have people screaming, *You're my kids' favorite, we love you, please show us more!*

I even pitched Kiki the Koala to Marissa. I did it fair and square, because if anyone would reject me instead of being forced to accept it because I'm sharing a bed with the now-permanent CEO, Marissa would do it out of spite.

Look, she's on the twelve-step programs. Getting sober. Doing well.

She's actually getting along with her mother, and grudgingly accepting that Clara may end up as her stepmother soon.

She even made amends with Merrick, coughing up the money for his granddaughter's education, plus enough damages to afford Rick a decent retirement. When he begged August for forgiveness, though, August agreed to let him do occasional deliveries and rides.

Against the odds, all is well again, even with Marissa.

But she can still be one hell of a fire-breathing bitch.

With a little negotiation, though, I had a book deal before I knew it.

A career of my own.

I can't believe that's a freaking prototype plushie of Kiki the Koala sitting on my studio desk.

The same plushie that's about to be in bookstores all over the world.

How did I get here again?

The answer grunts as he stomps into the room and dumps another box in the corner.

"How many sketchbooks do you *have*?" August demands.

"Enough to keep you sweaty." I gravitate toward him. He's gleaming hot, his sleeveless undershirt turned transparent by sweat, his arms streaked in dirt and his ripped jeans riding down low on his hips.

Such a devilishly good look for Mr. Upright.

I hook a belt loop and tug him close.

"Hold up. I almost never get to see you outside of suits, and I'd like to enjoy the view."

"You rip me out of my suits every night, you little wildcat," he growls, leaning into me, nearly drowning me in the masculine scent of exertion. The pet name's not wrong, when just smelling him makes me melt. "You see me out of them plenty often."

"I wouldn't mind seeing you out of this right now." I cup his cock through his jeans. He inhales sharply, rising up a little, already swelling against my palm as his eyes narrow.

". . . *wretch*," he growls, hooking me around the waist and dragging me tight against his burning body. "I kissed you ten minutes ago, and you shoved me away and said you had to finish unpacking and answering letters."

I wince.

I am a little behind on letters to Inky.

Clara and I take turns answering them now, but with the new programs, there are so many that we can barely keep up. At least six of the boxes lining the walls are handwritten letters from all over the world I need to respond to, and that's got nothing on the email inbox.

I smile up at him innocently.

"Quickie against the wall? We can finish in five minutes."

"I *never* finish in five minutes," he growls, bending to lick the curve of my neck. I'm sweaty, too, and I shiver as the heated moisture on my skin cools as his tongue passes. "I want to lick you clean."

"August," I moan, digging my fingers into his shoulders.

He might not be done in five minutes, but I could explode right now.

He always does that to me.

One look, one touch, one taste, and I could mount this bull of a man and ride him for days.

But he lets out a frustrated growl, pulling back with a skeptical look. One blue eye narrows. "You might actually change your mind after you see this."

I blink.

"See what?" I groan. "August, no. What did I tell you about at least sending me a text before you make plans?"

"If I texted this, it would ruin the surprise. Believe me. You're either going to hate me or love me even more."

I don't know how I could love him more.

But I let him take my hand and lead me into the hall. I'm only pouting a little that he's leaving me unsatisfied after one little lick.

Curious, I trail after him.

August leads me into our bedroom—hey, I thought he didn't want sex just yet?—then out to the deck. He's oddly tense as he leads me to the railing.

A little box sits on the wood, quiet and unassuming, but—

Oh my God.

Wait.

He clears his throat. "Perhaps this isn't as flashy as showing up at your grandmother's house with a ring box and demanding you marry me on the spot," he says dryly, squeezing my hand. "Still, there's no one here to watch us this time. It's just you and me, Elle. It's . . ." He breathes deep, letting go of my hand. "It's real."

My heart stops.

I'm dizzy as August picks up the box and sinks down on one knee.

It's nothing like the first time.

His first proposal was stiff and growly and clean cut and emotionless. Just a business transaction with a stranger.

We're not strangers anymore.

We're *home*.

On the horizon, a storm brews against the sunset over the sea, as if it's *us* where the sea and sky meet.

My wonderful August, kneeling in front of me, a scruffy mess of sweat and dirt and disarrayed hair because he's been helping me make his home into ours.

He's looking up at me with his whole heart in eyes that can never ice over again as he opens the ring box.

"Eleanor Lark," he whispers, his voice as ragged as my emotions. "You have completely turned my life inside out, upside down, and shaken it apart. You put me back together better than I was before. We're tangled together, and if we were ever pulled apart, I'd collapse without you. I need you in my life. Your brightness, your sweetness, the joy you bring, simply by existing. I love you, woman, and this time— this time I'm asking for the real deal. Marry me, Elle. Marry me for real because I can't live without you."

My eyes are so blurry I can barely see the ring, but I can tell it's very different from the one still on my finger. It's a simple band with swirling engravings, sweeping lines that make me think of subtle blowing winds.

In some weird way, it makes me think of Inky.

That silly penguin we both loved as children for totally different reasons, and whose creator brought us together and made us who we are now.

Us.

Together, our lives united as perfectly as I think that ring will fit on my finger.

I try to say *yes*, but my voice breaks.

Nothing comes out but a squeak.

August's brows rise mildly. "I speak Elle fluently, but I'm not sure I can translate that one."

That *ass*.

Because he knows.

He knows, and he's already smiling slowly as I throw myself against him and practically bowl him down to the deck.

"Yes!" I cry, kissing him hard, rough, clutching at him like I'll never let him go. "Yes, yes, you big lunk. I'll marry you for real."

◆ ◆ ◆

Months later

I still can't believe my parents actually showed up.

When I called them in Florida to tell them I was engaged, my mother actually sounded bored.

We know, dear. Yes, it's been all over the news. The neighbors wouldn't stop bothering us about it for a week.

. . . right.

They don't know. Grandma never told them.

No reason to, really.

394

Let them believe what the rest of the world does.

August and the people closest to us know the truth.

And it matters more than ever that they know we're in love with each other for real.

I'm definitely wildly in love with a man who can plan a wedding without forcing me to do a single bit of it, because my God, I would never be able to put this entire shindig together.

Remember that Hilton ballroom we never went to? That night we were supposed to go ballroom dancing and instead had sex in our formal wear on the beach?

Well, now it's our wedding venue.

Somehow, August put together an entire theme that went with my dress.

Because I decided I wanted to dress up like I was going full eighties punk with a modern twist.

My dress is an explosion of white taffeta with black-and-pink net patches, irregular and ragged and so *me*.

When I told him what I wanted, he just smiled patiently and said, "I know, brat."

It's so nice to have a man who *gets me*.

One who doesn't mind a wedding that looks like someone spilled pink-and-black paint everywhere to complement the traditional gauze, white silk, white roses like a mad artistic impression.

It's so me.

It's so *us*.

And I can't believe he put this together.

Everything from the napkins to the cake have pink-and-black accents. Even my makeup has pink and black in the wings around my eyes, and the white bouquet of roses has little sprays of pink-and-black-dyed flowers.

I cannot wait to be married.

So why am I about to hyperventilate as the guests file in and sit?

I peek out from behind a curtain in the staging area.

"Look at all those *people*," I mutter sharply. "Why are there so many people?"

"Because," Gran says mildly, adjusting my corset. "Your fiancé is a famous billionaire; you're a beloved children's author. Your matrons of honor are an even more famous author and her lovely girlfriend."

Behind us, Yvette giggles. "I still can't get over that. *Girlfriend!*"

"Get used to it, my darling." Clara nuzzles her cheek. She's smart and trim in a women's black silk tailored tuxedo with black embroidery and pink lapels. "You're not going anywhere again."

I have to look away from them, blushing. "No wonder Marissa refuses to be seen in public with you. You're embarrassing," I tease.

"We're in love," Clara throws back shamelessly. "And so are you, dear. Don't think I haven't caught you and August making out in the hall at every family dinner."

"You're not supposed to look!" I gasp, and Clara, Yvette, Grandma, and Lena all snicker.

Lena's awkward in her pink-and-black bridesmaid's gown. Not because the dress is bad, but because Lena hates dresses and turns into a human coatrack any time she puts one on. She saunters over to tweak a curl of my hair.

"Stop panicking. Go out there and get married already."

"So I can take this awful dress off," Marissa mumbles, sulking in a corner. "Why did you even ask me to be a bridesmaid? Are we friends?"

I look up at her.

Are we?

I just smile and look at her. "Because you wanted to be one, and your feelings would have been hurt if I hadn't. And because I like you. And you just don't want to admit you like me, and wanted to be part of this."

Marissa gasps, then glowers at me.

Yvette grins.

"She's got you pegged, dear."

"Mom, shut up."

Everyone chuckles. I shake my head fondly.

Marissa's practically going through a second adolescence with her mom, but she seems to be doing that much better for it.

It's crazy how much can change in barely a year.

Relationship dynamics, friendships, family, work, life.

I tripped over August and fell into the life I was meant for, and I wouldn't have it any other way.

"Everyone decent?" One of the ushers peeks in with his eyes closed.

"Decent enough," I answer.

He opens his eyes, smiling. "We're ready when you are, then. Everyone's seated, all guests accounted for, the priest ready, and the groom's party is waiting. Give us the signal and we'll start, ma'am."

My smile fades.

I take a shaky breath.

Gran grips my shoulders, squeezing tight.

"You're ready, sweetness," she reassures me. "You've always faced everything head on. Now go see your groom."

I nod quickly, breathing hard, and flash a smile at the usher.

"Okay. We're ready."

And away we go.

It's surreal to be standing here, listening to the music start up on the other side.

To feel like this is leading up to *me* and then to eternity as everyone files out—leaving only Gran and me. My parents are here, sitting there in the audience, but it's Grandma Jackie who's giving me away.

She's earned the right.

She's the one who's held me together my whole life.

Just like she's holding me together now, her arm tucked lovingly in mine, keeping me stable as I wait for the magic moment in the music that tells me it's my turn.

When it comes, we walk out together.

I get to see August for the first time since we woke up together, before we were swept away by our respective parties to get ready for the big day—and for the rest of our lives.

He waits by the altar, tall and straight and handsome in his tux. The perfect cut of it can't hide the powerful body underneath.

His militant posture reminds me how much he likes to control me in bed, even while he lets me drag him around with my whims everywhere else. His cummerbund and the neckband are the same deep vivid pink as the accents on my dress and the decor, and so is his pocket square.

His hair is picture perfect—except for that one wild strand, arcing over his brow.

But he's smiling like the sun.

Gone is the forbidding man who refused to acknowledge my existence.

In his place, there's a man who's grown into someone warm and wonderful.

Someone who used to hide his kindness and now wears it openly for all to see and love just as much as I do.

That intensity almost makes it hard to hold his eyes as Gran escorts me up the aisle to his side, but I can't look away.

As Grandma guides me to my place, I feel so *right*.

No more nerves.

But I have to stifle a giggle as Grandma Jackie pats his arm, leans in, and whispers to him.

"Don't you dare fuck this up, young man."

I choke back a sound. I don't think she's ever said *fuck* before in her life.

August's eyes widen, and he stares after her as she struts over to the rest of the bridal party and takes her place with a smug look.

"You heard her," I whisper, grinning. "Don't screw it up."

"I wouldn't dare," he whispers back, his lips twitching. "Also, when I agreed to the punk theme," he says through his teeth, "I didn't think you'd make me wear a pink cummerbund."

I reach up to flick that unruly strand of hair. "The bride and groom should match."

"Everybody ready?" the priest whispers.

We both nod so quickly we look like those little dashboard dolls, only to catch each other's eyes and realize what we're doing.

We grin while the priest begins.

Before, we'd talked about writing custom vows. But in the end, we agreed not to because the letters we write to each other are for us alone.

Not to share with the world.

It started with the letter where he confessed his feelings.

Then it turned into me missing him at the office one day and leaving him a little letter written on a bit of sketch paper with a smile and a heart from Kiki, waiting in his office.

Him reminding me he had to go in early for an investor meeting and couldn't stay in bed with me, so I found a note on my pillow reminding me not to burn the kitchen down while I was warming up the breakfast he'd made—and he loved me, don't burn the kitchen down (again), don't slip off the deck and drown; oh, and be naked when he came home.

Horny grump.

Over and over, we traded little love notes.

Some silly. Some sweet. Some downright filthy, and it's kind of our thing now.

I've kept every single one.

Even if they're for my eyes only.

And even if we've both bloomed with each other's love, there are some parts of us that are just for us.

But this, here and now, it's for us *and* everybody else.

Everything we're proud to show and prouder to say.

"I do."

Eyes never leaving each other, hearts beating as one.

You may now kiss the bride.

Screw that.

I'm kissing my groom.

As the crowd bursts into wild applause and cheers so wildly they send my heart soaring, I fling myself into August's arms, drag him down, and kiss him like the plane is going down.

The Mr. Marshall to my Mrs. Marshall.

I've never felt more perfect, more wonderful, more bright.

His mouth claims mine, and this kiss becomes the dawn breaking on my first day as his wife.

The very first day of the rest of our lives.

Together forever.

And as we've written our story, so it must be.

Epilogue

(AUGUST)

Years later

"And when she went home," I read, slowly and softly, careful not to raise my voice too high, "Kiki's grandmother was there with a nice cup of eucalyptus tea to relax her after a long day. And Kiki was proud and happy, because she'd helped the Platypus Twins be friends with Gruffykins the Owl once again."

The only answer is a burbling sigh.

My newborn daughter—*our* newborn daughter—squirms in her swaddling, smacking her lips adorably in her sleep as she turns her face into the crook of her arm.

I carefully close the cover of *Kiki the Koala: Mending Fences* and set the book aside, lightly flexing my ankles to make the rocking chair sway a little. Giselle settles quietly at the swaying, out like a light, with one fist half in her mouth.

My sweet, perfect little goober.

My darling baby daughter, with her tiny fingers and her button nose and her little fluff of wild strawberry blonde hair, just like her mother's.

She's already as amazing as her mother too.

As I look down at our little girl sleeping so soundly, so trustingly in my arms, my heart runs the fuck over.

I'm filled with so much love I almost find myself choking back tears.

Yeah, this daddy thing does that, turning even the toughest guys into great big saps.

When I first took over Little Key, I didn't have the slightest clue what to do with children. They didn't matter to me at all beyond being a distant target demographic. Little Key was Aunt Clara's legacy, and I was just there to handle the money and legal matters.

Somehow, Elle changed everything.

She changed me.

And when my gorgeous wife gave us our daughter, I realized I've always needed this.

Being a husband and father is etched in my bones.

Being a family, as strong and wonderful as the true families we both found for ourselves when our parents couldn't be there.

Elle's steps whisper behind me as she tiptoes into the room, then drapes her arms around my neck from behind, leaning over the back of the rocking chair.

"A little young to get it, isn't she?" she whispers against my ear, soft laughter edging her voice.

I look up with a smile, turning my head to catch her lips in a familiar kiss.

"Thought I'd start her off on the right books early," I whisper back. "Think she loves Kiki the best. She knows her ma's brilliant, so she'll grow up to be just like her."

"God, let's hope not. Tripping over random strangers in airports can only work out well once. She should be less of a disaster." Elle nuzzles me. "You're so good with her, though. She falls asleep for you like a little angel. She's a demon with me."

"Because she knows you'll let her get away with being a demon. You spoil her rotten."

"Like you don't?" Elle laughs. "Look at you guys!"

"Can't help it." I sigh, looking down at Giselle. "She's so perfectly tiny. She'll never be this small again."

"Oh, you'll wish she was when she's big enough to start crawling." Elle noses my cheek. "Come to bed. Early day tomorrow. Clara's got a signing, and I promised I'd be there."

"Yeah. Let me put her down."

Elle pulls back, holding the rocking chair steady for me while I stand and move delicately toward the crib. One tiny bit at a time, I lay Giselle down in her blankets before tucking her gently and safely away.

She doesn't even stir.

She just keeps chewing on her fist in her sleep, resting there like the little cherub she is.

Elle leans over the edge of the crib with a small smile overflowing with love. "Bitey little monster. She gets that from you."

"I don't bite *that* much."

Elle gives me a look that drips pure sarcasm.

Then she pulls the neck of her shirt aside to show the hickey I left on her collarbone earlier.

Oops.

"I have to wear a high-necked shirt to an outdoor signing in the middle of summer thanks to you," she says mildly. "And you're telling me you don't bite that much?"

"Well, now, if you're already going to wear a high-necked shirt anyway . . ."

Her eyes widen.

With a squeak, she turns to run.

Too slow.

With a growl, I chase after her.

She's trying not to laugh, trying not to wake the baby, but I can't help chuckling. It's so much easier to laugh now with her.

So much easier to be *happy*, to live in the moment instead of being trapped in my worries and fears.

It's so much easier to be with her.

Nicole Snow

I want to be with her as I catch her just past the threshold of the
bedroom, sweep her up, tumble her down to the bed under me.

She sprawls out beneath me, her hair spilling everywhere. Elle's
changed since our wedding—her hair longer, strawberry blonde tangles
almost to her waist. Her body is softer and thicker and curvier from
pregnancy, her breasts fuller and more luscious.

More to entice me.

More to kiss.

More to touch.

More to *bite*.

I groan like mad when I feel her plush flesh yielding, igniting me
instantly.

"*Fuck*," I whisper as her heavy breasts move against me with the
arch of her back. "You feel so good."

"Never thought pregnancy body would get you this hot," she
teases, but her breaths are hitching, her nipples already hard against
her shirt. We're always hot for each other, always needy, unable to keep
our hands to ourselves. "The way you're going, you'll end up making
another baby."

"Four, five, a dozen, I don't care." I rip her shirt away, stroking my
hands over her breasts. I sink my fingers into their lushness as I drag
the cups of her bra down feverishly and rub my cheek against that pale,
curving flesh.

My beard rakes her nipple just to feel it peak, to catch that scent
that tells me she's already wet for me.

"As long as I have you, Elle," I groan, sucking her nipple and clutching her ass. "As long as you're mine. As long as you love me."

"Forever," she whispers back.

Damned right.

We fit together so perfectly too.

Clothing shed, mouths locked, skin to skin, and then the perfect
plunge inside her, fusing us together.

"Forever," I agree. "Forever, like the way I'll always love you."

Read on for a preview of *One Bossy Proposal* by Nicole Snow!

One Bossy Proposal

While I Pondered

(DAKOTA)

The spring sun shines down on Seattle like a sword aimed at my own personal gloom.

I'm sad and hungry—a dangerous combination.

It's been a year to the day since I buried my heart—and the utter scumbag who dragged it through the mud, doused it in kerosene, and burned it to a blackened crisp—and it feels like an eternity.

Some things, you only sort of get over.

Some things, you don't forget.

Hold the pity party, Dakota. You're better off without him. You're a thousand miles from home, smack in the middle of a whole new life, I tell myself.

Eyeballing the gluttonous offerings in the bakery case helps.

It's true. I have rebuilt. Kind of.

I left that small-town dreariness and its regrets behind. I have an interview next week for a job that slaps, and if I don't get it, I'll keep applying until I land something with big-girl pay and a real opportunity to flex my writing muscles.

Without my great escape last summer in a halo of tears, I wouldn't be here in Seattle, practically *drooling* at the sugar-rich delicacies that all seem to have my name on them.

I'd have less time to focus on my writing, too, and I'd still be intern-ing in that one-room closet masquerading as a marketing agency.

Yay, heartbreak.

Yay, Jay Foyt.

His stupidity gave me a whole new life.

"You hungry or did you just come here to admire the goods? Can I get you something?" The barista appears behind the bakery case with a girlish laugh.

"Huh? Oh, sorry—" *Dammit, Dakota, get out of your head.* "Can I get a Regis roll and a small caramel nirvana latte?"

"Coming right up!" She smiles and uses tongs to grab a huge cinna-mon roll drizzled in icing. It's so fat I think it crosses time zones. "Lucky lady, you got the last one today! We're a little short. Cinnamon shortage in the morning shipment—go figure."

Lucky me.

If only my luck with pastries would rub off on other things. Like winning lottery tickets or cigar-chomping big shots in publishing ready to snap up my poetry. I'd even settle for a decent Tinder date who doesn't have a fuckboy bone in his body.

Nope. I'm asking for too much.

Today, Lady Luck grants bargain wishes. She delivers the very last mound of sticky cinnamon sweetness in the case and point-three more pounds on my thighs.

I mean, it's a start, right?

I move to the cash register and pay.

"Glad I got mine before you ran out," I say, swiping my card. "I'll be sure to savor the flavor—"

"What do you mean you're out?" a deep voice thunders behind me. "I've been here at exactly this time three times a week since Christmas. You're never *out*."

Holy crap.

And I thought I was having a bad day . . .

I look back toward the bakery case to see what kind of ogre crawled out of his swamp to rant and rave over a missing cinnamon roll.

"Sorry, sir. The lady in front of you just bought the last roll," the barista says, wearing a placating frown. "There's a bit of a weird cinnamon shortage going around—"

"Are you telling me there isn't another goddamned Regis roll in the entire shop?" The man is tall, built, and entirely pissed off.

"Er, no. Like I said . . . cinnamon shortage." Barista girl flashes a pained smile. "The early bird got the worm, I'm afraid. If you'd like to try again tomorrow, we'll save one for you."

Barista girl nods at me matter-of-factly.

The ogre turns, whips his head toward me, and glares like his eyes are death rays.

Red alert.

So, he might be just as bad-tempered as the average ogre, but in the looks department, this guy is the anti-Shrek. If the green guy had abs that could punish and tanned skin instead of rocking his brussels sprout glow, he might catch up to Hot Shrek in front of me.

My breath catches in my chest.

I don't think I've ever seen eyes like amber whiskey, flashing in the morning light.

If he weren't snarling like a rabid wolverine, he *might* be hotter than the toasty warm roll in my hand. The coolness of his eyes contrasts deliciously with dark hair, a furrowed brow, a jaw so chiseled it shames mere mortals.

He might be in his early thirties. His face looks young yet experienced.

The angles of that face match the cut of his body. He's toned like a former quarterback and dressed like he just walked off the set of *Suits*.

He is a Gucci-wrapped cocktail handcrafted for sin.

Every woman's dark vampire fantasy come to life—or maybe just mine.

When you're a Poe—distant, *distant* relation to Edgar Allan—it comes with the territory.

I definitely wonder if he woke up with a steaming mug of rudeness this morning to plaster that scowl on his face.

I'm starting to notice a pattern in this city. What is it with Seattle minting grumps who look like sex gods?

Is it something in the rain?

Worse, he towers over me, the picture-perfect strongman with a chip on his shoulder that entitles him to roar at the world when it doesn't fall down at his feet.

Although he's annoyingly gorgeous, and his suit probably costs half my yearly salary, I wonder. What gets a man this fire-breathing pissed over missing his morning sugar high?

Sure, I'll be the first to admit that Regis rolls are almost worth losing your mind over. *Almost.*

While Hades stares, I roll my eyes back at him and follow the curve of the counter to wait for my drink.

Precious distance.

After grumbling for a solid minute, he swipes his card like a dagger at the cash register and follows me around the counter.

Uh-oh.

Surely, he's not going to confront me.

He *wouldn't.*

Oh, but he's right next to me now.

Still glaring like I murdered his firstborn.

He pulls out his wallet, opens it, and plucks out a crisp bill, shoving it at me like it's on fire.

"Fifty dollars," Hot Shrek growls.

"Come again?"

"Fifty bucks. I'll pay you five times its value for the trouble."

"What?" I blink, hearing the words but not comprehending them.

He points to the white paper bag in my hand holding my little slice of heaven. "Your Regis roll, lady. I'll buy it off you."

"Wait, you just . . . you want to buy my cinnamon roll that bad?"

"Isn't that what I just said? And it's a *Regis roll*," he corrects sharply. "You know, the kind worth dying over? The original recipe cooked up in Heart's Edge, Montana, and approved by a scary burned guy who's been all over the national media and keeps getting cameos in movies?"

I laugh. That's exactly what Sweeter Grind's ads promise about the otherworldly Regis roll, a creation of Clarissa and Leo Regis, two small-town sweet shop owners made famous by some crazy drama a few years back.

"*Never mind*," he snaps. "You want to make this sale or what?"

"You should do commercials," I tell him with a huff. "Is that what this is? Some strange guerrilla marketing thing?"

I hold my breath. At least that would explain Mr. GQ Model going absolutely ballistic over something so trivial.

Also, it's the one-year anniversary of the most humiliating day of my life.

I need this roll like I still need to believe there's a shred of goodness in this world. What kind of psycho tries to buy someone's cinnamon roll off them for five times the price, anyway?

"Do I look like a comedian?" he snarls, his eyes rolling. "Fifty dollars. Easy money. Trade."

"Dude, you're insane," I whisper back.

"Dudette," he barks back, slightly more frantic. "I assure you, I am not. I need that roll, and I'm willing to pay you generously. I trust you need the money more than I do."

I scoff at him so hard my face hurts.

Rub it in, why don't you? I guess I should up and be amazed you're deigning to talk to us 'little people,' your pastry-obsessed highness.

"It must be nice, oh Lord of the Pastries. What do I get for an apple pie? A laptop?" I shake my head.

His *done with your bullshit* glare intensifies.

"Dakota!" A male barista calls my name and plunks my drink on the counter.

Awesome. There's my cue to exit this asylum and head back to the springtime sanity outside where birds tweet and flowers bloom and nobody goes to war over cinnamon shortages.

I grab my drink and start for the door.

"Wait!" Hot Shrek calls. "Dakota."

Ughhh.

My name shouldn't sound so deliciously rough on a man's lips. Especially not a man offering exorbitant sums to strangers for their baked goods.

Knowing I'll regret this, I stop and meet his eyes.

"What?" I clip.

"We haven't finished."

"Right. Because there's no deal," I snap, turning again.

Okay. Before, I was just looking forward to stuffing my face with sticky goodness. Now, I *need* this flipping cinnamon roll like oxygen.

If I spite the hottest freak who crawled out of the ogre swamp, I'll have something to laugh about later.

True to the promise I made the barista, I'll savor the flavor while wallowing in a little less of my own misery and reminding myself I'm living a better life now—which apparently includes handsome stalkers begging to throw cash at me.

"Wait. I need it more than you do. I swear," he says harshly, grabbing my shoulder and spinning me around.

I bat his hand away, doubly annoyed and taken aback.

"You're insane. Touch me again and I'll press charges for robbery. It's a cinnamon roll, dude. Calm down and come back tomorrow when they're replenished." I panic-chug my latte and walk out the door.

Hot Stalker Shrek is undaunted.

He trails me outside as I stroll into the Seattle sunshine, taking a deep breath.

"Seventy-five!" he calls after me.

"What?"

"Seventy-five dollars."

"Um, no." I speed-walk to the bike rack and unlock my wheels with one hand, balancing the Regis roll and the latte in the other.

"One hundred dollars even," he belts after me.

Holy Moses. How high will he go?

"One fifty!" he calls two seconds later.

There goes my jaw, crashing to the pavement.

A chill sweeps through me. I'm worried we're leaving eccentric waters for clinically crazy.

Part of me wants to keep him talking just so he doesn't carry me off to his evil lair. I imagine a storage shed stacked to the ceiling with crumpled cinnamon roll boxes.

"Did you really just offer me a hundred and fifty dollars for a cinnamon roll?" I place the latte in a cup holder on my handlebar and climb on the bike.

He gives me an arctic look, like he knows he's got me now and I've already accepted his bizarro deal.

"You're welcome. You can Uber and still have a nice chunk of change."

I scan him up and down, purposely glancing at his polished leather shoes a second too long. In another time and place, I'd take a nice big sip of my latte and spray it on his shoes but . . . that's not how I roll.

I have my dignity. I plan to have a little more of it when I'm safely away from here too.

"This may come as a shock, but not all of us worship money, King Midas," I say.

"What's that supposed to mean?" he says with a snort, squaring his hulking shoulders.

"You're a nutter. Like actually insane." My eyes flick to his wrists for good measure, legit wondering if I'll see a hospital band.

"I am not. Have you ever tasted a Regis roll? Seattle's top food critic described them as—what was it? A category-ten mouthgasm?"

My lips twitch. I try like hell not to burst out into a blushing laugh.

"Man, I am *not* discussing mouthgasms with you," I say.

"You're missing the point," he says sharply. "Help me and help yourself, Miss Dakota. We never have to see each other again and you'll be three hundred dollars richer."

"Three . . . hundred?" I say slowly, my mouth falling open.

"You heard me." His eyes flash with hope and triumph, and he starts reaching for his wallet.

Stay strong.

Invisible crucifix.

Latte holy water.

Do not be tempted by Lucifer.

"See, you're not making your case. Just further proving your insanity." I eye him warily. Maybe there's some wild story behind how he stole this suit and he really did just escape some mental institution.

That would be the most believable explanation for what's happening.

Honestly, a lot less scary than thinking guys who look like billionaires want to spend their time reverse robbing strangers for their pastries.

"Five hundred dollars, damn you," he rumbles. "Final offer."

My jaw detaches from my face.

Five hundred flipping smackers?

That's more than my student loan payment this month. Almost half my rent. I'm tempted to sign my soul away, but my fingers clench the bag tighter, demanding me to be brave.

Not today, Coffee Shop Satan.

A smile that's almost comically pleading pulls at his lips.

Damn. Somehow, he's even hotter when he smiles and makes those puppy dog eyes. A face like his should come with a warning.

"I see that got your attention," he whispers.

"Did it?"

"Your mouth dropped," he says, making me keenly aware his gaze is fixed on my lips. I don't even know what to do with that.

He closes the space between us and reaches for my bag, trying to get the drop on me.

"Hey—no! I told you it's not happening, crazypants." I don't like the way he so casually invades my space. I also have a pesky habit of not taking a single speck of crap from anyone. Especially this past year.

But there's also this tiny thought nibbling at the back of my brain that screams this man is no different from Jay.

Just richer, stronger, better looking, and possibly more arrogant.

Keeping this Regis roll out of his grubby paws is a little win for Dakota Poe against mankind. Against every swinging dick who brandishes his selfish ego like a club.

"I'm perfectly sane. I simply need that roll, and I can't walk away empty handed," he tells me.

"Y'know, I woke up inspired to write today. But I wasn't planning on getting real-world inspiration shoved in my face from someone so ridiculous."

"I have no idea what the hell that means, but I need the roll and you need money. Do we have a deal?"

"Why am I not surprised you can't follow simple English? Are you one of those guys who paid five hundred dollars for some poor geek to boost your grades too?"

He glares at me like an angry bull.

"Watch your step, bigmouth. You know nothing about me. Let's make a trade and be on our merry way for the sake of our blood pressure." He gives me a slow, assessing look, his eyes sliding up my body with a weight that makes me shiver. "You're on a bike. Don't tell me you couldn't use a few hundred bucks."

"Orrr I could be so loaded I run a green power company and need to look the part," I throw back. "Plus, biking helps blow off some steam. You should try it sometime."

Scowling, he grabs at my white paper bag again.

I shift away at the last second, slapping his big hand away.

Yeah, I've had it.

Narrowing my eyes, I glare back at him, reach into the bag, and pull out the warm roll. In slow motion, I bite off a massive chunk.

I chew it as loudly as I can, smacking my lips like war drums.

The most mouthgasmic *"Mmmmm-mmm-mmmm!"* I've ever mustered in my life rips out of me.

Then I drop the bite-marked roll back into the bag, lick my fingers, and wipe my hands unceremoniously on the front of my jeans.

"See? Not everything is for sale. No deal."

God.

I've seen my share of selfish men, but this one takes the cake—or rather, he doesn't take the cinnamon roll I won't let him have. The tantrum brewing in his face when I make it crystal clear he's not getting this roll would scare the best kindergarten teacher pale.

His jaw clenches.

His bearish brown eyes become brighter, hotter, *louder*. I can hear them cursing me seven ways from Sunday.

It's not fair.

When he's majorly pissed off, he's a hundred times hotter than he was at first glance.

His eyes drop to my lips and linger for a breathless second.

His gaze feels so heavy I hug myself, trying to hide from the intensity of his scorned-god look that feels like it could turn me into a salt pillar.

About the Author

Nicole Snow is a *Wall Street Journal* and *USA Today* bestselling author. She found her writing groove by hashing out love scenes on lunch breaks and plotting her great escape from the cubicle. Her work roared onto the indie romance scene in 2014 and quickly multiplied into all the contemporary romance butterflies she's known for today.

Snow now aims for the very best in broody book boyfriends you can't help falling for, tropes with meaning, and swoon storms aplenty. With over a million books sold, she lives for the joy of making two people fight with every bit of their soul for a happily ever after.